HIGH PRAISE FOR *TIME TRANSIT*!

D1415036

A TIMELY QUESTION

Maude's chronometer pulsed off the seconds. She should give it up. They were already overdue at Reacclimation. The now-deserted commons wouldn't stay that way, not if someone triggered a search and launched a retrieval team. If security squawked, she and Gil would be located, swarmed, and hauled off—Gil to Reacclimation and her back to Rogue Central for a well-deserved slap on the wrist. It was dangerous to linger. Her pulse hammered at her wrists, her throat, and her temples. Every instinct she'd cultivated and honed for Rogue missions recommended abort. But Maude's heart wouldn't yield. She had to know.

"Gil, do you...remember me?" she ventured.

Other *Love Spell* books by Kay Austin:

TIME ROGUES

KAY AUSTIN

TIME TRANSIT

LOVE SPELL NEW YORK CITY

LOVE SPELL®

January 2008

Published by

Dorchester Publishing Co., Inc.
200 Madison Avenue
New York, NY 10016

ISBN 10: 0-505-52715-4
ISBN 13: 978-0-505-52715-8

The name "Love Spell" and its logo are trademarks of Dorchester Publishing Co., Inc.

Printed in the United States of America.

10 9 8 7 6 5 4 3 2 1

Visit us on the web at www.dorchesterpub.com.

To the Rogues in my life, Pat and Mom; thanks for believing in me and applying swift kicks when I didn't. To Chris Keeslar, the best of the best; thanks for the challenge to explore the future and bring it to the page for SHOMI. To Meredith Bernstein, a class act; thanks for your unfailing support. To Veda and Bev and the rest of the Tacoma Readers Group; thanks for your passion for the written word. To the countless number of friends, family, and readers who inspired and blessed me; thanks for the gifts of conflict and compassion that nurture my dream. And to the chief Rogue in my life, God; without you, I am nothing.

PROLOGUE

Earth's Core, 2152

I'm dead. I'm still breathing but I'm also gut-shot, bleeding, hurting, and alone. If help is on the way, it won't get here in time. I'm doomed.

Death for a twentysomething gal, even a devil-may-care Time Rogue like Maude, was premature. She'd been forewarned, so it should have been preventable. Right? After all, Rogues saved lives and she was one of the best—a prodigy, they said. But she couldn't save herself. Could she?

Maude sniffed the air. Sulfur. Brimstone. It was cool and dark on this isolated tram platform within an inactive volcanic flume. Too cool. The enviro-sensors only activated with movement, and she hadn't moved for what seemed like hours but probably only amounted to a few minutes.

Her auto-transit from the past had been rough. Lacking safeguards, standard Core tracking devices and all but the basic time-travel protocols, her unauthorized mission to defy death and fix fate was iffy and dangerous for even the healthiest Rogue. And she wasn't healthy—not by a long shot. Less than an hour ago, a bullet had changed everything.

She moaned and gripped the edge of the mesh partition helping to keep her upright as another wave of pain spiraled through her. She'd never endured such agony. After two hundred missions logged on her identilog and countless brushes with death, her luck, her skill and her time had run out. She wouldn't survive the hour. She couldn't; she'd lost too much blood. She'd given up trying to staunch the flow pulsing from the wound in her belly. But she hadn't given up on rescue. Not entirely.

"Help?"

The cavernous dark space swallowed her voice. Maude released her hold on the partition and slid like a mass of ooze to the soot-coated tile floor. It was sufficient movement to activate the limited atmospherics. The ambient lighting swelled like a swift sunrise, accompanied by scratchy acoustics of chirping larks and rustling leaves. Without viewscreens, the simulated setting was incomplete but still a welcome comfort. Maude felt less alone. And when the flickering heat lamps struggled to life and dissipated some of the chill, she managed a smile.

Nominal accommodation. A default setting for atmospheric enhancements at isolated stations supporting minimal use.

But by the looks of it, this station hadn't been used or serviced recently. If the lingering odor of rotten eggs was a true indication of elevated magma activity, this section of the sub-orbital tram system might have been abandoned. From countless evacuation drills, she knew all too well that it wouldn't take much—a pyroclastic surge of heat or a burp of poisonous gas—to fry her stem to stern, teeth to toenails.

Drutz. Gut-shot or not, she needed to clear the area fast.

"Hellllp." It sounded like a pathetic bleat compared to the ear-bustin', hoot and holler volume she could manage effortlessly until a few hours ago. But it still might be enough for the sensors in Core to pick up.

She blinked back the sweat blurring her vision and focused on the chunky device mounted on the mesh partition. More rotten luck. First the bullet and now this, a communications relay fouled with grime and nonfunctioning. Her cry for help hadn't been received by Core.

Gigadrutz. What a day. With her transmitter smashed—the first casualty of the bullet that had also penetrated her flesh—her emergency and impending expiration were well-kept secrets from all who would or could save her life.

Core could. Thanks to the cadre of super-intellects like Charlie, technology existed that could do almost everything, including fix time rifts and repair seemingly lethal wounds like hers.

Seemingly lethal? Maude's lips twitched, curving into a half smile. It just wasn't in her to give up. She clung to the faint hope that against all odds her arrival on this platform had somehow registered on Core's grid.

By design, safety systems were full of redundancies. The presence of life-forms automatically dispatched retrieval trams: another system default for stations beyond Edgeville. But just how far beyond Edgeville was she?

She rolled her head from side to side, looking for some landmark to identify her location. She spotted a sign and gasped. *That can't be right. Outskirt 13?* This was where her mission to save herself had started nearly thirty rotations ago.

Or was it? She rubbed her eyes and looked again for confirmation. Awash in the lemony light from the fake sunshine, the letters were unmistakable.

Thirteen miles from Edgeville and help. She was almost home.

On foot and bleeding she'd never make it, but on a sub-orbital tram she'd be patched up and sucking down some of Charlie's bad tasting, cure-all liquid nutrient in no time. All she had to do was hold on until the tram arrived.

She glanced at the spreading darkness on her camo-colored garb. She'd hold on. She had to. Not only for herself but to prove to everyone that Charlie was always right. Time Rogues never died on his watch.

Maude grimaced as another wave of agony buffeted her senses. She fought the urge to give in and pass out. It was a struggle, but by applying her Rogue skills she managed to briefly detach herself from the pain. She focused on Charlie: boss, surrogate papa, and resident genius for Core's crucial maintenance and recovery department. He called her "Kid"—and maybe she still was one—but he'd also promoted her to Rogue status anyway, weathered her novice days, and saved her life more than once.

Memory of the first rescue—more than two thousand rotations ago—was sweet and vivid: Charlie pulling her out of the Children's Cabala, an Edgeville orphanage, after a skill-scan registered her Rogue potential. It had been a momentous event for Maude. She'd been gifted with a friend, the Rogue family, and the will and purpose to survive against the odds.

Thanks to Charlie, no matter how bleak her fate seemed, her faith was unshakable. She wouldn't yield to despair. Only cowards gave up. Rogues dug in and held on, no matter what.

Mega-mondo drutz. Where *was* the Rogue rescue squad, and more important, where was her hero and heartthrob, Gil? His image crystallized and pressed to the forefront of her thoughts.

Ah, Gil. For a brief moment, bliss buffered her pain and the rush of pleasurable memories supplanted her terror. She'd shared lip-scorching kisses and exquisite intimacies with Gil during their intense race to fix the future.

Strange, she mused, remembering her first Rogue mission to Gil's century. She'd sacrificed her passion for the man to restore his world, his time, and his memory—a memory then made devoid of all reference to her. But like the dogged determination the man himself possessed, the bond between them had persisted. Stretched taut through the fabric of time, the connection had pulled them irrevocably together in an alliance to save the future while in the past.

Reunited in passion and purpose, love had flourished. Wonderful, sweet, torrid, amazing, and everlasting love. And they'd weathered the worst, or so she'd thought. Transit foul-ups, pit vipers in the Frontier Zone, a close call with a discharging stunner—they'd survived all of it. But a tiny bit of lead had severed their union and now promised to change everything permanently.

Did he know?

She didn't doubt it. Gil's uncanny and unnerving knack for reading her thoughts—some before she'd even thought them—might still save her. If anyone could figure out she was a bona fide damsel in distress, that hunka-hunka cowboy was her guy. Gil, her love, her one chance.

The atmospherics ceased. The sudden stinking darkness was complete. Gone were the sounds of spring and the comforting warmth. Maude tried to swallow. Terror had a taste, and it wasn't good. She marshaled her remaining energy.

"Somebody help me!" she screamed.

Spent and hoarse, she didn't have the energy to blink back the tears. Her body shook with silent sobs.

Is this it? Am I giving up?

So much for her damned faith and cursed optimism; she

wasn't invincible after all. Soon it would be too late for anyone—Gil, Charlie, and her rough and rowdy Rogue pals included—to fix anything. That is, unless they could bring her back from the dead.

ONE

Pompeii, Italy, 2005

Damn. Gil groaned as a gale-force wind hit him without warning, plastering him against the ancient stone wall like a bug on a windshield. The roar was deafening. And the festive café around him dissolved into a swirling puddle of color.

I'm a goner, he thought. But his life didn't flash before his eyes. Instead, out of the feral wind and mash of color, a body—a powerful, curvaceous, and lush in all the right places female body—materialized and bounced against his. She grabbed him and held fast.

Eye-to-eye, nose-to-nose, and chest-to-breast, Gil instantly knew the strange woman. They'd met before.

Where?

She returned his grin of recognition and offered him a thumbs-up sign. *A-okay?* she mouthed.

He was. The world around them might be going to hell in a handbasket, but Gil didn't care anymore. He was better than okay. He was terrific and fueled with cocky confidence now that this blue-eyed beauty held his fate in her hands.

Gil knew all the tornado survival protocols. Growing up in Texas he'd encountered his fair share of twisters and had known enough to take note of the warning signs, even here in Pompeii, Italy. The sudden silence, yellow sky, the air still as death, and the abrupt skedaddle of birds: Signs were signs. It didn't matter one iota that Italy didn't regularly host tornados. Gil recognized trouble; smelled it, in fact.

Rotten eggs? That smell was a kick in the pants reminder that Pompeii was home to a snoozing volcano. Vesuvius.

Gil admittedly didn't know the indicators of a pending eruption. The other occupants of the hotel eatery from which he'd just emerged had seemed unconcerned or oblivious. But Gil couldn't dismiss the knot in his gut or the raised hackles on the back of his neck or the ache in his trick knee. Trouble—smelly trouble—was definitely brewing.

He flexed his jaw and popped his ears but the invisible pressure continued to mount, rousing age-old fight-or-flight urges. Did "duck and cover" apply to earthquakes or eruptions? Neither seemed appropriate. Hightailing it outa Dodge did.

He had reacted on instinct. Kicking back from his table he'd thrown down money and backpedaled out of the restaurant until his rump rudely connected with a wall, cutting off his retreat.

A mistake? He didn't think so. Certainly not now, not with his back against the wall and this friendly female body pinned against him. Not even though wild winds howled around them and tore at their flesh.

Looking magnificent and utterly fearless in the midst of the roaring vortex, the beauty slapped a curious blinking badge on his arm. She wore a short-cropped ebony wig, which was askew, and her brow glittered with sweat. Her eyes were bright with excitement.

Ready? she mouthed.

It took Gil less than a second to decide. For a Texas cowboy who thrived on risk and adventure, who still craved the eight-second thrill of his bull-riding days, the answer was a no-brainer.

Hell, yeah.

Whether she was the angel of death or the key to his salvation, he couldn't guess, but Gil wasn't quibbling. No, sirree. He'd already determined that whatever she was selling, he was buying—even if it was a one-way ticket to Hades.

Okay, maybe accepting a one-way ticket to Hades had been a bad idea, Gil decided as the lights extinguished and the bottom of the planet dropped out from beneath his feet. Getting sucked into a black hole and stretched like Silly Putty triggered a mondo case of buyer's remorse. But before he could barter with the black nothingness that surrounded him and beg for a refund, the next leg of his trip to hell commenced.

Whoosh. Another thousand-story elevator drop. *Not* pleasant.

The concluding slam dance against an invisible force, pinging fore and aft, thankfully didn't last long. Weightlessness followed.

Was he alone in this blacker-than-midnight soup? It seemed so, but then . . .

Click, click, CLACK. A split-second image from his childhood flashed in living, breathing, Technicolor: a humid summer day on Padre Island, riding cousin Sandra Lee's filly along the beach, the salt-tinged air heavy with the scent of sweaty horseflesh.

Click, click, CLACK. Another image as vivid as the first: his college days, researching at the Alamo's archives.

Click, click, CLACK. Another: eating filched green apples.

The image assault continued. Each was a full immersion in a past event; a moment here, another there, this was a random seek-and-play selection from his entire life.

Faster and faster the images came. A barrage of smells, tastes, and sounds. Blisters that oozed and ached. Hot cinnamon rolls that melted in his mouth. New cars. Dead coyotes. Hugs from Grandma. Fistfights with his brother. He was slaphappy one moment and boiling over with anger the next. His brain felt like a giant Rubik's Cube with invisible hands twisting and matching the colored squares. *Click, click, CLACK.*

Another image. *Her.* His angel of death. The woman in the wig.

She was a knockout; the deliciously dangerous kind. Gil lapped up the image like a thirsty hound. Her lithe and powerful body was encased neck to ankles in a skintight electric blue bodysuit. This time her wig was long. That bullwhip-like ebony mane, a sleek and shiny faux ponytail, twitched like Lucifer's tail as she moved.

Hold on a dang minute. Her?

But the image was gone, replaced with another and another after that. He couldn't stall the playback or control his thoughts in any way.

Maybe I'm dying, Gil reasoned.

Whoosh.

The DVD of his life ended abruptly. He was off again, sailing lickety-split through a yawning abyss, headlong into a great boiling cloud rumbling with thunder and flashing sparks of retina-searing cobalt.

This doesn't look good, he thought. It wasn't.

The landing was hard and merciless. His surroundings were entirely unfamiliar. One saving grace: He wasn't alone. The angel was with him.

"Is he going to make it?" she asked.

Silly female, Gil thought before passing out cold. *After that ride, you're stuck with me.*

TWO

Transit Pad Echo, Earth's Core
Day 178, AD 2151

"Is he going to make it?" Maude cried. She leaned over the humming gelatinous slab cradling Gil's comatose body.

It was a legitimate question. Unbuffered time transits from Earth's past to the present were risky; scrambled molecules didn't always unscramble like good little soldiers.

Gil looked scrambled—irretrievably scrambled. And the transit pad looked like a disaster zone. Discarded treatment tubes, scanners, and probes littered the polished floor, evidence that a significant, and hopefully lifesaving, intervention had recently taken place on the prone subject.

No one replied. With their monitoring consoles adjacent to Gil's body, the diagnostic and medical technicians—heads bent low over their respective tasks—ignored her.

Silence wasn't a good sign, Maude decided. If all was well and under control, someone—one of these techs, at least—should respond.

She growled. But her fury was a sham. In truth, panic dominated as she hovered between concern and forced dispassion for the helpless male. The cold hard reality of leadership was new to her. She'd made this command decision to bring Gil back to Core for processing at Rogue Central, but was it the right one? She couldn't be sure. Questions and doubts plagued her. And her first mission as a certified Time Rogue wasn't over yet.

Drutz, will it never end? Success and failure still hung in the balance.

Maude knew only success—accepted nothing less. Top of her class and schooled in everything but practical experience, she had fought for the privilege and honor of her first mission being to rescue Dak, another Rogue.

She had succeeded. The trip to ancient Pompeii had finalized that. But there had been collateral damage to other timelines and Gil.

It was all Dak's fault. He'd broken his own rules. The kingpin of the Rogues had challenged the limits of time travel and established the safety limits for his elite rescue squads. But his last challenge had jeopardized humanity.

By resolving the threat and saving her mentor, Maude had launched her career. However, tying up loose ends like Gil were troublesome details she'd never anticipated as a certified Rogue. Frankly, she didn't know how to do it. Gil, Mackenzie, and Rick had been victimized by her rescue antics. Exposing the trio from the twenty-first century to time travel technology had compromised their ability to fully reintegrate with their eras of origin. Intervention efforts were necessary.

Mackenzie's and Rick's issues had been fixed. Allowed to retain their memories intact, they had accepted Core's offer to become "on call" Rogues, residing in the past.

But Maude doubted that solution would work for Gil. He had been minimally exposed. Perhaps reintegration only posed marginal risks to his psyche if untreated, but she couldn't be sure. Maybe a Core Bodyscan could assess the variables. She couldn't. Not now. She needed help, help that only Core could offer.

Drutz. Guilt plagued her now, a symptom of her flagging confidence and brought on by fatigue. Gil's splayed body looked nearly lifeless. *Had she done more damage than good?*

The diagno-med techs finally backed away from Gil. Detaching their consoles, they activated the emergency hoverlift carrying his gel slab and stowed their gear.

"Stop worrying, Kid. He's stabilized now. He'll make it," Charlie said, coming up behind her. His warm palm squeezed her shoulder and Maude felt her tension slip away. Charlie never lied.

She straightened and tried to dismiss the issue. Gil was as good as fixed; she could let go, forget him, and move on. That's what Rogues did, didn't they? They moved on. Another day, another mission. No ties, and definitely no entanglements.

Entanglements? This was another problem she had failed to anticipate on her first Rogue assignment.

Drutz. From the get-go, the mission had been fraught with problems. Fixated on the expanding time rift and her uncooperative rescue subject trapped in the AD 79 Vesuvius eruption, Maude hadn't expected bumping headlong into a guy who was all right *and* all wrong for her. As if the unique mission troubles weren't sufficient to complicate her life and budding career as a Rogue, somehow she'd also managed to stumble into love, too.

No. *Not love*, she silently insisted. Rogues didn't love. Rogues sacrificed. Everything. They sacrificed love and sometimes their lives. That was what had been drilled into her through the past years of training.

As critical services personnel for Earth's subterranean society, Core, Rogues served as an elite specialized squad. The embodiment of technological expertise, Rogues preserved and protected Core's time traveling population.

Maude remembered now that as a young girl she had known no alternative to Core's complex society. The Government of the Western Sectors administered countless regions through Critical Service Units, to secure and maintain quality of life standards for all residents throughout Earth's continuum.

In the sparse settlement of Edgeville, reared with other orphans at the Children's Cabala, Maude had understood nothing of the magnitude of force and intellect that had created her world. She had failed to grasp until much later in life how the perpetuation of life depended on the crucial balance between brains and brawn. Nor had she imagined the persistent friction between the two that challenged and spirited each change for the good of mankind.

Oaths to protect the future and preserve the past were meaningless to a girl who only craved fame and glory. The daring exploits of Rogues and magical creations from Scios had fostered her dreams as well as those of her childhood friend Cara Chay to one day join their ranks.

Maude sighed. She missed Cara. Her choice to join the Rogues had triggered a rift. An understandable but regrettable consequence, Maude reminded herself.

The lone survivor of the infamous Lima Transit disaster, Cara had sworn allegiance to the cerebral Scios and joined the league of extraordinary scientists responsible for restoring her life. Mentored by the irascible and brilliant Hickham, Cara belonged to the Scios now. And Maude belonged to the Rogues. Rogues were committed to Core, to the mission, and to each other. That left little room for anything else in life. Entanglements were a distraction.

Gil was an entanglement, a complication that needed to end here and now. Maude closed her eyes for a moment, willing it to be so.

It didn't work. If this was another Rogue certification test, she was flunking.

Charlie seemed capable of reading her mind. The jolly father of Rogue Central, the head honcho and surrogate parent to the elite personnel here, he eyed her with one of his probing stares.

"You like this male, don't you?" he asked as they walked, finally clearing the transit pad. It didn't sound like a question. His generous ear-to-ear grin brooked no debate. Charlie stated facts.

Maude pressed her lips tight as they both boarded a lift. Her feelings? She wouldn't admit them to anyone, especially not Charlie. Too much was riding on this first mission—her future and career as a Rogue, for one.

She powered up the lift but waited until the other hoverlift passed, the one transporting Gil and the diamed techs, then fell in behind. The flash of blue tunnel lights as they traversed the serpentine route marked their swift progress away from the transit arena.

"I want to do right by him," she said at last. The hoverlifts neared a junction, slowed, and banked into a satellite hub of Rogue Central flush with tiled treatment pods. Maude glanced over at Charlie. "It was my decision to bring him to Core. I know what he saw, Charlie. He saw our technology, our transits, the alternate timeline, and more. It was too dangerous to leave him behind."

Charlie considered her words and nodded. "It's been a messy mission, Kid," he said in somber tones. "Rogue squads are still repairing damage to the timeline."

Maude looked sharply over at him. "I did my best. I rescued Dak. I prevented the time rift and I—"

"You did good, Kid. You were the best," Charlie interrupted, and he waved her toward a lift dock. "Park this thing, will you?"

Maude complied, them accepted the flask of nutrient

he pressed into her hand. She consumed a sufficient quantity of the foul-tasting sludge without complaint. Charlie's bluish-hued nutrient, the bane of Rogues far and wide, was a necessary evil.

"Don't get me wrong," Charlie continued, "I'm proud of you. But you had better get used to disappointment. These aren't simulated missions, Kid. Nothing's text-book. Time travel isn't a perfect science. Constantly in a state of flux, the time line can be fractured by almost any mistake. That's what we're here for. Insuring our tech-nology is current with and up to that challenge keeps me up at night."

Maude barely heard him; the taste of the nutrient was too foul. She spluttered as she finished the flask and wiped her mouth with the back of her hand. "Some things never change," she muttered under her breath, then belched.

Charlie chuckled. "I'm working on changing that too."

Maude turned away from the dock. A life beacon flashed in a treatment pod. Gil's pod. Were they losing him?

Charlie ignored the flurry of activity, the influx of per-sonnel crowding into the treatment area, and a now audi-ble thumping noise broadcast throughout the hub. He watched Maude carefully, his mouth tugged down in a rare frown.

"Emotional attachment," he noted, as if marking a clinical checklist. "Did you procreate?"

Maude froze. She didn't know how to answer.

"Respond," Charlie demanded.

She shook her head. "No, of course not," she replied ve-hemently. "I didn't . . . procreate. I'm currently sterilized—it's standard prep for time travel missions. You know that."

Charlie broke form and snickered. "Oh, Kiddo, noth-ing about this mission has been standard—not even your Rogue prep."

Maude's mouth dropped open, an unuttered *Oh?* hanging in the air. Charlie held up a hand to forestall any response.

"I don't need to know everything. Keep your privacy. But I'm recommending a memory purge for both of you."

A memory purge? Anger flushed through Maude like a pyroclastic blast. It took every ounce of control, every micron of discipline she'd drilled into her body and brain to not lash out and reject his suggestion outright. Charlie knew best, didn't he? Mentor. Boss. Friend and stand-in papa.

"Not a purge," she managed between clenched teeth. "I'll agree to a data transfer. Download my memories of Gil to a chip."

"What about Gil's memories of you?" Charlie asked gently. His bushy brows rode high. Per usual, his wild red hair stood on end in that absurdly comical way, making one of the biggest brains of Core seem the friendliest of friends—a shoulder to lean on, to confide in—rather than the single most authoritative figure in the Time Rogue hierarchy.

Maude hesitated. This was another command decision. Gil's welfare, and Core's too, were at stake. Should Gil keep his memories of her? A total memory purge was best for everyone concerned. Gil especially. If he was to successfully reintegrate into his time and place in Earth's past, in 2005, a total memory purge was essential. Gil wasn't a Rogue, Maude reminded herself. He wasn't implanted with buffering hardware, trained to ignore impulses, or disciplined to detach from any subject of attraction.

"It's my decision?" she asked, even though she knew it was.

"I calculate Gil's involvement in the mission and exposure to the alternate time line as minimal," Charlie replied. He nodded toward the pod. "Our intervention efforts, of course, and all input to his active and subliminal memory since arrival at Core has been restricted. Inducing the coma is standard procedure for unbuffered and unauthorized transits. There's not much memory to purge. Our future is not in jeopardy."

"Erase it," Maude said suddenly. "Take me out of his mind."

Maude didn't cry easily. She could count the number of times she'd cried in her life. The moisture accumulating in her eyes was sudden and confusing. She collected a tear on the tip of her finger and stared at it.

"Curious," Charlie murmured.

Maude sniffed and agreed. "Indeed." She squared her shoulders and glanced at Gil's pod again.

"Alert me when he's stabilized for retransit. I'll provide the optimum coordinates for time and date delivery."

"You want to deliver him?" Charlie asked.

"Negative," Maude snapped with the restored officiousness of a newly certified Rogue. She was all business again, a Rogue once more. She'd passed the test. She was moving on. Another day, another mission. This one was finished as far as she was concerned.

Charlie nodded and replied simply, "Understood."

Thankfully, he didn't say anything more. She might look tough on the outside, but Maude was all aquiver inside. Mush. Mushy for Gil. And greedy too. She wanted to remember, and wanted Gil to remember what almost was but could never be: a Rogue in love.

THREE

Dallas, 2008

"Shhhhit." Gil dropped the replacement lightbulb and clung to the top rung of the metal ladder as a blast of frigid air hit him with tsunami-like force. His plane of vision flattened into a thin horizon of color and suddenly he couldn't tell up from down. The sound of the bulb shattering on contact with the rock-strewn chuck wagon exhibit somewhere far below him penetrated his mental fog. He swore again. If he didn't hold fast and regain his senses, he'd join the bulb in the fake fire pit.

Preston "Gil" Gillespe, PhD had made his share of mistakes as the new curator of the Dallas History Museum, but this one was a doozie. Damaging artifacts was a no-no. And, accident or not, tumbling headfirst into a valuable collection on loan from the right-and-proper Chicago museum wasn't going to be easy to explain. His after-hours project, a solo enterprise to tweak lights and replace bulbs for the showcase exhibit in the main gallery, was a prime example of his work ethic, of his need to do everything himself that needed fixing fast if he was going to survive the job. Overkill was threatening to snuff him.

Reminding himself of his squandered youth getting tossed and stomped by rodeo bulls, he sucked air into his lungs, opened his eyes wide, and willed himself to buck up. *It worked.* He came back to himself. Surveying his surroundings from his precarious perch atop the service ladder in the main gallery, he saw the numerous exhibit spotlights glowing warmly above his head. His sweat-slicked palms still gripped the railing. No hint of a chill lingered in the climate-controlled environment, and gone was the silent and invisible blast of air that had so surprised him.

"Imagined the whole damned thing," he grumbled under his breath, and fished around in his canvas tote for a replacement bulb. He popped it in, levered the lamp to center on the campfire, and scrambled down the ladder with the brisk efficiency that had hallmarked his sixteen-hour shifts every day for the past month.

Although he was a hale and hearty ex–bull rider still in his prime, Gil's burst of energy was brief—short-circuited by the cumulative effect of a month of insufficient sleep. The minor effort of stowing the ladder and tossing the remnants of the broken bulb taxed both mind and muscle. When he'd finished restoring the display to rights, he could barely move his leaden limbs.

"What I wouldn't give for eight hours of solid sack time," he muttered, snapping the final Plexiglas partition into place and standing back to survey the results. A futile prayer for several reasons, the biggest being: sack time didn't promise rest. Not with that damned temptress tormenting him in every dream.

No. He scrubbed his brow with the back of his hand. *Don't think about her. Don't give in. She's not real.*

But Gil couldn't stop himself. She slipped past his de-

fenses. More than a seductive image or a sultry shape
that merely teased a guy's anatomy, she stirred up deeper
stuff. Conquest. Commitment.

He could hear her voice. Her throaty laugh when she
slipped her arms around his neck and pulled his lips
close. Contact. Brief but powerful. And he was a goner,
sinking like a rock and loving every minute of the plunge
into the abyss of passion.

She was more than an idea. He remembered a gal who
matched him in smarts, inspired feats of daring, and also
soothed the savage beast. His beast.

Gil shook himself and concentrated on the exhibit,
on its security. Had he checked and rearmed the motion
sensors? Interning at the museum during the Pompeii
exhibit the two previous years had spoiled him. The
state-of-the-art security had been smooth, seamless,
and nearly impervious to human error. This current
traveling exhibit was sufficiently secure, with industry-
standard systems, but those required a bit of grunt work
to enable or manually reset.

Damn. I'll have to double-check the system, he silently
groused. It was one more task that couldn't wait until
morning, but thankfully it wasn't brain surgery. Grunt
work was all he was good for this late in the workday.
Hours earlier his higher cognitive processes had fled,
leaving him a virtual automaton.

Tired as he was, the straightforward chore took twice
as long to accomplish. Twenty minutes of effort finally
insured the gallery featuring the unique collection of
cattle drive relics from the Old West was sufficiently protected, but left Gil dead on his feet. His neck ached, his
calf muscles twitched, and the dull throb in the vicinity
of his gray matter threatened a migraine if he didn't
clock out and snag a nap. Everything else on his list of
tasks as the museum's new curator would have to wait.

Groaning, he fought back all complaints. The buck

stopped with him. That's the way he'd wanted it. It wasn't in his makeup to shirk any duty or back down from a challenge; not now, not ever. But damned if he wasn't eyeing one of the cowpuncher's bedrolls cozied up next to the fake campfire as an ideal place for a siesta.

The display of treasured cowboy artifacts had a realistic setting. There was a convincing twilight backdrop. The pungent aroma of weathered saddles and gear nested about an inviting campfire prickled Gil's nostrils, and the chuck wagon overladen with mock foodstuff—stacks of baking powder biscuits and spackleware brimming with pinto beans—made his mouth water. The overall effect very nearly inspired the dog-tired curator to become one with his exhibit. The surround sound acoustic track of milling longhorns and a prairie thunderstorm rumbling in the distance would lull him to sleep *no problemo*. Here he finally might get rest. Far away from his fantasy beauty and her bedeviling claim to his nights, he could snooze and perchance *not* dream.

The wall of cold hit Gil again without warning. His knees buckled. His breath froze. His five o'clock shadow felt like frozen bits of glass peppering his cheeks, chin, and throat. The objects within the gallery space blurred, lost substance, and faded, revealing another layer of images. It looked like the old Pompeii exhibit was superimposed on the Chicago collection. Impossible.

Gil staggered, struggling to take it all in. It was an extraordinary sight to comprehend, especially with his reason scrambled by exhaustion.

It can't be.

But it was. Two realities were competing for time and space. One from the past and the other from the present. One reality with the female—God in heaven, she was a beauty—and one without her.

The woman's cornflower blue eyes seemed to see right through him. Tall and athletic, her figure sheathed in a leatherlike garment, she stood next to the key artifact in the old Pompeii exhibit, the bodycast of a victim of the AD 79 Mt. Vesuvius eruption.

No. It wasn't possible. He'd helped pack up the Pompeii artifacts over two years ago. And this female couldn't exist then or now. She was imaginary, the same one who had haunted his dreams and his waking hours for a month of Sundays, driving him crazy with desire and want.

It couldn't have lasted more than a moment—the oppressive frigid air, the confusion of colors and shapes—before it was gone. The absence of chaos swallowed Gil whole. Like tripping the main breaker on a power supply, he plunged into a dark void that could only mean one thing. Overwork could kill.

"Zat," Maude howled as she surfaced from the pool's icy depths like a breaching whale, freely spewing water and curses. She'd lost her link with Gil and destroyed another memory chip. With a *poof* and *pop*, the fragile implant was no more; the frigid dunking had zapped it with finality and severed her access to the enhanced data on Gil. It was a colossal error, one that aborted the nightly relaxation ritual she'd practiced for the last two years since sending Gil home. The all-important, essential download. The torrid collection of sensual memories with the cowboy, some real, others fabricated, was the ultimate balm for her weary body. This mistake would rob her of the treat.

A mistake? Rogues didn't make mistakes.

Maude howled again: another mistake, as the curse echoed throughout the shadowy cavern. Too late she remembered where she was: The Frontier Zone was dangerous turf, a volatile, unstable region for man or beast.

She splashed to the lip of the pool and pulled her nude body out in one smooth move. Heedless of the water dripping from her chilled flesh, she listened intently. Activating her ocular implants and audio enhancements, she scanned the cavern. Far away in the midnight darkness of the bowl-shaped cavern's central plain, a smattering of molten pits intermittently belched tongues of fire and lobbed tram-sized hunks of flaming goo. Maude adjusted her field of depth. Zoomed out. Refocused. From this distance, the glowing pits looked harmless, like campfires. They were neither.

She continued her visual and aural survey. Close by, fitful percolating mudpots perfumed the air with a noxious steam. Maude relaxed. It seemed she was safe for the moment. Her scan hadn't detected the telltale rumble of shifting masses or heaving earth, so her shouts hadn't triggered a rockfall. But she wanted confirmation. The fractured rock ceiling above was unstable. Abundant evidence of the danger existed. An impressive array of building-sized boulders littered the ground.

Accessing her mapping implant, Maude filtered the scan data. The results were produced with a minor octave tone. The map overlay noted adjustments in the rocky rubble, but none was significant enough to trigger fear. The expanse between her present location, within a narrow leg of the cavern and her mission goal, an egress tunnel and lift storage pod on the opposite side, was still hazardous—a maximum life-risk rating. But she could continue if she liked.

Whew. Maude sighed and powered down her implants. She would negotiate the distance over the next rotation. It wouldn't be necessary to break camp, backtrack to bypass the arena, or adjust her training schedule. Tough as it was, she was looking forward to the most arduous trial, to the resulting euphoria when she completed the last challenge. One final push and then she could return to Rogue Central.

She rolled her head, stretching out her neck muscles,

and the residual tension evaporated. She could rest easy tonight.

Rest easy? That was *drutzed* unlikely. Minus her memory chip, she was solo in a bleak, off-grid danger zone. Sleep wouldn't come easy or quick.

Maude shrugged off her fear. The situation could be worse. Her camp had been chosen with care. Although largely primordial, Chadwick Cavern also possessed a rare amenity: a freshwater pool. The phenomenon was fed by Earth's glacial surface far above the depths of the Frontier Zone. And, after nearly thirty rotations of Rogue training, a swim in its bone-chilling waters had been a welcome relief. But it had also destroyed her last link with Gil.

She'd started this series of exercises with two chips. Each had been loaded with her collected memories of the male she'd loved and lost to time, even though such an indulgence wasn't practical. The training was challenging. The Frontier tested survival skills and strengthened abilities essential for her upcoming level twelve mission. Concentration was key. Equipment minimums were in effect, and memory chips weren't recommended. In fact, the Rogue prep technician had reminded her during installation: "The chips aren't Zone-certified. Both will be damaged or destroyed before you complete the exercise."

Maude hated that the technician was right. She'd exercised caution, as much as she could, to preserve them for the duration. She'd nearly succeeded. Nearly. Damn the *zatting* temperature change! Diving headlong into the pool, she'd forgotten about it.

Still dripping from her plunge, Maude fingered her short wet curls and laughed. *Hair?* She had hair again. Not much, of course, but hair of any length was rare for a mission-certified Rogue. Leaning over the still pool, she stared at her reflection. Her curling cap of white-blond hair ruefully reminded her of the distant past—her time as a youth at the Children's Cabala. A time before the Rogues, before she'd discovered and embraced her purpose in life, and before Gil. Maude didn't like the memory and dismissed it immediately. Her youth was over. And hair—long or short—belonged to her youth.

Maude turned her back on the pool. Snagging her discarded bodysuit and utility belt, she clambered up the pumice rock face toward her temporary sanctuary.

A *level twelve mission*, Maude repeated silently, as though a mantra as she neared the pockmarked ledge where she'd stowed her gear. She levered herself up and over the obstacle with flagging energy.

To prepare for the mission, she'd pushed herself beyond Dak's written expectations. Making sure to test her abilities every step of the way, she had increased her endurance and skill. L-12s were rare; they were missions that defied the Rogue norms, but Maude was confident that *now* she was ready. One last hurdle: crossing Chadwick Cavern.

Zat, zat, ZAT, she hissed. Rest was an essential component of her training regime. But to rest, she needed her crutch. Gil. Her nightly indulgence had quickly become essential. She'd developed an unhealthy dependency on the chips, one of which she was not proud. It smacked of weakness. But using the chip's data to rouse and release emotion had become the only way for her to find balance in this place, and so she'd done it. Now, with the chip destroyed, her crutch was gone. She'd lost Gil.

Gone was the special blend of reality and fantasy that could stir her blood to a fever. The musky smell of his body, the wet salty warmth of his tongue pressing into her mouth, and the weight of him covering her body. How it had shielded and soothed her in the wilds of the Zone and the dangers known and unknown. Night after night. Gone. All gone.

She collapsed on the rough ledge. The shallow recess

offered protection and an excellent perspective of the main cavern. Activating her ocular implants again, Maude was assured by one last survey that all was well within the vast blanket of darkness. The belching fires looked like shooting stars. The serenade from the percolating mudpots was a merry accompaniment.

Busywork served a purpose; unwinding with other activities might prepare her for sleep. Maybe she could manage one night's rest without a Gil fix. It wasn't impossible.

Her perimeter sensors coded within acceptable margins but she rechecked them anyway. With a final adjustment to her ambient temperature settings and stowing her supplemental power packs, she was set. Stretching out on her gel pad, she forced her eyes closed. She'd make do without the memory chips; she'd have to. Sleep would come eventually.

The slowly warming gel pad helped, relaxing knotted muscles, and then, as if wishing were enough, a fleeting impression of Gil's embrace skirted her thoughts. But wishing wasn't enough. And, the experience wasn't entirely pleasurable, she realized as a delicious tonal fragment reminiscent of Gil's throaty chuckle degraded into a raspy hiss.

Maude's pulse jumped. The hiss wasn't human. She slowly opened her eyes and froze.

Snake!

Cozying up with a pit viper hadn't been in her training plan. But, their nearly nose-to-nose proximity indicated the snake had its own agenda. The Zone was a prime viper habitat, and evidently Maude had pitched camp on a ledge of preference for the creatures.

The sharp wedged snout, flicking tongue, and blind eyes were pointed at the strike zone: her vulnerable throat.

Maude swallowed, rechecked her impenetrable perimeter field, and forced herself to relax. She trusted her equipment; Charlie had never failed to provide the right gear.

"Go away," she growled through clenched teeth. Squeezing her eyes shut, she ignored the snake's continued complaints. Perhaps the serpent wasn't averse to cross-species snuggling, but Maude was. Sharing her warm nest with anything other than her dream cowboy was out of the question.

FOUR

"I'm dying," Maude cried, and thumped her stomach. Tight as a tick, full of burgers and fries, she was happily miserable. This monthly mission back to Dallas had perks, and one of them was the abundance of junk food, which was obsolete in her time. The other perks were sitting across from her in a commodious outdoor booth at the Sonic drive-in: Rick and Mackenzie Mason, two of her best friends and confidants. This monthly lunch date—Maude be-boppin' to the twenty-first century to eat, laugh, and keep current on her friends' lives—was something she always looked forward to, especially before she went out on a rough mission. Sure, she had dozens of pals in her time, but nothing equaled her trial-by-fire connection with the newly wedded couple from Earth's past. After they'd helped her save Dak, they'd become the family she'd always wanted. They cared, groused, and lectured ad nauseum. Maude loved them for it.

"I'd be dying too if I'd just polished off two chili-cheeseburgers and a Big-Tex basket of curly fries,"

Mackenzie said. She eyed Maude's slim build and frowned. "Are you eating right and taking care of yourself? You know you can't survive only on Charlie's nutrient supplements. You need a balance of real food too."

Maude grinned. She liked being fussed over, and Mackenzie, a card-carrying daughter of Texas and first-class mother hen, knew how to fuss with the best of them, in that annoying but endearing big sister–like fashion.

"Ease up, babe. Maudie's a big girl. She's looking good," Rick interjected.

Maude sighed. Rick's deep voice could melt her bones and set her all aquiver if she wasn't careful. Discipline—practice at managing distracting emotions such as envy, jealousy, and first heartbreak—was essential for a Rogue. And, boy oh boy, did she envy Mackenzie and Rick. She envied their loving partnership, and flat-out coveted Rick. Dr. Handsome-as-Sin Mason wasn't first, but he was still near the top of her list of dream lovers.

Before meeting Mackenzie, Maude had endeavored to make her romantic fantasy a reality. But, she'd never had a glimmer of a chance with Rick. That deliciously dark and distant man had never once indicated anything but fraternal interest, in spite of Maude's overtures. Rick had been, was, and always would be devoted to one woman: the woman now sitting next to him, her trim figure flushed with a healthy glow that might be just love, but Maude knew better. Mackenzie was carrying Rick's child.

"I don't care how good Rick thinks you look." The little mother-to-be wagged a finger in Maude's direction. "I'm not so sure you've got sense enough to come in from the rain. Rogues are gluttons for punishment, and I won't allow Charlie and that bunch to use you up or burn you out. Do you hear me, missy?"

"I'm with her there, Maude," Rick added, casually looping an arm around his wife's shoulders. They exchanged a silent, smoldering, and utterly intimate gaze that united them body and soul.

Giga zat. Maude swallowed hard. She was nearly tempted to slap her transit device and bug out, give them some privacy, but it was also delicious to watch love in action.

A heavy dose of envy swamped her senses. No, she didn't want Rick—not really. But she could dream about a guy like Rick—a guy of her own—and a dab of the brand of romance he offered to a female. All she needed was the time to indulge in a manhunt.

Ha. She nearly laughed out loud at the irony: a time traveler shortchanged on the essential ingredient for romance—time? But it wasn't odd. Actually, all Rogues lacked that luxury. Emotional attachments weren't easy to begin or maintain when one's job description required instantaneous leaps across time, transits back and forth between millennia. As a new Rogue intent on logging missions, learning skills, and building a career, "romance" was rarely more than an occasional one-night stand with a friend. It was efficient, effective exercise— just that and nothing more. Commitment complications were nonexistent. And Maude had fully accepted the constraints when she'd signed on as a Rogue—at least, she thought she had. Did her mounting interest in these affectionate newlyweds indicate otherwise?

Drutz. She bit her lip and forced her wayward thoughts to surrender to reason. Given her schedule of upcoming missions, including prep, debrief, and reacclimation, there wasn't time to spare for a quickie, let alone a leisurely slow dance with romance. Given the demanding schedules they kept, some Rogues opted for shortcuts, taking interludes with strangers, but Maude wasn't that desperate yet. Allowing an anonymous Mr. Lucky to climb into her sleep dock and service her between missions didn't sound appealing in the least.

If only Gil were . . .

No, not Gil. She wouldn't—shouldn't—consider it, even though Gil pegged out her hunk-o-meter. Gil was hot. But he was off limits. That was why she'd had that chip made, the one that could be inserted when she wanted to remember him and fantasize—and removed the rest of the time. Perfect, ideal, mouth-watering and all male, Gil was lost in the mists of time. Their brief association and flesh-searing, blood-pumping, breath-catching mutual attraction had been unraveled and erased.

Gil couldn't even remember their meeting, because it simply hadn't happened—at least, not to him. He was back in his regular life, and Maude was still grappling with the fluke of fate, falling for a guy 150 years her senior.

Yeah, Gil was hot. Right guy, but *wrong* century.

Another glance at the cozy Rick and Mackenzie, and Maude's jealousy won out. She cleared her throat and reminded them they weren't alone.

"Hey, stop playing kissy-face, will you? Save it for the bedroom."

Rick shook himself like a wet dog after a drenching; Mackenzie was the shade of molten lava. Then all of them laughed—even Maude, who suddenly knew that somehow, some way, she'd find the time for romance. Not the enhanced and fanciful memory chip version, but something real, substantial, and satisfying. The sooner the better.

"Damn." Gil didn't cut much slack for fools, himself included, but after thirty stress-filled days on the job he was grateful that his boss and the rest of the staff did.

He swore again, but under his breath, as he juggled a stack of reference materials, his briefcase, and a sack of doughnuts in a fruitless search for his employee badge. He'd forgotten it again. This was one more sign that he was losing his edge and turning goofy from overwork and no sleep.

Thankfully, it was Harry the security guard covering the staff entrance to the museum. Gil shook the Krispy Kreme sack and Harry buzzed him through.

"This is the third time, Dr. Gillespe," Harry said after confiscating two chocolate-frosted doughnuts. His scowl was comical, totally at odds with his jolly features. Although a runner-up in last year's Santa lookalike contest— Harry's Scottish brogue was a ho-ho-handicap—he could be hard-nosed about breaches in protocol.

Gil squared his shoulders and prepared himself for another lecture. Clearly, the doughnuts hadn't bought him a free pass. He didn't deserve one. Security was a huge issue for a facility that housed priceless artifacts. Aside from the main holdings, which ranged from porcelain and medieval tapestries to spurs and barbed wire, the exhibit on loan from Chicago featured a rare collection of relics. And as Gil well knew from his experience with the Pompeii exhibit while still an intern, anything on loan magnified the importance of security. One breach, however minor, could jeopardize the museum's ability to compete for the best exhibits.

Gil unloaded his burdens on a handy rolling cart and poured Harry a cup of coffee from his thermos. "Wet your whistle before you lay into me, Harry. I know I deserve it."

Harry couldn't maintain the scowl and sip coffee too. Harry sipped. He pulled out Gil's staff badge and tossed it on the counter between them. "Maintenance found it in the chuck wagon exhibit last night. Want to tell me how it got there?"

Gil blanched. *Hell, no.* He didn't want to tell anyone about that. It was the main reason he was late, dog-tired, tied up in knots, and alarmed that he might be losing his mind.

Harry munched on one of the doughnuts and tipped his snowy-haired noggin toward the bank of security screens that monitored the exits and gallery areas of the museum. "I checked the tape on camera six."

Crap. Is it all on film? Gil swallowed hard, his thoughts bursting from his head like fire from a Roman candle. In a moment his whole world would burn out. The sham of the last thirty days would be revealed, out in the open. He'd have to admit it, tell Harry everything, spill his guts and confess he didn't know what, why, or how it was happening.

Crapola. He couldn't even name "*it.*" Was "it" a vision, an illusion, a hallucination, or maybe a manifestation?

Any of the above and he was a dead duck. In the all-too-proper and upright world of academics, few historians survived a challenge to their credibility. Rational thought based in pure science legitimized their reputations. Sprinkle his newly established professional status with a bit of interaction with the inexplicable, and *poof*—Gil's future as a museumologist and curator would be history.

Gil wasn't a stranger to the occult. One kooky and entertaining ex-girlfriend had dabbled in the fine art of manifesting "good spirits." However, his playdates with Lucy Skydiamond hadn't ever manifested anything tangible or concrete that couldn't be explained away with scientific know-how.

He slowly picked up his staff badge and clipped it to his shirt. Then he looked Harry straight in the eye. "What's on the tape, Harry? What's it show?"

"It showed how you earned those black circles and bags under your eyes. You fainted."

"Huh?"

"Tim-berrrr! Stiff-legged, eyes rolling back in your head, toppling like a felled Ponderosa pine, and clipping your chin on one of the exhibit signs on the way down. You bled all over the floor."

Gil fingered the square of gauze he'd taped to his chin.

One puzzle solved. He didn't remember much from after he entered the main gallery last night to check out the spots on the alpha grid. He had pulled out the ladder, replaced a blown bulb in the exhibit, climbed down, and . . .

Suddenly he remembered all too well: stone-cold fear hitting him, an emotional sucker punch triggered by an extraordinary sight. Two realities, one superimposed over the other. The old Pompeii exhibit and the Chicago collections. And, *the woman*. Her intense blue eyes and leggy, well-shaped figure seemed unnervingly familiar . . . and yet alien. Imaginary or real, friend or foe, she was a knockout.

Gil tried to shake free of the memory, but it held him fast, seeping into the moment and taking control, etching conflicting images with startling precision. No wonder he'd keeled over. If there'd been a calibrating device for psychic phenomena, it would have pegged out. There was too much to take in, assimilate, and accept. Even now, buffered by time and diluted in memory, the situation threatened to liquefy his backbone.

Gil blinked, sucked in air, and the fear and conflicting images faded as suddenly as they had come. The second hand on the wall clock pulsed, the rise and fall of Harry's barrel chest continued, and nothing, absolutely nothing, appeared changed in this world. Save one thing: his sanity. He was losing it for sure. Yep, he was cooked, fried, and certifiably whacked-out.

Gil felt the wall against his back and locked his knees to keep from falling down. He plastered a smile on his face and nodded as Harry continued to talk; anchored between the counter and wall he could fake it until he'd fully recovered.

"Women, like my Bernadette, call it a swoon. She's done it a few times too. Gets herself all worked up over some fool nonsense, doesn't get sleep, eats like a bird, and next thing you know she's listing like that tower in Pisa."

At last, Gil's urge to mimic unmolded Jell-O passed.

He interrupted Harry's diatribe. "You're telling me I fainted?"

It was a handy explanation for the whole shebang: the vision, the female, the smell of brimstone, the overlapping images of reality. *Yeah, fainting could cover it.* It was a blow to his manhood—guys didn't faint—but it beat the hell out of the alternative explanation. *Crazy* didn't wear well.

The phone rang and distracted Harry. Gil seized the opportunity to escape down the long hall with his rolling cart in tow. Early in life he'd learned how and when to "beat feet" to avoid his dad's protracted inquisitions. Eluding Harry was a cinch.

Two more stops on the main floor and he was home free—up the elevators and sucked into the multistoried maze of holding areas, storage cubicles, conservation labs, offices, and conference areas that supported the grand public galleries.

Just two more stops.

FIVE

Nailed. Harry caught up with him at the staff lounge. Gil didn't have to fake looking busy; the stack of messages he'd just retrieved from his mailbox promised another very long day. He pocketed the messages and added a lab coat and gloves to his expanding load on the rolling cart.

Harry's girth blocked most of the doorway. It'd be a tough squeeze with the cart, and Gil briefly considered abandoning his payload and sprinting for the elevators. However, Harry's reflexes were phenomenal. He was renowned around the senior tennis circuit.

"You look like you've been tossed and stomped by a rogue bull. And it's not just because of last night," Harry said. He leaned against the door frame—polite, respectful, but persistent.

Not much escaped old Harry, and Gil told him so.

"It's my job," Harry returned, and slapped the walkie-talkie strapped to his belt. "Plus, I'm nosy."

Gil had to laugh. Harry was nosier than Jimmy Stewart in *Rear Window*. He had the skinny on half the town. There wasn't anything that slipped past those keen eyes, ears, and nose. He'd been a top-notch detective before retirement, but in his current security role at the museum, he'd probably found few opportunities to utilize his skills.

Until now.

"You're not crazy enough to still do piecework with the rodeo. And I'm figuring it's not a new girlfriend. You've been burning the midnight oil ever since you took over as curator, and no lass is going to put up with that malarkey. They need romancing, even from one of Dallas's ten most eligible bachelors."

Gil groaned and shook his head. "Oh, brother. Is she at it again?" He elaborated when he glimpsed Harry's puzzled expression. "Aunt Willie never gives up on trying to improve my image. She planted that seed in the society pages, didn't she?"

"Society pages? Bernadette's my source on that one," Harry replied.

"Whatever the source, if you've heard it, then it's in the wind and I'm toast. She did the same thing last year when I tacked on the doctorate. Criminy. Every mama in the Golden Triangle with a marriageable daughter invited me to dinner to check out my bankability and manners. What a joke. They all ought to know by now that I'm definitely not the upper-crust, CEO-of-the-family-business type. That's my brother Chad's gig, not mine. I'm the black sheep of the family."

"Black sheep? Your job here at the museum isn't exactly small change," Harry protested.

"No, but I'm also a bull riding, pick-up driving, burger-and-fries eating, beer swilling kind of a guy. I like the Texas two-step over the ballet. I prefer a weekend in Lukenbach to one in Paris. I'd sooner float the Brazos than cruise the Med. And I like gals who aren't afraid of sweat, sunburns, or broken fingernails. I'm every society mama's nightmare. I'm a trustfund baby with no class."

Harry snorted. "Maybe. But you're a *hardworking*, no-class trustfund baby," he corrected. "Too much so. When are you going to back off, lad? You're not Mackenzie's intern anymore. You graduated. You got the job. You're staff now, don't y'know? You don't have to put in a fifty to sixty-hour workweek to prove yourself."

"Don't I? Mackenzie's a pretty tough act to follow," Gil replied, and forced a grin—trying to keep it light, even though Harry's comments hit pretty close to home. He *was* trying to prove himself. That much wasn't new. As one of Colonel Quinton "Blackjack" Gillespe's heirs, he'd been reared on competitiveness and mentored to pursue, attack, and conquer life. His mom's untimely death seven years earlier had changed his goals—he'd balked at the colonel's plan for his future—but it hadn't changed his personality.

In life, Lellie Mae had gifted her passel of menfolk with a loving and supportive haven, and nurtured each with her distaff devotion to kith and kin. After her passing, her legacy to Gil had been the courage to defy convention—and three generations of patriarchal empire building in the oil industry. He'd shifted gears, changed course, and set out to stake a claim, so to speak, on his own merit.

When he was awarded his doctorate and accepted the coveted position as museum curator, Gil believed he had finally hit a gusher. Thanks to his mom and genetics, Gil never doubted for a moment that he could do the job or make the grade. With Mackenzie as the new Director of the Museum, taking over her job as curator had been great. They'd worked well together as mentor and intern. And he was looking forward to continuing their business relationship. He had plenty to prove, but second-guessing his own abilities didn't fit into the equation. Until . . .

Day one on the job changed everything. Suddenly Gil

was operating in an alien sea. Fear nipped at his heels. It twisted his belly, skewed his thinking, and ravaged his reserves.

Two years earlier, during the Pompeii exhibit and as Mackenzie's intern, he'd virtually lived at the museum, learning the ropes from the resident master. That plebeian role was a thankless and exhausting test, but one that he passed with flying colors. The invaluable experience had confirmed his commitment to the discipline and encouraged his passion for ancient relics. Ultimately, he'd proved himself worthy to succeed Mackenzie as curator. So, what had gone wrong? After thirty days on the job he had nothing but egg on his face, at least in terms of his sanity. Last night hadn't been the only fathomless and bone-chilling event he'd experienced in the museum. So far there'd been three. And *one* was too many. Fear shadowed his every move. At a dead run, he was two steps ahead of utter panic. If he tripped or fell, it would overtake him.

And then what? When would people realize he was cracking?

"Take some advice from an old war horse?" Harry asked. He didn't wait for Gil to respond before offering it with a generous dollop of gruffness. "Don't be so gosh-all fired up that you miss the important stuff."

Gil rooted around in a storage locker and added a field laptop and its otter case to his now overburdened cart. He noted his bag of doughnuts was empty, and so was his thermos of coffee. *Damn.* He didn't remember consuming anything. He glared at Harry.

"Do you have something specific to suggest, or is this just your version of 'take time to smell the flowers'?"

Harry shrugged. The gruffness was all bluster. Harry's eyes twinkled like those of an elf eager to share a secret Christmas cookie recipe. "Take it or leave it. If you've got the smarts I think you have, lad, you'll take it."

"You're not just talking about fine-tuning my sixty-hour workweek," Gil said. He kicked the metal supply locker door, which popped back open and rocked on its hinges. Harry's face was a mask of calm as he leaned over and gently closed the door.

"You're due, Gil. Take a break. Hell, take two." Then, without fanfare, Harry departed, his utility belt jingling like bells on Santa's sleigh.

Good advice. Excellent. Only Gil couldn't oblige him now.

He maneuvered his cart out into the hallway and toward the nest of service elevators. The smells of mortar, metal, and age dominated this special world, soothed him. Even the flickering fluorescents and the squeaking wheel on the cart upon the slick-floored corridor helped. The muffled hiss from the ventilation system explained away the cool breeze that teased his brow, cheek, and neck like a lover's kiss.

Yes, it was a tumultuous love affair. This discipline dedicated to the conservation of artifacts had snagged him hook, line, and sinker. He loved it. But like a bridegroom after the wedding, Gil realized there was a lifelong journey ahead of him. Getting the job was just the first step; keeping it would be the real adventure. Especially the way things had been going.

Yeah, I'm working long hours. Yeah, I've got a lot to learn. But that's all a load of horseshit. There's no excuse for cracking up.

Gil grunted. He wouldn't rationalize his recent failures. Something akin to self-doubt was eating him alive, and for the umpteenth time since he'd stepped into this job, he wondered: *Am I up to the task?* He would make sure of it.

It was a quick ride up to his new office on the top floor, and any notion of inadequacy evaporated the moment the elevator door opened. The business-as-usual setting supercharged Gil, as it usually did.

Phones were ringing and people were chattering in, over, and around the work cubicles that lined the wall of windows with western exposure. The Chicago exhibit concluded in two weeks, and the deinstallation and prep for the next exhibit was a top priority on everyone's agenda—especially his. This was going to be another one of those fanny-busting, tongue-hanging, brain-draining workdays.

After sixty nonstop minutes of returning mundane phone calls, delegating tasks, and pushing paper, he was almost convinced—again—that he'd imagined the whole weird woo-woo thing. Of course, he begrudgingly admitted, he had a fascination with woo-woo, despite being a scientist. Maybe he attracted it like an MRI magnet. He'd been a conspiracy theory whacko most of his life. His quest for "the truth" had been ruthless. From Area 51's captured UFO to the JFK assassination theories, he'd dogged leads, sniffed out real and manufactured "documentation," and wearied librarians and historians alike with his earnest efforts. He'd joined groups, led some, and debunked others. Squirreled away in his tie-clip and cuff-link drawer was his charter member card for the Grassy Knoll advocate group. As an academic and museumologist, he'd narrowed his focus, applying his skills and energy to ferreting out historical facts. Seeking truth was his motive, his mantra. And as a museum curator, he had a privileged and revered responsibility to do just that.

He shuffled around in his drawer and pulled out a special project folder filled with a hodgepodge of notes and data about a mystery near and dear to his heart. It was an outrageous proposal. The symposium topic and companion exhibit had a target date: 2013, the fiftieth anniversary of JFK's assassination in Dealey Plaza on that warm, bright, November day. That date was five-plus years off, but the museum would need extra time if they were going to do things right.

He tossed the folder on his desktop and scrubbed his face with his hands. He hadn't run it by Mackenzie yet. He had been waiting for the right moment. Sure, she knew about his JFK obsession. Maybe he was too close to the subject to be objective, but he didn't think she'd shoot it down outright. It had promise. But it was also fraught with problems—the prickly kind. It could garner respect and admiration for the museum or make the institution vulnerable to attack as a hotbed for conspiracy kooks.

Gil scratched at the bandage on his chin. The adhesive tape was itching, his belly was growling, he needed more coffee, and a stretch of the legs wouldn't hurt his neglected muscles either. Harry's recommendation resurfaced. *Take a break.* Yeah. He'd take a break and finally try out the idea on Mackenzie. It was long overdue, frankly, and if the wacky woo-woo world would give him a break too, maybe he could win Mackenzie's approval to get on it. The sooner the better.

"They're at Sonic," Mackenzie's secretary told Gil when he popped in to make the pitch.

Ms. Jane Broome was ageless and indispensable. The fine lines scattered among her features formed a roadmap of joy, but her firm, no-nonsense attitude and command of museum operations would have impressed General George S. Patton. When Ms. Broome said jump, people jumped.

"It's a standing date with Rick that helps her keep her priorities in balance. You ought to follow her example. You're starting to look like death warmed over."

It was futile to protest. He'd taken a good long gander at the circles under his eyes in the washroom mirror; still, Gil tried to look insulted. The grandmotherly bastion of efficiency either missed or ignored his look while applying herself to the brutal task of ripping off his bandage and replacing it with a fresh one. The dousing with alcohol stung like wildfire, but Gil bit his tongue—that is, until he'd fled into the elevator and the thick walls could muffle his agonized yowl. He had some pride left.

The doors opened on the main gallery level, and Gil tensed. He'd jumped ship last night, fled like the hounds of hell were chasing him. This was the scene of his visions. But now, less than twelve hours later and with visitors milling through the exhibit, the atmosphere was inviting and hospitable.

He stepped out of the elevator, two giant steps, and braced for any assault from the unknown. The doors shut behind him and cut off the most expedient avenue of escape, but he didn't need it. Nothing happened. Devoid of demons and darkness, everything seemed normal.

Had last night's episode been a mere flight of fancy? Bits of memory twisted around a dream? *Whatever the hell it was, it was hell.* Because it was impossible to explain. And Harry had said it himself: This was the third time.

Hell's bells. If only he could get some sleep—the dreamless kind. It was all adding up. Night and day. After a month with no solution in sight, he was out of ideas, out of energy, and probably out of his gourd.

Maude checked her chronometer as she slipped back into the seat across from Rick and Mackenzie. She was maxing out her transit window and lingering long past the typical two-hour session, pushing the safety limits and frankly resisting every urge to stay on schedule.

"You're dawdling," Mackenzie said between slurps of her cherry lemonade. "Something bothering you? Or do you need another dose of junk food before you zap back to the future?"

Yes, something was bothering her. She scanned the boisterous crowd clustered about the popular drive-in and groaned. *He* wasn't here. Cars packed with teens maneuvered in and out of stalls. Kids raced up and down the zigzag median dotted with speaker poles and backlit menu boards. Day-care moms with strollers claimed the metal-skinned picnic table to her left, a senior foursome the one to her right, and a rash of cuter-than-cute servers mingled throughout the scene, balancing burger-laden trays with ease. People. People everywhere, but no Gil. Two years without a single, solitary accidental-on-purpose glimpse of the guy who could trigger a cascade of shivers up and down her spine just by smiling in her direction.

"How's Gil?" she suddenly asked. Her cheeks superheated and her tongue nearly twisted into a knot.

Drutz. She didn't want them to know about the war raging within. It was a futile engagement between her head and her heart that she entertained every time she dropped into this time. She wanted to see him, to meet him anew and feel the delicious and dangerous attraction ignite between them. But she knew she couldn't risk it. Gil belonged to the past and she didn't.

"How's he handling the new job is what I meant to ask, of course."

Maude knew she didn't lie well, at least not well enough to trick close friends. She caught the silent message exchanged between Rick and Mackenzie—her Mona Lisa–like smile responding to his raised brow.

Mackenzie reached across the table and patted her hand. "You've still got it bad?"

Maude's stomach lurched, and not just because of the side order of jalapenos she'd consumed. "Yeah," she admitted, and tried to laugh it off. "Silly, isn't it? I mean, even if he remembered and wanted to do anything about it, he couldn't."

"Or you either." Mackenzie offered a wry smile and clicked her tongue. "Right guy, wrong time."

"There's someone else out there for you, Maude," Rick said. "Besides, Gil's no Prince Charming."

Mackenzie elbowed him and cut off further consolation from that quarter. "That's debatable, Rick. Gil's a catch in any century, but that's beside the point. Isn't it, Maude?"

Maude struggled to find her voice, and nodded. She said, "I don't have time for any extracurricular activities. I really, really don't. I'm scheduled out for the next sixty rotations for a level twelve mission."

Rick whistled. "A level twelve? That's something. You're moving up fast, Maude."

She grinned. It was a big step for a fairly new Rogue. She shrugged her shoulders and rolled her neck to work out some of the persistent kinks—a minor side effect of frequent short-term transits. At least Charlie had at long last managed to almost eliminate her hives, the head to toe raspberry-hued splotches that felt like she'd tangled with a thousand bloodthirsty mosquitoes.

She shifted the topic away from herself and focused on completing her briefing. She was running out of time, she reminded herself. Rick and Mackenzie relied on her to keep them current with Rogue business.

"There haven't been any recent problems with the data gaps in Core's records of Earth's past," she began.

Mackenzie sighed with relief. "Good," she replied. "As long as Core maintains time travel restrictions for those eras, our task of infilling those facts are a lower priority."

Rick jumped in like he always did when the subject of Core's incomplete database was introduced. "Did they successfully upload the presidential histories? That's important stuff. I sweated bullets double-checking Core's gaps and supplying the missing nineteenth- and twentieth-century data."

Maude nodded. "Done. In fact we used it to confirm a non-interference consequence factor for my next mission."

"Don't tell me that," Rick growled. "Damn! What if I overlooked something?"

Mackenzie rolled her eyes and groaned. "You didn't miss anything. Did you forget that you're not operating solo, buddy? I'm your backup."

Maude laughed. Her struggle with envy was constant during these monthly visits. The banter between the marriage partners was both a source of pleasure and painful to witness.

"While I'm gone, you'll have to transit back to Core for the monthly briefings, Rick," Maude said. "You're off the hook, of course, Mackenzie. You're past your first trimester, and Charlie told me to tell you that he's activated a safety block on you until Lara is born."

"Ah, Charlie. Right on schedule," Rick said, grinning ear to ear. "No more time travel jaunts for you, little mama."

"Or doses of Charlie's vile nutritional sludge either," Mackenzie returned, and toasted them with the last of her lemonade.

"*There's* a benefit to being pregnant in the past," Maude interjected. "Evidently Charlie's immuno-boost and pre- and postpartum swill are the bane of every procreating female in Core. If I ever . . ." She stopped abruptly. Her laugh sounded hollow even to herself. "Guess I won't have to worry about that for a long, long time."

"Hey, you didn't finish your story," Mackenzie said with forced joviality, reminding Maude of what they'd been discussing before thoughts of Gil took over. "What's up with Charlie's latest invention? Why is Core keeping it hush-hush?"

Maude giggled. "Because it's a wild concept, even for Charlie. Dak calls it the Superman chip because it's supposed to be bulletproof."

"Even Superman has his Kryptonite," Mackenzie said. "They think they are, but Core, Charlie included, isn't perfect—not by a long shot. The damned wardrobe folks at mission prep sent you to Dallas 2005 dressed like a film noir heroine from the 1930s. It's a prime example of the damned flaws in Core's so-called perfect time transit system, damn it."

"Don't get started on that gripe, babe," Rick interrupted. "That was a long time ago, and we're on repair detail now. We're fixing the problems. Besides, Maude's got to meet her transit window soon, and I want an update on Dak."

Mackenzie hissed, folded her arms and glared at him, but also acquiesced. Rick blew her a kiss and continued. "Is Dak recertified? I thought Core forced him to retire, and permanently revoked his time travel privileges because of that Pompeii stunt."

Maude nodded. "He's off the active Rogue rolls, all right. Of course, Dak and Charlie go way back. They started the Time Rogue program, and there's nothing they wouldn't do for each other. Dak's always tested Charlie's prototypes and although he can't test them on an actual mission, he can still run them through the initial stages at his fortress near Edgeville. He's got quite a setup." Maude held a finger up to her lips. "Another hush-hush tidbit is his stash of techie trinkets. You wouldn't believe the equipment he's acquired from unnamed sources. I think he's even got a secret transit station in an inactive volcanic pipe beyond Outskirt."

Rick raised his eyebrows. "Anyone else know about it?"

Maude shook her head. "Nope. I'm sure the Scios— you know, the league of scientists I'm always saying are more machine than human—would shut him down in a heartbeat if they thought he was transit-capable again. The time rift he triggered with his jaunt to Pompeii is the main reason we've got all the new protocols and safeguards. Strict auto-transit mandates also apply throughout Rogue classes, from scout to mentor. Everyone's getting the retrofit."

"Sounds like a dog collar with a short leash," Mackenzie said.

Rick scowled and nodded. "Sure does. We haven't had a retrofit yet. What about you?" he asked.

Maude pressed her lips tight. "No. Charlie's classified me as exempt. I'm newly certified to test his prototypes now that Dak's grounded."

"What?!" Mackenzie and Rick said in unison.

"It's okay, really. It's not dangerous," Maude interrupted before either could protest again. "I'm just the lucky Rogue who tests the gadgets in multiple transit scenarios. I'm getting the Superman upload for the next mission."

The short, shrill beep was unmistakable. Maude's chronometer alarm was sounding the five-minute warning before initiating auto-transit.

Rick cursed. "You're pushing it, Maude. You better get going."

Maude grimaced but agreed. The new mandates dictated that auto-transits were now class-one emergencies. Since the change, they had become a major headache for Core Transitors. Auto-transits could back up traffic through the system, snarl schedules, reroute routine time travel protocols, and skew arrival priorities. They could even trigger a full system shutdown. Maude's transit status didn't merit the emergency classification yet, but in 4.75 minutes it would. Missing a scheduled transit window, defaulting to the auto-transit safeguard, wasn't something a career savvy Rogue did without cause or consequences.

She checked her chronometer, her finger hovering above the manual transit button. Four-point-two-five minutes? Just enough time for one final taste of heaven.

She grabbed her Blue Lagoon coconut slushie and sucked hard on the straw.

"Yeow!" She scrunched up her nose and groaned. *Drutz.* She'd forgotten about slurping slushies too quick. Her eyeballs felt frozen and locked in the upright position.

"Pinch your earlobes, silly," Mackenzie cried.

Maude complied with the ridiculous command, and was genuinely surprised to discover it worked. "How do you come up with these things, Mackenzie?"

"We have a brain trust in the past, too. That bit of sage advice was handed down via my Granny Moon. Pass it on."

Maude nodded. "We don't have slushies in Core— yet." She had to grin. As one of Charlie's pet Rogues, she'd coerced the superbrain into supplementing the nutritionally balanced food selections by inventing replicant junk food products in his spare time. Nothing beat the taste of real junk food, of course, but it was a compromise between taste and essential protein that worked in a pinch.

She stood up and stretched. "I'm going to miss you guys."

"Sixty rotations on a level twelve mission," Rick said and scowled. "I don't understand all the turf war stuff between the Rogues and Scios yet. But, I tell you something, everybody back there better have all their ducks in a row to cooperate on a level twelve mission." He glanced at Mackenzie. "Wish I could come along." He winked at Maude. "But, the little mother needs me."

"The H-E-double hockey sticks, I do," Mackenzie retorted. "Promise me, Maude, if you need Rick's help, recall him. Level twelves are serious."

Maude's protracted groan brought smiles to all their faces. "Stop worrying. I'll be fine."

"Promise," Mackenzie demanded.

Maude's response didn't make it past her lips; beyond the sea of patrons was the answer to her prayer. Gil! Her tummy flip-flopped like a beached tuna. His quick smile, a flash of white amid bronzed features, triggered the delicious shiver she both craved and feared. He saw her and his smile stretched into a Cheshire cat grin . . . and froze.

"*Megadrutz*," Maude hissed under her breath. Rick and Mackenzie turned as one.

Gil's gaze shifted. His brow furrowed as he glanced first at Maude's companions, then back to her. His smile faded, and a dark and stormy countenance succeeded his normally friendly demeanor. He began to stagger toward them.

"Take off, Maude. I'll distract him," Rick offered under his breath.

"Something's wrong, you guys," Maude growled. Wrong? What an understatement.

"Huh?" Mackenzie said.

Maude spared her the briefest of glances. "He *knows* me," she whispered. She fished around in the leg pocket of her camo-colored bodysuit. "Think level-twelve time rift, *squared*," she grunted, and pulled out two small buffed disks.

"What's that supposed to mean?" Rick hissed.

"Core's mother of all boo-boos is my guess," Mackenzie snapped.

Maude nodded. "A disaster. Migrating time lines or worse."

Rick whistled. "What do you need me to do?"

Maude didn't have time to weigh the options. "Recall," she cried, and tossed Rick one of the buffed autotransit tags just as Gil stumbled stiff-legged into the table. She slapped the spare on Gil's brawny chest.

"Grab his other arm, Rick."

Rick didn't protest or demand explanations. On-call Rogues were trained to act first and save questions for later. He affixed his tag, blew his bride a farewell kiss, and lunged for Gil in one smooth move. In the split second before transit, Maude swallowed hard and glanced back at Mackenzie. Emergencies could get messy. She needed Rick's help, and after all, a promise was a promise.

Thankfully, Mackenzie proffered a nod and a thumbs-up to the unuttered request to borrow her husband. Maude opened her mouth to voice her thanks, but it was too late. Her chronometer toned with finality and the world around Maude and her traveling companions blurred into a mass of color accompanied by a deafening roar. Auto-transit commenced.

One, two, three—back to the future.

SIX

Ugh. A wordless grunt was all Gil could manage as he struggled for breath in the thick, jasmine-scented pink fog. He needed to sneeze but couldn't summon the energy.

What the hell just happened? He couldn't be dead. It hurt too damned much. He'd felt better after getting tossed into the stock-pen gate by his first bull than he did at that moment. A slug probably possessed more sense and twice as much stamina. He was as spent as a wingless moth; he was flat on his back on a chilled, slick surface with the wind knocked out of him and muscles that felt like goo.

The ringing in his ears subsided with a sudden pop and he heard murmurs of comfort echoing about him. The fog had thinned and the swirl of color swimming before his eyes seemed friendly and familiar. So did the punch on his nearly lifeless arm.

Rick?

"Hang in there, Gil. It takes time to recover. I felt like cow dung after my first transits," the voice from the formless, flesh-colored hue hanging over his head proclaimed. "After the techies shoot you full of nutrients and balance your enzymes, you'll get your sea legs."

Cow dung, transits, techies, and sea legs? Nothing made sense. Was he having a heart attack?

"You're doing fine," Rick said. "You're not a natural—few of us are except for Maude here—but you're better than average."

Good. Better than average at what? Gil's mush mouth twitched in response. He could count on Rick to make dying interesting.

The slick floor beneath him warmed, lights swelled, and the last of the pink fog dissipated. A quick inventory assured him that maybe he wasn't dying after all but rather making rudimentary progress in the other direction: He was blinking and breathing and moving the pinky toe of one foot. In fact, he was sure he could move a good deal more, except the weight on his chest wouldn't budge.

"Hey," he blurted when his vision snapped into focus. The shapely tush of the female straddling him was a beautiful but unexpected sight. Was she real? He poked at the curvaceous bottom and she slapped his hand away. She was real, all right—and spoiling for a fight.

"Knock it off and don't move," she cried with a quick glance over her shoulder at him. "You keep thrashing around and we'll never get untangled."

Gil wasn't sure that was a bad deal. Being snuggled intimately against his feisty dream gal was about as close to heaven as he'd imagined.

However, in the next moment an off-color comment by Rick—a suggestion that appealed to the emboldened sentiments of his libido—subsequently flattened his ardor with the delicacy of a steamroller. The female in question flushed pink to the top of her . . . *bald head?* Maybe introductions were the first order of business.

"Got it," she cried.

The sound of shredding fabric and a final tug on Gil's Levi's signaled the abrupt disconnect. The woman bounced to her feet and held up a chunk of denim—still entangled in her jeweled wristband—like a trophy snagged by the infamous hula popper at a fishing derby. She sliced away the remaining cloth and pressed a flashing red jewel. A pronged extension hummed and retracted back into the wristband.

She turned to Rick and said, "Whew. That was close. We collided during transit and it unleashed my stunner. I think he took a jolt." She leaned over and inspected Gil, checking his vitals with a clinical intensity that scared the hell out of him. "Say something," she demanded as she gave his jugular two taps with her fingertips. Her lips were pressed tight; her sky blue eyes reflected the same concern probably visible in his features.

With effort Gil mustered his voice. He wanted answers, a status report on his well-being, and help getting his limp body off the damned hard floor. But most of all he needed to know: "Who the hell *are* you?"

Her smile was instantaneous and infectious. It lit up her whole face, added sparkle to her eyes, heated her cheeks, and fairly danced upon her lips like a sweet melody hummed by a ravishing siren. "I'm Maude, of course," she said, and offered her hand.

Gil's thoughts were stuck on repeat. *This is not a dream. This is not a dream. This is not a dream.* And the moment their palms touched he was convinced.

She was flesh and blood, and within his grasp at last. The truth consumed him like a spark set to tinder, unleashing a torrent of testosterone that, if he hadn't already been flat on his back, would have knocked him off his feet.

* * *

"I imagine you've got a few more questions but they'll have to wait. We need to clear the transit pad," Maude said.

Gil didn't move immediately. His was staring at her with a dumbstruck expression that was both disturbing and flattering.

She'd wanted to meet him again, to prove that the attraction between them had been just a fluke, or one-sided, or temporary. It wasn't. The look on Gil's face was something akin to a sexual call of the wild. Maude's silent and potent response was an unconditional surrender, a wonderful and thrilling free fall into bliss that surpassed her dreams.

Her pulse pounded with a primeval thud that matched his. Her body still tingled from their prolonged contact. But her mind was a morass of emotion—perhaps a delightful state for a woman of passion, but a disaster for a Rogue. The highs and lows zinging and zapping within Maude's cranium very nearly hindered all but the basic command functions.

"Move. Now." She waggled her free hand in front of Gil's face. "Let me help you. They can't hold up retrievals indefinitely."

Gil didn't move.

Rick glanced over and shook his head. "My guess is he's still too stunned to move. I'd better get one of the lifts for him," he said, and hopped off the elevated pad to collect one of the hoverlifts stowed beneath.

Maude nodded and silently swore. It was a struggle to quell her merry musings about nuzzling Gil. She needed to focus on the task at hand, and one glance in the direction of the transit station's command booth helped her win the battle.

Drutz. The frown on the face of the lead Time Transitor, who was bellied up to the console, confirmed her suspicions that they'd exceeded processing parameters. If they didn't hustle, they could cause a delay loop.

"I'll have to file a report." She groaned and noted the Transitor's badge number and name: *Bob 13*.

A delay loop didn't qualify as a system crisis, but lead Transitors, especially those who handled auto-transit retrievals, were universally arrogant nitpickers obsessed with nanosecond precision. Maude knew a thing or two about the obsessive folk. Since Transitors and Rogues were dependent upon each other for mission successes . . . well, it just wasn't wise to piss off a guy who could pull her out of a dicey mission without irreparably scrambling her molecules.

"We've gotta get going. Give me your other hand," Maude shouted at the unresponsive Gil. When he finally obeyed, she pulled him up, shoved him onto the lift Rick had retrieved, and climbed on behind.

"Sit tight," she added, and thwarted Gil's struggle to right himself by planting a fist on his chest.

As pleasant as it was to maintain contact with the hunky male, she knew it wasn't going to last. Gil's strength was returning faster than she'd anticipated. It was taking most of her muscle power to keep him subdued.

Bob 13 didn't wait for them to clear the pad before flooding the area again with pink sterilizing fog. Rick maneuvered the lift off the pad and gunned the silent propulsion jets just in time. A shrill blast from the alarm alerted the station of a pending retrieval. The steady red glow from the status globes flicked to flashing amber, the foot-thick transparent blast panel sealed off the pad, and the spiral-jointed aperture on the far wall opened a transit portal onto the inky vastness beyond. Green light.

Maude turned back to watch as Rick jetted them away from the station. Transits were fascinating events.

Even with sound buffers, the deafening roar emanating from the black vortex registered within the station. The control booth vibrated and the pale blue track lights illuminating the length of the egress tunnel shimmered from the momentary power drain. The lead Transitor lowered his visor and focused on his console, his fingers a blur as he quickly locked in countless command protocols to receive the next transits.

"What in the hell?" Gil cried and sat up.

He'd knocked off Maude's restraining hold with little effort and was staring back at the yawning hole and spotlighted pad, his features twisted into a grimace. He looked as dangerous as an Outskirt pit viper, and as surly as a Reacclimate just roused from deep discharge. The man wanted answers.

Rick paused the hoverlift. He didn't say anything, and Maude thought it wise to follow suit. Explanations were inadequate at the moment. Gil was on sensory overload, possibly damaged from the emergency transit, and definitely juggling some confusing and psychotic aftereffects due to the tangled time lines. Mere words couldn't begin to fix this guy and restore him to rights. This time Gil needed the works. He needed Charlie's buffering implants or another memory purge. Or both.

Another shrill blast came from the alarm, more pink fog, an indistinct thud within the transit pad, and finally the all-clear tone. The blast panel lifted and a boisterous family of five with a dog in tow emerged from the dissipating fog: a routine scheduled retrieval for the general Core population.

It was obvious to Maude that the family had just completed one of Core's routine five-year tours to the past. The auburn-haired children sported waist-length tresses— something possible to cultivate only on longer trips. The Returnees' attire suggested they'd visited one of the agrarian cultures, a popular destination for Core parents rearing young children. The family looked healthy and happy—a testament to the population relocation program the majority of Core residents selected during their child-rearing decades. But periodic retrievals were essential to safeguard Core's time traveling residents and maintain their connectivity with their era of origin.

Maude didn't envy what lay ahead for the jovial group. After lengthy immersions in the past, Returnees endured a deep discharge renewal—an invasive but vital treatment. Compared to Renewals, Reacclimations were pleasure jaunts. Renewals included a series of tests and processes, and could take a long time depending upon the Returnee's resilience. Maude sighed and shook her head.

Of course, after Renewal came Recovery—the interval between time transits and before Reassignment and Relocation, when the Returnees reentered Core's general population. Recovery could be an exciting, confusing, and life-altering experience. Core residents were free of time traveler encumbrances and restrictions. Adults seeking partners could survey and acquire compatible mates. Couples desiring children or larger families could suspend their procreation blocks and conceive. And children could opt for enhanced training in any particular skill or talent identified during their Renewal scans.

Maude grinned at the thought. A genetic scan had identified her Rogue-applicable characteristics and career potential. The survey had altered her destiny, lifted her out of the Children's Cabala settlement in Edgeville at age thirteen, separated her from her close friend Cara Chay, and introduced her to the Rogue life. Would one of these children embrace a similar path? Maude's brow furrowed as she considered the question.

Not likely. They have a family.

The sight of the Returning group sliced deep into Maude's subconscious and routed a memory from her secret stash of desires. She'd missed that part of life. No mother or father, brother, sister, or dog. Besides Cara, another orphan from the Cabala, the Rogues—including Rick and Mackenzie—were the only family she'd ever known.

"Looks like they were visiting the 1930s. Prewar America," Rick mused as the group piled on a lift and floated past.

Gil's head swiveled like an automaton. He watched the process in stunned silence until the hoverlift with the family disappeared down the egress tunnel. "Okay, Rick—if that's really who you are—it's time for answers," he suddenly demanded. "Did I overdose on *Star Trek* or *Twilight Zone* episodes or something? Who are you guys? What happened? Where are we? And when exactly is this?"

Rick hooted. "We better get him to Rogue Central, fast, Maude. I know that tone. He's ready to tear off a few heads."

Gil glared at him. "Yours first, old buddy."

"You have tonsils!" Charlie crowed.

The head guru of Rogue Central, to whom Gil had been introduced several hours before, bore an uncanny resemblance to Carrot Top. No, more like Hollywood movie director Ron Howard minus his ball cap, he revised. But the similarity to either was disconcerting in light of the fact that the grinning redhead was currently inches away from his throat with ready access to sharp and pointy medical instruments.

"Marvelous," Charlie added, tapping the high-beam spot on his headgear and leaning even closer to inspect the back of Gil's mouth.

Gil squeezed his eyes shut. He didn't feel marvelous. Swarmed by innumerable technicians, he'd been overpowered from the get-go, suffering a host of indignities because Rick—damn him—had assured him they were necessary. As the prime target of every tech in Charlie's lab—a cavernous space that resembled a retrofitted New

York subway tunnel or a defunct missile silo or both—
he'd been probed, prodded, scanned, and scrubbed until
he felt a kinship with scourged saints. Countless hours under hot lights had seemingly blistered his denuded chest
and thighs. And the chilled slab had numbed his butt.

Would this torture ever end? The "treatment" had
abolished almost every micron of modesty he possessed.
He clung to what remained. A tongue depressor effectively prevented coherent speech, but he could howl
threats with the best of them. He began to do so.

Charlie jerked the tongue depressor out of his mouth
and apologized effusively, tried to push another beaker of
vile-tasting liquid nutrient into his hands. "Drink up, Gil."

Gil slapped it away and swung his legs over the edge of
the slab. "No. I'm done playing guinea pig. It's time for
the third degree. I want answers. I've earned 'em."

The soft murmurs that heretofore formed a comfort-
able auditory backdrop to the proceedings ceased. The
stark silence was stunning. From the innumerable treatment consoles cluttering the surrounding space, heads of
patients and technicians turned as one. Someone
dropped a metal probe and it clattered to the tiled floor,
but no one moved to pick it up; only the distant rumble
of some massive generator continued unabated.

"You sure have. But all in good time. Let's finish up
here first." Charlie's toothy smile was irrepressible. He
shook his head at one of the assistants, whose hand hovered above a flashing knob—a security alarm, no doubt.

Gil tried to gather his bearings, note exits, identify
friend and foe, and failed. Rick was AWOL, and so was
the beauty from his visions.

His urge to escape was fleeting, however. Stripped to a
loose-fitting pair of boxers and outnumbered, he was decidedly at a disadvantage. Plus, he was too damned curious and too damned pissed to depart before solving the
great mystery of where the hell he was.

Charlie rocked back on his stool—it was hovering in midair—and folded his arms. "It was necessary to bring you here to treat you, of course. Maude saved your life. You were suffering from a rare form of psychosis. Unchecked, it could have been lethal—or worse."

"Let me get this straight. There's something worse than lethal?"

"To me," Charlie replied. His grin flagged for a moment. He blinked, his big brown eyes full of startling honesty. "I'd prefer death over insanity."

Gil agreed. "Who wouldn't?" he asked.

"Precisely." Charlie slapped his knee and chortled. "But, there's no danger of that happening now. You're right as rain. Or, you will be as soon as I finish taking the titanium out of your leg. Rick said you broke it bull-riding. Well, you won't need the rod and pins anymore; I repaired the damage. And, your buffering implant is an industry standard. Most Rogues have them now, including Rick and Mackenzie."

"Rick and . . . ? Wait a minute. Buffering implant? Rogues?"

Anger kicked in, squeezing bile into Gil's gut, blood out of his brain, and air out of his lungs. He clenched his hand into a fist and pounded his other palm. He doubted that he could swallow much more of this baloney.

Lethal psychosis be damned, he launched himself off the slab hell-bent on ending this nightmare. But as soon as his tootsies touched down on the icy tiled flooring, his fury cooled. His old rodeo injury, the perpetual ache that had accompanied every swift move for a decade, seemed nonexistent. He flexed his knees. No stiffness. No pain. In fact, there wasn't even a scar on his shin, knee, or thigh.

Charlie chortled. "How do you like it? It'll feel better after I get you into Reacclimation and extract the titanium."

Gil flexed his knees again. He hadn't felt this good in

years—not since the infamous bull Texas Twister had stomped out a two-step on his right femur.

"It feels great. But I don't understand any of this," Gil growled. "And maybe you don't want me to, Charlie. But get this straight here and now . . ." He paused. The mule-stubborn tendencies he'd inherited from dear ol' Blackjack, his dad, were muscling to the forefront. They could be counterproductive at times like this, and slamming his fist through the nearest wall to vent his frustration was out of the question; it looked like solid concrete.

"Get this straight, Charlie," he began again, tucking his thumbs into the waistband of his shorts. Leaning against the slab, he crossed his feet at the ankles and offered Charlie one of his best no-nonsense frowns. "It's time to tell me everything, because I'm not budging an inch until you do."

SEVEN

"Err . . ." Charlie's fair-skinned features flushed crimson. Beneath his furrowed brow, his twinkling eyes shifted left then right, then back again. Gil's hunch seemed to be panning out. His instincts had been on target. Charlie was as jovial as a Munchkin and as easygoing as Harvey the giant rabbit, and that made him an easy target for some bullying. Gil didn't like to push, but this man was the scalpel-wielding potentate of this fantastic treatment center and was holding out on him.

Gil quashed a self-satisfied smirk. He wanted the truth, the whole truth, and nothing but the truth from Charlie. But he didn't repeat his demand. He didn't have to. He could outwait and outstare a rattler, if necessary, and he figured a nice guy like Charlie would fold and spill his guts in a few more minutes unless—

Providence intervened. The swoosh and mosquitolike hum of a hoverlift entering the chamber and discharging a passenger distracted Charlie, who glanced over Gil's shoulder at the new arrival. His frown vanished.

"How's the implant working?" a female voice asked.

Gil didn't need to turn around to identify the source. *Maude.*

"Within parameters. I just tested it," Charlie replied. He continued in a rush, his voice betraying his relief for the convenient and shapely distraction. "When Gil returns to 2008, he'll tolerate the conflicting images from the parallel time lines without noting the discrepancies."

"No more double images, no overlapping memories?" she asked.

Charlie shook his head. "None that will register in his conscious mind—and the Technicolor dreams are a bonus; that's the way I designed it to work," he finished.

"Hey. Don't stop there. Fill in the details," Gil demanded, confused and annoyed.

Maude circled the slab. She spared Gil the briefest of glances with those bewitching blue eyes, leaving him dumbstruck. She was jaw-droppingly beautiful, and Gil's libido responded. If he was drooling, Lord, help him, he was too stunned to care or remedy the situation. Her sheer, metal-flecked azure tunic clung to her curves, highlighted her delicate throat and wrists. Lust pulsed through Gil's veins.

If Maude noticed his reaction, she didn't show it. She seemed at ease in her skin, and as agile as a lioness, she hopped up on the slab and claimed one corner, tucking her long shapely legs beneath her bottom. Her tunic's filmy fabric pooled about her like spun gold and shimmered with every breath she took.

Gil's thoughts about his surroundings vanished. He was stupid with sensation, soaking in the sights, sounds, and smells that were uniquely Maude. He wanted to lose himself in her eyes, those pools of sky blue, and run his fingers through her . . .

"You're bald," he blurted.

Her eyes widened. She stole a look at his head and snickered. "So are you."

Bald? He scratched his head and laughed when he felt she was right. "Oh. Yeah. I suppose it's necessary?"

"Not always, but it helps." Maude shrugged. "Most Rogues opt for it. We transit a lot." Her gauze-draped breasts rose and fell provocatively as she breathed.

Gil's mama wouldn't have approved. Proper menfolk didn't stare at a woman's chest, or drool, or acknowledge inappropriate demands from the divining rod between their legs. He suppressed a groan and forced his gaze heavenward. His silent prayer for a cold shower went ungranted.

"It's an extraneous safeguard," Charlie said. Grateful for the distraction, Gil shifted his attention to the man.

The redhead uncoiled his smock-shrouded frame, stood, and tucked Gil's chart under one arm. "I didn't want to take any chances with you, Gil. You mean a lot to Maude."

Gil was slow on the uptake. "Huh?"

"*Zat*, Charlie, don't tell him stuff like that."

Gil's head snapped around. The beauty wouldn't look at him, and she cleared her throat.

"Try to remember he's new to Core, will you? And spare him your litany of safeguards and protocols you've invented. He doesn't need to know any of that right now."

"Whoa. I sure as hell do," Gil interjected.

Maude finally looked at him. Damn, but those blue eyes were killers. He'd never experienced such laserlike brilliance outside of Doc Roy's annual eye exam: His rods and cones felt scorched. He stared like a deer caught in the headlights until, mercifully, his autonomic system kicked in and broke the spell. Blinking, he surrendered his snake-staring title on the spot. Maude was the new champ, damn her lovely hide.

Charle interrupted Gil's admiration. "We manufacture 'strange' here in Rogue Central," the man said in a mugged whisper that could be heard throughout the complex.

Gil mentally shook himself. *Hey, cowboy. Stop thinking with your equipment. Tear your eyes away from the babe and listen up.*

"Strange is our job," Charlie continued, "and my techs are the best."

Several techs, listening in, laughed. One proclaimed Charlie the King of Strange, and a universal nod passed among the crew.

Gil scowled. He hadn't learned anything yet. "Strange? Okay, yeah. Keep going."

"We're an anomaly, a special unit attached to Critical Services that few Core residents know about or understand until they need us. You needed us. And we just gave you the works." Charlie's generous grin stretched wider, if that was possible. Pride seeped from his every pore.

"Thanks?" Gil couldn't quite muster a sincere tone, but with the force of that smile it was a struggle to maintain his scowl.

"You're welcome," Charlie replied, and waved in the direction of his white-smocked team. "But, as you can see, we're really just glorified repairmen."

Gil couldn't see anything of the kind—certainly nothing that he recognized as standard repairman-type situations. He was on tech overload. Everyone and everything here, from the treatment slab to Charlie's laserlight headgear apparatus, belonged on a *Star Trek* film set. "Strange" kept getting stranger by the minute. Lethal psychosis, implants, and now, "the works"? Damn, but this all added up to a hell of a lot more than a little body-and-fender work on his dinged-up packaging.

Gil started to point out that Charlie had clearly omitted some important details, but the King of Strange suddenly frowned. The man obviously didn't frown often; his facial muscles twitched from the effort.

"Umm," Charlie mumbled as he sat back on his stool

and levitated close, flipping a magnifying visor over his face to scan Gil's features. He checked pupils, pulse, and respiration, and noted them on his clear chart with a curious laser pen. Gil suffered the spot inspection in silence. And when Charlie's scowl disappeared, so did the knot in Gil's belly. Something about this guy bolstered Gil's confidence that everything was okay . . . or would be.

"Any potential complications or rejection?" Maude asked. "He took a jolt from my stunner during transit." She leaned in, giving Gil another of her dispassionate once-overs.

Now why does that break my heart? he silently mused.

Charlie answered her question: "I'm advising Reacclimation on what to watch for, but I'll be checking in on him too." He paused long enough to scan Gil's chart once more. "Hmm. Titanium extraction on third rotation," he mumbled under his breath. "Maybe I should move it up? Viable. Prudent. Yep, up one rotation and I'll do the extraction myself."

Gil watched Charlie note the changes, tuck the chart under his arm and produce another Cheshire cat–like grin, bobbing his head in silent confirmation that the revisions were right, good, and final.

"Thanks," Maude replied in even tones. Her sigh of relief amounted to little more than a hitch in her breathing, a softening at the corners of her mouth: She was one tough cookie to read. However, Gil's libido didn't sweat the details. Absorbing and translating her reaction, his brain transmitted a breaking news bulletin: *She's hot for me.*

"I like to finish what I start," Charlie said. He eyed Gil like a gem cutter sizing up a diamond in the rough, and for some reason Gil's confidence in the kingpin of Rogue Central mounted with each passing second. Gil was A-okay with the proposed . . . *Good grief. Extraction?* It had been said before, but he'd just processed it.

Charlie reached over and chucked Maude under the chin. "You know my golden rule. Nobody's lost on my watch."

"But it's not going to be your watch much longer," Maude returned. "I can't believe you chose Raymond to replace you." Gil glanced from her to Charlie and back.

"He's one of the best Scios suited to take over for me while I'm on sabbatical. He'll manage. He's scheduled to relieve me within the next ten rotations, and boy-oh-boy, I'm ready. My research is suffering."

"I know," Maude retorted. "I'm still waiting on your replication of a Blue Lagoon coconut slushie, by the way. But Raymond doesn't know how or when to bend the rules." She crossed her arms and huffed. "I can only imagine how he would have handled Gil's treatment. He probably would have insisted on another full memory purge instead of the buffering implants."

Gil noted the moment when Charlie's smile faded. He wasn't grasping all of the conversation, but a term like *memory purge* didn't require much translation.

"That's something I agree with," Charlie said. "A purge is mandatory."

Gil flinched.

Maude's response was short. She bit off her gasp by stuffing her fist in her mouth. She closed her eyes and seemed to regroup in less than a heartbeat, transforming into an ice princess, hard and impervious. Her long lashes lifted and, without a glance in Gil's direction, she nodded to Charlie.

"Understood."

That flat tone cut Gil to the quick. He swung his head in Charlie's direction. The King of Strange wasn't smiling now. Something had tugged those jovial features into a grimace of pain. No surprise. Charlie couldn't bluff. Not at Go Fish, and definitely not at a high-stakes game of Texas Hold 'Em.

"I'm recommending one for you too, of course," the man added.

Maude snorted, folded her arms, and looked as resistant to the idea as Gil. Questions plagued him. *What is a purge—a damned lobotomy?*

"Purge declined," Maude snapped. "We'll execute another download to a memory chip."

"Agreed," Charlie responded—a little too quickly to suit Gil. Maude had options. It seemed he didn't.

"He's ready for Reacclimation," Charlie said suddenly. His voice cracked. He cleared his throat before continuing. "You want to take him down, Maude?"

"Stop talking about me like I'm not even here." Gil drilled his index finger into Charlie's chest and glared into his kindly eyes. "I'm not *ready* for anything, let alone acclimation or purging. I've had enough shit done to my body today to last a lifetime." He kicked at the service cart laden with liquid nutrient vials. "I'm tired and hungry—and don't you *dare* push that nutrient sludge on me again. I want *food*." He swung around and faced Charlie again. "And if you'll stop probing me for an hour or so, I can grab forty winks."

They blew him off like so much wind, although Maude swiped at her eyes. *Were those tears?*

"I'll take him down," she said in a clipped voice. "How long? Fifteen rotations?"

"To be on the safe side, yeah, fifteen ought to do it." Charlie put his hand on Maude's shoulder and squeezed gently. "I'm sorry, Maude."

"I know you are," she replied, and shrugged off his hand. At last she turned to Gil and waved him ahead of her. "Let's go, cowboy. And it's *Re*acclimation, by the way."

"Do I have anything to say about this?" Gil said, clearly agitated. His hackles were raised, and his heels dug in for a fight. All he needed was a way to protest and someone to back him up. "Where's Rick?"

"Rick? Oh, I sent him back to 2008," Charlie replied.

Back to 2008? Gil couldn't catch his breath. It felt like he'd just lost a rematch with Texas Twister. Affirmation of his earlier fears was staring him smack-dab in the kisser.

"I'm in the future, aren't I?" he said. He'd been easing into the idea bit by bit, accepting information like pieces to a puzzle, trying them out here and there in his brain till they fit. This last piece fit. And the expression on Charlie's face confirmed things.

"Yeah, you are." Charlie snagged his hand and pumped it vigorously. "Welcome back to Core."

EIGHT

A full memory purge for Gil? Again? Maude struggled to keep her disappointment in check as reason warred with passion. Wasn't it enough that Gil was here with her now? Time Rogues, by trade, had a healthy respect for "now"—wherever and whenever that happened to be.

Maude smiled at Gil and extended her hand. After all, Gil was in Core. This was her home, her time, her turf, and she wanted to welcome him—though not really with a handshake.

Gil stared at her outstretched hand. His eyes were shadowed, wary. Her universal gesture of goodwill wasn't bowling him over.

Maude didn't insist. *Take it easy. Don't rush him*, she reminded herself.

She dropped her hand but not her smile. Gil's proximity triggered delightful sensations, chiefly a teasing and taunting itch that begged to be scratched. She slid off the slab and inched toward him. Kissing the cranky cowboy didn't seem wise or appropriate under the current circumstances—Gil still considered her a stranger—but what if she changed the circumstances?

Maude was close now; not close enough to touch him but close enough to allow his body heat to slip-slide over and around her. That warmth helped thaw what little resistance remained between her head and heart, her duty and desire. Awash in hormonal juices, she felt inebriated—high on lust, wildly romantic, and illogical to the extreme. Gil's presence tested her frayed grip on detachment. And she couldn't think of a sane reason to hold fast.

Gil wasn't off-limits now. Technically, neither was she. She'd performed her Rogue duties with regard to Gil, and until her next mission she was off the clock. If they could connect, it would do no harm . . .

Was his implant working? That question suddenly seemed critically important. Some adjusted swiftly to the technology, but others struggled. Even prepped Rogue scouts sometimes grappled with the conversion, and Gil's conversion had been especially complicated. A retrofit on Gil was a major feat for Charlie, given that his subject was not a Rogue and almost a virgin time traveler. But, Maude didn't doubt for a second that the implant would work eventually. Charlie could do anything.

Still, Gil's adaptation might take time. Sorting conflicting memories, reconciling alternate realities, expanding and enabling capacities to understand and embrace that knowledge with full awareness was a tall order for anyone past or present, Rogue or not. *Be patient*, Maude chided herself. But quelling her impatience was a losing battle. Especially when Gil suddenly lost his scowl and misplaced his grump. Staring at her with those sexy bedroom eyes and unabashed curiosity, he looked ripe and ready for a reunion.

NINE

Dallas, 2008

"How was your day, dear?" Rick asked as he sauntered into Mackenzie's office and claimed one of the leather chairs flanking her desk—a polished mahogany monstrosity inherited from the former museum director.

Mackenzie's wailing wall of anxiety vanished. She pushed aside the stack of busywork she'd used to tax her brain during his absence, rose, and cleared the distance between them.

"Tolerable," she snapped, and planted a kiss on her husband's lips.

Rick pulled her into his lap and prolonged the smooch. The mouth-scorching, spine-tingling, heart-melting smack unraveled the web of concern she'd woven during the eighteen hours and forty-three minutes he'd been gone. Waiting and thumb-twiddling while Rick handled a Rogue mission without her was a challenge she'd not anticipated.

"I won't ever get used to this," she murmured against his mouth.

Rick chuckled. "Better not." He reclaimed her lips and played her senses like a violin till they throbbed with pleasure.

"I'm talking about going on missions without me," she said in a breathless rush. "Counting the seconds while you're blitzing through time is nerve-wracking." She glanced down at her belly and laid her palm over the swelling knot. The pint-sized life force within her had a gender, a name—Lara—and a future that she instinctively protected with every thought and deed.

Mackenzie never once questioned the transit prohibition for pregnant Rogues. But that still didn't resolve her regret that Rick, her partner in life and work, would be a solo Rogue for the duration. Since joining the Rogues as on-call specialists, they'd worked only as a team. Some things, Rogue missions in particular, were best with every redundancy possible.

Her hands balled into tight little fists. Squeezing her eyes shut, she fought the overwhelming frustration and flush of hormones that often triggered her temper. *Holy Hades.* If she couldn't back up Rick . . . somebody else sure as heck had better step up to the plate.

"Relax, babe." Her husband stroked her cheek until she opened her eyes and looked up at him. "Per usual, Charlie has a plan." He winked and chucked her under the chin.

Ah. Charlie. Mackenzie unclenched her fists and her jaw. She wasn't entirely purged of skepticism, but the wave of relief was welcome. Ignoring an irrational urge to rip a new hole in the time line to kiss the Time Rogue boss on both cheeks, she merely nodded.

"Okay, let's hear it. What's the plan?"

"We've got a new assignment," Rick said. "Yes, *we.*"

He laid a finger against her lips as she started to protest. "The baby won't be endangered, because we don't need to transit."

"No? Then what . . ." Mackenzie stopped midsentence. Her features scrunched with thought, she puzzled it over, filtering possibilities until only the obvious remained.

She gasped. "Gil. Damnation. I forgot all about him." Tears filled her eyes. She pushed out of Rick's embrace, grabbed a wad of tissues, and blew her nose. She swallowed her guilt and squared her shoulders. She could handle this. She had to.

"Is he okay?" she finally managed. "Can Charlie fix him?"

"He's still got fifteen or so rotations with Reacclimation and a final memory purge ahead of him, but yeah, he's going to make it."

Mackenzie nodded. "Good. Good. And then what?"

"That's where we come in," Rick replied. "When Gil transits back to now, he's our mission."

Mackenzie raised one brow. "Our mission," she echoed. When Rick supplied the surveillance and implant testing details as dictated by Charlie, she summarized, "So, in essence, we're glorified babysitters?"

Rick nodded. "With Lara coming, we'll need the practice."

Hoverlifts solved many problems, Gil decided as they departed Rogue Central for Reacclimation: principally transportation through Core's rough terrain and maze of tunnels, shafts, caves, and conduits. Being on foot would have been tricky, requiring more stamina than he currently possessed. No wonder Core personnel looked incredibly fit. But the miraculous lifts also partially resolved another basic—and carnal—need for Gil by necessitating prolonged contact with Maude, something he craved more than food, sleep, or answers.

Maude had commandeered the helm, such as it was, while Gil pulled on a T-shirtlike, woven jerkin Charlie supplied. Preflight was nonexistent. She'd checked their safety tethers and set off without fanfare, skillfully exiting the Rogue compound and jetting them through a snarl of tunnels without a hitch.

This kind of flight took some getting used to. The craft's unconventional seating arrangement—side-by-side with their feet dangling over the lip, and with only a thin corded restraint anchoring their fannies—reminded Gil of a futuristic magic carpet minus the fringe and piping.

Eat your heart out, Aladdin.

Lift cruising speed apparently maxed out at ten miles per hour, more or less. Gil relaxed as much as he could, given that Maude's leg, by accident or design, was snugged against his from hip to kneecap. Her filmy shift was an insignificant barrier and everywhere they touched was registering intense pleasure. He was fresh out of drool—bone-dry. But lust continued to burn hot and deep. Unfortunately Maude didn't appear equally affected.

"Whoa, mama!" Gil roared as the lift shot free of the confining labyrinth and sailed high above a vast subterranean expanse. An underground city!

The lift skimmed the topmost structures, which were capped with flashing navigational buoys. Forward progress forced chilled air against Gil's exposed flesh and into his lungs. He sucked in the earthy scents that sweetened the great cavern. Far below, lamp-lit avenues and open forums hummed with activity.

"Is this Core?" he managed between clenched teeth. Fainting was bad enough. Now vertigo too? Damn. His woven T-shirt—another technological marvel, with sensor-feeds—warmed just enough to compensate for the temperature disparity. It cut the chill, but the last of his pride, the fragment he'd salvaged from Charlie's treatment, was gone with the wind.

Maude grinned and shook her head. "Not all of it. This is just the Scio Quad, home to the big brains and TTT—the Transit Think Tank."

Gil marveled at both Maude and her world. Nothing seemed to bother her; not heights nor the palpable tension between them. The tension that burned him where flesh met flesh.

"Want a closer look?" Maude asked. Without waiting for a reply, she dipped the nose of the hoverlift. It banked to the left and started a slow downward spiral.

Gil cursed and grabbed her around the waist to stop her from falling. She didn't move. "If you're trying to scare the hell out of me, you're succeeding."

"Not really," she replied, and leveled out the craft. "You don't have to hold on, you know. We can't fall off. I set the force field."

"Not that I don't trust you or the damn force field, but I think I'll hang tight if you don't mind."

Maude laughed and rested her head on his shoulder for one blissful second. "No. I don't mind, actually. But that's not the real reason I'm taking you on this detour."

A *detour?* Gil ruminated on that for a split second. If it meant more time with Maude, yeah, he was up for it. And that went double if it kept him away from a memory purge.

"We can't play around too long," she continued. "The Reacclimation department is clocking your transition from Rogue Central, and they'll mobilize a collection squad if I don't deliver you. But . . . I thought I owed you this."

She settled the lift down on one of the rooftops and cut the propulsion unit. "You want to know about the future? Come take a look. A picture is worth a thousand words."

TEN

How'd I lose control of this situation? Maude silently groused as she struggled to keep pace with Gil. She couldn't confine or control Core's newest guest any more than she could outmuscle a time line fissure or temporal migration. Gil was more than a handful; he was—she groaned—gone. *Again.*

Her inspiration to give Gil a peek at her future world had royally backfired. Deactivating the lift's tethers and force field had effectively unleashed one mega-curious cowboy in Core's Think Tank turf. A quick inspection of the Scio Quad from their lofty perch had only whetted his appetite. And before she could stop him, he was gone.

Gil had taken off via the building's personnel egress chute—a transparent cylindrical vacuum conveyance system—and hit the ground running with Maude in hot pursuit. So far they'd scoped out a six-block radius in about as many minutes . . . and Maude was getting winded fast.

"Hey," she cried, and snagged his arm before he outpaced her again. "Wait up. Gotta catch my breath."

That was an understatement. Maude needed to stretch out and finish her own Reacclimation rotations. After a prolonged debriefing and a stint with Processing to check her implants, she was physically exhausted. Gil should have been too, but he sure didn't act like it.

"This is fantastic," he crowed. "I want to see more. I want to see everything."

"Here. Eat this," Maude said, and tossed him a nutrient bar she obtained from a vending kiosk. It might not meet Gil's definition of food, but at least it was solid and chewable. Plus it was all Maude dared offer, given his impending Reacclimation.

Gil consumed the offering without noticeable reservation. Fortunately, he seemed distracted by the limited view of the Quad, too distracted to complain about the rubbery texture or bland taste.

Maude scanned her surroundings, attempting to see them through Gil's eyes. It took some effort. As Core habitats went, the Scio sector was lackluster. Entertainment was scant. Functionality dictated design and detail for all constructs. Yet the programmed atmospherics, optimized for foot traffic along the avenues, counterbalanced the more utilitarian aspects. The heady aromas of lilac and earth, a gurgling brook and cooing doves, and a whispering warm breeze complemented the simulated spring twilight. A violet hue washed the exteriors of the structures lining the popular Scio commons, and hanging lanterns marked the meandering footpaths.

"What's with *that?*" he managed between bites. He nodded in a northerly direction.

Oh, no. He *would* notice the tram station, of all things. But Maude also had to admit it would be hard *not* to notice the squat structure with cantilevered platforms and ramps. The pop and flash that presaged a routine staging between departures and arrivals were spectacular on purpose; a myriad of cautionary warnings and safety measures for Core's principal transportation system insured a virtually accident-free record. And at the moment, the lift storage and surface tram station looked like a fiesta. The header illumination was currently a flame-hued, eye-blistering wattage. A flashing light trail of the same brilliance and color defined the perimeter of the facility and the activation of a temporary containment field.

Maude cleared her throat, but before she could supply an explanation, hidden jets expelled fog in three short bursts. Soothing green light displaced the orange. The tote screen flicked on and streamed transport data. A saccharine voice announced the 17:36 westbound arrival.

Gil's brow furrowed. Riveted to the spot, he chewed and swallowed the last of his nutrient bar as he watched a surface tram whoosh to a stop and offload passengers.

Maude's relief was measured. From the age mix— family units and couples wearing embellished tunics— Maude surmised that the Quad was hosting an event that attracted Core's general population. Since residents rarely dealt with heightened security protocols, this event would mean only wary and ultrasensitive Scio and TTT personnel would notice and challenge her uncredentialed guest.

"Time to get going," she said as soon as the crowd had cleared the commons and filed into one of the blocky lecture halls.

"Nope, not yet." Gil's tone was firm, his gaze lingering on the station.

Maude couldn't guess his actual intent. But the set of his jaw and his defiant stance made her nervous.

Drutz, drutz, drutz. Nothing short of a blast from a particle beam could prevent him from boarding the next tram if he wanted. Minus her Rogue gear or even a handy stunner, she had only her wits and muscle to convince him otherwise.

"Feels almost real—like we're really outside," Gil finally said, and spun around with his arms outstretched.

"The Scios don't splurge on much, but this is pleasant enough," Maude agreed. "Now, let's go."

As she'd hoped, few Scios were afoot at this hour to monitor the commons for interlopers. It was an open-sector evening due to the event.

The Scio Quad still maintained its rigid adherence to security, a holdover from the decades when the Critical Services Units competed for limited resources, control of the labor force, and project approval. Once all the principal hubs had been constructed, equipped, and staffed, the friction and suspicion had largely dissipated. However, her infractions were compounding by the minute. From Gil's emergency transit to Core to this unsanctioned joy ride—to the Scio Quad, no less—she was bending rules to the point of breaking them, which was foolish for anyone intent on retaining Rogue certification.

Still, her empathy for Gil outweighed her ambition. She could only imagine the battle he'd waged for his sanity, and couldn't fathom how he'd endured both the cause and the cure with his intrepid spirit intact. Gil was a champion, a survivor, definitely Rogue material in any other time lines. For that alone Maude believed she owed him a brief respite before subjecting him to the final stage of his treatment. It was a payoff that couldn't be permanent. All too soon he'd be purged and returned to the past, no wiser about the future than anyone else in 2008, but for now, he'd earned the right to some answers.

Answers? That explanation didn't sit well with her conscience. Her motives weren't entirely noble. Selfishness, pure and simple, fueled her actions. She wanted . . .

Gigazat. What exactly do I want?

She knew. She wanted Gil to remember her.

Maude could feel her cheeks burning. It was true: She admired Gil, liked Gil, wanted Gil. And if this only amounted to a stolen moment that would eventually be extracted from his thoughts, one small connection was better than nothing and never. She was prepared. If Gil hit her with a plethora of probing questions, she'd answer.

As if she'd tripped a border alarm, a well-worn dictum flashed in her brain: Never tell people from the past about the future. Maude smirked, dismissive. Another Rogue rule bent to the breaking point and she just didn't care. After all, Gil's scheduled memory purge would erase everything. Emotion glutted Maude's brain. Dicta couldn't douse the craving ignited by Gil's proximity. She wanted all of the obstacles out of the way, all the rules and all the questions about the future, the Rogues, the transit, and the treatment. She wanted to *connect*.

So much data to cover, so little time. Maybe there wasn't enough time to get past it all. And even if they did, maybe he wouldn't ask the real question she hoped he'd ask. Right now his face betrayed nothing—nothing that Maude couldn't identify. He didn't have questions about her, about them, about the past; he was overwhelmed by the future.

Maude's chronometer pulsed off the seconds. She should give it up. They were already overdue at Reacclimation. The now-deserted commons wouldn't stay that way, not if someone triggered a search and launched a retrieval team. If security squawked, she and Gil would be located, swarmed, and hauled off—Gil to Reacclimation and her back to Rogue Central for a well-deserved slap on the wrist. It was dangerous to linger. Her pulse hammered at her wrists, her throat, and her temples. Every instinct she'd cultivated and honed for Rogue missions recommended *abort*. But Maude's heart wouldn't yield. She had to know.

"Gil, do you . . . remember me?" she ventured.

Gil's features shifted. His white teeth flashed in a grin, his brow twitched with amusement, and his eyes—those fathomless pools that could disarm her with a glance—surveyed her as though she were a juicy peach just waiting to be picked. His mischievous wink caught her off guard as much as his response.

"Oh, baby. I sure as hell do."

ELEVEN

Gil pulled Maude into his arms and spun her around until she was breathless. It was a heady sensation. Maude felt many things that she was not: helpless, tiny, light as a feather, girlishly silly. She wanted the moment to last forever. It didn't.

"Who's the intruder?" an officious female voice asked. Turning, Maude saw a svelte woman. Her handheld scanner hummed, pointed as it was in Gil's direction.

Gil showcased his heart-constricting smile, but Maude froze. In spite of the newcomer's "thin-skin," a lovely bronze flesh treatment that vibrated with health, Maude recognized her old friend, Cara Chay. Long ago they'd shared a room at the Children's Cabala—a time before either orphan dared dream of a future beyond their small community of Edgeville. How long ago was it? Five years? Ten? Maude had lost track of the time.

Maude wriggled out of Gil's embrace and offered the first greeting that popped into her head. "You're looking good, Chay."

Cara's chocolate brows furrowed momentarily. After a

barely perceptible nod of acknowledgment, she refocused and completed her assessment of Gil. Sure enough, her scanner triggered a minor-chord warning tone, a preamble to a Quad alert.

"'Reacclimation pending,'" Cara read out. The message was flashing on her scanner, and her frown deepened. "For both of you. What are you doing here, Kincaid?"

Zat. Maude knew that neither her past friendship with Cara nor her Rogue status would earn any quarter. If Chay determined she'd violated one of the countless sacrosanct Scio Quad restrictions, outdated or not, not even Charlie could bail her out of trouble. Scios still maintained the show that they guarded their secrets covetously.

Maude groaned. Her little detour might be costly indeed.

"I'm not sure I can explain it, Cara," she offered with a shrug of her shoulders. At least Gil had sense enough to keep quiet—another reason she'd fallen hard and hopelessly in lust with the man: His instincts were proving to be definitely Rogue-worthy.

"It's an open Quad tonight, Kincaid, but I should report this," Cara said.

"I can only tell you this much." Maude leaned in, her voice nearly a whisper. "I salvaged him from the past; a transit accident. Charlie was able to save his life."

A flare of emotion registered briefly on Cara's beautiful features. Maude was stretching the truth, playing dirty by appealing on behalf of one survivor to another. After the Lima disaster, Cara owed her existence to the Scios. The chief beneficiary of TTT intellect and Scio wizardry, a mishmash of flesh and electronics, she was one of a kind, a biological miracle. Rebuilt, she was very nearly perfect.

Would almost-perfect Cara turn them in?

Maude inched closer and studied her old friend. Since

becoming a Rogue, she'd acquired additional training and technology supplements, which greatly enhanced her threat-assessment skills. But, she couldn't read the equally enhanced Cara.

They probably looked ridiculous, standing almost nose to nose, practically sniffing each other and coming up empty. With Rogue technology versus Scio technology . . . it was a stalemate.

Maude struggled to keep her features impassive, her mind clear, her pulse normal. Any reaction might tilt the scales and give Cara an edge.

I'm *salvaged?* Gil was amazed at the equanimity he felt, considering the impossible information—like his near miss with death—he was ingesting. The full spectrum of the data filtering through his cranium should have unhinged him. But it didn't. Not at all. In fact, he felt better than ever. His kaleidoscopic memories of the past year were finally sifting and sorting themselves into neat, digestible bytes. Events. People. Time lines. And the bonus was, a substantial Maude byte had developed.

Recollections of her from an alternate reality had crystallized into perfect focus. Every thought, word, deed, smell, and hot inch of her. Maude. His dream girl. A smart, wild female wrapped up in one hell of a beautiful package.

No wonder he'd been insane with lust and tormented by her residual image. That represented the tip of a Titanic-class emotional iceberg afloat in his subconscious. At long last he could recount the minutes of their history together. It had been brief but intense. He'd been a goner from the get-go.

At that first meeting, it wasn't just her curves or the way that strange electric blue bodysuit shimmered with every little movement that aroused the beast in him; something within her spoke to him, something potent and provocative, a primal attraction that defied explanation. Whatever it was, it unleashed a jungle heat in his loins and fueled primitive—savage—urges to pursue, conquer, mate. It had been a siren call at life's most elemental level. That call he'd been hell-bent on answering until the Rogues intervened and warped his world.

Scrambling his marbles hadn't been intentional; he knew that now. He'd been collateral damage, one of the aggrieved but marginalized results of averting a disastrous time rift and saving the future. Thankfully, Charlie's fix had virtually erased the ill effects of the past two years. However, with his memory now restored, balanced, and buffered, Gil felt the urges—the uncivilized, all-male urges—renewed as well.

Maude. Gil was dizzy with desire. His tongue tangled on the glut of questions that begged to be asked. Struck dumb in more ways than one, all he could manage was a slaphappy grin and a few unintelligible grunts.

Danger? Who cared? He sure didn't. Every second with Maude felt like another slug from a fifth of Jack Daniel's. He was drunk with pleasure and stupid with sensation.

"Salvaged, huh?" Cara repeated, and teased the tip of her tongue with her teeth. A pretty frown marred her tanned features. "My scan notes an exceptional rating on his innate intellect. He's got Scio potential. Are the Rogues going to re-seed him in the past, or is he staying in Core?"

Staying? He could stay? Gil felt his jaw drop open. The idea sizzled inside his noggin. It danced around like a mouth-watering fritter in a hot skillet. Sweet and tempting, he wanted it. He *had* to have it. And damn anyone fool enough to tell him he couldn't.

"I have to report you, Kincaid. I know you, and I'm sure you're up to something," Cara said. She spared a glance in Gil's direction. A spark of interest that exceeded curiosity and stopped short of lust betrayed her otherwise well-schooled emotions.

Cara's moment of weakness reminded Maude of their childhood, and of the startling fact that Cara couldn't lie. That flaw bonded them as sisters more surely than blood. So, although jealousy plucked at Maude's body, tightening the frets on her vocal chords and sawing away at her nerves till she ached to punch Cara's lovely nose, she didn't.

"Of course you have to report it," Maude snapped. "I know you too, Cara. Even without all that hardware the Scios welded to your body and buried in your brain, even before that you lacked the ability to fib—even a little bit."

Cara's eyes narrowed to slits. Her finger hovered above the TRANSMIT button on her scanner. Maude half expected her to hiss like the pit viper she now resembled.

"Can too," her old friend growled. "I can lie when it counts. You asking me to prove it?"

Maude managed a nod. "I'll owe you one."

"Just like a Rogue. All emotion," Cara sneered. "Don't you employ reasoning? The mind is a terrible thing to waste."

Maude silently agreed, but emotion was an effective weapon against this half-human female. Scios didn't appreciate Cara's human qualities. But she did. She hadn't bonded with a zatting machine as a child. She'd bonded with another lonely orphan.

It felt like an eternity, a moment that stretched and tested Maude's patience almost to a breaking point. Finally Cara's frown softened and she slipped the scanner into her waist holster and folded her arms across her chest.

"Okay. You'll owe me one," she said. "Everyone knows you're one of the best Rogues. And I might need one."

Maude jerked. Every sense was suddenly on alert; she'd heard rumors and this reaction made those seem much more likely. "It's a go? The first human transit mission to the future?"

"In three rotations," Cara replied. She waved a hand over her well-muscled figure. "If you can still call me human. I'm the Eve One prototype—half machine, half normal, hormonal female."

Maude shook her head and they laughed together. The tension between them and the years evaporated. And for a brief moment, they were sisters again, united against the world.

Cara's beautiful eyes filled with unshed tears. "Promise you'll fish me out of the future if they screw up my transit. I think I'm scared."

Maude couldn't find her voice at first. Cara, vulnerable? Scared? Maude didn't blame her. Any human, Rogue included, would be too. The danger Cara faced was incalculable. Like with any specialist conducting a prototype transit, the risks often outweighed the rewards. But Cara's trailblazing venture would merit the ominous LR 50 rating: *Life Risk 50 percent*. At Rogue Central, they joked LR stood for Lethal Ride. If Eve One required retrieval, odds were high that the human portion would not survive.

"You don't even have to ask," Maude finally squeaked. "I'll bring you home."

Charlie tucked his long legs beneath the kneehole console and bent over to examine the data streaming across his screen. A sigh of regret slipped out. He glanced up, but no one on this upper tier of the Rogue Central complex took note. Clear, ultrathin acoustical panels isolated each pod. Here, silence reigned supreme. The unabated hiss from the hydration tube mainlining fluids into his tissues—a necessary pre-mission precaution to supersaturate his system—was the only noise.

He refocused on the screen and bit back another sigh.

Processing Subject Gillespe's files was problematic. He'd fixed what needed fixing in the subject, installed the buffering hardware he had mistakenly deemed unnecessary on Gil's first visit to Core. Yet there was more about this unique case that intrigued him and invited further study. Unfortunately, Charlie couldn't indulge his curiosity. He was about to leave on his long-anticipated sabbatical from Core. In seven rotations he was scheduled for prep and launch on his own research mission, one he'd postponed and delayed too long. Following a hunch, he hoped to determine whether a silent threat to the time traveling population existed or not. And though he would like to, he didn't have the luxury of time to indulge in a lengthy analysis of Gil's gene pool.

No, Gil's potential value to Core society was minimal. The cowboy was going back to his era of origin, minus all residual effects and memories of his encounters with his future.

The system blipped again. *Hmmm.* The temptation to revise his opinion was strong.

Charlie tugged at his chin as he reviewed the procedures. He had extracted typification facts from Gil's initial body scan, stripped the male down to the basics: genetic codes, random radicals, recessive and dominate DNA, et cetera. He'd captured and isolated all of Gil's damaged cells with a SCRUB bug. And he'd ensured optimum protection with the buffering hardware and specialized Reacclimation series.

Yet a tandem program kept triggering alerts. Gil, it seemed, was a wealth of untapped potential—the kind Core valued and recruited for its Scio career classifications. Should Gil's assessment be transferred to the Scios for consideration?

The system anticipated Charlie's answer. A transfer form popped onto the screen—a subroutine he'd designed to facilitate dissemination of Core-significant information. With a single click, Charlie merged Gil's data into the primary fields and transmitted it to Triad: a critical skills catalog maintained by the Transit Think Tank.

Maude's features clouded his thoughts for a moment. A blind man could see she was struggling with a bad case of lust for Gil, and Charlie wasn't blind or detached when it came to Maude. She was more than just the result of his procreant experiment, the engineered human he'd crafted like a cocktail from Core's storehouse of genetic material. He'd helped mentor her phenomenal ascent through the Rogue ranks, fully aware of the sacrifices she made in her personal life to become an elite Time Rogue. Everyone knew and accepted that Rogues and romance didn't mix.

He shrugged his shoulders, rolling around the idea of playing matchmaker between the two. He was tempted. Maude and Gil seemed right for each other in some ways, fitting together in a manner that sparked envy in him and reminded him of the deep-seated emptiness he concealed from everyone. What he wouldn't give for a taste of true tenderness with a woman! But long ago he had accepted his fate—the gift and the curse—that compelled him to eschew a mate and family and dedicate his life to securing a future for all. And Maude had accepted hers.

Just follow your own protocols, he schooled himself, noting the successful transmission of data. He quickly messaged his buddy, Hick, with a routine personnel alert noting Gil's file citation. Hickham, an opportunistic savant, still commanded the Think Tank in Scio Quad and dictated a no-holds-barred policy of harvesting intellect anytime, anywhere, any way. Charlie's gut twisted. He knew Hick would want Gil. And if Gil stayed in the future, Maude's life might get complicated—fast.

The system snarled, produced a rare static phrase that indicated a recheck was in-process. That stalled Charlie's internal dialogue. But when the recheck confirmed his initial summary, the confirmation screen immediately cleared and flashed a single message punctuated with a final minor tone:

CR: *Rejected.*

Charlie rocked back in his seat and closed his eyes. *Core Residency rejected?* How strange. He should be relieved: Gil's fate was out of his hands. But the knot in his gut twisted tighter, squeezing out bile in both directions and flooding him with bitter regret.

The minor tone sounded again. Charlie's features twisted in annoyance. He inched one finger toward the screen and tapped the bubble that acknowledged receipt of the notice and released the system. He hated doing it; he felt complicit in the decision rejecting Gil's option to stay in the future. But Gil had to return to the past. There was no flexibility on that score. The cursory time scan had triggered an autoblock for Core residency, which could only mean one thing: Gil was pivotal in his era of origin, an EE, "era essential." The past needed him. Using Mackenzie's new "Consequence Factor" measurement, the broad buffering net that identified significant persons in history, he rechecked Gil's status. Nothing. Was Gil EE or not? Charlie opted in favor of caution.

An EE? Drutz. Gil's Scio potential ranked among the ninetieth percentile. Regardless of the impact on Maude, Core could sure have used a guy with his prospective assets. But autoblocks were firm. Charlie knew better than anyone else. He'd drafted the manual, helped test and establish the inflexible rules essential for safe time travel. To Core, the safeguards were sacrosanct edicts to avoid screwing up the past. The past needed Gil. Case closed.

Charlie retrieved his stylus and clicked it against his

laser chart, weighing several options against innumerable restrictions and time line protection protocols. Hick would demand a full account, require options, and insist on a solution: a way—*any* way—to harvest Gil's intellect for Core. Charlie discarded all but two. Satisfied he'd appeased both his conscience and Core's needs, he made a final entry on his treatment protocol for Gil's Reacclimation.

Rotation three: sperm extraction.

TWELVE

"Hang on, we're almost there," Maude said as the lift silently floated up the slick black wall face of Reacclimation Block Three, Med Prep.

Gil grunted an acknowledgment. Word skills escaped him at the moment. Juggling sensory input was a bear. Human contact helped. Maude's bare thigh was once again pressed against his, and her whisper of a smile was a heartwarming reminder of the unfinished business between them. But his rapid pulse wasn't the sole result of a raging libido. Since their arrival in Reacclimation, his amorous urges had been largely supplanted by unspeakable terror.

The routine and expedient processing at reception wasn't alarming. However, as they moved beyond the brightly lit clinic area and entered a vast shadowland filled with acres of corridors wending through blocks of stacked monolithic ebony slabs, the enormity of what was to come hit him like a freight train.

The lift slid silently through the chilled passages, leaving plenty of time for Gil to contemplate his fears. The mythical bogeyman lurking under his bunk bed when he was a toddler couldn't compete with the real and present monster about to be unleashed in his cranium. He'd made it this far. He'd negotiated the turf of Maude's future world without succumbing to nerves. But the promised brain drain still awaited him.

A memory purge? What the hell was that going to do to him?

His newest acquisition, a slimline identilog cuff fitted to his wrist upon check-in, signaled the proximity of their destination. Maude adjusted the hoverlift controls and the vehicle slowed to a crawl. An amber beacon flashed above one of the hundreds of panels honeycombing the slick wall face. A thick shelf silently slid out to receive them. The padded platform resembled a gigantic file drawer.

Or a double-wide coffin, Gil thought.

Oddly enough, stretching out on or in anything—a coffin included—suddenly appealed to him. His body sagged with oppressive weariness. The burst of energy he'd experienced at the Scio Quad had played out, and terror supplied only a modicum of fuel. Some of his higher functions were flat-lined. His muscle memory was AWOL. The inclination to remain upright and alert was MIA, and his once stalwart collection of bone and brawn now felt more like derelict scaffolding. Gil had been dead on his feet more times than he could count, but this was a special brand of tired.

He managed another glance at Maude, his mind silently bargaining with the beauty. *Blow a kiss in my direction, babe, and I'll topple into dreamland without a fuss.*

"This will be your home for the next fifteen rotations," Maude said as she slid onto the platform, settled in, and patted the spot next to her. "Climb aboard and I'll hook you up."

"Any chance we're doin' this thing together?" Gil

asked. He levered himself onto the shelf and groaned as his limbs melted into the warm spongy surface. Damned thing felt like heaven to his aching body.

Maude blushed. "It's a great idea," she said, and activated the pad's interior lighting. Panels aglow with amber and red buttons lined the walls, foot rail, and ceiling. Vents hissed, and what looked like a mile of inky tubing snaked around the dials, knobs, and screens, and terminated at multiple feeder leads along the edges of the pad.

"I do have a few more rotations of my Reacclimation protocol," she said as she swabbed his forearms and slapped mesh circlets with metal-tipped nodes along the length of each from elbow to wrist. Her voice squeaked and she paused long enough to clear her throat and shake her head. "But this is Core's Med Prep Block. All Rogues are processed in Block Six."

"That so? Is that another one of those Core regulations you could fudge on my behalf?" Gil asked. He watched her intently as she knelt beside him, attaching lines to nodes. "You *could*, couldn't you?"

Her sigh was almost imperceptible. She wanted to—Gil recognized that much. Her reaction had been subtle, but with Maude he felt like he was tuned in and privy to some grand translator, or like he'd cracked some secret code.

"You want to but you can't," Gil volunteered.

She bit her lip and nodded again. "Med Prep chambers are single occupancy. No sleepovers allowed."

"You mean all this plumbing is just for me?" Gil asked.

"These chambers can handle multiple prepping protocols. Most won't be activated for your procedure and convalescence." She tapped a screen that unleashed a long wand with an instrument-wielding knuckle at the end. "This is your stasis nurse."

"Whoa." Gil ducked as the wand hummed and pivoted above their heads, then retreated back into its nest.

Maude snickered. "It's only an auto-arm. The staff at

Medical use it for minor patient and treatment adjustments. Droids and personnel typically don't require chamber access to effect Reacclimation protocols."

"Okay," Gil replied. Imagining why droids or personnel would need to access his pod unnerved him further.

"Lie down," she ordered, and pressed him back against the padding.

Gil didn't resist. Come what may, he trusted this strange beauty. That meant there was necessity for all the implants, prepping, probing, and memory purging in order to set his life to rights. Sure, he'd dug in his spurs initially. Who wouldn't, what with Charlie explaining every tedious step in the procedure, from the innocuous titanium extraction to the finale, a selective brain zap to erase all knowledge of Core, Maude, and the time traveling future? But Maude's short and snappy summary had cinched the deal for him, nailed his consent.

"It won't hurt a bit, and it'll add ten years to your life—at least," she'd said.

Ten years? He'd signed on the figurative dotted line and given provisional consent. After all, what was his alternative? Do nothing and risk developing a "lethal psychosis" when they dropped him back into 2008? Hell no. And although he'd had a few hours to think about it, he was still a go for launch. Sort of.

Cara Chay's comment indicated there were alternatives worth considering. Stuff he could and should mull over—if he'd had the time and energy to mull.

Gil sucked in a lungful of chilled air and shook out his muscles. Damn. He was nearly too trounced to attempt the alphabet backward or forward, let alone debate his fate with intellects like Charlie. At the same time, he was beginning to suspect that these future folk were in too much of an all-fired hurry to suck his brains and toss him back to the past.

"How are you with small dark spaces?" Maude asked as

she moved over him. Her diaphanous tunic trailed over his flesh, and her warm hands palmed his muscles and maneuvered him like limp clay till he was stretched and splayed.

Gil grunted an unintelligible response. Small dark spaces?

Still, Maude's touch had a way of dispelling his shadows, fears, and lingering doubts. And those niggling questions, the ones that had plagued him since first contact with her beautiful bottom and her bedeviling world, became almost nonexistent.

Almost. The biggies remained. *Memory purge? Staying in the future?* He struggled to voice the last one—the option of staying in Core. He'd asked Maude about it on the abbreviated jaunt from Scio Quad to Reacclimation, but her short and sweet response had been devoid of details.

"No."

Tough to argue with that. Her sudden mood swing from friendly to flinty and intractable—something that rivaled a Jekyll to Hyde reversal—had repelled every query he'd lobbed. When the gal said no, she meant it.

But that had been then. The Maude who had just brushed her lush breast against his arm wasn't prickly, or stoic, or impassive, or callous. Hyde was gone. And Jekyll—in a decidedly irresistible form—was back.

Plus, she'd wangled the right to tuck him into his Med Prep chamber. Maude's persuasive plea bargain with the Reacclimation techie checking him in had been impressive. It was another clue that the gal was soft on him and potentially open to a final appeal for a stay of execution. There *was* something between them, damn it all. Something worth exploring, acknowledging, and sampling before Core pulled the plug on him.

Maude couldn't be blind to his attraction. His heightened arousal was as blatant as a highway billboard with a flashing arrow pointing at his heart. The air between them fairly sparked with electricity, a compelling combo of magnetic and primeval mutual attraction. Only willpower had so far kept their polarized plus and minus forms from colliding. And with the curvaceous beauty checking him into this futuristic broom closet, preventing a collision was nigh impossible.

"Almost done." She paused long enough to stroke his cheek. "The enriched oxygen has trace sedatives. Primary venting is right above your head." She reached up, adjusted the nozzle until it hissed in protest. "I like to keep mine at about three. You're about fifty kilos heavier, so I've dialed it up to five."

She finished affixing nodes and leads to his lower limbs and finally settled down next to him. Propped up on one elbow, she faced him and stifled a yawn. "Ready for a briefing on the controls?" She didn't wait for confirmation. Instead, she reached over him, her fingers pressing buttons and turning amber lamps to green one by one.

It was a quick, no-nonsense briefing. Platform in and out. Lights on and off. Atmospheric selections set and activated—Gil picked a summer sunset at the Grand Canyon with a canopy of stars twinkling in the heavens. With the autofeed and elimination connections initialized, ta-da, they were done.

"Amazing. You're a natural," Maude said after pausing the system and extending the platform. She sat up and stretched. "I'd better check in to my own unit before the sedative takes effect."

Gil stalled her. Grabbing her wrist, he pulled her back down beside him. "Hang on a sec, babe, I've got several heavenly bodies I'd like to point out." He pressed a button and the platform slid into the wall face, sealing them once more inside.

"Gil, I can't stay," Maude insisted. But as Gil activated his atmospherics, the sudden visual and auditory transport from a small dark chamber to the chalky precipice before the vast canyon stilled all protest. The setting sun cast a rosy glow across the rim and upper canyon walls. A lone hawk soared effortlessly above the shadowed abyss. And a warm wind kissed their flesh.

Maude leaned back against him, her head pillowed on his chest. A wearied sigh eased from between her lips. "It's beautiful," she whispered. "I never saw it before."

"It's one of my favorite haunts," Gil returned. "I'll take you there someday. We'll hike to the bottom. Run the rapids. Camp on a sandbar. Make love under the stars."

She rolled over and faced him. "I'd like that," she whispered. "But . . ." She didn't finish. She didn't have to. Gil knew the score. His dream gal, this twilight temptress who fitted against him with utter perfection and completed his ultimate fantasy, belonged to the future. And somehow in the next fifteen rotations the essence of his passion for her would be extracted from his noggin—along with his titanium leg splint—and sucked into the bowels of this underworld, discarded and forgotten.

"We have now," she said, studying him intently, as if committing his features to memory.

Gil closed his eyes and savored the sound of her voice, letting it smooth away the rough edges of his weariness. Her body heated his where they touched, seeping into him as though a heavenly elixir, bending will and reason around the impossible.

Maude and the canyon. Life didn't get more perfect than this.

"I don't want to lose this memory," he said. "I don't want to lose you."

She held his gaze. She wanted it too—as much as he did, maybe more.

They eased together, heedless of the wires and nodes peppering his body, until at last their lips touched. Chaste, softly at first, breathing together, flesh pulsing, they kissed. Exploring the terrain that was his, hers, and the blurred turf between.

Maude chuckled as she pulled away, yawned, and stretched like a great cat. "The spirit's willing but the body can't oblige. The level-five setting on your oxygen flow is hampering all my best moves." She leaned over and nibbled his lips with such gusto that Gil groaned with delight just imagining what that might entail.

Lordy, she tasted good, like one of his father's tawny ports aged to pecan-sweet perfection. He couldn't forget this. Not her taste, not the sultry summer-rain aroma of her flesh—that silk-soft skin that stretched over every shapely inch of her body—and definitely not her Ferrari-like purr, the deep, powerful rumble of pleasure when she'd finally yielded to the kiss and melted against him with delicious abandon.

He *wouldn't* forget. If they tried to cut it out of him, he'd be scarred for life. Texas toast.

He shook her off and sat up. The frown marring Maude's dreamy lips and her growl of complaint bolstered his spirits.

"Here's the deal. I don't want the purge. I want to stay. And I want you to fix it. I know you can."

THIRTEEN

Can I?

Of course she could. She hadn't stopped thinking about how to do it for a split second since they'd left Scio Quad. The question wasn't could she, but should she.

She didn't give a drutz one way or another about Gil's percentile potential. The Scios would, of course; if given the opportunity, they would probably extend him a Core-residency option. But if they did and Gil accepted, she'd be in a gigadrutz dilemma.

Zat. She was tempted. In spite of every warning, she was seriously considering it.

She had to remind herself of the truth. Everyone said it. Everyone knew it: Rogues and romance didn't mix. Romance, the life commitment most core residents practiced, didn't fit into the Rogue lifestyle. An exhaustive training unit had stressed the rationale for avoiding emotional entanglements, and the ready supply of technological resources like emotion buffers and targeted memory purges existed primarily to repair damage to Rogues who didn't. But most Rogues simply developed a love 'em and leave 'em policy, or indulged in one-night stands with like-thinking individuals.

Maude squeezed her eyes shut and tried to concentrate. The sedative-laced atmosphere hampered a true effort, as well as her proximity to the object of her desire. A glance from Gil superheated her hormones and constricted her heart muscle—a delightful complication that wasn't troublesome, as it wouldn't last. It *couldn't* last. But Gil's touch? Now that was trouble. It sizzled her flesh, triggered sweat, and aroused a ravenous beast that couldn't be sated with a few kisses. So far, her craving for Gil had broken her rigorous adherence to the straight and narrow strictures for Rogues. She'd collected a half dozen infractions, including copping out of her Reacclimation protocol, just to indulge her libido with a high-risk partner.

No. For her sake and her career, Gil had to go home.

"I don't think it's a good idea," she finally replied, sighing heavily as she met his steady gaze. "My brain says it can't work."

"Your brain might be right," Gil shot back. "But then there's this." He tapped his chest, in the vicinity of his heart. "Tell me you don't feel it."

Maude's breath stalled. "Of course I do," she snapped. "We're biologically compatible. It's obvious there's an attraction between us. But you don't belong here. This isn't your time."

He grinned but didn't move—not a micron, not a muscle.

Amazing, she thought. He didn't try to convince her with any of the persuasive sensual weapons at his disposal; he spared tormenting her with another devilishly erotic embrace. Another motor-revving kiss and she just might crumble, agree to anything, admit everything—including love.

No, not love, she rushed to correct herself. *I just want sex.*

But that was a lie. If all she'd wanted was to meet a sexual need, she could have scheduled an anonymous Mr. Lucky to visit her sleep dock during her final Reacclimation rotations.

"Okay, I get it. This is the future. It's not my time," Gil said, interrupting her thoughts. "I don't belong. But what's the rush to get me out of here?"

Eh? Maude blinked. Gil had her there. What *was* the zatting rush, anyway?

"I want you. You want me. And since you guys are all about time, I figure it's not far-fetched to assume you can postpone the brain drain and extend my visit a few days."

Maude was stunned silly. The cowboy had a point. It was still zatting dangerous. She didn't really want to entertain anything as serious as a commitment. But a rotation, or maybe a half-dozen rotations, with Gil? How dangerous could that be? Immediately, her mind went to work on the problem. Shuffling mission-prep obligations, shifting most closer to launch, she could free up a fortnight.

He leaned over and teased her bottom lip with his finger. "You might not know this about me, but I don't ever give in without a fight."

"I *didn't* know," Maude managed. A smile popped up, like a submerged float escaping from the hold of a sinking ship. She was in trouble. Her stellar career with the Rogues was tanking, and all she could do was smile.

FOURTEEN

Males. Humpf. Maude sucked on the nutrient tube and glared at each man in turn. She hated the chalky food supplement she forced herself to consume, hated the formless and functional rock-hard lounge chairs in the Scio Quad process lab, but mostly she hated Charlie and Hickham. They were peas in a pod—eggheads lacking a modicum of romance in their mutual collection of XY genes.

"Gil can't stay," Charlie repeated.

He wouldn't look at her. Neither would Hickham. They stood shoulder to shoulder at one of the silvery analysis stations, their backs to her lounger. Gil's transparent treatment chart hovered above the station's surface scanner.

Charlie tapped a highlighted notation on the chart with his laser pointer. The text bubble ballooned, magnified, and glowed orange. "His Core Residency option was rejected. I can't override an auto-decline, T-code Echo Echo," Charlie added, and glanced over at his peer.

Hickham nodded in agreement. His frown somehow magnified the bad news.

"I know, I know." Maude snarled. "A transit code Echo Echo means Gil is era essential. He can't stay, he's got to go back. I heard you the first time, Charlie."

She pulled herself out of the lounger and stomped toward the men. "But if you were listening to me, you'd get that I'm not asking you to override the auto-decline. I'm just suggesting a fortnight-rotation delay."

Maude paused. Lust was making her loony. Challenging the respective heads of two of Core's critical service divisions wasn't a smart move. She doubted few certified Rogues or Scios ever had. Potentially career-sabotaging suggestion aside, it was foolhardy to tempt one of these two to deviate from Core mandates. Charlie's and Hickham's strict adherence to the policies protected Core's present, and their rigorous restrictions about disrupting the past were hard-won, hard-learned lessons for the tenacious time traveling society. Maude knew full well that bending a rule—even a minor one—could potentially trigger a chain reaction with devastating results. Gil might be the one man who stirred her blood, fanned her passion, and leveled every barrier to her heart with his touch, but he was also forbidden fruit and best forgotten. The longer Gil lingered in the future, the more the risk to the past.

Still, selfish as it was, Maude had to ask. Her attraction for the man had morphed into an obsession. She'd spent her final rotations in Reacclimation focused on crafting excuses to interrupt Gil's procedure. She had one—a flimsy one at best, but she couldn't back down now. The ache to surrender to desire was more powerful than anything she'd ever felt, feeding her carnal fantasies, whetting her appetite, tormenting her flesh, and starving her intellect of all but the most primitive urges.

The need to yield to those urges—just once or twice before Gil was lost to her forever—consumed her. Gil wouldn't retain the memory of their tempestuous tryst, but she would. No more uploading anything to a separate file. At last she'd possess her own snippet of passion, a prized recollection of utter abandon and delight, something of her very own to savor from time to time as she lived her eternity without him. And no one would take it from her.

"What's the harm in delaying Gil's return to his era?" Her cheeks felt hot, flamed from the craving she poorly attempted to conceal. She tried to shrug off the matter, minimize its import. "He asked me to try and arrange it. I'm only passing on his request. You haven't started the mental Reacclimation sequence or purging yet. Right?"

"Correct," Hickham responded. "Charlie just completed the titanium extraction." He continued to study Gil's chart. The holographic image of Gil's body glowed where invasive probes accelerated tissue regeneration and healing.

"Frankly, I like the idea, Charlie. The extraction was uneventful, and you've scheduled a generous transition period for healing."

Charlie snorted. "Not a fortnight. I've only scheduled two rotations."

Hick winked at Maude. "Two it is, then."

Maude's knees nearly buckled with joy. Two rotations! She'd see him again, taste the raw hunger of the man, feel his firm muscles knot and flex against hers. . . .

Hickham's strident voice interrupted her erotic daydream. "I'll need at least one rotation, though—to conduct a thorough gene harvest," he said.

Maude's jaw fell open. "Gil didn't consent to that, did he?" she asked.

Charlie didn't reply, but his expressive features confirmed the omission. Then he shook his head.

"A ninety-percentile doesn't come along every day, Maude," Hickham explained. "You know the Scios' central mission. Our part in Core's directive to protect the future and preserve the past warrants us to identify, evaluate, and protect human life, including the obligation to collect and store unique genetic material. Whether patient Gillespe authorizes it or not, I'm getting a sample."

"But you didn't bother to ask him, did you?" Maude was arguing a moot point. Collecting genetic material was a Core standard. It wasn't an invasive or dangerous procedure, and Gil wouldn't miss the sampled quantity. But she'd lose Gil—one complete rotation of the promised two-rotation reprieve.

"You don't need a complete rotation for harvesting," she said to Charlie. "Why don't you conduct the harvest during his Reacclimation?"

Charlie cocked his head, clearly bewildered by her query. "It's up to Hick. It's his procedure."

Hickham blinked like a great barn owl, frustratingly unmoved by her plea.

Maude rolled her eyes and groaned. She itched to bump heads with these two obtuse test tube junkies, mortified that she might be forced to reveal her true motive: an expedited and utterly gratifying orgy for as long as she had Gil after Reacclimation.

Gigazat. Do I have to spell it out for them?

When Maude didn't think she could stand another micron of frustration, Charlie finally offered, "An efficient alternative would be to pair the harvest with the scheduled sperm extraction."

Sperm extraction? Maude's curiosity quelled her craving for the moment. She pushed Charlie aside and studied Gil's chart, whistling as she read through the documented calibrations. She knew Gil's percentile ranking was important to the Scios, but not *this* important.

"Zat, Charlie. Is he really that special?" she cried.

Hickham responded first. "If he wasn't essential to his era of origin, I'd be recruiting the boy right from his Reacclimation chamber. He possesses a rare combination of attributes that the Scios and the Transit Think Tank covet."

"That means you'll clone him or make him a daddy without his knowledge or consent?" Maude knew the answer, but she still had to hear it.

"Conceivably," Hick returned.

Charlie's features were suffused with guilt, but not Hickham's. The guy looked cold, calculating, and unapologetic.

"You know it's how we survive, Maude. It's why we're still here. We harness all the resources at our disposal and ensure the perpetuation of our species. We always harvest genes from appropriate visitors."

"Of course I know it. I'm the *zatting* prototype for your perpetuating-the-species effort. I know you pulled my ingredients together from your stores and baked me up in a surrogate's oven."

Charlie grinned, and Hickham looked smug. Both were preening like proud papas—as proud as proxy papas could be.

Like Cara, Maude knew she too had been salvaged from the wreckage of the past. But unlike Cara, whose parents had conceived her in love before they perished in the transit disaster, Maude's parents had never met nor even existed in the same era. Reared as a lab procreant, she'd lacked a legacy, a heritage, and a history that all other orphans possessed. And although she'd come to cherish her friendships as the family she never had, the insatiable craving to connect to her blood roots persisted and shadowed her every happiness.

Maude shook her head slowly. Chewing on her lip, she struggled to stem the tide of longing that threatened to wash over her and suck her back into the pit of loneliness she'd escaped when she joined the Rogues. She didn't know how any of the other procreants felt, but she wouldn't wish that tortured fate on any child. Certainly not on Gil's.

"Don't do it," she whispered, looking at the floor.

Charlie lifted her chin. For the second time in recent history, Maude felt tears sting her eyes. She leveled her gaze at his kind face and blinked back the moisture.

"I'll never apologize," he said. "You were created with love, Maude."

Hickham turned away from them, busied himself at his station, and generally ignored the exchange until Maude collected herself. He cleared his throat when she did, and smiled—a rare treat from the stoic scientist.

"You were a successful prototype. It proved the procreant program was a viable option—if we should ever require it," he said. "Currently we don't. Genetic diversity and population numbers are holding at recommended levels."

"Glad to hear it," Maude returned. And, she was glad. Truly. But the gladness didn't erode the stunning realization of just how tenuous the existence of her society was, depending on the decisions of intellects like Charlie and Hickham.

"Rogues do it all the time, but exactly how risky is it to interrupt a Reacclimation procedure for someone like Gil?" Maude asked. She was suddenly alarmed that they might be doing this thing for her, misguided by their affection for her and their desire to grant her some brief joy. "Will it jeopardize Core or the time continuum?"

Hickham cleared his throat to respond. Belatedly, Maude remembered his penchant for pontification if an answer wasn't one of those easy yes or no types.

"There's a point-six-zero-three-five degree risk factor on the ZED scale with each rotation between his initial transit and retransit to his era of origin," he began, tapping his feet in syncopated rhythm with each word he uttered.

The arrival of cleaning droids and domed floor-mop bots signaled a pending shift change for the Scio process lab. The efficient service took only moments to complete, provided staff didn't hinder the process. Charlie and Maude snagged loungers and tucked in their feet. Hick paused in his explanation long enough to climb up on one of the lab's floating stools, his limbs dangling freely. While he did, Maude usurped his monologue.

"I gather it is and isn't risky," she said.

"Er, yes, however . . ." Hick replied, gliding his stool closer to the loungers and neatly avoiding the humming swarm of cleaning devices.

"But you're both willing to take the risk?" she hurriedly guessed, and shifted her gaze from one man to the other until they both nodded.

Hickham elaborated, his voice swelling above the din of the cleaning team. "Charlie's calculations indicate an offsetting positive for every three rotations. The patient's standard and nonstandard implants, the psychosis-limiting device in particular, effect all negatives as well. Of particular interest is the bonus positives derived from—"

"Hick," Charlie interrupted, jabbing a thumb into each ear as a whirring aerial dust bot briskly cleansed and blasted a nutrient stain from the yoke of his tunic. "You've made your point."

"Oh. So I have," Hickham blurted. He blinked owlishly in Maude's direction and proffered another rare smile. "The risk is within tolerances."

The men were blushing. It was all too obvious to Maude that they were bending the rules, weighing the odds, and granting one small wish for their beloved procreant because they knew and understood.

"Thank you," she said loudly as the clean team converged on their position, the last bastion of bacteria in the lab.

"What?" Charlie mouthed, and stuck thumbs in his ears again.

"I said—" Maude shouted.

Hick held up one hand as he clicked the heels of his

wedged shoes together. The spitting, spinning, and scouring bots squawked and stalled. Silence reigned.

Hickham snorted and glared at the innocuous-looking devices. "Ionic beasts," he snapped. "My Scio protégés must be messing with the zatting proximity buffers again. No shortage on intellect with the current crop of recruits, but most are sadly lacking common sense."

"New generation," Charlie chimed in. "Same situation with the newest scouts over at Rogue Central. Long road ahead of them if they want to measure up to the likes of Maude. I'm glad it's Raymond's problem now and not mine."

Hickham nodded. "Ray's a good man. Devoted to detail, rigid on the regs, solid foundation in the sciences. He's a good pick as your replacement. Might use him myself if and when I take a sabbatical."

Maude's groan was unconscious. The semipermanent swap in Rogue Central leadership had taken place during her last Reacclimation rotations. Raymond was her new boss. And with her level twelve mission on the docket, a wave of anxiety flooded her thoughts. She didn't shift her confidence easily, especially not to the upright and reserved Raymond. Instinctively she wanted to cling to the man who'd fostered her and preserved her life through thick and thin. Charlie's commitment to the Rogues was unmatched. His dogged determination and intense focus had demanded near perfection from every department and member of the team at Rogue Central, from scout to mentor, from technician to lead.

Yes, Charlie was a tough act to follow. Of course, if Raymond had passed muster with Charlie, Maude owed him her trust.

She swallowed and attempted a smile. "That's right, you're officially on hiatus now, aren't you, Charlie?"

Charlie's ear-to-ear grin was infectious. The knot of worry that had settled in Maude's chest softened a bit.

"As soon as I shift authorization to execute Gil's final Reacclimation protocols to Hick, I'm off."

"So soon?" Her voice quavered a bit. She coughed, squared her shoulders, set her jaw, and gripped the edge of the lounger for added support.

"Where are you going on your sabbatical?" Hick asked. Charlie grinned but didn't respond.

"Hey, yeah. Who won the bet?" Maude said.

Charlie didn't keep secrets. The guy was usually an open book—always had been with her, at least. But the purpose of his sabbatical and his destination had been an exception, and the secret had aroused a heady round of speculation and curiosity within and without Rogue Central—including one of Core's key administrators, the governor of the western sectors herself.

"Everyone was laying bets on your destination. I picked the 1950s, southwestern America. I know you're fascinated with the combustion engine, Route Sixty-six era. Did I guess it?"

Charlie chortled and tweaked her nose. "Nope. But neither did anyone else."

FIFTEEN

Mackenzie didn't mind filling in for Gil; it kept her finger in the pie and her mind off her favorite employee's fate. She had to trust that Charlie and the Rogues would fix him and send him home as soon as possible. Of course, anything was possible in Core. She and Rick were eyewitnesses to the fact that the future possessed some handy-dandy miracles that could right wrongs in the past, up to and including reviving a dead man from AD 79.

She shuffled stacks of papers on her old desk with roughshod efficiency. *This is Gil's desk now,* she reminded herself as she processed priority items in his inbox and stopped short of rearranging everything to her satisfaction. The cattle-drive exhibit teardown and prep work for the upcoming wildcatters installation had a few tasks that required delegation. She tagged the items, affixed routing slips with due dates, and dropped them in the outbox, then sighed, reveling in the brief respite when everything in her world seemed handled and on track. It wouldn't last. It couldn't. But for the time being, Gil's stack of mysteries were demystified, and workflow for his staff could progress without suffering greatly due to his absence.

It felt good to fuss around on familiar turf in a role that still fit her like a glove. Her new responsibilities as director and cushy digs didn't. Not yet. The challenging, rewarding, and often all-consuming position was everything she'd desired for her career, but then again, once upon a time, her tenure as curator had met that dream.

She lingered. Tweaking this and that, she reminisced about her recent good old days behind the scarred desk where she'd stretched and tested herself, taken on risky projects and won the right to host the coveted Ancient Pompeii traveling exhibit. The position had offered her countless opportunities for experience and advancement, which she'd reaped, and she was heartily proud that her former intern had taken her spot.

"He'll go far," she muttered to herself as she filed each of his dated project folders. She scanned his current calendar and nodded with approval; his notes for future events encompassed the next five years. *He's drafting potential thematic exhibits and annual research symposium topics that will attract the best of the best*, she thought.

She whistled when she stumbled across a diamond in the rough. It was still a maze of jots, notes, and half-formed task lists, but Mackenzie could decipher his scrawl and decode the brainstorm event for 2013. The call for papers. The exhibit. The compilation of all the research and artifacts to date. It was . . . brilliant. Hosting an academic symposium on the fiftieth anniversary of JFK's assassination could establish the museum—her museum—as one of the world's premier research and repository facilities on the topic.

Mackenzie hooted. Rocking back in her chair, she propped her feet up on the windowsill and steepled her fingers, contemplating the potential ramifications of executing such a pivotal event. Damn. Her blood was up.

She wanted to get going on it yesterday. It was utterly awesome.

"Get your butt back here, Gil," she fumed. "Pronto. This is your baby and I need you."

SIXTEEN

"Gil?"

The voice sounded familiar. Friendly.

Gil stretched and yawned as blue light slowly filled the small Reacclimation chamber. *Am I dreaming?* Monitors and transmission screens lit up around him. Rolling onto his side, he . . . stared into Charlie's clear eyes.

Gil jerked back and banged his head on the opposing monitor. "Damn it!" he roared.

Charlie's image flickered, then rotated ninety degrees. "You awake?" he asked after completing the adjustment.

Gil rubbed the back of his head and growled. "Am now."

Charlie laughed. "So, you're one of those."

"One of those what?" Gil snapped.

"A grouch," Charlie said with a grin. "Reacclimation disruptions stimulate adrenals. Some folks are pussycats. You're not. Bet you want to tear my head off."

"There's an idea," Gil said as he tried to sit up. He couldn't. He'd tangled his lines and was pinned.

Charlie's image on the screen flickered again, replaced briefly by that of a smocked technician. "I'm sending

Wendell to extract you. Refrain from assaulting him, if you please."

"I can't promise anything," Gil retorted. He tugged at innumerable connections, which resisted his efforts. "I'm pissed."

"Pissed?" Charlie's face clouded for a second. "Oh. Right. *Right*. You're angry." Charlie's smile returned and he chortled. "It'll pass. I'm balancing your electrolytes now. I weaned you off the nutrient tube during the last rotation. Your belly's empty."

Gil growled. "Yeah. When do we eat?"

"You are scheduled to break your fast in about an hour."

"An hour? That's not going to cut it." Gil finally freed one arm and tore the connections off the other. "Fuck the schedule. I want food. Real food—meat, potatoes, bread and butter. Lots of it."

Charlie scowled, his attention fixed on something off-screen. "You've disconnected your primary intake line," he noted with a heavy sigh. "I wish you'd waited for Wendell; this might delay us a bit. I'll need to backflush your system for residuals."

Gil's foul humor had begun to dissipate. "Sorry," he managed.

Charlie obviously didn't harbor grudges. He acknowledged Gil's apology with a nod and a wink. "You're feeling better already? Marvelous. Maude's right, you're a natural."

"Maude? Hey, hold on a sec," Gil said. "Did she do it? Did she swing it? She must have," he answered himself. "I remember her. I remember you and everything else. I'm in the future and you guys haven't zapped my brain."

Charlie's smile flagged. "Gil, you can't stay in Core," he said quietly. "It's not an option. You are era essential and you have to go home. Your memory purge is still on schedule."

"I don't understand, then," Gil snarled, his enthusiasm evaporating. "What's going on?"

"Maybe food is a good idea," Charlie countered. "Want a burger? Some fries?"

"I want answers," Gil said.

He felt like an emotional yo-yo at the moment. The urge to throttle Charlie returned. He bared his teeth, weathered another protest from his empty gut, and punched the monitor instead. That helped. Charlie's image flickered and the screen went black. Gil's knuckles throbbed, but the spent energy cut some of his tension.

The nozzle above Gil's head hissed. Someone was amping up his oxygen flow—and most probably his sedation levels too.

"Feel better?" Charlie asked from another monitor embedded in the enclosure's walls.

Gil glanced at the calibration for the air flow, which was at two—not enough to send him back to dreamland but just enough to take the edge off his anger. "Yeah. Thanks," he replied.

Charlie held up a steaming double-cheeseburger with a side order of glistening fries that Gil imagined he could smell. "Promise not to assault Wendell?"

Gil's mouth watered. He'd agree to just about anything for a bite of that burger.

"What about my answers?" he persisted.

"How about I leave that all up to Maude? We're having dinner with her," Charlie offered.

Maude *and* dinner? Hell, yeah. Gil finally managed a smile and nodded. "Throw in that burger basket to tide me over, and you've got yourself a deal."

"I'm going to kill Charlie," Maude spat. She paced the loggia that spanned the façade of Dak and Falah's homestead outside Edgeville. Patience didn't come easy for her, and waiting nearly an hour for Charlie and Dak to spring Gil from Reacclimation sorely tested what little she possessed. She shivered as she watched the night sky for approaching hoverlift lights. The vista was limited.

Edgeville evenings were pitch-black and chilly and long. Situated within the shelf caverns that buffered Core's heavily colonized sectors from the underworld's vast frontier region, the scattered settlement was technologically off-grid. Atmospherics simulating starlight and moonrise and moderating nighttime temperatures were unwarranted extravagances for a sparsely occupied district. Rated remote and reclusive, Edgeville wasn't popular but it was ideal for the likes of ex-Rogue Dak.

Maude caught snatches of a lullaby as Falah put her son to bed. She glanced back at the lovely villa. Warm light peeked from the shuttered windows and pooled at the thresholds. The savory scents of roasted meat and hot yeasty breads filled the air and teased her appetite till her belly protested. The bucolic homestead was the picture of perfection. And it was a drastic departure from the nested techie communal affairs Dak once preferred.

The notorious bad boy, Maude's mentor and former kingpin of the high-risk squad of Rogues, Dak had seemingly accepted his forced retirement and transit-restricted status. But Maude knew better. Relocation to Edgeville to settle down and raise a family with Falah was calculated. It maintained an out-of-sight, out-of-mind profile. Dak's wings had been clipped but he was *not* retired.

Falah called out from the portal. Maude shook her head.

"No sign of them yet," she replied, and rechecked her wrist unit. "They should have been here by now. Unless . . ." Her unit issued a flat tone: No communications.

"Zat," she said angrily. Logically she knew Charlie or Dak would have sent a message if there'd been any trouble, or if Reacclimation refused to release Gil. "They wouldn't frustrate me on purpose, or would they?"

Falah joined her at the railing and smiled. "No," the dusky, Madonna-like beauty offered. "They wouldn't." She showed Maude her ring unit, a sleek, hammered band studded with amethysts. One stone glowed brightly, the intensity and brilliance of the jewel noting the proximity of Falah's baby boy—less than twenty meters. The second stone in the ring flickered dully. Dak. Proximity one thousand meters and closing fast.

"Finally." Maude groaned, nearly giddy with relief. She released her grip on the rail and accepted the shimmery shawl Falah laid across her shoulders.

"You love Gil," Falah said simply as they watched the flickering amethyst grow brighter.

"Of course not," Maude countered. "I barely know him. I lust after him and crave him. I want to spend the next two rotations with him before my next mission. But I don't love him."

"Yes. Love." Falah sighed and held the hand with the glowing stones against her cheek. "As I love Dak."

Maude stalled her protestations. Arguing with her hostess on matters of the heart wasn't tactful.

Falah's greatest gift, other than her devotion to her husband and child, was her mulish matchmaking nature. Rectifying Maude's solitary status was a chief goal. The woman was indefatigable on the subject, something Maude had weathered and largely ignored during their brief acquaintance until tonight. Tonight, Falah-Cupid had found a new arrow: Gil.

Maude studied the diminutive, joyous female. They had little in common. However, Maude's fondness for the woman had been instantaneous, and their mutual affection for Dak helped span the gulf between the former slave from ancient Pompeii and orphan Rogue from the future. And although initially dismissing the importance of it, Maude acknowledged a blossoming respect for the instincts of Dak's ladylove.

"I love him?" Maude ventured, more as a query to herself.

Falah's tinkling laugh confirmed her opinion. "Yes, I believe you do."

The idea was stunning. Extraordinary. Maude mentally wheeled away from it. Right turn, one hundred eighty degrees.

"You're not using your translator," Maude blurted the moment the realization hit her. Falah's bulky audio apparatus was missing!

"But I am," Falah returned, and fingered her delicate bronze necklet. "A gift from Charlie."

Maude eyed the adornment with astonishment. "That man never ceases to amaze me," she admitted.

His was a clever solution. Creating a unique tool to expand Falah's language abilities had been essential for her successful integration into Core society. But the finely crafted piece was also beautiful. Simple yet elegant, it suited Falah's long, graceful neck and confirmed Charlie's limitless sensitivity.

Falah was still adapting to her new life and role as wife and mother. Her sudden immersion into a culture 2,100 years in the future had been brutal and permanent. Maude empathized. But to her knowledge, Falah had never uttered a complaint or a word of regret. For love owned Falah, more surely than any master ever could. It had spared her doomed life and claimed her heart, completely and eternally.

Of course, love had also felled Dak and destroyed his career. Maude knew some of the details: how the Rogue icon, this legendary leader of the lifesaving squad, betrayed the future, endangered the past, and surrendered all to the power of love. But she didn't know why.

She could guess, imagine, wonder about and fear it. But, she couldn't understand. Somehow love slipped under the skin and severed the connection between the head and heart. It corrupted reason. It compromised commitments. It challenged duty, devotion, and honor. It was dangerous. And debilitating to Rogues. There was no question.

Immunity to the state had spared her so far. However, if Falah's instincts were remotely on target, Maude's resistance was about to be tested.

The lift lights were finally visible. A hovercraft's approach activated the perimeter illumination system and highlighted several stuccoed outbuildings and Falah's trellised garden. The spring-fed pool that dominated the expansive tiled courtyard glistened in the muted light. Falah sighed and hugged her shoulders. She held her ring against her cheek again. The two jeweled stones glowed steadily. Dak was almost home.

Maude fumed. The zatting ring didn't confirm the other occupants of the lift. What if Gil wasn't with them?

Her patience evaporated. She sprinted the length of the loggia and stumbled into the courtyard. "If he's not with them," she growled, "I'll kill them all."

SEVENTEEN

Gil wasn't with them. Neither was Charlie.

Dak held up one hand in defense. "Nothing's wrong. They're coming. And, don't kill the messenger," he said the moment he stepped from the hoverlift.

Maude glowered but contained her frustration. Dak wasn't alone. Managing a civil tongue and demeanor, she greeted Dak's passenger.

"You're Bob 13, aren't you?"

The Time Transitor grunted in response as he loosed the tethers on a bulky container and transferred it from the lift to a rudimentary stowage sled. The task wasn't extraordinary, but Bob's attention to detail was.

"You processed my auto-transit retrieval," Maude continued. "It was perfect. Thank you."

Bob spared only a brief glance in her direction. And a nod. But his stony expression conveyed nothing in the way of recognition.

Maude extended her hand. "I submitted a commendation with my report, but I want to thank you personally."

Bob stared at her hand for a long moment. Then, wiping his hand along the leg of his jumpsuit, he took it with such trepidation that Maude herself nearly balked.

"Thank you," she repeated as warmly as she could, then surreptitiously leveled a questioning gaze at Dak.

"That's great, Bob," Dak intervened, slapping the slight fellow on the back. "You didn't tell me that you'd saved Maudie's life."

"And Gil's," Maude added. "He's coming for dinner. He'll want to thank you himself."

Bob froze. A slight breeze might have toppled him if there'd been one.

"Why don't you take our cargo on down, Bob?" Dak suggested.

That broke the spell. Bob reacted stiffly. Flipping levers mounted on the face of a nearby wall, he activated a ground-hugging conveyance system that bisected the courtyard and connected with the outbuildings. The machinery protested, sputtering to life and groaning, metal against metal, until the flat, track-fed belt engaged. With a jolt, the rubbery surface began to move. Bob deposited cargo from the lift upon it box by box. They were mysterious cases, suspicious-looking in Maude's estimation, and strangely similar to packages utilized almost exclusively at Rogue Central.

Dak called to Bob, who was trailing after the cargo, "If you're too busy with the installation and transit prep to join us for dinner, send up the droid for a platter."

Bob stopped and sniffed the air. A whisper of a smile tugged at his otherwise stony features.

"Smells like roast chicken tonight," Dak added. "Falah knows it's your favorite."

Bob nodded and turned away. Trotting after the cargo, he disappeared along with it into a ramshackle lean-to belching acrid smoke.

The moment he was out of sight, Maude turned on Dak. "What are you up to, Dak? And what is the lead

Time Transitor for us Rogues doing here?" she whispered hoarsely.

Dak folded his arms and shook his head in mock disgust. "You're letting recent events cloud your observation and analysis skills. Did you forget everything I taught you?"

Maude sucked in her breath. She had to admit that was possible. Off duty shouldn't ever mean offline. Chock-full of technology, trained by the best, and honed both by experience and enhancements, she'd never felt so detached from her brain.

"Oh, Dak." She groaned and collapsed on the stone wall surrounding the courtyard pool, buried her face in her hands. "It is Gil, isn't it? But he's something I can purge after he's gone and get my life back—and my career."

Dak settled beside her, then showed more insight than she'd expected. Or hoped. "Core possesses the technology to erase, buffer, and heal most minds. You can purge anything, Maudie, including lust and love. But do you really want to?"

She glanced at him through her parted fingers. "You didn't," she snorted, "and you lost everything."

"Did I?" Dak returned. "Look around. Tell me what I lost."

Maude furrowed her brow with the effort of taking everything in. The isolated farm offered clues that perhaps only another Rogue could pick up, but displacing distractions with details, she inventoried the known facts until the obvious conclusion emerged.

"Zat, Dak. You're building your own transit station."

"Not bad," Dak returned. "One minute, twenty seconds. Not a complete analysis, but a sufficient response in the time, given the circumstances and the lust factor."

"An EE? Explain that. Why am I 'era essential'?" Gil demanded between burps from the pseudo burger and fries he'd gobbled.

"Why? To be honest, it's a mystery at this point," Charlie began. He paused long enough to float the hoverlift into position. Engaging the autopilot, he settled back as the craft was sucked into a steady stream of traffic in the tunnel system, and elaborated. "I can't give you specifics because I don't have access to the Transit Think Tank's VIPER data."

"Viper? You lost me," Gil said.

"Viability Index for Pollution of Eras and Restrictions data, V-I-P-E-R," Charlie explained. "TTT uses it to measure, govern, and restrict transit pollution resulting from time travel. VIPER buffers all known significant factors in world history—key people and events—to prevent contamination. It safeguards the present and protects the past."

"From transit trash," Gil muttered.

"Never thought of it exactly in those terms." Charlie smirked. "But I like it. Transit trash."

"Era essential, huh? You sure about that?"

"No, not without seeing the data, but—how do you say it? Better safe than sorry. VIPER errs on the side of prevention. Significant historic events and people are 'sticky.' They attract contamination like magnets. And potentially, any contact can alter a time line. "A body scan provides a great deal of data on a subject. You've been supplemented with the buffering implants that record and project . . ."

Gil stopped trying to sort it all out; Charlie's response was a rabbit trail that included scientific jargon and a smokescreen of technical verbiage. He noted a few landmark terms and waited him out, listening more with his eyes than his ears. Charlie was sweating. Profusely.

After a few moments, Gil glanced around. So far, their journey to the promised destination of dinner and a date with Maude was lackluster. Jetting through the tubes of rock offered little distraction. And after his profoundly satisfying rest, Gil's powers of observation had improved a hundredfold.

No, they'd never *been* this good, Gil admitted. They were exceptional, in fact. He could pick up bits of chatter between lift occupants as their crafts passed in the opposite direction. Kids squabbling. Women gossiping. Men debating sporting statistics.

Gil interrupted Charlie's explanation with a shout. "Hey! Stop this thing for a sec, will you?"

"What's wrong?" Charlie asked, instantly slowing the lift.

"Shhh," Gil hissed. Clapping his hands over his ears, he concentrated on an approaching craft a hundred feet away. He could hear *them*. His eyes wide with wonder, his jaw fell open.

Charlie laughed and shook his head. "Another side effect of Reacclimation. Most of us take the heightened sensory acuity for granted," he explained. Releasing the brake, he engaged the autopilot again and pointed the lift forward. "Can you see the cutoff for Aquatics? It's approximately fifty-five meters ahead."

Gil nodded. Even within the marginally lit transport tunnel, he could pick up details. He sniffed the air, faced Charlie, and scowled. "Do you have another burger in that knapsack? Hand it over."

Charlie complied, laughing, but Gil, rather than wolfing it down, chewed each bite and swallowed with a new appreciation. "It's not meat or cheese," he said as he licked his lips appreciatively. "But *damn*, it's good."

"Is it?" Charlie preened. "Maude complains about the texture, but I've been working on that."

"Suits me as is," Gil replied.

Charlie flinched. Frowning, he checked his wrist unit. *Trouble*, Gil noted.

Charlie's demeanor shifted dramatically, and Gil glimpsed the iron within the man, this scientist who carried such a tremendous burden of responsibility. He wasn't sweating now, but he looked less in control.

Gil suddenly realized the truth: The future wasn't perfectly secure. And that meant neither was the past. His past.

"A minor emergency requires my attention," Charlie said, offering a quick, reassuring grin before shutting down the autopilot. "We need to take a shortcut."

He banked the lift. Maneuvering the craft into a steep, spiral dive, he dropped it neatly into a deep, dark, hole.

"Shhhhhhhit," Gil cried.

His survival instincts kicked in. Gripping the edge of the lift he held on for dear life, not trusting any invisible force field or microfiber tether to keep his fanny firmly fixed to the transport and safety. A blast of hot, smelly air from far below rocked the lift, slowing the descent and making it less of a free fall.

The urge to vomit was powerful. Gil had ridden most of the wooden roller coasters in the western hemisphere with nary a gurgle in his gut, but flying with Charlie at the helm had almost done him in.

"Got a barf bag?" he groaned. He didn't need it yet, he didn't think, but he rescinded his accolades for Charlie's fake burgers. Real meat or not, the backwash burned his throat. He might never eat another burger again.

"Haven't been down here for a decade or more," Charlie said, slowing the lift to a crawl. The darkness abated. The lower they went, the more a green algaelike substance coated the walls, phosphorescent and illuminating their path.

Gil's nausea subsided, displaced by a mounting curiosity. The diameter of the shaft was wider now, the temperature increasing the deeper they descended. Geology wasn't his strength—or vulcanology either, for that matter—but Gil was pretty sure they were traversing a volcanic pipe. He sniffed the air and said, "This pipe is inactive, I hope."

"There are safeguards against pyroclastic surges and the like. Pending lethal conditions, access restrictions protect life," Charlie replied.

"Right. More safeguards," Gil mumbled.

"Ah, here we go." Charlie chortled as the craft emerged into a larger, wider section, and as he rotated the lift, above them Gil could see the route they'd traveled. It was one of numerous branches of pipes, each clearly marked by manmade directionals. Beneath each was an up arrowlike symbol and an identifier. The one they'd exited was labeled REACCLIMATION AND AQUATICS. Not all the arrows glowed green. The SURFACE arrow glowed red.

The surface? Sure, he'd given that some thought—in passing. Overwhelmed by everything else in this future society, it hadn't been tops on his agenda. Now, suddenly, it was. What the hell happened? Why was everyone living underground?

Gil's questions were stalled when Charlie floored the lift again, exiting the main area through a lateral branch as another blast of hot, foul air—hotter and more violent than any previous—surged up from the depths.

"The pipes are handy. We utilize their geothermal properties as well as their being natural transportation routes," Charlie explained as the lift popped out into a smallish cavern.

Lights struggled to life as they passed, illuminating a minimalistic tram station, soot-coated and apparently derelict. The sign at the station entrance flickered. Letters were obviously missing. OUTS IRT 13.

"Outskirt Thirteen," Charlie added as he cut power to the lift, settling it next to a corroded mesh wall. "Thirteen miles beyond Edgeville."

Gil knew the drill. He released his tether, hopped off the hoverlift and helped Charlie stow it beneath the station platform. There weren't others—either lifts or people—and by the look of things, there hadn't been for quite a while.

Charlie rounded the mesh partition and settled himself on the tram station's seating slab. Overhead, warming units clicked on, accompanied by the pleasant sounds and smells of a summer rain, cleansing the immediate area of the scent of rusted metal.

"This will be faster than the lift. It's automated," Charlie explained, crossing his long legs and folding his arms. "Floor sensors register the presence of life-forms and launch a sub-orbital tram for retrieval." He nodded toward a boxy device mounted chest-high in the nearby partition. "Haven't seen one of those communication systems for ages. Primitive but effective . . . if they're still operable. The elements down here can foul the contacts. Identilogs and these"—he tapped his wrist unit—"made them obsolete."

He paused, glanced around at the station and beyond. "I remember Thirteen. A primitive settlement. Minimal resources. We stopped housing populations in these off-grid sectors a long time ago. Now most nonessentials opt for extended residency in the past."

Gil followed the course of his gaze. In the distance, beyond the pool of light that defined the perimeter of the station, he could identify silhouettes of blocky, low-level structures. A ghost town? He finally popped the question, point-blank.

"What happened, Charlie? Why is everyone living underground?"

Charlie tugged on his chin and eyed him. "Been wondering when you'd finally get around to asking that."

"I had a few distractions," Gil retorted. He claimed the seating slab opposite Charlie.

"Maude?"

"Yeah, Maude. And time travel. And the imminent brain-drain threat. And even that nutrient sludge you've been pumping into me from day one."

"But now you want to know everything." Charlie's brows lifted, as if in question.

"Everything," Gil confirmed. "From the beginning."

EIGHTEEN

Mackenzie sighed with satisfaction. The notice was out; the call for papers was begun, and Gil's project was in its initial phase. She'd gotten a preliminary go-ahead from the museum board after a rash of phone calls. Everyone agreed: Hosting a scholarly symposium on the JFK assassination would draw national attention to the museum—both popular and critical.

Thankfully, handling the logistics of the whole affair and the tedious little details was totally Gil's cross. His idea, his burden. Managing the attention they received was her responsibility. She looked forward to it.

Yes, she could leverage this interest to benefit the museum. First, she'd use it to promote and fund their growing collection of historical artifacts. Second, this would help establish a noteworthy reputation for the museum within the competitive society of its peers. Mackenzie rubbed her palms together with glee before unleashing her fingers on the keyboard. Although her desk was loaded with reference and trade books relating to the pivotal historic event, she was eager to surf the Net for the latest research.

Two hours later, Rick nuzzled her neck and almost scared the pee out of her. So absorbed was she in the search, she hadn't heard him come in.

"Sorry, babe," he said, rubbing the welt on her kneecap where she'd knocked it against the underside of the desk. "That looks like it hurt. What's got your brain in a trance? Lurid e-mail?"

"Well, it's lurid all right," she replied, scrolling down the screen for him to see. "But it isn't e-mail. Take a look at this, will you? I don't know all the assassination facts, but this doesn't look right. In fact, it looks way off base."

Rick obliged. After a few moments, they changed places at the console.

Mackenzie was grateful for the break. She had other fish to fry, pressing projects that had nothing to do with Gil's, but the temptation to dig into one of America's greatest unsolved mysteries was overpowering. It itched everyone's craw not to know the absolute, unvarnished, beyond-a-doubt truth of why America's thirty-fifth president had been felled that November day. And who had pulled the trigger. That was why this symposium would attract so many people.

Of course, it would also attract freaks. She'd have her hands full deflecting offers to participate from the ultra-ardent fringe conspiracy theorists and garden-variety wackos and quacks. But Rick and Gil could handle them. They would filter the nonlegitimate historians from the panels of speakers. The two of them seemed to know everything—pro or con, legit or otherwise—on the subject.

Mackenzie groaned. She remembered Rick and Gil male-bonding over conspiracy theories—a scene she'd witnessed soon after introducing them. It was too bizarre to forget. She wasn't so sure they didn't qualify for wacko status themselves. They even knew the color of Jack Ruby's tie the day he'd gunned down Kennedy's alleged assassin, Oswald.

Nevertheless, she was happy to yield to them the responsibility for checking out all the speakers. But now Rick was important in another way. Something had caught her eye during her Internet search, something odd and compelling; she'd stumbled onto an original and disconcerting premise about Oswald. Proffered by an academic, the theory appeared to be valid scholarship. Backed by selected evidence, the premise looked solid and factual. Impossibly so.

"It can't be true," she insisted as she shared the information with Rick. "Can it?"

Rick whistled long and low. "This guy's really smooth." He pushed away from the screen, folded his arms and grimaced. "However, the facts are wrong. He's manipulated information to support his premise. I can prove it. This is one of the times I wish I could use Core's data and clear up the mystery."

"Another data gap." Mackenzie frowned, wishing she'd been able to detect the fraud herself. "We're going to have to check all of the speakers when the proposals start coming in, Rick. They're going to have to be squeaky clean. The museum's reputation is at stake. Mine too."

"Stop worrying, little mother," Rick scolded, pushing away from the console. "I'm up to the challenge and so is Gil. Your museum's safe. I promise."

She didn't require convincing, but the subsequent toe-curling kiss from the father of her baby made her feel better in a heartbeat. "How about my reputation?" she whispered against his mouth.

"Well, that's in danger," he replied with a growl. His wicked grin matched the devilish tingle in her heart.

"Unless you lock the door and share in a little conspiracy of my own."

Mackenzie locked the door.

Gil fumed, but not for long. The rapid tram ride was yet another distraction forcing him to belay his gripes and demands for info that Charlie good-naturedly refused to supply, but it was also a blur. The cushy, automated tram cruised swiftly and effortlessly through the darkness until Charlie activated the entertainment unit. Then the full-media display overloaded Gil's newly enhanced senses—especially the ultrarealistic slog through an Amazon jungle. He surrendered to the assault for the duration of the journey, staring out the windows in awe.

I'll get the truth out of him soon enough, he swore when the tram deposited them at their destination. *I'm not going to back off just because he quoted a damned rule book and some sacrosanct oath to never tell anyone from the past about the future.* From Gil's vantage point, their rule book was shot full of holes, and their oath was as flexible as Gumby.

He recognized the Scio Quad instantly. Cara Chay's greeting was delivered on the fly as she corraled them through the commons and into a large squat structure. Soon they were deep within a complex that stirred Gil's blood. The brainlike high-tech labyrinth, with its myriad of air locks, levels, and labs, resembled his own home turf: the archival and preservation facilities beneath his Dallas museum. If Core had a heart, Gil suspected this made it beat.

Hickham's dismissal after a cursory introduction wasn't offensive; rather, it conveyed more to Gil about the gravity of the situation than the rapid-fire exchange that followed between the Scio head and Charlie. They'd convened in an elevated hub that overlooked a processing lab of sorts. Padded slabs encircled a central console. Soft, even illumination washed the walls, and task spots highlighted the stacks of clear charts. Hickham and Charlie had each claimed floating stools adjacent to the console, but Chay elected to pace the hub's length and breadth as the briefing progressed.

"It's her third message in the last hour," Hickham said, nodding toward Cara. "She's sending, but evidently not receiving. I think we should authorize receipt and decrypt. Do you concur?"

"By rights, Hick, Raymond should be here instead of me. He's the acting head of Rogue Central. If anyone checks the authorization logs to verify that two CS Unit leads authorized decryption, we'll be violating the very regs you and I established."

Hick grunted. "Zat, Charlie, I *know*. Let's just get on with it."

Charlie studied Cara in silence, tugging on his chin as he often did while weighing data. "What are the message values? Their duration and size?" he asked.

"Identical," Hickham returned. "It could be a repeated message, or a message in three parts transmitted through her encryption filter." He paused, studying Cara with a clinical detachment that was stunning in its coldness. "It's curious and compelling, considering the constraints of her Eve One programming. Her VIPER restrictions—and no contact commands—are obviously damaged or disabled. I believe the attempts to contact are viable and necessary. If you concur, I propose we decrypt the messages with all due haste."

"No. Don't do it," Cara interrupted, stepping between the males. "You programmed me, Hick, to prevent this precise event. It's ludicrous that I would override VIPER and inconceivable that I would imperil the present. I'm not contacting myself from the future. One of my enhancements malfunctioned. You'll have to abort my mission." Heaving a great sigh, she shook her head. "Drutz. It's over, before I'm even launched."

"Malfunction or deliberate? Both are possible," Charlie said. "However . . ."

"Does the oath apply to everyone?" Gil interjected. He'd selected a catbird seat on the periphery, settled in, and followed the exchange as intently as he usually did the finals at Wimbledon.

"What oath?" Hickham snapped, frowning as he suddenly remembered an outsider was present.

"*The* oath, Hick, the one that directs all of us to protect the future and preserve the past," Cara supplied, then faced Gil. "Of course it does. It's crucial to the time continuum. No exceptions. No one is exempt. *No one,*" she repeated, glaring at her boss. "Not even Eve One, your half-human, half-machine prototype."

"I'm exempt," Gil interjected. He shrugged his shoulders. "Until you melt my memory and boot me back to Big D in 2008, that is. But, my point is that there are always exceptions to every rule. Is contacting yourself in the past one of those exceptions?"

Cara protested vehemently. "Indefensible. We protect our future by preserving the past. It's the basis for every Critical Services program, the commitment of their personnel, and the inviolate condition for time travel missions."

Gil saw the look Charlie and Hickham exchanged: agreement. A decision of mutual accord effected without a word passing between them.

"These messages aren't the only communication attempts, Chay," Hickham announced. "There have been others."

Cara's near-perfect features shifted. "Others? I sent others?" she whispered. She'd stopped pacing. Fumbling for a stool, she tucked it beneath her.

"You've trained Cara well," Charlie said with a nod of acknowledgment to Hickham. "She clearly comprehends the risks and the responsibility." His tone was gentle but firm as he addressed Cara: "Your willingness to abort the mission is commendable—and prudent."

"Thank you, Charlie," she began. But Cara's sigh of relief and professions of gratitude were premature.

Charlie shook his head and continued. "However, it is for that very reason that I concur with Hickham's decision. You would not knowingly violate the directives, Cara, unless the consequences of not doing so compelled you to act otherwise. You are the first Scio to venture into our future. As with the first transits to the past, we could not anticipate or conceive of every instance when an exception to our directives is warranted. We're writing a new rule book, Chay. I trust your decisions to warn us. As with your previous messages, I consent to authorize receipt and decrypt immediately."

The discussion was over, the pronouncement final. Everyone but Hickham's protégé stood, ready to take action on the decision.

Cara was speechless. Her impregnable aura of confidence had slipped, exposing the youth and inexperience beneath. She disagreed, intensely; it was obvious from the set of her jaw and the glint in her eyes. But she didn't challenge the men's authority further.

She's a lot like Maude, Gil mused with mounting respect. These women of the future were something. Like Maude, Cara was tough and fiercely loyal to her mission, her people, and her world.

As the men were walking out, Cara finally rose and squared her shoulders. She made as if to follow. Charlie grinned and nudged Hickham—none too gently—in his underling's direction.

"Oh," Hickham grunted, perceiving at last the need to placate the human half of his prototype. "Right, right you are." At the threshold of the hub he turned back to her. "You cannot hear more than this now, Chay," he explained with some degree of awkwardness. He paused and cleared his throat. "But as Eve One, it is your humanity that I trust and value most."

Cara faltered slightly, midstride, but otherwise appeared unmoved by Hickham's declaration. "Understood," she replied in an even tone.

And even if he didn't understand, Gil didn't doubt for a second that Cara did. Because, as they all exited the hub, he was sure he saw a glimmer of a smile tug at her mouth.

Women. And he'd been stupid enough to think he'd had one of them—this one—all figured out?

Maude lounged. Played with her food. Said nothing, glared at everyone and ignored him. He didn't understand. Especially not after finally arriving. Gil had been expecting a hot date and a roll in the hay with his dream gal. That didn't seem as likely as it once had.

Well, either way there were a few obstacles barring his path. First, he had to get through dinner. Second, he had to make nicey-nice with these good future folk. Then he'd pull out his club and drag his beautiful mate off to some convenient cave for a night of whoopee.

He longed for the latter. Yet the sight and smell of Falah's grilled chicken and cream gravy won the war raging between his aroused anatomy and his growling gut, and thanks to his mama's knuckle-rapping efforts when he was a raw-boned lad, he could fake his way through fundamental social pleasantries.

Don't talk with your mouth full. Use a napkin. Compliment the cook. And don't grope the gal next to you. These were simple rules Gil figured he could follow, except maybe for the last. As soon as the parade of comestibles ceased, he was pretty sure he was going to break it.

Falah's steaming pastries and hunks of hot bread dripping with butter were two-fisted foodstuffs, keeping his hands well occupied while he chowed down and mopped up the mess. But the lounging couch he shared with Maude made his desire burn all the hotter.

Fortunately Dak and Falah were excellent hosts. The convivial setting, tables and loungers gathered around a central open hearth with a crackling fire, entreated their guests to relax and enjoy. While Falah gently prodded them to relish the feast, Dak skillfully probed them for anecdotes and recollections. Gil for one was smitten with the whole Ancient Rome theme that dominated both the decor and the eating, drinking, and merry-making. There wasn't a flask of liquid nutrient anywhere in sight. And, the taste of real food with his enhanced senses was driving him wild.

The wine sparkled like a heated ruby, enflaming his palate with the hint of smoke and bittersweet cherries. Sweet tastes were sweeter, and the sours and savories competed with his head and heart for favor. The lemon-splashed vegetables were tangy, crunchy jewels that teased his tongue into a knot of ecstasy. And the buttery nuggets of fennel-laced poached salmon melted his resolve to cease and desist before he exploded.

At last, stuffed to the gills, he was no longer in danger of embarrassing himself and Maude with untoward advances. Thanks to his gluttony, the polite little eating orgy had heightened his ardor but sapped his energy to do anything about it. One more bite of food would no doubt sink his battleship.

Lounging against the overstuffed bolsters, Gil indulged himself. He mooned after Maude like a lovesick bull and laughed so hard at the amusing table talk that he thought he was going to mess himself. It was Charlie's anecdote that nearly cinched the deal. His version of a bad day at the office—at Rogue Central—surpassed the best of *Seinfeld* for tickling Gil's funny bone. Maude's accompanying giggle ran up and down his spine like little fingers dancing a jig, and with tears trickling down his cheeks, Gil doubled over, clutching his aching, over-stuffed belly and wishing for a swift and merciful end.

"Gil?" Maude's nose was inches from his.

Drunker than drunk on her dreamy proximity, Gil was lost in that face, those eyes. The scent of heated honey pumped between their bodies like a blast from the summer sun. A kaleidoscope of color swirled around them, fractured images. His brain was fried. He knew only one thing. Maude. Here. Now. He stumbled as the floor moved beneath his feet.

Charlie crossed the room in a flash, because seemingly in the next second he was beside Gil, pulling out a sharp, shiny hunk of medical hardware and slapping it against Gil's bare flesh. The device pinched his arm and hung on like a damned bloodthirsty tick.

"Hey, that hurts," Gil snarled, and tried to brush it off.

The room stopped spinning. Charlie's features had replaced Maude's in front of his eyeballs. The heat pulsing between *their* two bodies was decidedly cooler and crisper.

"Try to tolerate it a few more seconds," Charlie said, guarding the now glowing device as it vibrated against Gil's flesh. "Just balancing out your sugars and proteins. Happens all the time with Reacclimants," he explained.

Gil glanced at the hovering females. Falah's sweet features were masked with concern. Maude's scowl threatened storms ahead.

On the other hand, Gil felt great—better than great, actually. He said so.

Charlie chortled. "Grand. Just grand."

"You're sure?" Maude demanded. "He doesn't need to return to Reacclimation ahead of schedule, does he?"

"Gil's fine. His mind might be Scio material, but his

body meets Rogue qualifications too. In fact . . . *drutz!* His recovery rate is off-scale. Wonder if riding bulls conditioned him," Charlie muttered as everyone returned to their loungers.

"Bull riding?" Dak asked, and accepted a clear tile from Falah piled high with frosty tidbits.

"Yes, tell us more about those cowboy sports Rick's always talking about," Charlie said, nursing a goblet of what appeared to be nutrient sludge as if it were Napoleon brandy.

The crisis over, Gil kept them fairly entertained with a general survey of the finer agricultural arts of his era, from roping cows to pitching their patties. And once introduced, the subject of Gil's favorite sport wasn't easily dismissed.

"Bull riding," he said, and shrugged his shoulders. "A hazardous sport to be sure, but I come from a long line of scrappers. Dad has wildcatting in his blood. But Mother swore I was the worst Gillespe of the lot." He lifted his goblet and, after a nod from Charlie, swallowed some wine. Maude, near enough again for him to see the soft rise and fall of her breasts beneath her sheer tunic, had abandoned her scowl and—hallelujah—looked fascinated.

"Mom did her best," Gil continued, "and tried to tame the beast within me. Coached me on deportment, dressed me up proper every Sunday and tucked the Good Book inside here and here." Gil thumped his head and heart and grinned. "And thanks to Mom, I don't get many complaints from my partners when I herd them around the dance floor. I'm waltz, two-step, and jitterbug proficient.

"After Twister stomped my femur, my bull-riding days were numbered. I loved it—nothing like sticking like a cocklebur to the back of a bull for eight seconds of hell.

The titanium kept me going for a while. But eventually I had to find another line of work, something that used less body and more brain."

Charlie's eyes glittered with unabashed envy. "I wish I could try bull riding, just once."

"Don't you dare!" Maude blurted, knocking aside her platter, spilling its contents. The sudden silence was deafening. No one moved to clean up the food or fill the abyss with words. "You're going to transit tonight, aren't you, Charlie?" Maude hissed the words, spitting them out as if they tasted foul.

Charlie raised his goblet and chugged the last of its contents. His eyes watered. He wiped his mouth with the back of his sleeve and burped.

No doubt now, Gil decided. The contents were pure nutrient.

"It's no secret, Maude," Charlie said gently. "You know about the sabbatical."

Maude shifted her glare to Dak. "No, your sabbatical isn't a secret. But an unauthorized transit mission is. It's unauthorized. It's illegal. And it's dangerous, isn't it? It'd have to be. You're breaking regs. You're risking Charlie's life, Dak."

Charlie wasn't capable of snarling at Maude, but Dak was.

"The sabbatical is scrubbed. This mission is necessary. It is Charlie's choice, and that's all you need to know."

"He might be okay for a resident standard transit, but a mission? No way," Maude persisted. "When was his last mission transit?" she cried, shifting her attention between both of them. "It isn't easy, Dak. Even prepped, Rogues can get into trouble out there, and Charlie is *not* a Rogue."

Maude kept at it, like a boxer, jabbing them with words, concerns, declarations. Grazing their egos blow by blow. Wearing them down, slowly and effectively. Gil could see it in their faces. Maybe they weren't sure of their plan. Maybe it was risky. Maybe Maude was right.

"I am one of the best. *Zat*, I'm certified for level twelve missions now—there's nothing higher for a Rogue. Send me instead," Maude demanded.

"No!" Charlie suddenly roared, springing to his feet, his face red with rage.

Maude flinched. She reached out, fumbled beneath the table until she found and claimed Gil's hand. Surprised but pleased, Gil covered her shaking fingers and gently squeezed. Maude's strength seemingly returned with what little comfort he offered. "Do you know what you're doing?" she persisted in firm, clear tones.

"I do," Charlie retorted.

Charlie looked magnificent, Gil realized. Tall, clear-eyed, and determined, he was the picture of strength and confidence. The lion within had roused and roared to life.

But why? What was going on here? What rules were being broken, and for what reason?

There was something driving this rare intellect, but Gil couldn't guess what. He could only hope and pray that Charlie's imminent deeds—noble, daring, and courageous—wouldn't be sacrificial as well.

Maude squeezed Gil's hand one more time, then stood. Snatching up her goblet, she raised it in tribute. Her blinding smile was fake as a toothpaste model's.

Dak slowly unfolded his body and stood as well. Splashing wine in his cup, he lifted it.

Falah joined him. Gil followed suit. With all their goblets refreshed, filled to the brim and raised high, Maude nodded to Charlie.

"To the mission," she proclaimed through clenched teeth.

"The mission," everyone save Charlie replied, and then drained their cups.

Charlie cleared his throat and glanced at Dak. "Is it ready?"

"Apart from a few last tweaks it's been ready for a fortnight," Dak replied. "We need to input and actualize the new transit coordinates, then your mission launch can commence anytime in the next two to twenty-four hours."

"Then tonight it is. I'm prepped as I'll ever be," Charlie replied, dropping and kicking his empty goblet. "And I'm sick to death of nutrient." His irrepressible smile was back in place and as infectious as ever. He crossed to Maude and chucked her under the chin. "That's the first thing I'm going to fix when I get back," he said, snorting. "Why didn't someone tell me how bad it tastes?"

NINETEEN

"I've tested the prototype countless times within the confines of this place," Dak grumbled. "It's virtually foolproof. It deflects bullets, knives, lasers, and more. Anything we put it up against, it offers limited protection. Enough, surely, to meet the standards you set."

"But you have reservations about me doing Maude's field mission. Why?" Charlie said, lowering his voice to a husky whisper.

Transit Station Romeo—the covert transit pad the two men had built—was small, a tight fit within an extinct flume. Charlie glanced over at Bob 13; the proximity of the man at the transit console would prevent Dak from engaging in a truly intimate exposition on the subject. Well, Charlie wouldn't question it. The mission had to go forward for reasons he didn't want to think about.

"Many reasons," Dak said. "Same reasons Maude mentioned earlier. You're not a Rogue, and it's been decades since your last transit."

"We did this thing together years ago." Charlie adjusted

the cinch on his waist pack, as if he'd just done it yesterday. Muscle memory. "We were the first transits. We worked through the weaknesses, the errors—fixed them, too. I can handle myself back there. Raymond upgraded my implants."

Dak scrubbed his face with his hands and growled. "I know you can handle yourself. But I should be doing this, not you. *Zatting* transit tether. Core's got me on a pretty short leash."

Charlie laughed and slapped his back. "Payback. You screwed with the time continuum, caused a class-six time rift, transited in and out of no-transit zones, hijacked a pregnant citizen from the past, and . . ." Charlie paused. "I lost track. Where was I?"

Dak groaned. "Forget it. I'll be on house arrest for the next millennium. Between the tether and the monitoring marker on my identification chip, I may never get to transit again."

"You know I can't do anything about the tether. But it's temporary. Tether implants expire. And when it does—"

"Have you done it?" Dak interrupted, his brows twitching up with excitement. "I knew you'd find a way around Core's monitoring system."

Charlie leaned over and hissed, "I've been working on it. The idea is to develop a false-positive tracking element that displaces your unique signal during transits."

"When is it going to be ready?"

"Not soon enough for this mission," Charlie replied. "But there's hope yet. Hick's been helping me with an ingestible goo. In theory, it should cloak identilog signals as long as it remains in the body."

Dak groaned. "Another goo? Your purgatives are anathema to the living. They can evacuate the system unannounced."

"I've been working on that too," Charlie returned with a laugh. "Holding tolerances are at about an hour."

"I'll wait," Dak snapped, "for something with more staying power—preferably an implant."

"Noted," Charlie said. Then, sobering, he stepped up to Bob's transit console for the final prep, shivering, his newly shaved flesh chilled within the one-piece camo garb that Maude had popularized. He rubbed his scalp. His bald head, robbed of its red locks, felt like an ice cube beneath his fingertips.

Bob blinked. Adjusting the console scanner, he positioned it over Charlie's head and shoulders till the chill abated.

Charlie groaned with delight and stretched. "Thanks, Bob. That did the trick."

"You could delay," Dak said. "Postpone the transit another twenty-four hours, just in case Chay sends another message."

Charlie shook his head. "Her last three contacts were repeats. Identical. Hick thinks she's limited to autotransmit now."

He tapped his wrist unit and activated each of the devices housed within. Bob nodded as each one cleared. The final device—the prototype—hummed as it emerged and activated.

"Is Superman ready?" Dak asked, leaning over to see for himself.

The innocuous-looking wand telescoped to its full extension, flashed a steady green signal, and issued a major harmonic tone. "Operable," Charlie said.

"Remember, the protection it affords fluctuates against the weapon type, number, and duration of contacts between the kill point and the victim."

"I designed it," Charlie replied, a bit testily. "I can do the math. A single contact is 99.63 percent nonlethal, whether knife, bullet, or laser. Multiple contacts accumulate error probability, and cumulative errors measurable on the ZED scale without offsetting negatives will eventually render the device ineffective for protecting life."

"That's why you ended up in the lab and I ended up in the field," Dak retorted. "What the *zat* did you just say?"

Charlie chortled. "That I only want to get stabbed, shot, or lasered once."

"Once is all we need to confirm protection. Once in each mode, that is. We don't know how she's going to be attacked. We've got to test them all," Dak replied.

Bob stiffened. His silent stare was potent.

"We'll save her, Bob," Charlie promised. "With your help, we'll save her."

TWENTY

Maude smiled as Gil docked the lift in Edgeville's quaint urban center and cut the propulsion unit. They'd just come from Dak's, after Charlie left. Hoverlifts in general weren't complex, but maneuvering them in and around Core with the autopilot deactivated was demanding for a novice. Gil had handled the task like a pro, transporting them from Dak's homestead. It was impossible to ignore his natural talent at almost everything.

"You'd make a great Rogue," she said as they disembarked and stowed the lift.

His mouth twitched. "Yeah?" That monosyllabic response was all he gave. He followed her silently through the limited nightlife, a confined hive of commercial activity along a two-block street; the bright lights, blend of conversation and twangy music blaring from a sidewalk café, and savory aromas wafting from a corner confectionary were obviously distracting him from the unspoken desire in her comment. She didn't elaborate. Why bother stating the obvious? It was a zatting shame and Core's loss, but Gil had to go home. Everyone said so.

Maude stifled her sigh of regret and led him up a wide ramp to the multilevel blocky structures housing residential flats. It was cooler and quieter on the elevated garden esplanade. Gil's wide-eyed curiosity seemed to miss nothing, not even the smallish patch of fragrant violets adorning the entry to her building. He paused, nodded with appreciation, and tossed her a grin.

They'd said little during the brief run from Dak's homestead to here, but their bodies had communicated nonstop, establishing a silent but potent dialogue between them. Maude's body cried out for intimate contact. Gil's did too, and his musky, all-male scent inflamed her blood and teased her pulse into a brisk trot. Her appetite whetted, the short flight seemed to last an eternity. She wanted sex, this man, and the sweet agony of surrendering to desire.

As Maude's impatience mounted, she fixated on the essentials: how to get from alpha to beta with swift efficiency. She wanted Gil, the feel, smell, and taste of him on and in her before another sixty-segment rotation passed. How to get down to business and accomplish the feat, however, wasn't quite as clear.

She'd done "it" before. The physical act of exchanging sexual gratification with a male wasn't entirely alien to her. Previous encounters with consenting Rogues had educated her anatomy to the gymnastics required to engage and excel in the endeavor. All in all, she'd found the act satisfying and worth repeating when and if time allowed.

However, in general she'd opted for more expedient measures to exocise her hormonal demons before missions. Pills blocked the demons; purges eliminated them. And Core's impersonal "equipment" option was always at hand, ready to relieve any residual tensions.

Yes, she'd done "it" before. But never with love.

But it wasn't love now. Maude was reasonably sure of that fact.

But it's just as dangerous, she reminded herself. What she felt for Gil approximated the amorous state enough to warp her judgment, arrest reason, transpose priorities, and gut all qualms.

She was in over her head and loving every second of it. And of course there was always the possibility that this union she craved with Gil might satisfy her most basic requirement and purge her passion for him.

Of course, it also might not.

"Wow," Gil said when they arrived at her domicile. She let him in and he strolled around, inspecting every square inch.

Maude held her ground at the entrance, content to watch him prowl the spartanly appointed flat she maintained as her primary residence. Outside, the flat's nondescript access was identical to the other dozen-odd portals dotting the tiered construction. Inside, nothing struck her as wow-worthy. Few trophies or embellishments enhanced the snug polygonal space. The service cubicles for hygiene, rest, and nutrition were Core-standard, basic tools to support health and habitation. Nothing more.

Maude's body vibrated with energy. These utilitarian Edgeville quarters suited her, calmed her, and nurtured her. They had been a convenient haven for the focused and unsentimental Rogue she'd become, meeting both her demands for proximity and isolation.

She was suddenly nervous. She'd expended effort imagining her spectacular one-night stand with mega-delicious Gil, but failed to factor in location. Without a second thought, she'd brought him here—to her sacred place, her sanctuary, to the hideaway that no one else had ever visited or shared. She'd brought him *home*.

Did he like it? She fretted, aware that it mattered to her more than it should. *What is there to like or dislike about a habitation shelter, anyway?* she countered.

Besides, Gil wasn't a permanent partner. He wouldn't remain in this world long enough to require a personal entry code, food preferences log, or individualized hygiene and rest protocols. Gil's impression wouldn't be lasting on the space. And after he'd returned to his own time, she could—if she wished—purge all traces of him from it so it was as if he'd never crossed the threshold.

Maude shook off the thought—the thought of Gil gone forever—and joined him inside.

Her fingers fumbled through routine tasks, flubbing everything from sealing the entry to powering up the environmental systems. She narrowly missed activating the emergency assist call when she bumped the prominent red disk affixed to the wall. Thankfully, the margin for error on the simple residential maintenance console was generous.

"I'll be done with this in another minute," she called over to Gil; she had to handle a few tasks required by Rogue Central.

He grinned and waved her on. From the rudimentary selection of amusements her flat offered, Gil had located her treasured collection of books and was fondling one leather-bound spine with covetous fingers. Maude's flesh twitched as she imagined those same fingers fondling her, skimming the length of her back as he claimed her.

Her knees nearly buckled. A wave of desire washed over her, swamping her senses and threatening to scuttle the ark of reason floating within her brain. She sucked in her bottom lip and nipped it between her teeth. The pain was nominal, but she used it, forcing herself to turn back to the console and refocus. Only one more task, she promised herself: Clocking in. That was essential for a Rogue of her status and certification class. She suffered the brief but necessary systems download and checked for updates.

Good. No messages. No agenda revisions.

A giggle bubbled up within. It was a rare treat to find herself so unencumbered; so rare, in fact, that a cloud of suspicion threatened her joy. She firmly dismissed it and adjusted her Rogue availability to *pending*—as close to off-duty as any certified Rogue could rate.

The quick check had assured her that the countdown for her first level twelve mission was proceeding without a hitch. She was looking forward to the challenge and the risks. Charlie had once called her a danger junkie, and maybe she was. But she wasn't the only one. Chay and Dak shared the same passion, and there were others too. Wonderful others.

She stole a look at Gil. He was a danger junkie too. She'd guessed it even before hearing his bull-riding stories. She'd seen it firsthand during the Pompeii mission. He was Rogue material, a Rogue at heart, with a balance of courage and impetuousness that was essential for saving lives, past or future. She didn't doubt that he was essential to his time; a man like Gil didn't just live history; he made it.

That thought was sufficient to re-arouse her ardor for him. Maybe it was a weakness, a flaw, but Maude didn't care. Heroics and bravery, men who dared to live large, lead, love . . . these were all turn-ons for her. And the male who seemed to embody the full range of her preferences was within twenty meters of her lips.

What was she waiting for?

Maude shook herself and glanced back at the console. *Damn!* A new obligation had appeared, and she grimaced. It would be her first scan without Charlie. Soon enough she'd have to suffer through Raymond's exacting, by-the-book prep for her level twelve mission—in thirty-six hours to be precise—and now a routine body scan? Well, all residents had them, not just Rogues, which meant she could handle it anywhere, even at the Scio Quad.

She checked availability and hooted with glee. There

was a body scan slot at Scio in twenty-nine hours. She could check in with Chay again before her mission. She snapped it up, received confirmation, and loaded the change into her console. Nothing else on her schedule demanded her attention. For the next twenty-nine hours, her time was her own. And so was her body.

Her palms were slick with sweat when she finally pushed herself away from the unit. She'd roughly sketched out her objectives for this free time in her head—too many to accomplish given the time frame, which was now seven hours shorter—but she was undeterred. Her how-to seduction plan required a cool head—and a stunner if Gil refused to comply. She didn't think he would, but foreplay and romance were factors she'd never experienced before. She'd observed the tempestuous nature of Rick and Mackenzie's love affair firsthand. Did sex in 2008 require something more than acknowledged consent between partners?

"Done?" Gil asked as she switched off the console and stood.

Maude nodded. But for some unaccountable reason she was rooted in place, transfixed as the man tossed aside the book and advanced on her position. Her mouth was dry, too dry for words.

"Good," he growled, body rippling with restrained power. He looked controlled but deliciously determined.

She silently cheered when he finally stopped, only inches away from her lips. She wouldn't need a stunner.

Her sheer tunic repelled nothing; Gil's body heat invaded her pores and blasted her senses. Sweat peppered her brow, tickled her upper lip, pooled between her breasts and slicked her thighs. The throbbing knot of her sex metered her heartbeat and measured her arousal. Her body was ready. And she could see Gil's was too.

She was giddy with relief. The encounter she'd planned for and anticipated had finally arrived.

This was it. *It*. Sex. Sex with Gil.

The business of sex isn't complicated, she reminded herself as another wave of nervousness pulsed through her. With awkward but efficient motion, she got down to it. Reaching out, she tugged down the waistband of Gil's shorts and exposed his swollen member. The tip was moist as she palmed it.

She heard him groan—or had she uttered that throaty cry? She couldn't be sure. She felt his hot, pulsing flesh, thick with engorged blood, bounce against her hand. It was a wild thing, a tool of pleasure bucking within her grasp. She moaned again, and maybe he did too.

A heated, honeylike wetness seeped between her legs, heralding the urge, the achingly sweet urge, to open to Gil and take his bucking wildness deep within her. Maude shivered, savoring the intoxicating aroma of him, relishing the spicy scent of his lathered skin as it prickled and puckered her senses, flooded her brain, and unleashed her feral fantasies. Suddenly feeling too vulnerable, she closed her eyes to the face, to the looks of the man who would gratify her. Shutting out the identity of her partner, she surrendered completely to the will of her flesh, became attentive only to the audible and tactile sensations of sex.

Sensations: the male's ragged breath as she bared her legs and hitched one up around his hip. Her own gasp of pleasure as she guided his thick member between her thighs to the center of her, caressing his stiff rod with her body. His fierce grip on her buttocks as she lifted, opened, and thrust him home, seating him deep within her in one swift move. Her body spasming in response, squeezing and welcoming the flesh that filled her.

Gil staggered as he accepted the weight of her. With his sex buried deep, he held Maude fast and firmly immobile. His accompanying cry could have been pleasure, shock, or something else. Maude opened one eye and peered at him.

Gil didn't look ecstatic. He was holding his breath, his features scrunched into a mass of wrinkles, and his face was red. He looked more agonized than ardent. And his bright-eyed gaze was fixed on a point above and beyond her. The wall? Perhaps the emergency call disk? Did he need help?

Drutz. He felt so good inside her. She didn't want to move, except in that inexorable pulsing way that would swiftly bring her to climax. Yet she knew enough from her limited exchanges with other partners to abort the connection if injury occurred.

"Is something wrong?" she asked, shifting against him.

Through clenched teeth, Gil said, "Er, no. But for pity's sake stop wiggling, will you? I'll explode."

But she couldn't help it; she shifted again, moaning with trembling delight from the thick, throbbing length of him within her. She couldn't focus. Gil's image swirled into a fuzzy mass that growled, groaned, and grunted as she arched and ground herself against him. Unbearably wondrous it was, and she pressed him deeper still.

Only another moment. She could feel the tide of gratification rising within her. Another sweet stroke from his throbbing length and orgasm would overtake her.

"Love, *stop*," Gil roared. He firmly stilled her twitching buttocks, held her, and entreated her with his palms and fingers for mercy.

But Maude's body refused to obey. She pumped against him mercilessly, and in spite of his protests Gil's body yielded. Both hands now gripped her bottom, guiding her, pacing her, and urging her to take him deeper. His rigid rod was swelling and lengthening with each stroke as he drove into her with a frenzy that rocked her body and battered her senses.

They were beyond words now. Moans and groans of pleasure passed between them. Maude cared little who spoke, for they were at last in accord, moving as one. She and Gil were one thought and one voice.

Gil ceded to her demands. Filling her again and again, he pushed her higher until she was up and over that precipice of passion. She was suddenly past the explosion of light and sound that accompanied feverish sexual release, beyond the threshold of physical needs. She was tumbling into a realm of rapture that shattered senses and stopped time. Maude hung there, floating, suspended in that perfect moment, a primeval cry of gratification caught in her throat. It didn't last. But when the bubble of perfection popped, Maude's last lucid thought before she succumbed to oblivion was one of joy.

With a roar, Gil drove into her body one last time. Maude wasn't alone in her ecstasy; Gil had joined her in paradise.

TWENTY-ONE

Gil stood upright, but just barely. *Hellfire.* He needed to sit down before he fell down. Spent and witless, Maude clung to his very nearly dead weight. Gil slid out of her without fanfare but tucked her body close, lifting her into his arms and molding her to him with a strength he mustered from somewhere.

He staggered forward glancing around in a quick search for something that resembled seating, bedding, or physical comforts that could accommodate his need. But there was nothing, *nada* in the apartment. Three wardrobe-sized cubicles didn't look promising.

The future couldn't have totally abandoned the requirements for a Beautyrest or Tempur-Pedic. Where did they sleep?

Gil stumbled toward the closest prop, the wall, intent on stealing support for a controlled crash and burn to the only sure bet: the polished white floor. The tile looked hard, unforgiving in its coldness, but it was the only option for his gravity-challenged frame.

Maude stirred in his arms and sleepily nuzzled his neck.

Gil's sex stirred. *Shit.* It might be a half-gun salute, but it was a damn miracle, and a valiant effort of his body so soon after the best and fastest sex he'd ever experienced.

He reached the wall—another miracle. His shorts were tangled around his ankles and his tight grip on Maude's beauteous body sorely tested his upper body strength. He backed against the wall and cursed. *Damn.* He'd found the only protrusion on the surface—a damned red button—and drilled it into his hide. He swore again as the button carved a hollow into his flesh as he slid downward, bumping his head on it as his bared buttocks finally kissed the . . . yes, cold and hard floor.

His discomfort didn't last. As soon as the back of his head cleared the button, all hell broke loose.

Deafening sirens, warning commands, flashing egress lamps and the arrival of the residential emergency squad wasn't part of Maude's planned seduction. She stumbled to her feet, jerked Gil to his and addressed the squad leader with her frayed but adequate composure.

Yes, she knew the penalty for false alarms. No, she didn't need a rebriefing on housing safety protocols. The squad leader noted her Rogue status with a sneer.

Yes, she could handle a full systems check without his help. It was a *zatting accident*. Accidents *did* happen. Even to *Rogues*.

She sagged against the wall after the squad departed. Gil had handled the scrutiny well: suffered their questions, politely refused their forceful suggestions for a safety briefing, ushered them on their way as if he owned the flat himself. He'd even made a joke to her as he shut the door.

Maybe this was a big mistake, Maude silently groaned, watching him study the residential console with a new-found gleam of comprehension. *He's imprinting. Drutz.*

*I'm imprinting. I'll need a full memory purge for my brain
and my home after he's gone.*

"Ah-ha," Gil crowed—and activated the entertainment panels.

He spun away from the console just as Maude's favorite surround setting flashed into focus. The glacial
whiteness of the simulated snowfield was almost blinding. Its icy surface reflected rainbows of color from the
glinting winter sun.

Maude hazarded a glance in Gil's direction. She had a
problem. The sex had been great—better than she'd
imagined it ever could be, actually. And the effort
hadn't purged her passion for him. She'd ridden him
hard, used him with a fierce, demanding, and calculated
objective: satisfaction. And she'd achieved the objective
in short order.

But unfortunately it wasn't enough. She wanted
more—more sex, of course, but something else as well as
carnal satisfaction. Something she couldn't exactly define.

Her flesh trembled, but she wasn't cold. Her nervousness was back. She was green, raw, a novice at this romance business. And her inexperience aggravated and
aroused her need to excel at everything.

Was Gil nervous too?

He didn't look it. He emitted another "Wow" as he
successfully launched and activated the contents of her
rest cubicle. He claimed the cushioned body-sling,
bounding into it with a smooth leap that landed him
butt-first into its cradling softness.

"This is the North Pole, right?" he asked, and nodded
toward the scene that had transformed her flat's walls
and ceiling into an icy wonderland. He laid back and
tucked one arm beneath his head. The sling still rocked
rhythmically, and looked inviting to Maude. There was
room for another occupant.

"I'm a South of the Border fan, myself," Gil continued after a quick glance. "I love the sun. Love the heat. But everyone who still believes in Santa would want at least *one* visit to his workshop."

"Huh?" It was Maude's turn for monosyllabic responses.

She considered the simple scene with new eyes. She'd never thought of this as a destination, a real place; until now, the cool, bright, clean and unfettered vista from the crystal-coated plateau had been merely a peaceful respite. A prescription. A recommendation from Charlie that worked. It had counterbalanced her harried, complex life and provided a sensory haven powerful enough to salve her loneliness and serenade her soul.

In fact, in just the few minutes since activation, it had worked wonders: Her pulse had slowed, her rangy and discordant emotions had settled into harmonious agreement, and the sole purpose of hauling Gil home to her sanctuary had crystallized in her brain.

Sex. Lots of it. With no strings attached. She had more than one chance at purging him through gratification.

Just thinking about her and what they'd just done, Gil felt his arousal return. Maude was still across the room, pacing like a caged lioness. Sleek, svelte, and sexy, she radiated subdued power as she moved about, adjusting illumination, adjusting ambient temperature, and driving him crazy with want and desire.

Gil focused on the arctic scene. Imagining a full-torso skid along the frigid surface saved him for a moment, keeping his libido from immediate and total meltdown, and him from jumping Maude again. After that slam-bam-thank-you-ma'am sex, he should have been flatlining, unable to muster the energy to straighten his pinky, let alone desire more, but his shoulds and coulds were jumbled. With little effort he could likely find completion before Maude even crossed the room and touched him.

Maybe Maude could too. Clearly she burned hot and fast. Finely tuned and expertly wired, she seemed capable of a zero to sixty acceleration without much help from him. Is this all sex was in the future—no foreplay, no pillow talk, no afterglow? Just mindless intercourse? Was it the KISS principle applied to physical intimacy?

Keep it simple, stupid. What red-blooded cowboy hadn't imagined a situation like this—prayed for it or paid for it? Mutual satisfaction minus the heartache. If that's what Maude expected, he could oblige. They could go at it like rabbits till his johnson fell off.

Gil snorted. Charlie probably had a cure for that too.

Raw with need, he was at war with himself. Craving to indulge his every carnal desire, he doubted that his forced concentration on Santa was going to help maintain control much longer. After all, Santa satisfied Mrs. Claus, didn't he?

Hellfire, but he wanted her. And not once or twice, but always and forever. In and out of bed. He wanted more from Maude than sex and KISS. She had teased his flesh, tantalized his senses, and wriggled her way into the deepest part of his psyche. If this wasn't love, it was as close as he'd ever come.

Maude had activated another cubicle. Gil was mesmerized. Feeling like the luckiest Peeping Tom on the planet, he watched her strip. The filmy garb that had left very little to his imagination now pooled at her feet. And, great day in the morning, the sight of her beautiful body, its lush curves and long limbs, nearly burned holes in his retinas. He stopped short of rubbing his eyeballs; he didn't give a damn about going blind. He'd seen Maude. That sight was enough for a lifetime.

Stepping into a clear chamber, Maude stretched and rotated as powerful water jets buffeted her flesh. Blasts of air swiftly dried her when she emerged. Steamy and pink from the treatment, she looked ripe as a Georgia peach.

Gil gulped. His pulse had accelerated from a brisk trot to a full gallop. This wasn't going to be easy—not any of it: the kiss, the sex, or the good-bye at the end. She'd wedded her essence to his dreams and welded her spirit to his. They were yin and yang, conjoined for eternity.

He slapped the cushioned section of couch next to him and crooked a finger in Maude's direction. "There's room for two, love."

When had that happened: calling her *love?*

Maude smiled. Her beautiful mouth twitched up at the corners in a silent and glorious portrait of joy that stirred him beyond his wildest imaginings. Gil knew then that he'd found his heart's true mate. That *love,* in name and deed, suited her.

Love felt right and true. And, when Maude acquiesced and stretched out beside him, it felt like forever.

TWENTY-TWO

Gil's version of sex—circa 2008—required more participation than Maude had imagined. But she wasn't complaining. The entire event, from start to finish, had far exceeded the standards of satisfaction she'd come to expect from intercourse.

"Open your eyes," Gil demanded as she straddled him again.

Maude hovered over him, ready anew for the feel of him inside her. She was ravenous, aching for the release he'd denied her with his slow and patient tutelage. She'd quickly acquired a taste for the man and the industry he applied to the task of pleasuring his partner. Gil's attention to detail was remarkable.

"Good old-fashioned lovin' isn't about beating the time on some damned stopwatch," he had told her when he had rejected most of the orgasmic stimuli enhancements from her world. He'd twitched an eyebrow, grinned that grin, traced a lazy circle around her erect nipple with his fingertip, and suggested a novel concept: "Let's get to know each other."

Maude had balked. She had a timetable, objectives, and a deadline—now with less than ten hours of free time remaining. To get to the good stuff, she'd been prepared to sacrifice a few things. Adding new objectives to the list seemed absurd.

Still, Gil could be persuasive. After a delightful shower for two where he'd rubbed and lathered her to a sudden and explosive climax, she'd tossed aside her list and yielded everything to Gil's capable and astonishing hands.

He wanted to know her. Wanted to acquaint himself with her body's every curve and blemish. And that took time. Hours. Hours with no penetration.

After she'd resigned herself to his languorous courtship, she'd slowly found herself caught in the ebb and flow of its sensual tide. He intrigued her, baited her, lured her past the brisk rutting thrill, and drew her deep into the heady stream of a perpetual bliss. His hands and lips kissed, stroked, worshipped. Again and again. She'd savored the feel of him driving her to the brink of ecstasy numerous times, giving herself over to his touch and tongue with complete abandon. But now she was ready, past ready, to yield to the mountain of heat building within. She needed him inside her.

Her limbs trembled. Her breasts, the nipples teased to taut peaks by Gil's hot mouth, swung loose and heavy as she hung above him. The briefest of contact against his sweat-drenched chest was electric, sending tiny shocks that spiraled deep into her core and unleashed spasms of pleasure.

"Open your eyes," he gently repeated as he eased her onto her back and kissed her senseless.

The brutish tactic worked, of course. Gil's kisses were hot, toe-curling, and convincing. Maude opened her eyes and fixated on his mouth. The things he could do with those lips and tongue were phenomenal.

A lazy grin spread across his lips, and he bared his

GET UP TO
4 FREE BOOKS!

You can have the best romance delivered to your door for less than what you'd pay in a bookstore or online. Sign up for one of our book clubs today, and we'll send you **FREE* BOOKS** just for trying it out...**with no obligation to buy, ever!**

HISTORICAL ROMANCE BOOK CLUB

Travel from the Scottish Highlands to the American West, the decadent ballrooms of Regency England to Viking ships. Your shipments will include authors such as CONNIE MASON, CASSIE EDWARDS, LYNSAY SANDS, LEIGH GREENWOOD, and many, many more.

LOVE SPELL BOOK CLUB

Bring a little magic into your life with the romances of Love Spell—fun contemporaries, paranormals, time-travels, futuristics, and more. Your shipments will include authors such as KATIE MACALISTER, SUSAN GRANT, NINA BANGS, SANDRA HILL, and more.

As a book club member you also receive the following special benefits:

- **30% OFF all orders through our website & telecenter!**
  (Plus, you still get 1 book FREE for every 5 books you buy!)
- **Exclusive access to special discounts!**
- **Convenient home delivery and 10 days to return any books you don't want to keep.**

There is no minimum number of books to buy, and you may cancel membership at any time. See back to sign up!

*Please include $2.00 for shipping and handling.

YES! ☐

Sign me up for the **Historical Romance Book Club** and send my TWO FREE BOOKS! If I choose to stay in the club, I will pay only $8.50* each month, a savings of $5.48!

YES! ☐

Sign me up for the **Love Spell Book Club** and send my TWO FREE BOOKS! If I choose to stay in the club, I will pay only $8.50* each month, a savings of $5.48!

NAME: _____

ADDRESS: _____

_____

TELEPHONE: _____

E-MAIL: _____

☐ I WANT TO PAY BY CREDIT CARD.

☐   ☐   ☐

ACCOUNT #: _____

EXPIRATION DATE: _____

SIGNATURE: _____

Send this card along with $2.00 shipping & handling for each club you wish to join, to:

**Romance Book Clubs
1 Mechanic Street
Norwalk, CT 06850-3431**

Or fax (must include credit card information!) to: 610.995.9274.
You can also sign up online at www.dorchesterpub.com.

*Plus $2.00 for shipping. Offer open to residents of the U.S. and Canada only.
Canadian residents please call 1.800.481.9191 for pricing information.
If under 18, a parent or guardian must sign. Terms, prices and conditions subject to change. Subscription subject
to acceptance. Dorchester Publishing reserves the right to reject any order or cancel any subscription.

JOIN NOW!

teeth as he prepared to mount her. Maude's pulse sky-rocketed to Alpha Centauri. Her body was already open and waiting. Her brain went to mush, spellbound by the promise in his eyes.

He pressed into her, filling her with a suddenness that stirred her desire to a fever pitch. She lost all complex thought. Basic instincts took command, and her frame acted and reacted with the wisdom of the ages. Her polysyllabic communication skills eroded, limiting her responses to a series of sighs, exclamations, and gratified grunts.

"Mmmm," she moaned. Her body quivered, swimming to the edge of satisfaction. The dance was familiar but also different. Gil made it different. Staring into his eyes she could see her own passion and her sweet surrender to it—to Gil.

She squeezed her eyes shut when the rocking sea of sensation began to suck her under, towing her relentlessly toward a deep and dark delight that was hers and hers alone.

"Don't stop," she groaned as Gil suddenly pulled out of her body, leaving her bereft with want.

"I won't, love, not this time," he said against her lips. "Only, look at me. *See* me."

She obeyed. From the start, Gil had demanded much, exacting a toll for sex and rewarding her complicity. He'd pleasured her in countless unimaginable ways, courted her flesh, and tantalized tender pulse points to hypersensitivity where a single kiss from his lips was bliss. And still he asked for more.

She watched him through half-closed eyelids. She could see the flame of passion in his eyes, and something else, something potent and mysterious that stirred her even more than his touch. She trembled with delight as his warm breath teased her lips, her throat, then snaked lower, billowing from his mouth across one breast, the other, and still lower.

She gasped as his tongue tangled with her throbbing nub and prodded inside her swollen flesh, truly tasting her heat. She arched against him, opening wide to his feasting mouth. A strangled cry of protest rushed out of her when he pulled away.

"*See* me," he growled again, levering his rock-hard member to the point of penetration. Poised above her, he reclaimed her mouth and thrust inside her body, burying himself to the hilt.

The spasm seized them both. Ripping through them, it bucked their bodies and liquefied limbs and ligaments. Muscles molded into one quivering mass as they rode the crest of the wave of passion together, past the penultimate climax to a surreal and sanguine harbor beyond.

And throughout it all, Maude watched. She witnessed Gil's complete surrender to the tide of ecstasy they shared as one. They were joined in body. Joined in spirit. Joined in bliss.

Twenty-odd hours later, Gil decided the fake sun at the Aquatics facility felt like the real thing. He rolled over and sopped up the warmth like a sponge. Maude had dropped him off on her way to some damned body scan, and he'd lacked the energy to protest the brief separation.

The sandy beach with loungers under umbrellas, the long tall fruity drinks that helped rehydrate his system, and the sights and sounds of the lovely Caspian-colored waters lapping at the pool's edge very nearly replicated a resort from Anywhere, USA. After epic sex with Maude, this relaxation under a counterfeit sun was a crackerjack cure for most of what ailed him. But his mondo case of lovesickness would require something more drastic: a purge.

Gil felt cross-eyed with exhaustion. He'd loved her long and well. He'd given her more than she could ever know, this woman of his future. He'd given her his heart.

Damnation. He was getting sappy. Stupid. He'd known it was hopeless right out of the gate. He'd tried to lock down his feelings during their fantastic close encounter. He'd cinched up his stirrups and hung on for the ride of his life. But eight seconds on Twister couldn't begin to match the power of one second with Maude. And they'd gone at it for hours—eighteen or nineteen, he guessed.

His anatomy was pulverized, but his mind was in a feedback loop. His thoughts replayed her cries of passion, sweet sensual sighs of surrender that, even after hours of being worn down, his sex still responded to.

Yeah. He'd obliged Maude. He'd delivered sex. But the price had been dear. He'd given everything to the female, including his soul. It'd be a bloody miracle if Charlie could effectively purge the woman from his gray matter.

But, they sure as hell better, he silently swore. Because if one iota of memory about the girl persisted when he returned home, he'd be tormented by unrequited love for the rest of his days.

TWENTY-THREE

"Did Chay leave on her mission?" Maude asked as Hickham adjusted the leads attached to her body. The Scio body scan process differed little from one at Rogue Central, and she submitted herself to the prep and fitting with a minimum of attention.

"Affirmative," Hick replied. "Hourly checks indicate Eve One's first mission to the future is a success."

"So far," Maude muttered.

Hickham snorted and ran a finger along one of the numerous bruises peppering her flesh. He didn't express himself on their existence; he merely noted it on her chart and affixed the final two connections to her wrists. He tapped the thick clear slab next to the body scan unit.

"Lie down and let's get this over with."

Maude climbed aboard and stretched out. With Hick's adjustments, the slab softened to near gel consistency and accepted her body weight, allowing her to sink deep. She gripped the firm edges of the slab as the gel molded to the contours of her backside from scalp to heel, up and over her kneecaps and thighs, encircling her throat, waist, and ankles before rehardening. The cool sterile air in the Scio lab tickled the quarter of her flesh that remained exposed. The slab held her fast. She was unable even to move a muscle to scratch her nose—which always itched at this particular moment in the process.

But if it itched now, she wasn't aware of it. Her mind had shifted elsewhere. Meeting Gil back at the flat. Squeezing in a few more hours with Gil? Maybe three or four, but not more than that. Gil's Reacclimation cycle and her mission prep commitments wouldn't allow for a protracted farewell.

Drutz. Long or short, that scene was going to be tough. Their last kiss. Her last glimpse of the cowboy. The emptiness afterward.

But she had wanted it this way, wanted to feel everything—good *and* bad—about sex with Gil. She'd chosen a path less traveled by Rogues. She'd stalled her buffering implant—the tech that relegated choice memories to extractable, supracranial storage—and with virginal curiosity had shunned the cloaking protection that would have numbed her to the legacy of her first romance's residual emotion.

Gil's gift had been substantive. She'd been bombarded with feelings. Deep ones. They were curious, compelling, complicated, and carnal. They were potent flesh and neural linkages that far surpassed the whispers and rumors and fanciful tales she'd heard. When she'd taken Gil into her mind and body, wholly and unreservedly, she'd turned her back on caution. And she wasn't sorry. From head to toe, inside and out, she'd learned how it could be—how it was *meant* to be between a man and a woman. Her head was full of Gil. So was her heart.

Maude sighed, a self-satisfied hiss that settled her pulse. She didn't care. She'd risked the consequences and completely lost her heart to the man.

"Here we go," Hick said. He dimmed the lights, lowered his clear visor, and initialized the sequence that would slice and dice her molecules to assess and forecast health basics.

The slab vibrated and warmed. *Nice,* she mused. A nested light-ring apparatus lowered from the ceiling until it encircled the slab and unfolded its multiple bands to surround Maude's body with a ribbed sphere. The lights switched on and a myriad of tiny beams cast a green survey grid over her nude form.

It won't take long, Maude reminded herself as the urge to get back to Gil threatened to storm her patience. Her inability to concentrate completely and not think about him, even to handle this housekeepinglike activity, proved one thing: She'd gone too far. She'd experienced too much with Gil to retreat to her former state of confident detachment without help.

Yes, she accepted that her transition to mission-ready status was going to be tough—the toughest ever. And, not just because Raymond was leading Rogue Central instead of Charlie. The harsh reality was that she would have to request and submit to a deep-probe memory extraction. It was the only way. Effective and permanent, it would clear her system of the headiest and most dangerous of all distractions for a Rogue: love.

The first flare startled Gil. Arcing above the pool, it got everyone's attention. Playtime ceased and controlled panic ensued as bathers and Aquatics staff exited the facility as directed by a monotone voice and flashing egress lights.

Gil fell into step without comment. Past or future, emergencies weren't a time to debate directions. The orderly descent into a strobe-lit bunkerlike space wasn't alarming; however, he balked when he realized the ultimate destination: one of three tubular chambers thick with familiar, floral-scented fog.

"Whoa, mama. That's not for me, buddy," Gil snapped to the staff manning the hatchlike door. He sidestepped the entry and held his ground. "Emergency or not, I want a few fucking answers before I seal myself inside that tomb. What's going on?" he demanded.

The staff blinked at him for a minute. "Oh, you must have just come back from the past," one man replied. "Well, trust me, nothing much has changed while you've been away. These monthly drills are still a Core standard. Mega-cautious Scio freaks," he hissed under his breath. "This area hasn't experienced a surge in decades."

A surge? Gil stepped back farther and the chamber reached capacity.

The Aquatics staffer simply redirected foot traffic into the adjoining chamber. Slamming the hatch on the first, he spun the wheel on it till the illuminated green seal switched to red. He turned back to Gil.

"I hear they still have surges in Outskirt. I haven't been out there in ages, but my podmate works transpo-maintenance and rides the loop. He's got some stories about how wild it can get out there in pipe- and flume-land. The surges can fry you in a second."

"Frying. That doesn't sound good," Gil said.

"It's quick and painless, I guess," the staffer replied. His ghoulish grin reminded Gil of Freddie Kruger. Add a striped shirt, hat, and long nails and the gabby doorman could pass for the child murderer's double.

The ghoulish gabster nodded toward the chambers and snorted. "The Scios planted these safety pod bunkers all over the place. Even in Outskirt." He sounded apologetic, almost like he was sorry that technology had mitigated the risk.

"My name's Jonesy, by the way," he offered, and urged Gil toward the last chamber. "We better go in now. Won't get the all-clear until all life-forms in Aquatics are safe and accounted for."

Gil glanced around the inside of the pod after Jonesy sealed them in. The space was slowly filling with pink fog. Microwave-sized service cubicles lined the expanse. No doubt each contained life-support equipment.

"How long can people survive in here?" he asked.

Jonesy had made himself comfy on one of the cubes. He shrugged again and fanned the fog floating between them. "Specifications indicate a maximum of forty rotations. But I don't think anyone's ever been stuck in one for more than forty hours. Critical Services rescue teams are launched automatically—when it's not a drill, of course.

"Good thing, too," Jonesy continued. "I hate small spaces. It's a syndrome. I have implants, so I'm fine for now, but even with the implants, they still have to zonk me before those zatting annual body scans. I get to sleep through the whole thing."

Body scan? That was what Maude was getting.

Gil mused about the term for a half a second. Was it a futuristic X-ray or MRI? He was saturated with Core terminology, and blank on the rhyme and reason for all the sophisticated treatments. This one sounded routine. She'd told him it was nothing to worry about, innocuous—an annual event that only terrorized characters like Jonesy.

The staffer was exhibiting warning signs. He checked and rechecked his wrist unit and continuously pressed his nose against the thick square portals that resembled airline windows, when he wasn't fixated on the glowing red seal on the chamber's hatch.

"It doesn't usually take this long," Jonesy snapped. He glared at Gil. "You might need to zonk me if takes much longer."

"Okay," Gil returned. He'd zonk the guy. He'd punch his lights out with a left hook if necessary and put him out of his misery for about two or three hours.

"Sedatives are in the med-pak by the hatch," Jonesy added with a nervous laugh. He'd seen Gil's fists clench.

Gil nodded and smiled. But he wasn't counting on the zonking value of something from a med-pak. The little guy was starting to twitch like a squirrel. It might get ugly, quick. And Gil's fists were handy.

Klaxons sounded. "All clear," Jonesy cried, and bounced up. His relief was palpable. His efficient exit from the chamber amounted to blowing the hatch and running pell-mell from the bunker without a backward glance.

Gil shook his head and fell in with the stream of other occupants exiting the chambers. He was one of the masses, fitting in, blending—maybe more so than the Jonesies of this era. It was stunning. Not for the first time, he was amazed about his relative adaptability to living in the future. He felt like he belonged here, with Maude, living this adventure. It made his next questions all the more important.

Were they right? Did they really, *really* know he was essential to the past?

TWENTY-FOUR

Gil extracted a hoverlift and activated it. Divining the route back to Maude's flat didn't require much effort. He punched in the keycode for the destination, which he'd seen on his first trip there, activated the autopilot, and held fast. He still wasn't sure about the invisible force field and didn't entirely trust the lift's nearly transparent monofilamentlike tethers, but his faith in the guidance system was solid.

The autopilot nosed the lift into traffic without his help and allowed him to ogle the sights. This cross-country route was a new one for him; evidently autopilots gauged traffic and selected options accordingly. This hadn't been the expeditious tunnel path Maude had used when she'd dropped him off. The lift soared high, skimming the jagged peaks that dissected the narrow cavern and propelling him up and over the range to the other side.

He looked down on the rugged terrain. A rainbow and waterfall were stunning surprises. Nested in the slopes was a village of longhouses and lodgelike structures. A simulated noonday sun cast little shadows on the walking paths that loosely connected the buildings, and fingered routes through and around plateaus and outcroppings. He assumed the steamy atmosphere was due to the numerous hot springs at the heart of the district. Vivid-hued pools emitting vapor clouds were spanned by bridges or edged by railed boardwalks. And, by the look of it, these were popular soaking sites for families.

Earth's natural hot tubs, he guessed. Another example of how the future had harnessed some of Earth's bounty. The possibilities of what else this society had mastered in its colonization of the underworld intrigued him immensely.

He deactivated the autopilot and dipped the hoverlift for a closer look at the waterfall. Manmade or Mother Nature? He couldn't decide.

Real or bogus, it didn't diminish his amazement or his sudden desire for Maude—the impulse to bring her here and share his discovery. It didn't matter that she'd probably been here before and seen it with someone else; it only mattered that they share it together. He wanted to forge a bond with her that was stronger than steel, a union that would outlast their memories and echo through time.

He stalled the lift and jumped off. A quick sprint up to the lip of the falls provided a spectacular view of the rainbow and village below.

Rainbows are all about hope, aren't they? He closed his eyes, letting the water spray freckle his flesh while he dreamed his dream, hoped his hope, and prayed his prayer. *Maude.*

Damnation, he had it bad. And in a few hours, he was going to have to say good-bye to the female and the future forever.

He had to shake it off, get over it. But all admonitions failed to break the spell. Love had decked him, knocked him senseless. His heart was smiling, swelling his chest to near the point of bursting.

Ah. This must be what all the dang cowboy poets and Sons of the Pioneers were poeting and singing about. Gil snorted with amusement. The shoe fit. Almost.

If he was going to ride off into the sunset with his heart on his sleeve, he needed a damned horse.

"What's wrong?" Maude asked.

Even behind Hickham's clear shield visor, Maude could see his furrowed brow. His lips were pressed into a thin white line. He wasn't saying anything. But Maude was suddenly knee-shakingly scared. Only old people, injured, and terminal people flunked bodyscans. Rogues didn't. She tried to relax. Glitches weren't uncommon considering the competing and potentially conflicting technology employed to keep Core habitable and its precious population forewarned, forearmed, protected and preserved. However, a glitch in Scio equipment? Strange.

Hickham rarely showed emotion, either in his features or speech. Like most Core scientists, he maintained the facial expressivity of fixed concrete when dealing with subjects. He hid his feelings well. Maude had seen him smile, of course, but only with Charlie—Charlie could make anyone smile—and Hick's protégé, Cara.

She'd seen him angry once, too. Once was enough. When Dak had gotten trapped in ancient Pompeii and triggered catastrophic time rifts throughout the continuum, Hickham's cold, seething rage had been terrifying to witness. However, that had proved to Maude that Hick's still waters ran very, very deep, despite all outward appearances. She'd learned to read his subtle quirks of character. And she now respected any shift in his otherwise passive countenance as a warning signal that something huge might be going on inside the man.

"I'm going to repeat the cranial segment," Hickham finally responded.

A nod was impossible. Maude twitched her nose. "Understood," she added. Her tone sounded level and controlled, but she wasn't. Panic raced through her.

In the dimly lit space, Maude watched Hickham's face. The sub-lit scan console cast his features in an amber light. They were now settled into a mask, but she wasn't fooled. She'd seen the eyebrow, the white-rimmed mouth, and his thousand-meter stare as he read and reread her body scan data.

Routine body scans were just that: *routine*. The assumption was cold comfort. It didn't quell her mounting suspicions that her routine scan had just shown something that wasn't routine.

At best in the past, her annual checks had merely amplified the existing analyses collected from previous scans. They reinforced classifications weighted by skill and talent ratios identified and tracked from birth. As a procreant prototype she'd been scrutinized from her first snooze to her most recent ovulation. Nothing about her development from zygote to adulthood had been a surprise. Her scans never turned up anything alarming.

But there's a first time for everything, she firmly reminded herself.

Hickham initialized the cranial grid again, but instead of closing her eyes Maude watched him. His visor reflected the soft blue beam of light as it sawed across the section with lightning speed. A sudden red flash stalled the process.

Maude flinched when she saw it, the slab confining and intensifying her reaction. She'd felt and heard nothing when she saw the flash, but she knew the color of trouble. Red. And she also knew in that instant that the stoic scientist had been trying to hide it from her. He had deactivated the audible alarm in advance.

Yes, Hickham had expected the flash, planned for it, and silenced the telltale signal that she'd just flunked a routine body scan. Twice.

Maude bucked against her restraints. "Get me out of here," she cried, suddenly sick to her stomach. Her thumb inched toward the emergency switch that, if activated, would eject her body from the scanner.

"Trust me, Maude," Hickham interjected. That stalled her panic long enough for him to adjust the slab and free her limbs.

Maude sat up and knocked the light-ring apparatus aside. The urge to bolt was strong. Jerking out the leads that still tethered her to the body scanner would hurt, but she wrapped her fingers around the lead on her chest and started to tug.

"Deep breaths," Hickham advised her. He held up a beaker of gray sludge. "Consume three CCs."

Maude ignored the sludge and the advice. "You were expecting this, Hickham. You knew I'd flunk the scan."

"Yes." He lifted his visor and blinked owlishly.

She should have been used to Hick's abruptness and abject honesty, and she was, but she had always relied on Charlie's spontaneous explanations to balance the scales. Without it, Hickham's response left her wanting.

"More," Maude demanded, and flicked her fingers for him to continue. "Tell me more. What's going on? What's wrong with me? And how do we resolve it?"

"Three CCs," he returned, and forced the beaker into her hand. "No arguments. Drink it; it is essential."

Maude complied. The sludge wasn't bad. It wasn't Charlie's nutrient recipe.

"It will cloak your identilog signal temporarily," he added, "and prevent you from tripping Core's general alarms if you leave Scio Quad."

"Trip alarms? Holy gigadrutz, Hickham. What the zat is the matter with me? Am I contagious? Dangerous?"

She didn't feel different or deadly. She flapped her arms. The leads that connected her body to Hickham's scan console limited motion a great deal.

"Can you take these off yet?" she asked. "And turn up the lights?"

Hickham blinked. "No."

Maude rolled her eyes and groaned. "More. More info. When? Why?"

"We haven't completed the scan and submitted it," he said, and blinked again.

"No? I flunked it. That's fairly complete, don't you think?"

"Yes. It would be if I had hooked your leads directly into the console, but I didn't. I'm using one of the portable body scan units. Rather than a constant feed, it submits results to Core's mainframe when connections are terminated with the subject. Core doesn't know." He paused, then added, "Yet."

It was Maude's turn to blink. Her processing was slowing to a crawl. Being one on one with Hickham required more concentration than she'd been applying. She was going to have to detach from the sticky, distracting emotions gumming up her cogitation. Fear, for one. Panic was another.

She breathed deeply. In, out. Settling her soul, shifting out of her frame mentally and into a guarded space reserved solely for observation and reason.

"From the beginning," she insisted. "I flunked the body scan. Tell me why we're hiding it from Core."

"I'm going to die." She said it simply, a statement of fact supplied by the body scan summary. She gasped and clapped one hand over her mouth, but it was too late. The words were out of her and between them.

For all his honesty, Hick hadn't put it quite so bluntly. Though he'd set the stage for the life-changing revelation, activating a warming spotlight above her slab that cast the surrounding lab in an inky shadow, he'd offered a two-word explanation and nothing else. *Scheduled Expiration* was meaningless until it was linked to a subject. Now it meant something. It was linked to her.

"I'm a Scheduled Expiration? An SE?" She'd forgotten about the implant. Another first. Something else to test for Core's benefit. Something connected to Chay's mission, her implant communicating with Cara's, a signal across time.

She tried the words out, rolling their sounds around her tongue with an effort to spin them into something less final. It didn't work. Separately, *scheduled* and *expiration* lacked clout, but knowing they went together, said fast or slow, the end result was final. She was going to die. Soon. In thirty rotations. In less than 720 hours. Dead.

This wasn't a minor inconvenience that a memory purge could correct. It was a major complication. And, if she said so herself, it was a tragic waste of resources: her training and experience, the glut of implants and programs housed within her. Those were all unsalvageable.

The lamp above her hummed with warmth. Surrounded by the cool, dark lab, she felt the seconds tick away, hemorrhaging from her diminishing supply even as she grappled with the facts.

She had to think about her fate in the abstract. If she didn't, if she allowed herself to dwell on the horror, she could easily topple into a black abyss. The labyrinth of darkness was both her comfort and her foe. She could feel fear snaking up from the depths, coiling and squeezing the courage from her drop by drop. She fought it blindly with the only weapon she possessed: fury.

"So I'm doomed," she snarled, unable to conceal her resentment. "Thanks for the advance notice."

This automatic SE alert was a new innovation developed by Hickham and Charlie. She'd originally thought it was brilliant—but now, as a recipient of the alert, Maude couldn't be entirely pleased by it. Knowing the day and hour of her own death wasn't helpful, especially as a major part of the puzzle was still missing.

"How am I going to die?" she asked.

If he knew the answer, he wasn't sharing. Hickham just blinked.

Maude groaned and kicked the scan console with her bare foot. What good was the *drutzed* early-warning technology if the manner and means of expiration was still shrouded in mystery? It could be *anything*. Her cause of death could be her next Rogue mission, or a lift accident, or choking on nutrient, or even an implant malfunction. Freakish and untimely deaths plagued humanity regardless of the era. However, once Core received the SE alert and identified the subject, she'd be quarantined—for her own protection and Core's.

Maude grimaced at the thought. She'd seen Quarantine. Those darkened corridors in Reacclimation were solidly silent and forbidding. How many were housed within, sleeping away the centuries until the reason for their confinement could be resolved and their lives restored?

Stasis offered hope for terminal residents, she supposed, but for Maude it symbolized a fate worse than death. From her earliest memory, her greatest fear had been being alone. As an adult, that fear had manifested into a firmly rooted and secret belief that she might outlive everyone she knew, humanity itself, somehow arising from some sleep only to discover that she alone had survived, an Eve without an Adam.

Only Cara Chay knew of the phobia. Only Cara would understand. Only Cara could be trusted, having taken a childhood blood oath to prevent stasis for Maude at all costs. But Cara was gone. And without Cara, Maude could only trust herself to prevent her nightmare from becoming reality.

Quarantine was out of the question. When Hickham released her body scan results, she'd be a marked woman. He'd said his gray sludge would cloak her status, but for how long? Maybe an hour at most? After that, she'd be hunted down, collected, and "saved" from her fate—indefinitely.

Regulations and restrictions on changing the past were ostensibly inviolate. But fixing the future wasn't. That's what Cara's Eve One mission was about: amassing knowledge and launching the sonarlike technology for SE alerts. Which gave her pause. Could Chay's mission save her? If not immediately, perhaps eventually? A flicker of hope helped dispel some of her bone-chilling terror.

Quarantine. Locking her up might just work. Until the Scios and the Think Tank crew harnessed the power to alter the here and now, isolating the subject was their only viable option. But cowering in some isolation chamber for what might be the last hours of her life, unable to change her fate or fight back, was an awful end. Her eyes burned with unshed tears.

Hickham leaned over and hugged her. The moment was awkward, because Maude's leads were still attached, because he'd never displayed emotion well or often, and because Charlie wasn't around to handle speaking for him. After a few seconds, he released his stiff-armed embrace and sniffed.

The gesture connected Maude to Earth again. Awkward or not, she'd needed this.

"I've failed you," Hick said in a hemming-and-hawing, Charlie-like fashion. He looked like he'd been sentenced to death, too. His whole frame sagged, a scarecrowlike figure with the stuffing plucked out. His eyes were sunken in their sockets and heavily shadowed.

"I'm not unique. Everyone dies." Maude's tongue tripped over the last word. She squared her shoulders and continued. "I'm apparently just scheduled to die sooner rather than later."

Hickham nodded and coughed mightily. The phlegm must have been excessive; it took a while to clear his throat.

"What are you going to do?" he asked quietly.

She hugged one knee to her chest, propped her chin upon it, and scowled thoughtfully. "Any suggestions?" she asked.

His nod was barely perceptible. "You won't like it. But stasis is the recommended procedure."

"I don't need you to regurgitate protocol, Hick," she growled. "Suspended animation? That's the best you've got?" She fidgeted with her leads. She was suffocating. Tethered to the console, she couldn't escape the decisive moment. Hickham had bought her time to process the implications of her failed scan and consider her options. He'd stalled the process, but he couldn't prevent the delivery of data to Core the moment the leads were disconnected from her doomed body.

"We don't know what's going to kill me, do we?" she hissed. "I'm not inclined to snooze through my last hours, only to have my heart stop anyway."

"You don't have options, Maude. Quarantine. Face it."

"Don't do it, Hick. Don't make me do it," she added more forcefully. "Give me a fighting chance."

"What can you do that we can't?" he asked. "Trust us. The regs are designed for a purpose. Charlie's working on the alternative. But he won't be back with the Superman prototype in time to save you. Quarantine is not a choice. It's a mandate."

"I've been out there, Hick. I take risks. I don't play it safe." She gulped and admitted it. "I don't play by the rules all the time. There's a time for rules and there's a time for breaking them.

"I'm asking for options—something brilliant. *You've*

got the zatting big brain. Blow me out of the water. Give me something, and zat the risk. I'm an SE. I'm doomed. How much worse can it get?"

Hickham jerked back. Her words had assaulted him and beaten through the thin veneer of dispassion he'd tried to maintain. She could see past his mask now; he wasn't detached. He'd lost the ability to conceal his inner thoughts from her. His emotions were laid bare: a father's love, a parent's fear, a scientist's defiance, a thinker's wisdom, a warrior's courage.

"I *said* you wouldn't like my suggestion," he remarked. A rare smile surfaced. He'd made a joke, albeit a minor one. It was his first within earshot of Maude.

"There's another option," he added, but paused. Concern filled his face. "It's against regs. . . ."

"You know I'm a fighter," Maude said. "I saved Dak against all odds." She lifted her chin and stared at him long and hard. Unflinching and resolved, she shared her decision. "I deserve a chance to save myself. And you're going to give me one."

TWENTY-FIVE

"I only have an hour?" Maude confirmed as she pulled on her service tunic and leggings.

Hickham nodded as he adjusted the lights to maximum wattage and stowed her wafer-thin chart. "You'll have to clear Scio Quad and any other predictable destination before your signal-cloak expires," he said. "Core will check your frequency logs and direct collection squads accordingly. Your lodgings will be a primary search target."

"But this *works*, right?" she persisted. "My identilog won't trigger an alarm for an hour, no matter where I am."

"An hour is my best guess, Maude," he said. "It varies, depending on how long the body can tolerate the ingredients. The average is an hour." He handed her several sealed vials. "Take these with you. But I wouldn't recommend more than one dose per rotation. The identity inhibitor serum is a prototype concoction Charlie's been developing for Dak, so he can jump again without Core detecting him in the matrix of time. The side effects haven't been fully tested yet."

Maude sighed in relief. "It'll work. And I won't need an hour to get away," she assured him. "My plan isn't complicated."

Hickham folded his arms across his chest and turned away from his console. "Don't tell me anything more," he said firmly.

Maude noted that he was studiously ignoring the silent alarm flashing on the screen. It required a response, a confirmation and reaction to the auto-alert generated when her body scan results and SE status were absorbed into Core's mainframe. He was buying her more time. Time to escape.

As she'd said, Maude didn't need an hour to disappear. An expedited egress from the Quad required only minutes. She would need several more to regarb at her flat and collect necessities—she might not get another chance.

"You can't contact anyone at Rogue Central for help," he reminded her. "Raymond's procedure for a Scheduled Expiration will require him to deactivate all your access protocols. He'll do it too, as soon as Central receives the alert. Other Critical Services units will perceive you as a hazard as well. Every program will initiate similar access restrictions coded to your identilog that will be effective until you are isolated and contained. You won't be able to transit, cross through most Quads, use surface trams, or enter public facilities without alerting Core," he finished, and scowled at the pulsing timepiece on the lab wall. "It's how we set things up."

"You and Charlie thought of everything," Maude hissed as she swiftly finished donning her wrist unit and modified utility belt.

The slick, thin rope affair—an insubstantial and decorative version of her Rogue-standard field belt—hugged her hips. She swatted the vanity pouch dangling from it.

It reminded her of the unfinished business waiting at the flat: Gil.

His image triggered a surge of regret. She wouldn't need any of the tiny vials of scent and edible glosses she'd stowed inside the pouch. Any farewells they exchanged would have to be brief. No lingering kisses. No breathless whispers or eternal promises. Her flight to freedom couldn't be delayed by love.

She mentally shook herself and followed Hickham out of the lab complex. She didn't even have time to indulge herself with regrets; she'd set the chronometer on her identilog for an hour, and ten of those precious minutes had already expired.

"The SE status alerts are new and untried, of course. No one will be expecting this. Reactions might be delayed, but you better not count on that." Hickham said quietly as he escorted her up the ramps and through checkpoints. Once safely outside, with no apparent hindrance in sight, Hickham pulled her aside. "We designed the system and developed procedures to address unspecified catastrophic threats." He coughed and shrugged his shoulders, dipping his head close to hers. "But we didn't anticipate this situation so soon." He meant that he was helping her out. "Factor that information into your plans."

Maude nodded. Her plans were rough, cobbled together in the last moments before Hickham detached her leads and freed her body from the scanner. Phase one; the getaway. Phase two? Well, that needed work.

"And you can't know what my plans are?" she reiterated.

He shook his head vigorously. His blood was up. Maude could see it simmering within, coloring his cheeks.

"It's too risky. If I don't know where you are, I can't help Core locate you," he said. Pausing, he glanced around the utilitarian quad with a look of loathing. The springlike day and chirping birdsong conflicted with the quiet desperation tugging at his features and weighting his words.

"You won't reconsider Quarantine?" he demanded. "It's not a guarantee, but it is one hope I can offer."

Maude swore under her breath. "You know I can't. I've got to try to save myself."

"I know," Hickham snapped. He grabbed her suddenly by the shoulders, his fury and frustration cresting. "*Drutzed* Rogue training. *Zatting* genetics. Headstrong, brash—"

"I know," Maude cut in. She lifted her chin and grinned.

Hickham's fury broke. He folded her into another brief and awkward embrace. "Don't just try," he whispered hoarsely in her ear. "*Do* it. Save yourself."

Maude had beat him home; on his way into the flat, Gil nearly knocked heads with her. The oversized pack strapped to her back, as well as her hell-bent-for-leather pace, were mondo clues that she was on her way out— and not just for coffee.

She pulled up short, her pack's weight nearly bowling her over. Gil helped steady her.

"Hi," she managed with a tight smile that cut him to the quick.

"And bye?" Gil offered. He dropped his hands. His gaze flicked over her body and processed the abrupt change in attire and demeanor. Maude the Rogue was back. Fully garbed in her camo bodysuit and field boots, and geared to the hilt. The sight sucker punched Gil. Fighting every instinct to tackle her, he stepped out of her way, clearing a path to the exit.

Maude didn't budge. With nary a muscle twitching to

take her in either direction, in or out, she held fast to her gear like a superhero figurine. Poised—for fight or flight?

Gil resisted the urge to check the sky for a bat signal. Instead, he chucked her under the chin and stepped inside. "Nice knowing you," he quipped, and added over his shoulder, "Don't worry. I'll clean up after myself and put the key under the mat when I leave."

It was hard turning his back on her. The flat had been reset to its standard spartan look. He stared at the stark walls and the innocuous service cubes. All evidence of habitation was stowed in semipermanent housings.

Was it over? Had last night ever happened?

A twinge in Gil's well-used anatomy assured him it had. And it could happen again with just the punch of a button.

In seconds, the insular space could be converted back into the pleasure palace he'd come to know and love in those last twenty-odd hours. He had easily mastered the residential controls and added some additional atmospherics—sex at the North Pole was okay, but he'd supplemented Maude's limited selections with steamy, sultry, deep-South settings. They'd visited nearly every backdrop he'd downloaded. But he'd saved the best for last. There was still one moonlight-and-magnolias fantasy he hadn't shared, one that involved a bayou cabin and a big brass bed.

And it looks like I never will.

He heard the hushed hiss as the portal sealed. He spun around, but Maude wasn't gone. She had slipped out of her pack. She dropped it on the floor, leaned back against the closed portal, and sighed heavily.

"I didn't plan to leave this way," she said quietly. "Without saying good-bye. I wanted to . . ."

She didn't finish the thought. Gil interrupted with the only weapon he trusted: his lips.

"Saying 'good-bye forever' isn't going to be easy now or an hour from now," he finally said when he pulled back from the kiss. Maude sagged in his embrace, holding on for dear life. "Good-byes aren't a cinch in any century."

It was a bad joke, meant to ease the tension between them. But Maude didn't return his smile.

"I don't have an hour," she whispered. Her cornflower blue eyes looked big as saucers. Serious, sad, and moist with tears, they were melting his bravado by the second.

This farewell was hard on her too, he realized. Their torrid rolls in the hay had wooed and won her body—he'd seen plenty of confirmation of that. But he hadn't been sure he'd won her heart.

"Hey?" He crossed his fingers and waggled them in front of her. "Should we check? Any chance I got a reprieve?"

Maude stiffened perceptibly and shook her head. "No reprieve."

Keeping the smile plastered on his face was damned difficult. The first step? Ignoring the knot in his gut. His lucky streak was over. No reprieve or alternative for the brain drain had magically surfaced. His hours were numbered, and so were Maude's kisses.

He sampled another—and another, as Maude met his demands with her own. Contact ignited the smoldering heat in his loins and dropped the floodgates on his desire, and belied the idea that leaving the lady was going to be anything but sheer hell.

Damnation. Kissing her was torture. Even her mouth was a study in perfection. Maude was sinfully delicious, and he was certifiably obsessed, addicted, and stupid with love. He'd never get enough of her. And he wasn't fool enough to try.

He sucked in his breath. It was now or never. With a low growl, he wrenched himself away from her.

"You better get going. I can get myself back to Reacclimation." He said it fast, spitting the words out like bullets.

Maude flinched like they'd struck home. She wiped her nose on the sleeve of her bodysuit and sniffled. Tears leaked from her eyes and dripped off her chin. Her lips trembled. It wasn't a confirmation of love, but Gil didn't care. The gesture was enough. It had to be, because in a moment she'd be gone.

One last look: the body he'd loved. The woman he'd craved to know better, and had learned to admire. Mysterious, generous, sensuous, and serious. Maude. Keeper of his dreams, mistress of his heart.

Going. Going. And in a moment, gone. Forever.

The residential console activated. What looked like a self-scan sequence commenced with a fanfare of humming and bleeping. Maude spared a glance in its direction and checked her wrist unit. Her lips were pressed tight again. Her face was a mask of resolve.

"I've got to go," she said. She hoisted her pack in one swift move that looked effortless and familiar.

And, wrong. There was something seriously wrong with this picture.

Gil snorted. He'd been thinking mostly with his johnson again, and suffering from the consequences. He'd been deaf, dumb, and blind

"Hold on a sec, babe." He reached over and snagged her by her heavily accessorized utility belt. "What do you mean, you don't have an hour?"

TWENTY-SIX

She should have stunned Gil and left him behind, Maude silently chided herself. Survival was a solo venture. Flights for freedom didn't include tourists. Still, it felt great to have him along, his leg pressed against hers.

"Here we go," she said a split second before she nosed the hoverlift into a narrow, dark flume. Gil grunted and ducked.

He probably deserves one, Maude admitted to herself, *but explanations will have to wait.* She had other priorities. Negotiating the poorly mapped maze of interconnecting caves, flumes, pipes, and manmade tunnels couldn't be left to an autopilot.

She concentrated on the 3-D mapping screen, slowing the lift to a crawl as she picked her way through the intersecting avenues. Every venture into the highly volatile frontier region was fraught with danger. She'd learned one immutable law of the land: It was oh-so-easy to get lost.

Her spontaneous escape plan had flaws. Taking the shortcut to Dak's was risky. It cut across one corner of the dangerous district, and a sparely equipped Rogue with a guest, and on a limited-distance lift, was handicapped even before entering the expanse. But with a small supply of auxiliary sonar beacons, she hoped to minimize risk.

At the first major juncture, she stalled the lift and spun it slowly. Nothing looked familiar. Checking her chronometer, she groaned. Her hour was almost up. She couldn't second-guess every intersection; she had to keep moving.

She fished around in her pack. Pulling out a beacon, she activated it and dropped the lift's surrounding force field long enough to affix it to the nearest wall surface.

"Trail of bread crumbs, I take it?" Gil offered. The glow from the hoverlift's mapping screen illuminated his grin.

"It's a sonar beacon," she replied, and reactivated the force field. "Just in case."

He nodded. "Bread crumbs.

"I understand you're under a time crunch," he added. "But, I could be more help if I knew why the hell we're on the run."

"I'm not running," she snarled, and powered up the lift again. Directing it into the central pipe, she gunned the vehicle full speed ahead.

She didn't lie well. Gil's grunt supported that opinion. "Okay. You can't tell me. I'm all right with that."

Maude groaned. "I should have left you behind," she said.

Gil chuckled. "It wasn't optional, if you'll remember. I was coming along whether you wanted me or not. No self-respecting cowboy leaves a gal in distress."

He was right. It hadn't been optional—that is, unless she'd stunned him. And she couldn't bring herself to do it. The most obvious reason? She wanted his help.

"I don't need your help," she clarified.

"Too bad. You've got it," he returned, in that same infuriatingly jovial tone.

She growled. But she'd been lying; she needed help.

Fortunately, Gil was an able navigator, learning quickly how to translate the shapes on the map and interpret the resolutions and proximities of solids.

"Hey. Watch it," he groused. "More to the left."

"I see," Maude said with matching volume, adjusting the lift's course to edge around a massive stalagmite.

At the next Y intersection, she stalled the lift again and grabbed another beacon. Gil delayed her and pointed to the junction on the map.

"Just a minute," he said, and rotated the lift forty-five degrees. "I think I know where we are."

"Impossible," Maude snapped, watching him as he surveyed the directional header above the nearest tunnel with her handheld flash.

"There it is—'S one K'. The surface: one kilometer. Right?"

"Yes. So? Surface directionals are all over these tunnels and caves."

"Maybe so, but this one looks familiar," he returned, and spun the nose of the lift another forty-five degrees. The directional marker above them was missing, like most had been along this primitive transport route, but that fact didn't seem to erode Gil's confidence. "I know where we are," he crowed, and pointed straight ahead. "Take that tunnel."

"You don't even know where I'm going," Maude replied.

"To Dak's," he said simply. He laughed when her chin dropped. Then the brute distracted her with a kiss.

"But, how?" she asked when he pulled away, and nosed the lift down the specified tunnel.

"There's only one destination for you, Dorothy," he quipped. "And that's to see the Wizard."

TWENTY-SEVEN

"That's your plan?" Gil roared. "That's not a plan. That's a joke."

The three collaborators shifted on their packing-crate seating. Slowly, Bob, Dak, and Maude turned in Gil's direction. Cast in green light from the glowing time map, their frowns looked sinister. But at least for the moment, they were listening. And they'd all forgotten the blackboard-sized holographic image representing Earth's past.

"You don't know what you're talking about, Gillespe," Dak said.

The weird guy, Bob, supported his criticism with a nod. Maude hissed loudly, a wholesale rejection of Gil's comment.

Debating lifesaving options in Dak's sealed command center with nothing but nutrient sludge to wet their whistles had made everyone testy. Gil was itching to slam a few heads together.

"I know one thing," Gil said, soundlessly pacing the mud-colored rubber floor. "A plan involves action. Sitting around on our thumbs and waiting for Maude to drop dead isn't a fucking plan. Maude's idea had balls— more balls than the two of you have combined."

Maude arched a brow. She absently clicked her nails against her wrist unit, a habit Gil had come to associate with her rare struggles with indecision. Gil silently cheered. He'd reached her, piercing the glut of nonsense Dak and Bob had thrown at her. She was thinking again.

In the past few hours they'd backed her into a corner, pummeling her with promises that everything was going to be okay, damn their hides. They'd almost convinced her to stand down and desist—something Gil knew would undermine Maude's morale in short order.

"Waiting is safe and sensible," Dak argued. He shoved his laser pointer around on the punched metal tabletop with his fingertip. "Bob's plan has merit." His deep voice carried a throaty warning that Gil refused to heed. He wouldn't back off. Couldn't, for Maude's sake.

"So does Maude's plan," Gil replied. He stepped behind her, rested his hands on her shoulders, and glared at Dak. "It's proactive. And it gives us all something to *do*—including Maude. Let's run it up the flagpole again and see who salutes."

A collective expression of confusion was the response. Bob looked stunned, his mouth forming a silent O. But Dak rallied and slowly stood.

Gil wasn't nose to nose with the former Rogue; he had three inches on the guy. But Dak outweighed him by almost forty pounds. If it came to blows, he wasn't sure that he'd survive fisticuffs. But he had the advantage of brains over brawn, he reminded himself. At least he hoped he did.

A fresh cool blast of filtered air from the ventilation grill chilled Gil to the bone. His thermal tunic wasn't adjusting. It seemed that gizmos everywhere, even in Core's wonderworld, could malfunction.

He gritted his teeth. This interminable, civilized discussion about Maude's death was killing him. He'd been stunned senseless when she'd first blurted the news to Dak. Maude. Vibrant. Alive. And soon to be dead. He was still reeling from shock, but fury and frustration had devoured the worm of fear. And the others acquiescing to the wait-and-watch solution boiled his blood.

The silence was deafening as Gil and Dak sized each other up. *This isn't a pissing contest between us*, Gil reminded himself. Everyone wanted to save Maude, including Maude herself. And that was his point. Maude had great instincts.

He said as much.

She twisted around and looked at him. Her smile was worth a million bucks. For a split second, Gil felt like a hero.

"Her instincts are good," Dak snarled, "but mine are better. We're going with Bob's plan—the original plan. Maude stays here, where she's safe, until Charlie completes the test of his Superman bodyshield prototype and brings it back for implantation."

Gil rolled his eyes, counted to ten and took a deep breath before he continued. "I get it and I agree—it's a stellar solution *if* the Superman chip works. But let me get this straight: Charlie's got the one and only chip on him. He doesn't know Maude's got less than thirty days left, and there's no guarantee that he'll be back in time to plant it before she croaks. Correct?"

"Affirmative." Dak's frown was potent. It would have terrorized the Dallas Cowboys defensive line.

"And you're okay with that? Waiting? Doing nothing?" Gil persisted.

"It is the safest plan of action for the situation." Dak enunciated each syllable. His cheek twitched. It was evident he was clenching his teeth, controlling his temper, and wrestling with some internal demons. "Core's intent to put her into deep hibernation is our contingency plan. We won't need it, of course, but it's available—and the system was designed by the best minds I've ever known, Charlie and Hick." Dak folded his arms and glared. "So, what is *your* idea?"

"Trying the plan Maude suggested," Gil said. "Her idea sounds prudent and smart. I may not know a damned thing about transits, but if Maude wants to track down Charlie, I'd let her do it. Not cut off her options, tie her hands, and ask her to cower in your inner sanctum and watch the clock." Gil squeezed her shoulder. "Just look at her," he snapped. "This gal is all about kicking butt. I'm all for empowering her to do it. Damnation. I'll help her do it."

Dak's scowl shifted. "Is that a threat, Gillespe? Or are you volunteering to travel?"

Gil suffered Dak's steely-eyed gaze without flinching. "What the hell do you think?" he retorted.

Dak laughed suddenly. "*Drutz,* you remind me of myself. Full head of steam with no place to go. You don't have the training, but zat, Gillespe, you're a Rogue at heart." He sighed and flopped back down on his crate. Unclenching his fists, he shook out his fingers and cracked his knuckles. Gil noted the scars and calluses on those plate-sized mitts. Dak wasn't a stranger to hard work or pain. He was a man of action.

"None of us are cowards," he said. "Rogues don't play it safe. We break rules every day. But Maude's situation is different. It's tricky. And, I'm not objective." He glanced in Maude's direction. The muscle in his cheek twitched again.

To Gil, Dak suddenly looked guilty. Guilty as sin. Gil had seen the same look on his brother Chad's kisser every time he'd broken a heart and moved on to greener pastures. Gil's white-knight instincts kicked in. One thing was damn sure: No one was going to break Maude's heart or there'd be hell to pay, and he'd do the collecting.

"I'm not objective," Dak repeated. He gulped like a fish out of water, searching for the words. Finally, they spilled out of him unchecked, uncensored. "I can't risk it. I have to trust the original plan. We all agreed to it when we first learned about your death."

"You knew?" Maude cried. "Before my SE alert? How?" She stared at Dak, her face expressing a mix of bewilderment and consternation. Gil could feel her shoulders square up under his palms.

"We all did," Bob replied defensively. "Even Charlie and Hickham."

"Gil," she whispered. "They knew about it before I did, and they didn't tell me."

Gil growled. His first instinct was to slug Dak and thump Bob. White knights got away with that kind of thing, stomping and thumping and such. But Gil fought the instinct. Getting physical with Dak wouldn't contribute one iota to solving the chief problem they all faced: saving Maude.

"I'm sure they had their reasons," Gil gritted out, nodding in their direction. "Right, boys?"

Neither man replied at first. Bob dipped his head and stared at his notes, studying them intently, as if he'd just discovered how to read. Dak, however, had regained his stoic aplomb and leveled an unapologetic gaze first at Gil, then Maude.

"You didn't need to know," Dak said simply. "Standard containment protocols."

"I didn't need to know?" Maude echoed. "Containment? *Drutz,* Dak. It's my life."

"No exceptions. You know the regs," Dak replied.

His cold calm didn't fool Gil. Dak's rough and tough exterior was a smoke screen. The glint in his eye, the grit in his tone, and the involuntary twitch told a different story to anyone with a knack for spotting weakness in green bulls. Gil had the knack. Dak was scared stiff.

"Containment protocols?" Gil asked. "As in information containment?"

Bob nodded, his features twisted with conflicting emotions. "A breach in authorized transit communications restricts dissemination of information. We couldn't tell her."

"But, how . . . ?" Maude started, her perplexed tone carrying more meaning than the actual question itself.

"We're messing with the future, Maude," Dak replied, somewhat cryptically. He folded his arms and waited.

"Cara," Maude said after a moment. She slowly nodded. "It was in her report, wasn't it?"

"It's not an Eve One malfunction," Dak explained. "Chay purposely violated Core directives and communicated information from the future to effect a change in our present. A Breach Six, transit communication."

Maude nodded again. "A Six? *Zat*," she hissed.

"No one caught it at first," Dak continued. "Chay inserted an encoded message in each scheduled report. Looked like an error message to everyone, including Hickham."

"A transmission glitch at the end of every sequence. Or a transit malfunction hallmark. That's why it caught my attention," Bob added. "I brought it to Charlie after Hickham helped clarify Chay as the source; then I connected the string and decoded it." He stopped suddenly. His color was up, his eyes bright.

Dak raised a brow and shrugged his shoulders. "I guess we can share the basics now," he finally said. "Decoded, Chay's repeating message is: 'Kincaid dead.'"

"That's it?" Gil roared.

Bob blinked and swallowed nervously. "We d-don't know much else," he stammered.

"The zat you don't," Maude shot back. "How am I going to die?"

"B-b-bullet," Bob returned. "I decoded that from Chay's last message."

"A bullet?" she repeated. "You mean, from a gun?" She slapped her thigh and grinned. "*That's* why we need Charlie's prototype. It's bulletproof."

Bob frowned. Slowly shaking his head, he opened his mouth to elaborate.

"That's enough," Dak said. "Stop feeding her info." He leaned in close to Maude, his eyes mere slits. "Trust me," he said, his voice a snarl of concern and bluster. "This new info doesn't change anything. We've considered all the options. We're sticking with the original plan. End of discussion."

It wasn't the end of the discussion. Everyone had opinions about Bob's revelation. Gil took a swig from his nutrient flask and launched the debate. Maude jumped in. And Dak volleyed between them, basically agreeing to disagree.

The volume of the exchange increased to ear-numbing decibels as everyone but Bob recounted the pros and cons of each plan. Action versus inaction. Defense versus offense. Minimizing risks versus maximizing options.

Although loud, the three-way debate was sensible, Gil noted; but also a waste of time. Dak wasn't flexible. There seemed to be no apparent middle ground for compromise.

"This is pointless," Gil said, pulling back from the group. Gil was furious. He wasn't contributing much. Supporting the woman in jeopardy was something, of course, but not enough. He was packing some intellect and itched to apply more than mere body mass to the problem at hand.

"I don't get it," he finally said. "This should be easy to fix. After all, you guys broke the code on time travel. You can go anywhere in time . . . not to the future yet. I mean, I know Chay's the first there. But you can go anywhere in the past. Right?"

"Yeah," Dak sighed and stretched. "*Some* of us can still transit anywhere."

Everyone was tired, Gil noted, himself included. Good decisions might be impossible under these conditions. But he wasn't throwing in the towel yet.

"Mind explaining the basics? I'm safe. Any supersecret stuff will be sucked out of my brain with that damned purge."

"Doesn't matter to me," Dak replied and shrugged his shoulders. "There are 'no transit' zones. And, of course, Core's info gaps equate to black holes and make those off-limits too. Even the 'free transit' zones have duration restrictions. But other than that, we can transit anywhere in time."

He nodded in Bob's direction. "He can supply the details about warp versus non-warp time travel; Core utilizes non-warp, by the way."

"Non-warp? Do you mean you're traveling in real time?"

All three of the future folk reflected various expressions of surprise.

"Of course," Bob replied after a moment and laid out the basics.

"Warp transit for humans was disastrous." Adding, "Sorry, Einstein," under his breath before continuing.

"Until non-warp technology was invented and implanted, we couldn't successfully relocate the population or travel through time and maintain viable contact with our era of origin. Real-time travel prevents adverse physical and psychological impacts and maintains a viable connection between the time traveler and Core society."

Dak chuckled and added, "He's trying to tell you that the two hours a Rogue spends in the past equals two hours in Core. Got it?"

Gil nodded. He got it, all right. Real time? Amazing. It explained a few things, enough to move on and chew on the problem at hand. After pacing throughout the discussion, he felt like he'd just run a marathon. He was sweating and parched. Reluctantly, he snagged his flask and downed the remainder of his nutrient.

Maude pushed herself up as well, heaving a sigh of frustration. "It's already Day 185?" she hissed, glancing at her chronometer. "Zat. Only twenty-nine rotations left." She slumped against one wall. "I'm doomed."

"No," Bob interjected. His head was still bowed over his notes. His tone was firm, authoritative. And, Gil noted, his comment got Dak and Maude's unequivocal attention.

Maude straightened, her ebbing life-clock forgotten.

"No?" Dak echoed. "You've got something else for us?"

"Another option," Bob said. "A compromise."

The sober fellow fiercely gripped his laser pointer and stood. Turning back to the holographic time map, he tapped the image, highlighting three spots on the tangled mess of lines and bubbles that represented Earth's past.

The pulsing spots meant nothing to Gil, but Bob's gleaming expression of inspired revelation did. Gil recognized a "Eureka" look when he saw one. Bob had the answer.

"Interface with Charlie is possible at any of these points on his mission," Bob said.

Maude gasped. "Interface? We can communicate with him?" She glanced over at Gil. Hope temporarily flushing through her and softening her strained features, she grabbed his hand and squeezed.

"We maximized Charlie's testing fields. They are complex and diverse arenas," Dak interjected. His frown intensified as he leaned in close to study the locations. "Aren't these all no-transit zones?"

"I've been working on something that . . . well, I can

punch a hole in the zone and drop someone in," Bob explained. He tapped the spots again. "Here, here, or here."

Each location in turn was maximized and scrutinized by Dak. He nodded slowly.

Dak looked up from the time map, but he didn't look at Maude. His gaze skewered Gil from across the room. "It might work," he admitted ruefully. "If it can be done."

There it was: the challenge. Gil instantly knew what Dak's silent stare implied.

"I can make contact," Maude whispered. "I can update Charlie on my status, tell him about my SE, tell him to hurry."

"Hurry?" Gil stormed. "Fuck that. I'm going to haul his ass back here to implant that damned Superman chip *now*—before it's too late."

TWENTY-EIGHT

Now was relative, Maude reminded herself five hours later, after another interminable discussion. They had outlined, prioritized, and assigned the necessary tasks to launch another unauthorized mission to the past. But time was running out. Intimately aware of the minutes bleeding off from her destiny, Maude craved a quick fix.

Bob's drop-in idea had sounded simple. It wasn't. Planning a clandestine transit for a doomed Rogue and a tag-along cowboy was a complex and time-consuming operation. Especially when the transit to connect with Charlie involved an innovative hole-punching feat.

Bombarded with details, Maude's brain felt fried. But, at least she was busy. Gil was right. Doing something was immensely better than waiting. And she wasn't alone. Brains and brawn were helping her subvert her mortality issue, with everyone shouldering a piece of the project.

Of course, the true test was for Bob. Creating the science that would allow her to violate a no-transit zone was his burden and his alone. It was illegal, and up until now had been inconceivable. And no one could help.

Without any collaborative input from big brains like Charlie, Hickham, or the Think Tank, the lead transitor with a reputation for understated brilliance was facing the challenge solo. His work up until this point had all been theoretical, but that was about to change.

Bob's assurances helped salve her fretful spirit. This was possible. He could do it.

Still, Maude's orderly mind was in chaos. Any Rogue skill she'd possessed to displace emotion, even temporarily, had been ravaged by the SE alert. It had been a rough day. She had lost her job, most of her family and friends to Core's protocols, and gained a death sentence all at once. The SE had changed everything forever.

Unable to adequately sort fact from fear, Maude shut out all distractions. With a fierce determination that had never failed her, she focused on her prioritized tasks. Everyone did, scattering with purpose once Dak bellowed, "Let's get going. Maude's on a clock."

Bob departed for the covert transit pad to map the route, and Dak abandoned the complex to collect and check mission equipment. As directed, Maude's champion and transit partner, Gil, stoically ingested another liter of nutrient.

Maude scowled and refueled too, but not without complaint. With her energy stretched thin keeping all her flaws and fears in check, she didn't waste any on concealing her revulsion for Charlie's cocktail. She gagged, burped, and groaned with undisguised distaste.

"I hate this part of mission prep," she managed between swallows. She shivered as the chilled, chalky syrup slid down her throat. It didn't have a kick. She wished it did.

"It's a necessary evil for time travelers, especially Rogues," she added, more for herself than Gil, as she finished her allotment. She elaborated on the benefits beyond mere nutrition, and how the sludge supersaturated tissues and organs and effectively protected Rogues from contagion when venturing into hazardous arenas.

"I guessed that was the case," Gil said as he tossed his empty container into the buffed metal sanitation chute. "But, I'm not really able to appreciate the finer qualities right now." He looked green, and not just because of the glowing time map.

"You going to toss your cookies?" she asked. She liked the term. In fact, she liked all of Gil's terms. Even though she didn't understand most of them, she understood Gil. And she loved that he was fearless.

"Nope," he snorted, and forced a fake smile. "I'm not gonna swill that muck *twice*."

He was true to his word. He kept it down. Still green but grinning with gritty resolve, he cleared his throat.

"Worst is over. What's next? Bring it on," he demanded.

She wanted to throw herself in his arms and lose herself in that bastion of manhood, grateful for his resilience. Grateful for his broad shoulders that seemed capable of bearing any and every burden. And, grateful for his smile—the smile that constricted her heart with gladness and reminded her that she was alive.

But, she stopped herself. She had been in Gil's position countless times. Glutted with nutrient, he still managed to look fierce and formidable, but she knew it had to be mostly bravado. Until the energy boost from the nutrient kicked in, he was probably about as tough as a wingless moth.

"What's next?" Maude echoed. "How about hair removal?"

"Again?" Gil frowned and scrubbed his scalp. Very little regrowth was observable. "Not that there's anything wrong with it, but is baldness essential?"

"It isn't standard for all missions now. But . . ."

Gil rolled his eyes with feigned exasperation. "Forget I asked. I'll do it. This isn't a standard mission. . . . And I suppose it's going hurt like Hades again. Right?"

Maude admitted it: Denuding flesh did hurt. Every time. It was one of those things that never got better or easier. Like the nutrient, it was a necessary evil.

"Well, bring it on."

Gil mugged agony, as if he'd agreed to ingest a dozen liters of Charlie's sludge, then winked. Maude sighed with relief. The cowboy was committed. She loved him for it, and for his dogged determination to save her life.

Her *life*. The terror was back, kicking her senseless, wearing her down, wearing her out. She still couldn't fully accept the facts. Her frayed nerves sawed at her courage. She knew all the symptoms of exhaustion, and the cure. She needed rest. She needed Gil, and she needed time.

Don't think about time. And don't think about Gil.

But she couldn't help it. She was doomed and desperate. As the chronometer ticked off what remained on her life-clock, her doubts multiplied. She second-guessed everything. Trusted nothing. She quaked with indecision, uncertain about her next thought, her next word, her next deed.

She tried to brace herself and rise above the paralyzing fear, remember her training. *Rogues don't fall apart. Ever.*

Silently cursing—every foul-mouthed curse she knew from A to Z—she squeezed her eyes shut and fixated on the facts. Knowledge was power. Her fate wasn't a mystery. She had two pieces of the puzzle: when and how. In less than thirty rotations, a bullet was going to end her existence. *Unless?*

Gil folded her into a wordless embrace that blocked out the world. His energy was back, and so was the devilish twinkle in his eyes.

"We're going to get it done," he finally said. "We're going to stop that bullet."

And in that moment, safe in his arms, Maude was convinced she wouldn't die. But the knowledge was joyless, because she also knew why. Gil was tenacious. She could feel his resolve, see it in his eyes behind the twinkle. He was going to make the intervention work.

He intended to take the bullet for her.

TWENTY-NINE

Gil appreciated Maude's Time Travel 101 briefing. Finally away from the fretful Dak and twitchy Bob, he could drop his bluff and bluster routine and figure out what the hell he'd just agreed to do—and how to do it.

His last-ditch option was clear, and stepping in front of a bullet would be a cinch for a guy with more passion than sense. But his selfish goal was to save Maude with his hide intact. A win-win option had to exist. However, getting one step ahead of these time traveling Rogues and transit eggheads required finesse, an edge, and luck.

Maude's explanations were grist for the mill. In a matter of minutes she had cleared up some basics and was dishing specifics about the ultramysterious no-transit zone.

"Core prohibits transits into some zones," she explained, splashing her face with citrus-scented water and toweling off.

He took his turn at the copper basin and doused his head. It had been a quick and sweaty climb up and out of the secret transit complex via a tight access tunnel beneath Dak's villa, but the cleaning station available in the dwelling contained essentials to remedy any immediate discomfort.

The cool water cut through his film of sweat, but Gil was still steamed. Maude, doomed. Her life cut short by a bullet. It was incomprehensible that a nugget of lead could punch through her perfect flesh and stop her heart, erase her smile, steal her future.

"Are you okay?" she asked, concern furrowing her brow.

Damn. His mask must have slipped. He wanted Maude focused and worry-free—if possible. He forced a grin. "Nothing a few beers and a steak wouldn't cure," he replied. "Please continue. The zones . . ."

Maude didn't look entirely convinced, but she picked up where she'd left off. "They have boundaries. Critical events in Earth's history are mapped and defined by spatial buffers," she elaborated. "Insulated from contact by Core's mainframe, the past is preserved and our reality is protected. So are time travelers."

Gil grasped the concept and the rationale. It was fairly easy to assume the impact to history if a time traveler inadvertently distracted Sir Isaac Newton while he was under the apple tree, interrupted Jack the Ripper's spree, or diverted the Titanic. But, what about intentional acts? Or accidents?

Maude shook her head in response to his unspoken questions. "It's nearly impossible to penetrate a no-transit zone, either by accident or on purpose," she said. "There's some law of physics that makes it difficult— don't ask me to explain."

"But Dak managed," Gil interjected. "I'm assuming the AD 79 Mount Vesuvius eruption that destroyed ancient Pompeii qualifies as a critical past event."

Maude agreed. Stripping off her gear and donning a form-hugging tunic and leggings, she continued, "Natural disasters are one category. There are event classes and sub-classes, each with unique proximity and duration restrictions. But, yes, Dak managed it," she admitted. "He exploited a flaw in the system and penetrated the Pompeii event deliberately."

"And got trapped," Gil added.

She glanced over at Gil, a hint of a smile curving her lips. "Rescuing Dak was my first official Rogue mission," she said, stowing her waist pack and field boots.

"Remind me to thank him," Gil said, and pulled her into an embrace. She fit against him like a missing piece to a puzzle. Gil felt complete, restored to wholeness, one with the universe.

"For what?" Maude murmured against his lips.

"For triggering a rift that screwed up time lines," Gil returned. "And dumping you into mine."

Maude flinched suddenly, pulling back and staring with wide-eyed concern. "Zat, Gil," she hissed. "I forgot. And so did the others. You *can't* help me. You've got to go back to your era. You're essential there."

"I'm pretty damned essential here, too. The mission's set. You can't transit without me," Gil said.

"The zat I can't. I can do it solo. It's not a rescue, it's just an interface," she snapped.

"And the whole hole-punching thing?" he prompted. "What about the big stink Bob raised about aligning time threads and holding the window open with sufficient body mass? I might be ballast, but I'm essential ballast."

Maude's mouth hung open. He'd undercut her argument beautifully.

She recovered. Snapping her mouth shut, she scowled, her eyes mere slits. "Here's a time travel fact you might not have grasped yet," she said quietly. "You are coded as EE, era essential. Like my SE code, it is registered in Core's mainframe and will trigger a retrieval squad if you don't return to Reacclimation on schedule. In fact, it probably already has. Charlie only cleared you for three additional rotations. We're well past that now."

"So we're both on the run?" He felt his engine rev. The outlaw in him liked the idea; it fired him up and spurred his passion to rebel for a just and righteous cause. Saving Maude's life qualified.

"You're smiling," she cried. "Don't you understand? Any additional delay in returning you to your era could cause irreparable damage to the continuum."

"One crisis at a time," Gil said. "I'm not going home until the fat lady sings."

Maude's expression was rebellious. Gil admired her strength. She was doomed, but she was fighting. Independent, loyal, brave—she had all the superior human characteristics that fueled a fearless psyche. In short, she was a Rogue—and Rogues were certifiable superheroes in his book.

He'd seen the Rogue motto on the wall in Charlie's lab: *Preserve the past to protect the future.* That's what these superheroes fought to accomplish.

He wouldn't like it, but he would go home. He had to, for everyone's sake, including Maude's. He wasn't going to risk damning this future world if he was essential to preserving Earth's past.

At the same time, he wasn't about to enable that annoying superhero habit of self-sacrifice. Nothing short of a team of wild horses was going to pry him away from Maude until he'd saved her life.

Falah skillfully deflected the queries as she circled the unannounced guests and collected the remains of their refreshments. Pleading patience in halting English, she thumped the blocky translation device tethered to her sash.

Three of Core's finest, a retrieval squad with an appetite, had courteously sampled the rare foodstuffs she'd offered. But now they were all business. Maude's SE alert had triggered a search-and-recovery effort. Her logs indicated this homestead as a frequent destination, including a visit at 182.25 through 182.90, one of her last tracked locations. Did anyone at the homestead know of other destinations for the subject?

Falah smiled beautifully and thumped her translation device again. Shrugging, she merely repeated Dak's message.

"Husband gone. You wait."

Dak scowled. He monitored the invasion from his hidden transit station. He'd advised Falah on the delaying strategy, but he knew all too well that retrieval and collection squads were doggedly devoted to duty. The squad was conducting a reconnaissance mission, but the longer they tarried at the remote homestead meant increased risk of exposing the illegal enterprises concealed below. If they didn't leave soon of their own accord, he'd have to get up there and motivate them to depart—before one of them started nosing around the outbuildings.

"I better go up there," he told Bob. "*Drutz.* This delay better not put us behind schedule. I want those kids out of here before Core launches a locator probe in this sector that might pick up their signals."

"The static screen for the complex should prevent it," Bob said. "However, I think we should power up one of the alternate stations. This close to launch, it is hazardous to switch the codes and realign the coordinates, but I want to retrieve them from another pad. One of them might purge the identity inhibitor serum before retrieval. If they do, their signal will be hot."

"Prudent," Dak agreed. "Which station?"

Bob tapped on a handy surface grid and highlighted a map of the hidden complex and its ancillary sites. His head bobbed over one in particular. He enlarged the view.

"Outskirt 13? Your old homestead," Dak noted, peering over Bob's shoulder. "Good choice. It's the closest."

He started for the villa tunnel. "I'll get rid of this squad while you activate Thirteen," he called over his shoulder. "Better send an SOS to Rick," he added. "Don't recall him. And don't make it imperative, either. Send him one of your coded messages, just in case Core is monitoring communications for leads on Maude and Gil."

Bob's brows furrowed with thought. "I'll do my best."

"Rick won't understand what the zat we're doing. I'm not sure I do, either, but we need backup, and Rick's our best bet."

"So, what's the plan again?" Gil asked after strapping on his waist pack in Dak's equipping hub and locker room. "If I arrive alive, that is."

Dak looked up from his task of collecting gear and assured him he would. "Don't linger. Either Charlie is there or he's not. Don't get distracted—it's easy to do when you're new to transiting. Get back within the hour, and everything should be okay."

"What's our destination, by the way?" Gil said. "Nobody's mentioned that tidbit yet."

"Doesn't matter," Dak snapped. "I can't prep you for the era with mapping, or wardrobe, or language enhancements."

"Language enhancements?"

"You're going to Rome," Dak supplied.

"Rome? I can do Rome. I've mastered the rudiments of the language enough to eat, drink, and make merry. That'll come in handy."

"No." Dak shook his head. "It won't. You won't be there long enough. Like I said, the entire transit is less than an hour. Stay focused. And *your* job isn't to find Charlie, it's to keep Maude safe for the duration." He stopped checking the supplies in the equipment locker and slammed one fist against the thick acrylic shelving. "I should be going," he seethed. "If Core hadn't chained me to this time, I'd be out there now. Testing Superman or collecting Charlie."

Gil didn't respond. There wasn't any profit in dwelling on what couldn't happen. Core's transit prohibition had hobbled this fearless Rogue, end of story. Whether it was a just punishment for Dak's massive boo-boo wasn't up for debate; the fact remained that there were only two people at present who could transit through Bob's hole in time. Dak wasn't one of them.

"Maude will get the job done," Gil assured him, "and, I'll keep her safe."

Dak stared at him long and hard. Gil could see it wasn't easy for him to concede the turf, yield the responsibility, or trust a stranger.

"Just keep her in the transit window," Dak growled. "Don't let her venture beyond it and enter the event, no matter what. Stun her if necessary."

Stun Maude? Gil flinched. But he'd do that and more if it would keep her safe.

"Let's launch this mission already," he said. "I'm as ready as I'll ever be."

"Not quite," Bob replied. Waving him over to the screened console adjacent to the transit pad, Bob fired up and tested each of the gizmos Gil had just donned. Gil watched with rapt attention. Dak's briefing on the equipment had fostered a false sense of well-being.

The technology here was awesome. He had gear any commando would envy. His transit skills might be zilch, but he had a stunner, a chronometer, auto-transit triggers for himself and Maude, and a futuristic *Top Gun*-like bodysuit that coated him from neck to ankles with a web of light deflecting and camouflaging sensors.

"Hey, you look great. Just like a Rogue!" Maude said as she entered the chamber.

Gil returned the compliment. Of course, she'd looked great every time he'd ever seen her—clothed, nude, bald or bewigged, in his dreams or in his arms.

She came close and surveyed Gil, noting the accessories supplementing the outfit. She frowned and ran her fingertips over the surface of the bodysuit. "What's this?" she asked.

"It's a poor substitute for implants and experience," Bob replied as he activated the sensor web and attached a long lead to Gil's wrist unit. "But it should help stabilize Gil's physiology upon arrival."

"Transits are rough on everyone," Maude said, and rolled her eyes. "I used to get hives."

"Hives are rare," Bob returned. "But transit sickness is common. Everybody gets it at least once."

"Thanks for the warning," Gil replied, "but if I didn't toss my cookies after a wooden roller coaster marathon with my nephews on the notorious Rattler, I'll probably be good for the duration of the mission. You said we're only popping in and out."

"Short jaunts are sometimes the worst," Maude said. "Wreaks havoc on the body. We have to build in rest protocols—auto shutdowns to allow recovery—between each transit in a series." She stretched, flexed her long legs, and shook out her muscles as if she were warming up for a 10K run.

Gil had a killer warm-up routine, one that had always prepped him for lashing his body to a two-ton cow. But he rejected the idea before converting it into action. As soon as Bob completed the gizmo check, Gil resorted to the old standby. Push-ups were universal. He dropped and did reps until he broke a sweat.

"He'll be fine," Dak growled. He crossed the room and stood over Gil, eyeballing him critically. "That zatting suit will temporarily fool your body and delay any reaction until you return."

Partly to ignore Dak and also to show off, Gil punched out another ten push-ups before he stood and checked his pulse against his wrist unit. The multipurpose item equated to a deluxe Swiss Army knife. Packed with devices, weapons, and tools, the small split screen displayed his vitals. The HR and BP readings fluctuated as he caught his breath.

Ah, he was alive. But one of the incomprehensible details on the bio-screen was only at 50 percent and flashing red: the Greek symbol for time. That couldn't be good.

"You're ready to transit," Bob called from his console.

Ready? Gil frowned. Bob had seen his vitals. Maybe the pulsing red time symbol wasn't significant, or maybe Bob wasn't telling him everything.

So what. He scrubbed his face with his hands. After Dak's briefing on his technology-packed garb and gear, his brain was saturated with info. If Bob was holding out, Gil realized he didn't care. He was ready—past ready— to get this show on the road.

"Keep her within the transit window," Bob said under his breath as he detached the lead to Gil's wrist unit. "Prevent her from penetrating the era. No matter what happens."

Both Bob and Dak had stressed the point. Penetrating the era was a no-no.

They didn't have to tell him twice. Bob's graphic description of a collapsing transit window had sounded a lot like the birth of a black hole—or worse. Dak's description had been marginally better. It boiled down to insider Rogue stuff about getting stuck in time, and how to get unstuck. Stuck was problematic and situational. Getting unstuck required one skill: speed.

If a window collapsed, a time traveler, if he survived the collapse, might be too damaged to somehow get beyond the geographic limits of the no-transit zone to allow for a safe retrieval. It was a moot point that in addition to the physical dangers of a collapse, the time crunch on the cloaking serum and getting beyond the no-transit zone before Core picked up their identilog signatures was virtually impossible.

Solution? Gil and Maude couldn't get stuck. Get it?

Oh yeah—Gil smirked—he got it. He understood his role here completely. They didn't need his brains for this mission; they needed his brawn, pure and simple. He was a glorified bodyguard, Maude's physical anchor to the transit window. He could do that. To keep her safe, he was expendable.

THIRTY

Maude giggled and fought the urge to scratch; her denuded flesh felt soft as a baby's bottom—and ticklish. She loved that feel, loved the man standing next to her, and loved life. She was doomed but also deliriously happy. Maybe it was something only another female could understand, because the three males staring slack-jawed with horror at her didn't seem to get it.

Admittedly, standing on the transit pad, primed for the mission of her life, wasn't traditionally the time or place to indulge a giggling fit. Her companions apparently agreed.

But she was going. Moments earlier she'd swallowed the contents of one of the vials of goo Hick had supplied, and tossed another to Gil. Bob had confirmed their signals were cloaked, and she'd sighed with relief. Their transit wouldn't trigger an alert. For the next sixty minutes, Core wouldn't be able to pick up their signals within the continuum.

The launch was going to be tricky. This interface procedure was untested, and the tagalong cowboy was an inexperienced time traveler, which added an unknown and incalculable variable to the enterprise.

Bob, usually stoic and monosyllabic, quietly repeated cautions. Dak sported his legendary do-or-die mission face, which she always saw as perfectly conveying the heart and mind of a fearless Rogue. Gil, resplendent in his Rogue attire, shadowed her every move with an air of confirmed success. Each was poised to execute the endeavor and sell their very souls, if necessary, to save her.

But not if they thought she'd lost her mind.

"I'm not hysterical," she assured them between gulps of air. She fanned her flushed cheeks with her hands.

Gil leveled his gaze on her, surveying her from top to bottom. "She's good to go," he said brusquely. "Just letting off steam."

To prove him right, Maude forced her demeanor to seriousness and tucked away her joy. Straightening her body, she squared her shoulders and assumed the position: her tush facing the spiral aperture at the rear of the transit pad, her smile toward her scowling mentor.

"You're a Rogue, but you're going to have to fight your instincts," Dak said. His features were drawn and flat. For a split second, Maude remembered him frozen in time as the victim of Vesuvius. Dak had once waged a similar war with his instincts and lost.

"If you fail, I can't rescue you," Dak added.

"Acknowledged," Maude replied. The sobering reminder helped focus her attention.

Although she couldn't imagine the conflicts ahead, she gathered from Dak's expression that the most powerful and experienced Rogue in Core could—and that they could be grueling. Dak was telling her he had envisioned and prepared for the worst. And, for the good of the mission, she needed to prepare as well.

Gil flexed his muscles a few times and growled. "If we don't get this show on the road pronto, *I'm* gonna lose it.

Ready or not, Rome, here we come," he added with mounting verve. "Do what you have to do, Bob. Hit it."

Dak grunted his agreement and Bob complied; lowering his visor, he faced his console and commenced the sequence. Lights, pink sterilizing fog, then the thick clear blast door lowered, sealing off the transit pad.

Maude glanced over at Gil as the fog swirled between them. He'd mimicked her position and stood resolute, grinning. Maude's heart jumped. She loved him. Oh, how she loved him.

With countless transits recorded on her identilog, she'd thrilled to each and every one. They were never routine. However, this one was special—it could be her last, and she was sharing it with Gil.

A rush of air whipped at her body and tugged at her gear as the aperture slowly opened behind them, exposing the vast, inky void of the transit tunnel. The noise was deafening. Maude's pulse raced as adrenaline surged through her body; blood pumped at her temples and wrists till she felt like she was purring. In spite of the chill from the tunnel, sweat from her energized body soaked through her garb. Gil was still grinning.

"Ready?" she shouted above the din. Solids surrounding the pad shifted and blurred into masses of spinning color; Bob had activated the transit.

Gil winked, and Maude realized one immutable fact: This cowboy was born ready. It was another quality that seemingly tethered her, body and soul, to this megalicious male.

"I love you," she blurted, the ever-increasing maelstrom sucking the words into the clamorous soup that swirled about them.

Gil furrowed his brow. "What?" he shouted, and cupped one hand to his ear.

She could only smile and shake her head. It was enough.

She'd said it for the first time in her life—and maybe the last.

"Here we go," she mouthed instead, and offered her hand, delighting to the spark of heat igniting when he snagged it and pulled her close. Palm to palm, their fingers entwined, the pad nudged them into the yawning darkness till it swallowed them whole.

THIRTY-ONE

"It's obviously not a recall from Core," Mackenzie repeated, staring at the split screen on Rick's buffed slimline unit. "I don't get it. And what's all this gibberish supposed to mean?"

Rick had apparently downed half a pot of coffee trying to figure it out before she'd stumbled onto the tableau in the kitchen nook. The two males in the household—one human and the other an ottoman-sized, pumpkin orange feline—were bent over the device front and center on the café table. Yosemite Sam swatted at it from time to time as Rick replayed its tonal message.

Mackenzie heated some milk before wedging her thickening body next to Rick's on the bench. Clutching the steaming cup in both hands, she sipped slowly and glanced at the clock. Midnight. Then she went back to considering the screen display between flicks of the cat's tail. Sam had lost interest in the beeping object, shifting his massive body and fixing his penetrating gaze on her drink.

"What gives? Core's *never* sent a message like this before," she said, teasing the cat from its unauthorized perch with a splash of milk in her saucer.

"Nope. It's not official," Rick agreed. "But it's important."

"You sure? It could be a joke—or maybe someone managed to tap into Core's Rogue transmissions and this is spam," she suggested.

"Futuristic spam?" Rick laughed. "Unlikely. This is deliberate. The symbols are ancient Phoenician graphics, of course, alphabetical equivalents to our A through G. But they are meaningless in this sequence without a code-cracking Rosetta Stone. The music, however— well, that's from the movie *Casablanca*."

"'As Time Goes By'," Mackenzie cried. She grinned suddenly, and slapped the table. "You're right. It is. I didn't recognize it at first—those off-key notes threw me. Play it again . . . Sam." She scratched under the cat's chin.

Rick snorted at the pun but complied. Meanwhile, the symbols marched across the screen in no apparent order or correlation to the music.

He started to state the obvious when Mackenzie waved for him to hush. Closing her eyes she sang the lyrics, the ones she remembered. She opened her eyes when she finished. "Anything?"

"You've got a beautiful voice," Rick offered.

She slapped at him. "Any *clues?*"

"Afraid not. What about the movie itself?"

"That's a thought," she returned. "Well, you have the same first name as Bogart's character. The plot is all about expatriates trying to flee for freedom. And, there's all that blackmailing and bloodletting to get letters of transit. . . ." She stopped and shook her head. "Criminy, I can read a lot into the message-within-a-message idea. It's tempting but, no, that's too far-fetched. The future is calling you, not the past. Core wouldn't know or care about classic movie details like that."

"Hmm? I suppose not." Rick stretched and yawned big. "Let's keep it simple. On the face of it, it's not a recall. But it's an alert of some kind. Something's up in the future."

Mackenzie sat bolt upright, nearly toppling her milk as she jerked her hand to her heart. "Is it Gil? Do you think he's in trouble and sending us a message?"

Rick frowned. "Gil? *Negatory*. Besides, Gil's musically challenged. Have you ever heard the kid sing? God Almighty himself probably cringes."

"It would explain the wrong notes," Mackenzie said.

"Nope. That's a stretch. Gil knows how to bellow for help. A simple SOS would suffice."

"So, if it's not Gil, then who? I'm nixing both Maude and Charlie for the same reason—they'd be direct. Who's left?"

"Dak." They both said it at once, and stared at each other.

"He's unconventional," Rick said.

"A rebel with a heart," she added. "Maude told us he's been wheeling and dealing behind Core's back." She pursed her lips as she considered the info Maude had supplied at their last briefing.

"I'm starting to put two and two together," she said.

"And?"

She blinked as the foggy remnants of sleep lifted from her brain. The wrong notes—they weren't accidental. And neither were the symbols.

"Come with me," Mackenzie suddenly crowed. Snagging her husband by the neck of his T-shirt, she pulled him along as she fairly skipped through the house and flicked on the lamp beside her piano. Plopping down on the bench, she opened the lid and fingered the keys for a few moments, picking out the melody and singing along.

"You've broken the code," Rick whispered, and planted a kiss on the top of her head as she worked through the tune until she'd inserted all the wrong notes, scratching lyrics in the margin of a handy hymnal as she proceeded.

"You would have too after another pot of coffee. The message isn't gibberish."

Rick studied the display again. "Damn. You're right. Any other archaeologist with half a brain would have figured it out an hour ago."

"That the symbol sequence correlates with the wrong notes in the tune? Give me a break. This message is unique, tailor-made for the two of us to decode."

"But my ego deserves a butt-kick for this one. I'm the purported king of sleuthing in this family, and I nearly missed the damned link to the lyrics. Criminy."

She played through the piece again and shook her head. "Wow," she said. "Dak, or whoever, is one clever dude."

"What's the message?" Rick asked, squinting at the notes she'd made.

"I'm guessing on the punctuation, but here goes," Mackenzie said, and started reading the highlighted lyrics. " 'You fundamental. You can matter. Future woman needs man. Man can deny. It's old fight. Glory or die.' "

"Maude's in trouble," Rick growled. "I knew it. Damned level twelve mission. Pushing her into it before she's ready. I'm gonna kick me some butt."

"Whoa, cowboy," Mackenzie broke in, spinning around on the piano bench to face him. "I agree with some of that. Maude's in trouble. But, there's a twist. There's gotta be. Core's got Rogues out the yin-yang to rescue her if she's in *that* kind of trouble. We've got some Rogue training, enough to qualify for on-call status, but we're not the bona-fide cavalry."

"No?" Rick grumbled, his scowl a fiery expression of disagreement. "I don't give a damn what the other

Rogues can do, it's *Maude*." He snarled as he stalked the length of the living room. "We can do something."

Mackenzie pressed her lips tight, waiting for the storm to subside. Rick was right; they—or rather, he—could do something. The message was a specific request from Dak for help. Rick's help.

But how? And when?

She hissed after glancing at the lyrics again. The clues were terse. The last phrase, "glory or die," had frightening implications. But "man can deny" seemed like an escape clause. Rick had options. It wasn't a command performance. He could just say no.

She shared her insight. Rick nodded, stopping in front of her. It appeared that he'd exorcised some of his frustration and could contribute to a rational analysis of the message now.

"You think so? Let me see that again," he said, and scanned the highlighted text. "Dak needs me. I'm fundamental. Maude's in trouble. It's an 'old fight'—whatever the fuck that means. And my participation is *optional?* What the hell kind of message is that?"

"You two bonded, right?"

"So?"

Rick didn't get it, obviously. But she did. Dak was already heavily indebted to them. They'd helped Maude save his hide in Pompeii, so he felt bad asking for help. They didn't owe Dak anything. They didn't have to throw in with him or help out in any way.

But? Rick and Dak were birds of a feather. And "future woman needs man."

"In summary, it's illegal and dangerous," she translated. "It's a damned call to arms for you damned heroes. And I know you're going to answer it."

Rick grinned, his brow smoothing out as the burden of indecision slipped away. "Yeah."

THIRTY-TWO

The force of their landing knocked Gil to his knees. *Shit*. Marble flooring hurt. He squeezed his eyes shut and grimaced through the pain till his kneecaps numbed—hypersensitivity to all things had a downside. But the utter silence after their riotous journey stumped him.

He popped one eye open and surveyed the scene. The swirling vortex of color and light that had propelled them through time and space was dissipating.

Maude was with him, still gripping his hand, but she was crouching behind a massive marble column. She held one finger to her lips. He nodded, tried and failed to move closer. His limbs were rubbery and powerless. If a gnat called him out right now, the bug would win.

His peripheral vision improved and expanded by the second. Formless features crystallized into recognizable shapes. There were more columns—lots of them, he guessed from the line of shadows cast on the wall behind him. There would have to be plenty to support the weight of the veined milk expanse of Carrara marble sheathing the floor-to-ceiling surfaces of the spacious templelike structure.

Dak had told him their destination: Rome. Maybe their arrival was in one of the city's countless landmark monuments. He didn't recognize it, but then again, his one and only visit here hadn't included a grand tour of the city's architecture.

With a pop like that of a huge soap bubble, sound returned. The sudden clamor was unnerving. He clapped his hands over his ears and blocked some of the din created by a multitude of voices echoing within the spacious structure. It was a debate, and a heated one at that. But, about what?

Hellfire. His Italian was rusty. The echo was horrific in the edifice, but still he should be comprehending something.

Maude tugged him closer, and Gil realized that thankfully the strength had returned to his limbs. His body had adjusted to the comforting feel of terra firma under his . . . knees. He adjusted his position and squatted next to Maude and tried to remember Dak's directive to stay focused. But it was tough. The mystery of the shouting match occurring offstage from his box seat on history was tantalizing.

Maude pivoted her wrist scanner and pointed. "Charlie," she mouthed, and counted down the seconds with her fingers.

She moved fast, too fast for Gil to do anything gentle. She bolted from their hiding place like a barrel-racer out of the chute. He tagged her within two or three seconds, his full-body tackle knocking the wind out of her and leaving them both sprawled on the floor, exposed. She cried out with the smidgen of breath remaining in her flattened lungs. She flapped her limbs in the general direction of the crowd, scanning it with her wrist unit and ignoring—an admirable feat—the fact that he'd pinned her like a butterfly.

When Gil was fairly confident he had contained her within the transit window, he dared a glance at the throng. The sight slapped him silly. The toga gang didn't appear aware of their arrival. Their camouflaging garb had worked. But Gil couldn't be sure because at the far end of the chamber, another scene unfolded, riveting every eye. Two time travelers tumbling into the dramatic event went entirely unnoticed.

Rising en masse, the gathering cheered a stark and stately figure draped in royal purple as he entered.

"Caesar! Hail!"

Gil had seconds to assimilate his eyewitness account with a lifetime of historical facts he'd crammed into his brain.

Holy Bejeezus. *The* Caesar? Julius?

This wasn't the Rome he'd anticipated. It was Rome, all right, but it was circa 44 BC. And the toga-wearing set had to be the Senate, a fraternity of Rome's elite about to do more than haze their notorious leader.

No wonder Gil's rusty language skills weren't helpful—ancient Latin and Greek were spoken in this era. But Dak had been right—he didn't need a language refresher to comprehend the significance of the day. This was Caesar's ill-fated Ides of March.

To Gil's horror, he was powerless to intervene, but equally powerless to turn away as the tragedy unfolded before him.

It happened swiftly. With daggers drawn, the Senate rushed Caesar. The point of one blade caught the emperor's left shoulder. At first blood, a mighty roar rose from the throats of the attackers, fueling their frenzied assault. Bearing down on the man from all sides, they struck wildly, wounding others as well as their prey.

It was worse than a car wreck. Gil couldn't tear his gaze away from the grisly scene. Blood splattered marble, stained snowy togas, and dripped from shiny blades. He felt Maude flinch beneath him as she too witnessed each blow of Caesar's foes.

An intrusive figure flashed into the scene. So involved were they in their haste to murder their emperor, no ancient Romans noted Charlie's presence joining their mob.

Maude trained her scanner in the direction of the scene and activated something.

"What in the hell?" Gil grunted.

Maude struggled beneath him. "It's Charlie," she wheezed, and kept her scanner on her target, tracking his dash through the melee.

"I know. *Shit*. What's he doing?"

Maude shook her head. "My job. Drutz. I can't contact him now. It's too risky to distract him while he's testing the prototype," she hissed, and thrashed around some more. "Can't breathe. Get off me."

"Keep him in your sights," Gil snapped, not budging an inch. "It's not over yet. You might have a chance for contact when Caesar goes down—if Charlie doesn't go down first. It'll happen any minute. Right in front of Pompey's statue."

Maude twisted around and glanced at Gil. "You know this event?"

"Stay focused," Gil growled.

It was brutal. The final blows: Long after Caesar ceased defending and deflecting the attack, the conspirators persisted. As he clung to the base of the statue, the mask of death upon him, the killers continued. Even when he slowly slipped to the ground at the foot of the marble tribute, Rome's elite huddled around his corpse, driving their blades into him, until Gil knew they all owned the death of their leader.

"Now!" he hissed and pointed.

Charlie stood apart from the murderers. His garb was blood-spattered, his face pale with an alien expression twisting his features—a silent scream of horror. Maude activated the unit and directed a short burst of light, a brief but brilliant blue beam, in Charlie's direction.

Dak, Bob and Maude had told Gil during the planning stages that the contact code was standard, something all Rogues recognized as an inaudible visual recall to Core. Was it too little, too late? It was for Caesar, Gil realized. But he prayed to heaven above that it wasn't for Maude.

THIRTY-THREE

"Unscheduled transit?" The lead Transitor at Transit Station Bravo frowned as Rick stepped off the pad. Rick acknowledged the fact but supplied little else. He had discussed it with Mackenzie, and determined the prudent strategy involved not arousing undue concern.

As an on-call Rogue, every transit to date had been initiated by Core, both to and from the future. However, self-transits for his Rogue classification weren't forbidden. They weren't even that unusual. He said so.

The Transitor nodded wearily and processed Rick without further inquiry, logging his arrival and clearing him for entry. Bravo was a high-volume transit station. Rick had selected it for that very reason.

The warning klaxon sounded, lights switched to amber, and the blast door automatically lowered. Another transit retrieval was pending.

Rick grabbed a hoverlift and powered it up. A surreptitious glance at the busy lead Transitor assured him that phase one of Operation Casablanca was a complete success. He'd slipped past Core's first threshold of scrutiny without challenge.

He nosed the lift away from the station and set a course for Rogue Central. It was an obligatory stop; a check-in with Charlie's replacement was phase two of the plan.

With luck on his side, he'd succeed there too. One more hurdle and he was free and clear to lend Dak a hand.

Maude landed on her butt—a first for a certified Rogue.

"Ouch." Gil howled beneath her, rubbing the back of his head where it had made contact with the grid flooring.

She smiled at him but Gil didn't return it. Another first.

They were tangled again, like they had been on the earlier transit from Dallas, her bottom resting comfortably atop Gil's groin. But that's where the similarities ceased. Gil wasn't enamored of her behind—he was crimson with anger and spoiling for a fight. And this wasn't one of Core's standard transit retrieval stations, full of pink sterilizing fog and able personnel. They were in one of Dak and Charlie's covert transit sites.

Maude processed the situation immediately. She might be an SE, and a persona non gratis Rogue at this moment, but she still possessed stellar transit recovery skills; she adjusted quickly. Pulling herself upright, she offered Gil a hand up.

"Thanks," he grumped. He was still rubber-legged and understandably foul-tempered. Both were byproducts of transits, and were temporary. Once he was on his feet, he rejected her support and stomped around, shaking out his limbs and swearing under his breath with every step.

Maude admired Gil's stamina. His natural abilities were telling. With only a few transits to his credit, it was miraculous he was functioning and fuming. And he looked better than functional. He looked ferocious and clearly intent on recovering without her help.

She smothered her appreciative smile and swung away from him, surveying their surroundings more closely.

They had launched the mission from Dak's illegal transit pad, dubbed Romeo, but clearly Bob had switched them to plan B for retrieval. Cold, sooty, and dark, this covert transit site in Outskirt 13 wasn't cushy. The sublit triangular grid was elevated and temporary. Dubbed Juliet, the arrival location was little more than a landing bay. It lacked the necessary equipment and connections to Core's mysterious transit vortexes to qualify as anything other than the most limited emergency transit site. It obviously couldn't launch. And, Maude guessed by the look of things, it had only been activated to receive transits for their benefit.

Maude brushed at her sooty garb and coughed. Their unceremonious arrival had stirred the air, and minute particles of ash and dirt were still settling to earth.

She jumped down from the grid. Utilizing the flash from her wrist unit to supplement the glow from the grid, she explored the immediate area. She headed down a smallish tunnel, followed by Gil.

"Ah-ha," she cried when the flash's beam defined a familiar object. As she approached the mesh screen and bench area of Outskirt's neglected tram station, atmospherics activated, illuminating the immediate platform, tram line, and intersecting approaches with menial lighting. She circled the station, carefully avoiding the floor sensors that would automatically route a tram to their location and alert Core to her presence. She checked the lift storage and was relieved to find one freshly charged unit.

Gil trotted over and joined her. He was tight-lipped and terse. "Plan B. Better check your unit for messages. I don't have any."

His clipped tone alarmed her. Either he hadn't completely recovered or he was legitimately angry. Consideration for either would have to wait, however. She activated her split screen; scrolling through data, she highlighted a directive from Bob.

"The alternate-site retrieval was a precaution," she said with a sigh of relief. "If one of us heaved the cloaking serum, they didn't want Core to pick up our signals when we arrived at the complex. We're cleared to return to Dak's."

"Fine," Gil snapped. He stepped around her, activated the lift, and climbed on board. "The sooner, the better. I'm feeling strongly compelled to jettison this damnable goo. Hop on. I'm driving."

She started to comply, but the notation suddenly flashing on her bio readout stopped all progress. Her chest constricted. Her breath had vanished. Her heartbeat, too. She couldn't blink, cry, or think, because something was terribly wrong.

Gil's voice penetrated the fog of emotion stirred up by the message. He sounded far away, too far to catch her if she fell. And she thought she would.

She stared at her SE alert, at the addition to her bio screen tracking the rotations remaining on her life-clock. *It isn't right!* She silently screamed the denial, her eyes flicking over the display, willing it to reset and fix itself. Prior to the Rome mission, the life-clock indicated that twenty-eight rotations remained. Now it indicated twenty-three.

There were possible explanations: a transit fault, an implant failure, et cetera. But explanations were cold comfort for a female staring at her own mortality, watching it pulse away by the second.

She felt Gil's arm slide around her body. She wanted to close her eyes, sink into the blissful oblivion his strength and heat offered. And maybe she had, because she'd lost track of how he'd moved her onto the lift and secured her within his embrace.

"What is it?" he asked. His voice was thick with concern. The anger was gone and her hero was back.

She wouldn't speak—a childish and cowardly ploy to put off the truth and ignore it away. But that didn't work. Gil snagged her wrist and checked her split screen. He swore when the realization struck.

His agonized groan echoed within the desolate cavern and sent shivers up her spine. Like a wounded beast, Gil was territorial, defensive, dangerous. If only he could confront their enemy. But he couldn't turn back the clock and neither could she. Time was a formidable foe.

The mission to contact Charlie had been costly. Another peek at the data-byte confirmed it was all too real. During that fifty-minute jaunt to the past, she'd lost five precious days of life.

"We need a new plan. Another attempt to contact Charlie is out," Gil stormed, refusing to step back onto the transit pad. They were gathered at the transit station beneath Dak's villa. "It's obvious. Maude can't transit again."

Bob's drawn features were flushed from a similar outburst. He'd diagnosed the defect in Maude's SE reading and declared it problematic and fixable. Another mission *should* work. He had Charlie's coordinates for the next contact opportunity loaded into Romeo's transit console. The pad was prepped. The clock was ticking. He was ready to launch.

Dak withheld his opinion on the matter. His knuckles were white where he gripped the console's edge, and he was staring glassy-eyed at the display that indicated no acknowledgment of the recall or deviation in Charlie's mission stats.

Gil kept tabs on Maude as they talked. She was unresponsive. Stoic and silent, she slowly skirted one corner of the launch area looking like the fight had been kicked out of her.

I've got enough fight for both of us, he silently declared. He was determined to succeed. They might have lost the battle to contact Charlie, but he damn sure wasn't going to lose the war. There had to be another way to save Maude's life.

"There has to be an alternative," Gil announced.

Dak detached his hold on the console and faced them. He cleared his throat. "Charlie didn't acknowledge the recall because he didn't receive it. It's visual and silent, a noninvasive signal that is meant to pass without comment by era-inhabitants. It could easily escape the notice of a Rogue intent on testing a prototype."

"Caesar's assassination was a bloodbath," Gil agreed. "I'm not sure how Charlie blitzed through the thick of it without injury."

"He's testing the range and duration of protection the prototype affords against diverse weaponry. Deflecting multiple dagger thrusts is risky. I didn't know he was trying that. You indicated he was blood-spattered?"

"But apparently unwounded," Gil clarified.

"Then that will suffice for his test. He's established tolerances and collected data."

"A dagger isn't a bullet," Gil reminded him.

"Correct. It's safer."

"That was safe?" Gil shouted. "That was suicide."

Maude flinched. She glared at him with her big blue eyes and defended her mentor. "It is part of what Rogues do, Gil. It's what I'm trained to do too. We need to be prepared for this sort of danger, and Charlie's trying to see how his device will work after transit—and in variable situations."

Gil felt the anger rush through him like a mighty wind, stirring up everything he'd stuffed down the moment he'd glimpsed Maude's SE data. "Nuts," he snarled, and shook his head. "All of you. Certified wackos."

Bob blinked, looked around at all the faces and interjected the correction. "Certified Rogues," he said quietly. "They risk their lives every day to protect Core and save people."

"We don't need to defend what we do to you," Maude growled, crossing to Gil. He was heartened to note that she'd abandoned her corner and was coming out swinging. God love her, but she was a survivor.

She drilled a finger into his chest. "I don't expect *you* to understand. How could you?" she said. "You don't know what we're up against, how we've survived, or what we've sacrificed to save humanity and preserve its intellect and culture."

Gil shook his head. "No, I guess I don't. And I suppose you can't tell me, seeing as you took that oath and all. But you've got my respect and admiration."

"You called us all wackos," she snapped.

Gil chucked her under the chin. "Well . . . it takes one to know one."

She smiled then. Her color was back. Her determination too. She climbed atop Romeo's transit pad and backed up against the aperture.

Gil knew he couldn't stop her; she was going, regardless of risk, with or without him.

"Then you're coming with me?" she asked.

He sighed. "Love," he growled, "I'll go to hell and back with you, if it'll save your life." And to prove his sincerity, he jumped up onto the transit pad and sealed the deal with a kiss.

THIRTY-FOUR

Another day, another glitch. Mackenzie scowled at the text she'd just read on the Kennedy conspiracy. Either her memory was faulty or there was a flaw in the fabric of time. The errors in data were collecting one by one, piling up slowly like falling snow.

She'd inherited her Granny Moon's talent for sleuthing, a gift that thrived in the small hours of the morning. So, after sending Rick off to the future with a kiss at the crack of dawn, she had settled into her cushy chintz wingback with her laptop and indulged herself by researching the JFK event. The effort was calculated to keep her two steps ahead of her worries, and it almost worked.

However, nailing down facts as a basis to build legitimate queries was more troublesome than expected. The mysteries and curiosities that still shrouded the assassination were compounding. Her research, so far, had exposed more issues than it had resolved.

She'd stumbled onto more errors in history. They were minor, subtle alterations that individually had no impact, but collectively they suggested something significant to her. Something significant and sinister. A new worry had temporarily displaced Mackenzie's concern about Rick's mission.

The errors might be symptomatic. Was the future messing with the past again?

"Hmm," she mused aloud, her pulse jumping as she pondered the theory. "It *is* possible."

The cat beside her stirred, leveling another complaint about the disruption of his sleep cycle.

"Sorry, Sam." Mackenzie shifted in her seat. It was a tight fit with the cat, the computer, and her bottom. But, the optional element—the feline—held his ground, apparently committed to guarding her during Rick's absence. The sweet comfort of his raspy purr did help moderate her mounting concern.

Mackenzie stroked Sam's silky head as she glanced through her notes. Dak's message had included the lyric "old fight." He'd triggered a time rift once before with his Pompeii jaunt. Could another one be the crux of their current problem?

It was a reasonable question, given the life-changing events she'd experienced two years earlier. Since becoming a time traveler and an on-call Rogue for the future world of Core, her concept of the probable and possible had expanded tenfold. Connecting the errors with a pending rift or migrating time line wasn't far-fetched.

A Rogue primarily because of her expertise as an historian, her data collection and analysis skills had enhanced Core's understanding of Earth's past. Not all changes resulting from time travel were significant or warranted fixing. Her contributions, and Rick's too, had helped establish a Consequence Factor, applicable when determining priority missions to repair or restore timelines. She applied it to her data findings. Did it warrant sending an alert to Core?

Her nose itched—a valuable clue that she was either on to something and this was a psychosomatic hint, or she was having an allergic reaction to the surplus of shellfish she'd been consuming lately. She opted for the former.

Her blood was up. Her pulse chugged along at a jackrabbit clip. Adventure was calling, but unlike Rick she couldn't answer.

At the same time, she was still a Rogue, even when forced to the sidelines because of her pregnancy. And Rogues could do something. If she was correct, a cosmic storm was brewing. Just where, when, or how it would hit wasn't clear. But if she was going to help everyone weather it, she needed to prepare.

THIRTY-FIVE

"Okay, we're agreed," Gil said as he flexed his knees and backed against the aperture. "We're going to do this thing, no matter what. It's the only way."

Maude admired him. Gil committed quickly and decisively—another Rogue-worthy trait that pushed all her buttons.

"Hey, Dak," he hooted as the blast door started to lower. "Destination?"

"Washington—the capital, not the state," Dak called out. A moment later the panel snapped in place and the space flooded with pink fog.

Gil frowned and turned to Maude for confirmation. "Did he say when?"

She shrugged as the jasmine-scented cloud tickled her nose. If he had, she hadn't caught it. "Does it matter?"

"I'm curious. Aren't you?"

She admitted she wasn't. Her curiosity had evaporated. Her courage too—although she didn't share that with Gil.

He kissed her palm and nodded.

Does he know? she wondered. Could he see she was crumbling inside, that her shell was hollow and brittle? This wasn't a typical mission. It wasn't even the challenging level twelve she'd trained for and anticipated. It was worse than an ordeal. It was a nightmare rife with dread and unspeakable terror. It lacked transit essentials. The cadre of her peers, the other Rogues, was absent from the scheme of planning and rescue. Without the basics and the backing of Rogue Central, Maude's cloak of confidence felt like a sham, a ruse.

The familiar whine, thump, and pressure adjustments warned her. She braced herself as the aperture opened.

The racket from the inky vortex assaulted her ears and triggered a shock wave of panic. The sweet residue of Charlie's signal-blocking goo lingered, but her mouth was dry. Her knees were stiff and achy. And the implants that should have buffered most of her fear couldn't filter its flinty stench or stall the quavering of her voice.

She gripped Gil's hand and pulled him closer. She felt she had to brace herself for the possibility: "If we aren't successful in contacting Charlie on this mission," she shouted above the thunderous din, "we'll have to go again."

"Don't worry, love," Gil yelled back. "If this one doesn't work, third time's the charm."

Maude stifled her sneeze. These proscenium curtains were thick with dust. She pinched her nose and Gil did the same until the cloud of particles the transit had kicked up dissipated. Their perch above the theater stage below appeared ideal, albeit filthy and hot from the gas-fired lamps below. Hidden among the shadows, rigging, scene drops, and extra curtains stored in the fly loft, they could survey everything without discovery.

"Drutz," she growled after checking her wrist unit. Bob's hole-punching technology wasn't perfect. The readout indicated they were off the mark relative to Charlie's coordinates.

It was a minor flaw—one of elevation. But it was something she needed to resolve quickly if she hoped to contact Charlie before the event instead of after.

Gil scowled. "What now?" he whispered.

She showed him her split screen and he rolled his eyes. With an exchange of heated whispers and sign language, they discussed their options.

Their current perspective afforded a full view of the play in progress far below, but a limited view of the audience beyond the flickering footlights. And somewhere beyond the lights was her target. They were going to have to abandon their catbird seat.

Maude checked her mission chronometer. They had time.

Climbing down without arousing attention wasn't difficult in the sublit backstage area. After Gil scanned the fly loft to confirm the parameters of the transit window, he took the lead and Maude let him. They were down the ladder and crouched behind props within moments. The backstage hush was profound. Actors awaited cues. Wardrobe matrons tucked ingenues into massive hoopskirts or powdered their painted faces. And the stagehands, those not bent to tasks, were riveted on the little comedy center stage.

Gil's viselike grip held her fast as Maude rechecked the coordinates. They were good. She could hear the dialogue exchange—the clever banter that titillated the audience, and the sporadic applause when certain characters entered the scene. But she couldn't see anything. Her line of sight with Charlie's impending arrival point was blocked. The back curtain and a layer of scenery were formidable obstructions, and a pile of props and costumes another. They needed to move again, as far as the transit window would allow.

Maude leaned close to apprise Gil of their situation, but she didn't get a chance. He jerked away from her suddenly. Even in the shadows, Maude could see the look of surprise on his face.

"Stay here," he hissed. "Your word on it. Don't budge till I get back."

In a smooth and silent move, he backed into the darkness and disappeared. He wasn't gone long. When he returned, his demeanor had changed dramatically. His face was drawn and serious. His eyes were dark as midnight. Gone was the glint of devilish delight; in its place was a fixed intensity that was fearful to regard.

"What is it?" Maude whispered, pulling him into the dimly lit corner to study him more closely.

Gil looked through her, not seeing her but imagining something that captured both his heart and soul. His anguish was unmistakable, and Maude wanted to force it out of him.

"What's wrong?" she asked quietly.

"This is Ford's Theatre." He stopped and buried his face in his hands for a moment. "My God," he moaned. "It's Good Friday."

Maude's palms were sweaty. The taste of fear was back. She was afraid again, blood-chillingly and bone-quakingly afraid, but not for herself. She was scared for Gil.

"I know where you must contact Charlie," he said.

She tried to swallow. It wasn't easy.

"Where?" she finally managed.

"In President Lincoln's opera box."

THIRTY-SIX

Gil couldn't breathe. His chest was tight. He knew the facts; few didn't. And in the next few moments he would hear, see, and feel the horror of Lincoln's assassination firsthand. He couldn't prevent it, although every fiber in his being wanted to. Dak had reminded him once again before transit: "Stay focused on Maude." But remaining detached from the impending calamity required strength Gil lacked.

"You know this event." Maude didn't pose it as a question or an accusation; she whispered it like a prayer.

Gil could see the concern in her eyes and felt a tremor race through her body as her fingers touched his cheek. A spark of understanding linked them in that moment. She knew his heart; she knew his mind.

"You can't save him," she said quietly.

But he could. One of America's darkest hours could be averted if he could stop Booth's bullet. He had to try.

He had seen the state box and the figures within. The poignant picture had pierced his resolve. Lincoln's tall frame reclined against the horsehair rocker's seatback; he looked relaxed. The weight of the long and bloody civil war that had threatened to destroy the nation was lifted at last. His wife, her dark curls bouncing, was clearly enjoying the play. Fluttering her fan in animated delight, she exchanged whispers with the other guests in the box. A night out. This was a bereaved couple still recovering from the loss of their beloved son, persevering through adversity and gleaning small pleasures in the company of friends.

It wasn't too late. Lincoln was alive.

"You can't," Maude repeated firmly. "You can't change the past."

Why? Gil's brain demanded. Nothing made sense to him. It was 1865, and he'd just seen Lincoln smile.

Maude didn't try to restrain him. The choice was his. He knew the risk; Bob had explained it to him in detail. If he exited the transit window, it would collapse and, if they survived it, strand them in the past. Without a timely rescue or any other protections afforded to her in Core, Maude would be doomed to a swift and certain death.

And what if I do stop the fatal bullet? Gil asked himself. *What then?*

Dak had drilled him on the inherent dangers caused by bungling or meddling time travelers. The resulting rifts, paradoxes of unimagined proportions, could ripple through time and forever change Earth's history and future.

Gil had been cocky and stupid. Historian that he was, he'd considered himself immune to the temptation to meddle. But he wasn't immune. Far from it. He wanted to horn in and meddle big-time.

Gil gutted up. It had to be done. Although he had the power to intervene and make a difference to one man and a nation, he didn't have the right. Lincoln belonged to the ages. Maude might still have a future. His choice was clear.

Maude's unit flashed a warning. Charlie's transit signal. They had less than a minute to prepare for his arrival.

"I need to move," Maude said.

Gil nodded. "Follow me."

Booth's garbled cry of retribution as he leapt to the stage was the actor's last performance. It was a showstopper, and shocking to all who witnessed but failed to comprehend the magnitude of his foul deed. So stunned were they, Booth made good his escape, exiting through the wings and backstage without pursuit.

Mary Lincoln's shrieks resonated throughout the theater. Her cries galvanized aid for her husband that was too late to matter but incited alarm among the audience and actors alike.

Gil caught Booth as he passed. Wrenching him up by his neck till his feet dangled, Gil squeezed. All around, pandemonium ensued. Actors and stagehands bolted for safety. Somehow, no one took notice of him or the slight man twisting in his grasp.

"Know this," Gil snarled as he tightened his hold on the murderer. Booth clawed at Gil's fingers. His eyes bulged and his skin purpled as he desperately gasped for air. "You will die within a fortnight," Gil raged. "Shot like the mad dog you are. Your corpse will be spit upon, buried in unhallowed ground, and your name cursed for eternity."

Booth stopped struggling, and Gil tossed him down like a piece of garbage. "God have mercy on your soul."

Gasping for breath, Booth crawled away and pulled himself up by the doorframe at the rear exit of the theater. He stared back at Gil, his eyes wild with fright.

A portent of death from a futuristic soothsayer? Gil could only imagine Booth's thoughts. But he was sure that he'd smothered the killer's gleam of maniacal triumph with his prophecy of doom.

"Stop that man!" The shout from the wings and the

thunder of footsteps spurred Booth through the doorway and onto his waiting horse. The chase was on.

"Stop! Stop!" Booth's pursuers shouted. As they passed, Maude jerked Gil back into the shadows, held him fast.

It wasn't necessary. Gil wasn't compelled to join the chase. This wasn't his time. This wasn't his fight. He'd made his choice. He was all about Maude and the future.

And, thankfully, their mission was complete. Maude had seen Charlie and transmitted the recall seconds before Booth fired the bullet from his derringer into Lincoln's brain.

"Ready?" she whispered.

Gil had lost the power of speech for the moment; he could only nod.

Maude seemed to understand, and she hugged his neck as she initiated transit. Gil closed his eyes to this sorrowful place. He was heartsick and drained of anger. And as their retrieval commenced, he took comfort from the feel of Maude's warm, firm body next to his.

They'd done it. Maude would live and be safe.

THIRTY-SEVEN

Raymond queried Hickham again; he needed advice, from one director to another.

He looked around the brightly lit lab. Staff and Rogues alike were busy. The prepping slabs were filled. Consoles were staffed and humming with industry. The heartbeat of Central, as everyone called it, the great pumping station housed within the complex, continued unabated. Everything looked normal. But it wasn't.

Raymond's concerns were mounting. The retrieval squad had failed to secure the SE Rogue, and until that issue was resolved and mitigated by established procedures, he was in danger of losing his first Rogue.

At first he'd assumed the SE alert was a test of his skills planned by Charlie. It challenged his adherence to protocols and eased the transition in leadership. Everyone had performed well, utilizing the conventions recently established for the new early warning classification. He too had done everything as prescribed.

However, that wasn't enough. The valuable Rogue had not been collected and processed.

Raymond flinched. Another chart thudded into his inbox. The pneumatic routing system connected staff pods with the central hub, and his workload was piling up. He needed to press on and forget about the errant Rogue.

But he couldn't.

Sticking to regulations was more problematic than he'd expected. Not that it mattered, of course—a Rogue was a Rogue—but the SE happened to be Charlie's protégé. Kincaid. Losing one of the best and brightest Rogues wasn't going to look good on his record. There had to be something more he could do, something that Charlie would do if he were still here, something more than deactivate Maude's access protocols to Central and wait.

He looked around at the hub workstation that housed all of Charlie's toys, gadgets, inventions, and prototypes. He'd taken Charlie's place, but he wasn't Charlie.

Picking up a shiny gadget and puzzling over its purpose, he twisted and turned it until he admitted defeat. He couldn't build or devise anything to change Maude's fate. He had to either trust the regs or start stretching his imagination. Options for Scheduled Expirations were nil. Quarantine. No exceptions. And her time was running out.

Zat. What was Maude doing? It was her obligation to turn herself in for the safety of everyone in Core. She belonged in stasis.

Rick Mason's unscheduled visit to Central had given him an idea. The on-call Rogue was unorthodox, and a wild card. His input on other missions had demonstrated innovation and courage—of course—but also a bit of the imaginative daring and risk that the now-disabled Dak had once contributed as Charlie's peer. Relying on the retrieval squads to save Maude didn't sit well with him. Raymond itched to stretch his authority and do more. Did he dare?

"Is this how it begins?" he asked himself, and tossed down the gadget. "Bend one rule? Break another?"

His console communication link beeped. Hickham's response: *Follow procedures.*

Raymond whirled away from the screen and stood up. He didn't blame Hickham for failing to offer options; he blamed himself. He'd asked for this opportunity with the Rogues. He was technically qualified to fill in for Charlie, but the rush of power and the knee-quaking responsibility for every decision had tangled his orderly mind into a disquieting knot of doubt. The role as the Rogues' director was tougher than he had ever imagined.

He folded his arms across his chest and surveyed the efficient teams at work. Could he lead them? He could dodge the responsibility for the duration and cower behind Charlie's console till the man returned from sabbatical. These teams were well trained, independent, and resourceful. All he really needed to do was spout the regs and process paper. But with this crisis . . .

Hide or lead? The choice was his.

"Recall Rick Mason," Raymond barked to a passing assistant.

The assistant jerked to a halt. "Rick? I think he's still in Core's research zone."

"I don't care if he's in the Frontier region or a no-transit zone, get him back here. Send a retrieval squad if necessary. I need him."

"This idea is going south fast, guys," Rick commented to everyone in Dak's villa after he'd been briefed on the plan. "Just my two cents, of course."

"The idea is good," Maude countered. She wanted to hug Rick and hit him at the same time. She was glad to see him, but *drutzed* if he was going to throw everyone off course when they were so close to their goal.

She looked around at the others. The loungers were full; Falah was busy feeding and fussing over the lot, and the men were bonding in ways to which she couldn't relate.

Men. She knew what they'd come up with next, the muscle-bound brutes. They were probably going to outvote her on Quarantine and tuck her into that deep, dark sleep indefinitely. For her own good? She wasn't going to stand for it.

"I know what I did wrong," Maude stated as forcefully as she could between burps from nutrient. The mouthwatering aroma of Falah's roasted meat and buttery russets was torturous. But while Dak, Bob, and Rick tucked into their meals, she could dominate the conversation and plead her case.

She didn't doubt for a second that her partner, her lover, her hero, Gil, would back her up. They were a team. His encouraging gaze warmed her heart. It amazed her how a look or a touch from that smiling cowboy soothed her soul and bolstered her confidence.

"I know why Charlie didn't receive the recall code this time," she continued. "The excessive illumination at the edge of the stage conflicted with my signal."

"Stage?" Rick mumbled between mouthfuls.

"Ford's Theatre," Gil supplied. "Lincoln's assassination."

"Damn," Rick returned, nearly choking on a hunk of potato.

Maude cleared her throat. "As I was saying," she began again, and shared her analysis of the first and second missions to contact Charlie and how she planned to correct her transmission on the third. She concluded with a smug assurance that she would succeed on the next transit. She *couldn't* fail.

No one responded at first. Gil's obligatory intake of nutrient kept his mouth busy. But Dak and Rick looked identical, sporting expressions of concern and skepticism.

"Third time's the charm," Maude added.

Rick's head swiveled in Gil's direction. "Where'd she get that one? From you?" he asked.

Gil shrugged. "Well, it is."

"You can't be serious," Rick said. "Every time she transits she loses days on her SE. Right? What's the count now?"

Bob answered. "Thirteen. She lost *ten* rotations on the last transit."

Gil squeezed Maude's hand. When they'd returned to Juliet in Outskirt 13 and discovered the significant adjustment to her SE countdown, he'd taken it hard. He'd stormed about the desolate settlement, cursing fate and demanding justice. Maude's bones still ached from his crushing embrace. Her lips were still bruised from his hungry kisses that breathed life and hope back into the moment. And her heart and mind were still full of his empowering love, sustained by his sworn oath to right the wrong and save her life.

"She lost ten rotations?" Rick was incredulous. "Damn."

"But," Bob added. His eyes shifted from face to face, with an expression of unshakable conviction accompanying his explanation. "It is a ninety-eight percent probability that the data is incorrect, a malfunction on her chronometer resulting from my targeted transits in and out of no-transit zones—cumulative errors on the Zed scale that my programming cannot purge. We have limited capabilities with the Romeo equipment."

"But if it's not a malfunction, and if she loses another ten—or God forbid, all—of her remaining SE days, we've killed her."

"Exactly," Gil said. "That's why the mission is on, but Maude's scrubbed."

"What?" Maude cried, whirling to face him. "Not you too."

Gil grinned.

It was a huge mistake. Maude thumped him soundly with her half-filled nutrient flask before she could stop herself. The sludge splattered everywhere, and the glob hanging off Gil's nose looked like bird poop. Rick laughed. Maude gasped. One of Gil's brows twitched up, but otherwise he didn't respond except to lose the smile.

Instantly contrite, angrier with herself for losing control of her temper and her life, she sopped up the spillage. Choking out an apology to everyone, she felt hot tears collect and start to blur her vision.

"I'm not betraying you, love," Gil whispered. He stalled her efforts to clean him up. "But Rick's here now. He'll take your place and we'll get it done. It's the safest way."

"I'm not going to Quarantine," she said.

"You won't need stasis," Dak interjected. "Rick and Gil will contact Charlie and be back before it's necessary."

"Uh-oh." Rick was staring at his wrist unit. "We better jumpstart the launch unless you've got a place to hide me too. Raymond just issued a recall."

"*Drutz!*" Maude cried. "Do you think Central is on to all of us?"

"There's your answer," Gil cut in, and pointed to the perimeter alarms flashing on the villa's residential console.

"Go. Now," Falah cried, jumping up from her place beside her husband. "I will send them away."

Dak cursed and quickly assessed the nature of the intrusion. "It's another collection squad. One kilometer. I'd better handle it this time."

He hugged his wife and nodded to the others. "Take them down, Bob, and set the static field to block everyone's identilog signatures."

Maude let Gil tug her up from the lounger, but she hung back. The access hatch for the covert complex was cleverly concealed and convenient. Bob popped it open and waved everyone over. It would only take a moment for all of them to enter the tunnel and set the signal blocking field. But would the safeguards deter a determined retrieval crew?

She glanced about the dining area. Evidence of multiple guests and the substantial feast was fast disappearing; Falah had activated mop bots and scullery droids.

"Get going, Kincaid," Dak stormed at her. "I'll be down as soon as I've ejected them."

"I *can't* go to Quarantine," Maude returned in a hoarse whisper.

Dak leveled a stern gaze in her direction. "I'm giving you my word, I won't let it happen unless we're out of options."

"And we're not, Maudie," Rick called back from the hatch. "So get your butt down here. You've got to prep and brief me on this charmed mission, ASAP."

THIRTY-EIGHT

Dak quickly joined them in the complex. Explanations on how he had handled the threat and instituted all possible precautions against discovery satisfied the others. Gil had to take him at his word as well.

What the hell do I know about evading retrieval squads, anyway? he consoled himself. Beyond ingesting more signal-blocking goo, getting lost in the Frontier Zone, or attempting to outrun and outthink the roundup teams, he lacked options.

Dak's clarification about the scanning limits of the deep probe launched in the sector sounded plausible. But the news that Rick had now joined them on Core's Most Wanted list of missing personnel raised the stakes for everyone.

An SE, an EE, and now a missing on-call Rogue. Gil added up the score and figured someone at Core had to be pissed. Eluding the squads indefinitely was impossible. He didn't doubt that there were some big guns ready, willing, and able to employ all available measures to collect the strays. This was definitely their last shot at collecting Charlie and saving Maude. Gil didn't need confirmation. It was obvious. Time had almost run out for the collaborators.

They couldn't launch immediately. The scheduled transit had been set for Day 195, 05:32. Altering the commands wasn't practical or advisable; Bob had complained when Rick suggested it.

"Like the previous transits, the third launch is sequenced to coincide with others elsewhere in the transit vortex." Bob's strident tone quelled Gil's planned rebuttal. "It is the only additional means I have to cloak our activity from Core's intricate tracking system."

"Understood," Dak replied, undercutting the tension in the room with his booming voice. He noted the time on the pulsing clock affixed to the Romeo launch arena. "Five hours it is. We need the time to get you fully prepped anyway, Rick. Start sucking down nutrient while Bob uploads the contact hardware to your wrist unit."

"Five hours," Maude whispered. She leaned her head against Gil's chest for the briefest of moments. Then she announced, "I'll grab the nutrient," slipping away before Gil could snag her.

He bit back a groan. The contact left her lingering scent, the intoxicating bouquet of simmering honey that drove him mad with desire. It gave him pause. He didn't need five hours to prep. And thankfully, neither did Maude.

But before he could indulge his baser needs with the woman of his dreams, Gil had a few practical issues to bring up with the head honcho here.

"Where and when are we going?" he demanded of Dak. The man's remonstrations that *it didn't matter and the less he knew the better* weren't acceptable. Gil stressed the point. "Unacceptable," he growled. "It *does* matter. Hell of a distraction, getting dumped in the middle of two historic murders."

Maude returned and tossed a flask of nutrient to Rick.

She settled beside Gil on the padded slab, reminding him just how much spine-melting heat transference was possible from thigh-to-thigh contact. The delightful distraction didn't last.

"Murders?" Rick said as he surrendered his wrist unit to Bob for the upload. "What was the other one?"

"Caesar," Gil supplied, and rolled his eyes. "It was a damned bloodbath."

"Wow. Charlie's field-testing the prototype at murders." Rick whistled and looked around for confirmation. His gaze settled on Maude. "It was supposed to be your level twelve mission."

"By rights it was mine," Dak growled. "I planned and plotted the field tests. But the mission fell to Maude when Core married me to my transit tether. And then, of course, it fell to Charlie."

"Brief them on the next destination," Maude suddenly demanded, spinning around to face Dak. "Tell them anything that will help them succeed."

Dak scowled. "They won't need any help from us on this one," he said quietly. "It's Dallas. 1963."

Gil sat up straight, surprised, and assimilated the info. After a moment, he nodded. The destination fit the pattern; he could see it now. The testing locations weren't just murders. They were all assassinations.

"JFK," he said.

Rick groaned. "We've got our work cut out for us, Gil, if we're going to contact Charlie. There are so many variables. Is he going to be in the car with the victims? Or in the depository with Oswald?"

"You'll get two pending alerts with coordinates," Maude explained, thinking back to how her wrist unit had warned her. "The sixty-second and five-second alerts will be sufficient for positioning yourself in the line of sight of your target. You should be able to do it, no problem. Third time's the charm."

"Oh, baby." Gil snorted. "You can't begin to know how wrong you are on that point. Believe me. This one's not gonna be a cakewalk. And not just because of Charlie's damned camouflaged getup."

"Don't blame them," Rick said and shook his head. "They're time travelers but—and it's a big but—what these guys don't know about history is frightening." He glanced over at Dak and offered a shrug of apology. "What'd you do—plug the ideal testing scenario into the damned computer and go with the list of events that matched?"

"We were selective," Dak returned, and nodded for Bob to continue.

"We limited our selections to those with a plus or minus variance of three percent," Bob added. "Those were ideal for testing purposes."

"But not for us contacting Charlie," Gil argued. "We need an alternate location, Bob. Go back to the drawing board; find us another. This one won't work. There are too many places he could go."

Bob protested. "All three contact points you've seen meet my specific requirements, and only those three. I applied a filter and additional criteria for my transit requirements into no-transit zones."

He launched the time map and spun around on the group. "Look for yourself," he demanded, and traced a thin blue line through the holographic image that bisected eras. "Of the multiple incidents chosen for Charlie's mission, only these three settings can be penetrated for contact purposes."

Gil leaned close, noting more than a dozen nodes along the blue line. Three were highlighted in red.

"The Roman senate," Gil said, and pointed to the first red dot. He ran his finger to the next one. "Ford's Theatre."

"Yes, yes," Maude interjected with mounting impatience. "And the third one is here." She leaned in and stabbed the last red dot. "Dallas, 1963." She was cheek to cheek with Gil. He could hear the quick pace of her breathing and felt the tension building between their bodies.

"It will work," she hissed after a moment's pause. "The third time's the charm." She jerked back and glared at him, then Rick. Her pupils were pinpricks of black in seas of blue, her lips a thin, tight scowl. "If you can't handle it, I *will*."

"Whoa, whoa, whoa," Rick cried. "No need for charging in wildly, Maudie. Gil's just exhausting our options, that's all."

"There aren't any," she snapped.

"Okay," Rick replied. He gestured toward her vacated seat. "So, now we're back to discussing strategy. Gil?"

Gil couldn't take his eyes off Maude. He loved her fight and her courage. They made a damned fine team. Their bond had been building with each challenge and, with it, the uncanny ability to anticipate and meet each other's needs. He knew how badly she wanted to go on this mission, to take her destiny in her own hands.

It broke his heart when he realized he didn't want Maude with him on the Dallas jaunt: she had already used up too much of her remaining rotations. He didn't want to throw the rest away in desperation.

As well, this mission required more than courage for success; it needed Rick. Together, he and Gil could make it work. Their encyclopedic knowledge about the JFK assassination and major, minor, and wacko conspiracy data would be extremely handy. It didn't hurt that they were Texas boys, either. Their shared heritage included a heavy hand in the seat-of-the-pants decision-makin' department. Given all these factors, he could almost offer one of Bob's plus-or-minus-2-percent assurances that they would succeed. That was higher than he could assume for any other partnership in the room.

"Gil?" Rick repeated, and cleared his throat. "This is when you make nice. Stop staring at the pretty lady and tell us how the *fuck* we're gonna make this work. Speak up, boy."

Gil tore his gaze away and sucked in a fresh dose of brain-clearing oxygen. "It's going to be tricky," he started. "Covering the depository angle isn't good enough. If Charlie knows something about the multiple-shooter theory and testing the prototype against one of those, he could pop in anywhere. We're going to have to consider the grassy knoll."

"What about the guy with the umbrella," Rick said.

"You can't be serious." Gil grimaced. "With all of the photo documentation from Zapruder's footage to the still shots, we can eliminate most of the red herrings."

"Including the man with the black dog?" Rick added.

Gil sneered, figuratively rolling up his sleeves and digging into the subject, producing all the information he'd recently read on the subject. They continued the debate, hashing out the details and options for another hour before Bob called a halt to the proceedings.

"We've done enough planning," the Transitor declared, and stretched his slight body. He pushed away from the others, calling over his shoulder, "Launch in less than four hours. Everyone get some rest."

Nobody needed prodding. Rick followed Bob. Dak scampered up the tunnel to the waiting arms of Falah.

"Four hours?" Maude sighed. "It's not five, but it's better than nothing."

The deep-throated chuckle she gave soothed away some of the tension that had tightened Gil's every thought, deed, and word since realizing their second mission failed. He was feeling the pressure. It was now or never for his ladylove, and the stress had manifested into a noggin ache not unlike a migraine combined with a jackass's kick to the head. The ringing in his ears sounded like a swarm of cicadas nesting in his brain. The pounding in his skull felt like a pile driver was busting up concrete between his eyeballs, and the purgative side effect from the repeated doses of Charlie's goo left him weak and woozy. Dialing it down a notch or two and grabbing some shut-eye would help him regroup before the final mission.

But when Maude slipped her arms around his neck and pulled his mouth to hers, all the symptoms of stress sloughed off. The woman had magic fingers. Her breathy kiss stirred his senses to a fever pitch in a split second. And her long, lean body melded to his like superglue. She tagged him with her smile.

Pulling away she whispered, "Follow me."

Fortunately, she didn't lead him far. All Gil's limbs were stiff. He trailed her to one of several Reacclimation pods Dak had salvaged from surplus. The outmoded chambers lacked sophisticated atmospherics, but for two lovers intent on privacy, they filled the bill. For a few hours, pod six would be heaven.

Yes, heaven. It wasn't the sensual finale Gil had programmed into the system at Maude's flat. They didn't have a big brass bed. It wasn't a hot night on the Bayou, thick with the scent of magnolias. And the milky moonlight wasn't streaming through slatted blinds or kissing their bodies with its silvery glow. But the absence of atmospherics increased their ardor. It made everything more . . . real.

Maude loved him slowly, reverently, knowing him in quiet and profoundly surprising ways. She teased away his tension and lifted the burden of tomorrow with her tender kisses. Gil's unquenchable passion for her—the sight, smell, feel, and taste—consumed every thought. Tomorrow didn't exist. Only now mattered.

When she finally fell against him with a joyous cry and drifted off to sleep, Gil's heart filled to bursting. Too moved to sleep, he held her close and watched the slow rise and fall of her breasts, treasuring the sound of every breath. She had uttered words of love. She had yielded more than her body to him; Maude had gifted him with her soul.

The padded pod's interior glowed blue. That soft azure light surrounded their entwined bodies in an endless horizon, and Gil imagined he was on top of the world, embracing eternity. He felt perfect. Privileged. Pleasured. At peace. And the woman beside him had made it possible.

THIRTY-NINE

Maude's blissful dream included Gil but nothing else. Awake after a short nap, she rolled around, nestling her back and bottom against his hard body.

"Nice," he whispered into her ear. He folded one arm over her and pulled her closer. His hardness prodded her flesh, seeking and finding that delightfully intimate niche that was slick and hot. They fit together perfectly. He slid into her. Pulsing with a rhythm and course that had become as familiar as breathing, their bodies danced. Their sighs and groans of pleasure accompanied a flawless duet they knew by heart.

Gil met her needs and shared her desire. And when the wave of their passion again crested, carrying them far beyond the delicious spasm of physical climax, they dove deep into a sea of sensation that blended beauty and bliss.

"I love you," she cried breathlessly as they clung together, spent and joyous. It was the third time she'd said it to him.

Happy tears slipped down her cheeks, and she swiped at her eyes. The ardent glow persisted, yielding a new awareness of something profound within. She knew she could share everything with this man.

"I've never loved a man before," she said, her voice breaking with the admission. She rolled in Gil's arms till she could see his face, his eyes, his mouth. "I won't ever love again," she whispered.

Gil's eyes were dark and solemn. He understood completely.

He didn't protest her fatalistic comment. He didn't assure her that she would live long and love again. He knew this wasn't about the hours left on her body-clock. He got it: Maude was talking about eternity.

"I know I won't either," he replied. "Not like this. Once is enough for a lifetime."

He had loved her body many times, in many ways. And he had told her with his eyes and smiles that he loved her, too. But Gil's actions told her how much. He would do anything to save her. Anything.

"Say it again," he demanded, his voice thick with emotion.

She laughed. "I love you," she conceded, and stretched like a great cat. "Love you, love you, love you." She winked. "Is that sufficient?"

His devilish grin was back. "Thanks. That'll hold me for now."

"You'll love the side effects of this goo," Gil said to Rick. There were only two vials left, and he tossed one to his friend with a warning: "Three cc's of this stuff works like a swig of Ipecac or a box of Ex-Lax. But either way, up or down, at least it tastes okay."

"The hell you say?" Rick growled, eyeing the vial with trepidation.

Gil chortled. "Down the hatch!" He swallowed his

dose in one gulp and offered Rick a challenging look.

Rick groaned and followed suit. Bob nodded the moment their signals were masked.

"I take it we're good to go," Rick said, giving one last check of his wrist unit.

Maude nodded and wagged her finger. "Watch out for Gil. He'll tackle you if you get close to the transit window perimeter."

Rick cut his eyes over to where Gil was stretching and knocking out some deep knee bends. "Thanks for the heads up, Maudie. The kid looks like he could pack a wallop."

Gil saluted and continued with his knee bends.

"Anything else you good folks want to tell me now that it's too late to back out?" Rick joked.

"Yeah," Maude said. "Thanks."

Rick laughed, chucking her under the chin before he hopped up on the transit pad. "Any time, kid."

Time to transit, Gil reminded himself. *Keep it upbeat and positive*. It was a tall order. He could see through Dak's mask; worry edged the man's resolute expression. Even Bob 13, ever the confident brain, blinked excessively. Everything was riding on this last attempt, and Gil was hard-pressed to keep his grin in place. This was going to be a hell of a mission, the worst yet. But with Maude's big cornflower-blue eyes watching his moves and propping him up with that gaze of utter trust, he knew he could mug it long enough to clear the launch.

He encircled her biceps with his hands, lifted her entire body up off the floor and kissed her soundly. "Love you too," he growled against her mouth before he put her down.

He leapt up on the pad and took his place beside Rick, and in a matter of moments the two cowboys from Big D were headed home.

* * *

"Ouch. Get your foot out of my mouth," Gil snarled.

Rick grunted, rolled over, and sat up. "Sorry. My fault. I took you down on that one."

Gil picked grass out of his ear and caught his breath. The soft landing had been great; an upright, two-footed success, until Rick had slammed into him. The tumble down the grassy knoll had knocked the wind out of both of them.

Rick suddenly scrambled to his knees and took off, sprinting back toward the bushes. He plowed into their thickness and collapsed against the snowy white wall behind. Retching sounds were unmistakable. Gil followed but there was little he could do; vomiting wasn't usually a team sport.

Gil groaned with empathy, adding Charlie's cloaking goo to the list. Too much whiskey. A bad toss from an even badder bull. A memorable case of swine flu. What did they all have in common? They caused him to heave his guts out.

Rick recovered quickly and marched out of the greenery, madder than a one-winged bumblebee. "Damn," he snarled.

"Your signal's not cloaked anymore," Gil said, checking his wrist unit.

"No kidding," Rick replied.

"Have we blown it?"

"Nah. We're good for now," Rick said. "No-transit means that retrieval Rogues won't be able to get to us. They'll either have to drop in beyond the zone and walk to our location or wait until after the event. Either way we'll have ample time to contact Charlie and accomplish our mission. Let's get to work."

"Roger."

"You got your bearings yet?" Rick asked.

Gil spun around and surveyed the scene. "Grassy knoll. Check. Dealey Plaza. Check." He had to squint.

The November day was warm and bright. Sunlight sparkled off windshields and chrome bumpers as a trickle of traffic pulsed through the heart of Dallas. Office workers were collecting curbside, and gawkers leaned from upper-story windows along the L-section of the motorcade route that cut through the plaza. The excitement, the anticipation, was palpable. The president was coming.

"School book depository?" Gil craned his neck and looked up the street. The redbrick structure was a prominent anchor at Elm and Houston. "Check."

Live oaks fronted the facade, but above the treetops Gil could see the sixth floor. He glanced over at Rick. "Oswald's window is open," he said.

"Damn," Rick growled. "This is going to be tough."

"Understatement of the century," Gil agreed. "What's Charlie's ETA? Got anything?"

Rick glanced at his wrist unit and shook his head. "Nada. But we've got five minutes till the cars make the turn from Main onto Houston Street. Police haven't blocked all the local traffic yet."

Gil nodded. He was relieved to note that their arrival hadn't aroused curiosity. A lucky break. Although their drop-in behind the bushes at the pergola was off-target—they had wanted a higher spot, one along the triple underpass—the spectators had largely ignored their pratfall down the slope. The approaching motorcade was paramount. From the skinny-tie business-suit types to the laborers in T-shirts and coveralls, all eyes were fixed elsewhere. Although their garb blended with the landscape, they weren't invisible. Fortunately, no one took exception to a couple of jumpsuited time travelers joining the assembly.

"The transit window is broad," Gil said as he completed his scan of the parameters.

"At least Bob was able to adjust the dimensions in his

hole-punching. We can't cross Elm or get out of the general vicinity, but one of us can stake out curbside. No problem."

"That'll be you, kid," Rick returned. "I'm keen on this piece of real estate. High ground is the best vantage point in this fishbowl to drill Charlie with my laser."

"Stay clear of Zapruder's movie cam," Gil said under his breath. "We'd look like a blur or distortion, but we can't chance it. We don't want our mugs on any film footage."

Rick stretched and glanced furtively behind him in the general direction of the wall. Zapruder had just climbed up on it, and seemed to be testing his camera's panoramic capabilities. "Can't be helped," he said quietly. "We've already changed something in history."

Gil whipped his head around. "How's that?" he hissed.

Rick quickly briefed him: the glitches in the assassination factoids Mackenzie had unearthed. They'd already been here and done this.

"They are minor," Rick assured him. "While it's definitely a change from how we knew things, they haven't triggered a time rift yet. I checked when I was at Central."

Gil nodded. "Good. We need to keep it that way."

"Amen," Rick said. His features were stony.

Gil didn't need to ask about the inner turmoil he knew Rick was experiencing; he had been through it himself. That didn't make being an eyewitness to this event any easier to stomach. Just like with Lincoln, his brain rebelled. They had the power to intervene.

Gil's ears twitched. Police radios squawked, and uniformed officers adjusted barricades and diverted traffic. In the distance, he could hear the echo of roaring engines from the motorcycle escort as the motorcade passed between the tall structures lining Main Street. The shouts from the upper windows of the old county courthouse announced a visual on the approaching parade. Excitement rippled through the throng in the plaza. The crowd pressed forward. Fire escapes filled; faces lined windows.

Rick scanned the plaza again. He shook his head. "Still nothing," he said. "Either Charlie's not here yet or this damn wrist thingy can't pick up his signal. Start using your eyeballs, Gil. Ferret the guy out before it's too late."

"Roger that," Gil replied, and trotted toward the edge of Elm. Stopping next to the freeway sign, he concentrated on the immediate vicinity of the kill zone. With help from his scanner and the knowledge of what to look for, he studied every blob and blur. Charlie's tall lanky body wasn't in the area; he was sure of it.

His thumbs-down gesture back to Rick wasn't well received. Rick returned a like gesture and mouthed a curse.

Gil cursed as well when he checked his event chronometer. It was 12:29 P.M., and as the pilot car for the motorcade popped out onto Houston, its red lights flashing, Gil realized it was too late for pre-contact. The moment had arrived. Preceded and flanked by motorcycle escort, the sleek ebony Lincoln carrying the ill-fated Kennedy was now on Houston Street. Deafening cheers erupted from the crowd, outmatching the roaring engines.

A flash of pink from the First Lady's suit caught Gil's eye. In moments she would be a widow and America would lose its youngest president. He tore away his gaze. One look at Rick and he knew they were in trouble. They hadn't located Charlie.

Where was he? Gil frantically searched the faces near and far for the errant time traveler, but nothing.

Kennedy's limo turned onto Elm. From both sides of the street, spectators rushed the sidewalk, crowding closer for a glimpse of the Massachusetts boy and his beautiful bride. And still no Charlie.

There was something wrong. The other missions hadn't been like this. Charlie's pending signal and his arrival had been constants for each.

Above the din, the first pop rang out: The end had come. Gil felt the report pierce him as surely as the bullet itself could have. It tore through his illusions. It shattered the shroud of mystery for him forever, searing an image of tragedy in his brain unfettered by any filter of time. He'd witnessed the assassination.

Other gunshots followed in quick succession, echoing over the heads of these witnesses to history. And the deed was done.

Silence. Gil's brain froze, gifting him with a microsecond of noiselessness to fight his instincts and contain his fury before the world reacted. And then it did. Screams and sirens converted the riotous exuberance into voices of horror and outrage. The images were jagged: the dark limo speeding away from its snaking train, which was left headless and disoriented; the tumblebug scattering of men in uniforms, guns drawn, seeking prey.

Gil forced himself to look away. Picking through the huddled masses—those shielding their children, running for cover, or hugging the ground—he searched for a face that still wasn't there. He looked to Rick, who mirrored his confusion. Charlie had stiffed them and bypassed the event. They had failed both the past and the future. Kennedy was dead and Maude was doomed.

Gil didn't have time to weigh all the ramifications, because suddenly Rick was down. His friend's roar of protest cut through the chaos as two males muscled him to the grass.

Even in era-appropriate garb, the men were unmistakable. Their uniforms weren't vintage Texas, and neither were their sidearms. Stunners didn't fire bullets. These were Retrieval Rogues. Core had caught up with them.

However, events didn't quite occur like he expected. One second Rick and the Rogues were wrestling on the grass; the next, they were gone. Without Gil. Bob's hole-punched transit window collapsed with a *whoosh*. Gil gripped the freeway sign as the whirlwind force buffeted his body, nearly knocking him flat. The nauseating swirl of vivid hues, a blur at first, slowed as the whistling faded. A deadly stillness followed.

Gil slid to his knees. He didn't need to check his wrist unit to confirm his fate. Core had gotten its wish. He was back home in Texas permanently.

Big D, 1963.

FORTY

"I can't count the number of Core directives you violated, Mason," Raymond roared, standing in the headquarters of Rogue Central. "An illegal mission into a no-transit zone is sufficient reason to end your career." He pounded the main console with one fist and groaned.

Rick winced. The briefing loft at Rogue Central was packed. It was tight, hot, tense, and it was standing-room only as the acting director addressed him. He didn't begrudge Raymond's impromptu and public grilling; the man had a right to be furious and toss him out of the program.

"I'm speechless," Raymond raged.

Rick smothered a grin. Clearly Raymond wasn't.

"Explain yourself, Mason."

The limited information he gave only infuriated the acting director further. Rick shifted on his feet. The inquisition was justified, but he didn't feel compelled to spill his guts either. He said he was checking into the anomalies Mackenzie had recently uncovered.

"Are you mad? Independent research within historic

events is *not* sanctioned. If there are glitches in history, your penetration most assuredly contributed to them," Raymond cried, scanning a current list of time errors. "You couldn't have done all this alone. Who helped you?"

Rick stood tall, sweating under the spotlights, but stared straight ahead, unrepentant and fairly uncooperative. Freshly scrubbed, scanned, and stripped of hardware, he was essentially under house arrest. All he'd give up was his version of the old *name, rank, and serial number* surrender of information.

He had already been upbraided once by Raymond, his list of offenses itemized and weighted against the regs. But the egregiousness of his actions had rankled the director and prompted this showcase event for the benefit of all Central staff. Rick could even foresee a season of censure and restrictions if he remained with the Rogues. But he would willingly accept anything Core imposed. He didn't care, so long as Dak and the others saved Maude.

Raymond repeated his request for more details, demanding the names of any collaborators and the true purpose of this penetration into a no-transit zone. He wasn't buying Rick's lone-Rogue assertion any more than he was buying the research nature of Rick's jaunt to the past.

"I'm not qualified to supply an explanation for anyone other than myself," Rick replied. "I contributed my mean skills to investigate a developing deviation in historical fact. If or when the issue merited consideration, I was prepared to bring it to your attention."

The Rogues in attendance reacted favorably. Raymond didn't.

"This department exists for a reason, Mason." His growl quelled the enthusiasm stirring among the ranks. "Our mission is critical and highly regulated. We resolve problems. We do not create them. It is highly suspect that you acted independently. Or that you have been entirely forthright regarding your motives. The illegal penetration into a no-transit zone for any reason is unconscionable. I refuse to entertain thoughts of, endorse, or encourage deviating from the regs, now or in the future. Do I make myself clear?"

The silence in the room was stunning; no one moved for a full minute.

Raymond sighed heavily. "Thankfully, there is minimal damage to the time line. Initiate mop-up scans," he ordered. "Realign any detectable migration. And I want an immediate investigation into Mason's transit to flush out and apprehend his collaborators." He scowled at Rick and added, "Focus all efforts on Dak's villa."

Rick had been cagey long enough. Lives were at stake. Under Raymond's direction, the super-efficient Rogues could very well storm onto the scene, discover and shut down Romeo, and jeopardize everything.

He cleared his throat. "I wouldn't start rounding up suspects and throwing them in the pokey just yet, Ray. We've got some unfinished business on the Dallas mission."

Raymond's features twitched as he nodded knowingly to the other Rogues. He folded his arms across his chest and glared at his informant.

"Explain," he demanded.

"You left a man behind," Rick supplied.

FORTY-ONE

Gil's stomach growled. He was cold. Finding a good hot shower was on his list of priorities.

He was alive and undamaged. So far, so good. Was this luck or something else? The vitals section of the split screen on his wrist unit indicated one change: his time percentage—the troubling red indicator—had decreased from 50 to 25 percent. Like a deflating tire, it had a slow leak. A leak on any of his vitals didn't seem good.

He felt okay. Hungry, and so on, but otherwise great. He decided not to dwell on the mystery of his time percentage. He'd survived the collapse of a transit window. Now he needed to focus on surviving in general. Surviving without money required ingenuity and refreshing himself on the lay of the land. He was home, but Dallas 1963 had thrown him a few curves.

Number one was the dress code. The concealment qualities of the Rogue jumpsuit were limited. It would probably pass as maintenance attire. Few uptown establishments invited penniless laborers to exploit their creature comforts, and spending nights at the bus depot wasn't a long-term, five-star option. He was sure that his noodle could come up with something better, but he needed food first.

His smile bought him a free cup of java from the fry cook at the depot's lunch counter, and a tip: Brother Nehemiah's Saturday-morning eat-and-preach at Ebenezer Baptist Church. It wasn't a secret. The indigenous foot traffic was "beatin' feet" to Brother Nee's door. As street bums and hobos emerged from their nests and headed purposefully to the little brick sanctuary in West Dallas, Gil fell into step and was soon shoveling in buttery grits, crisp bacon, jam-soaked biscuits, and fried eggs. Heaven on earth.

"Sad business," Brother Nee said as Gil helped him clear the tables and wash up after the generous meal. "God's test of faith."

"With more to come," Gil responded automatically, fishing through the sudsy water for the last of the silverware.

"Amen," Nee replied.

He nodded toward the boxy Philco television in the corner of the basement kitchen. A knot of homeless men circled around it, listening with rapt attention to the broadcast. The black-and-white images were fuzzy, but the voice of the newscaster was not. The local channel was replaying Friday's historic broadcast when Walter Cronkite informed a nation in somber, weighted tones that "President John Fitzgerald Kennedy is dead."

The program cut back to current events with the local affiliate, one of a half dozen networks with cameras crammed into the corridors of the Dallas jail. A scene of contained bedlam flashed onto the screen. Stalwart figures guarded the frosty-windowed interrogation rooms. Reporters with popsicle-sized mikes bumped shoulders in front of their live-feed connections, and the wearied reporter for the local station, his bow tie askew and fedora listing oddly to one side, maintained a stream of garbled updates as to the fate of the alleged lone assassin contained within.

"That boy, Lee Oswald? I'm praying for his soul," Brother Nee said, his clear eyes bright. He polished each chipped plate with care and added it to the mismatched stack on a cinder-block shelf. "He's one of God's own. And, like Judas, he's carryin' a mighty big cross today."

Gil hadn't thought of it quite in that light. Outrage still glutted his brain. He wasn't numb. He wasn't impartial. He wanted blood. Oswald's. He'd crossed over the line from dispassionate historian to a man of vengeance. He had witnessed a coldhearted act of murder. And yet he knew that retribution was nigh. In twenty-four hours, Lee Harvey Oswald would pay for the deed with his life.

He also knew that Oswald's death wouldn't satisfy the grieving nation or its quest for answers, now or for generations to follow.

"Somebody's gonna kill that boy," Brother Nee declared. His sad voice rang loud and strong in the low-ceilinged space. "I knows it. Lord have mercy on his soul, I knows it."

The homeless men shifted in their metal folding chairs, eyeing Brother Nee with newfound awareness. Even one shriveled gray drunk, half insensate from his mind-robbing addiction, nodded, exhibiting a brief flash of awareness.

"Vengeance is mine, sayeth the Lord," Brother Nee said.

A timely reminder, Gil silently thought. *Unfortunately for Oswald, Jack Ruby is across town and missing the message.*

"I know. I am back early," Chay commented as Hickham met her at Transit Station Bravo with his personalized hoverlift and ferried her back to the Scio Quad for a thorough debriefing. "How is Maude? Has her SE cleared yet?"

Hickham jetted them through the maze of access tunnels. "Negative," he snapped. His features were waxy and drawn, and Cara quickly divined that he was more than angry. He was enraged.

"Your programming is obviously flawed," he snarled. "I did not incorporate random communication capabilities in your Eve One system implants. Overrides should have prevented your illegal messages."

"It isn't flawed," Cara replied. "Unless you are including and condemning my personal judgment. I'm more than a machine, Hickham. You sent a human into the future, too."

Hick didn't reply at first. He slowed the lift as it popped out of a tunnel and into the cavernous Scio Quad, nosing it into a downward spiral.

It was night in the sublit sector. Crisp and quiet. Maintenance bots scoured hard surfaces. A fine mist hydrated the plants along the walks and throughways. Vending kiosks were dark. The central plaza was empty. Cara was home. Back from the future.

Her LR 50 mission hadn't been a failure. She had survived phase one. That achievement was totally at odds with the fretting figure beside her; her mentor wasn't happy. But if her breach of the communication directives had impacted the project, Cara didn't care. She could justify her actions.

Hickham settled his lift on the rooftop of the main structure, a rough landing for even a skilled pilot. With stiff motions he nested the lift within the charging bay and finally addressed her.

"I value your human components," he started, but shook his head. "However, employing them to subvert mission objectives is . . . questionable."

"Because I did it, or because it didn't change Maude's fate?" she asked quietly.

"I understand why you did it. And yes, Maude's fate is still in question. However, Scio consensus concludes that you be afforded no quarter for your actions. Your communication effectively dismantled established protocols, endangered countless lives, and altered the true course of our present in incalculable ways."

He towered over her as she settled herself on the roof ledge and listened. She had been aware of her expected behavior prior to the mission, and which actions had been authorized to proceed. So she had expected censure. She was Hickham's creation, after all, and he was as much a stickler for the rules as anyone. His deliberate marriage of technology with biology had saved her life. The Eve One improvements, implanted progressively as she grew into adulthood, were his design, balanced in a precise ratio of human and enhanced cybernetics. He understood her capabilities. But did he understand her challenges?

"You were wrong to subvert the procedures, Chay," he said again.

Cara nodded, but she wasn't sorry. She was human first and Core's instrument second. In spite of her cybernetic implants, she had been compelled to prevent death by any means available. Her Eve One programming had provided those means.

"Your programming is flawed," Hickham insisted.

"My programming is not the issue. You designed me. I collected data from the future and responded appropriately."

"You've attempted to change our present," Hick returned.

"My friend's life was at stake. I felt justified." She rose to her full height and faced him. "You would do the same for Charlie."

"No," Hickham replied.

"No?" Cara raised one eyebrow. "Scios value science, but I know you value life more. I came back early to tell you, to give you the chance to make a difference, to change the present, not for science but for humanity."

Maude would be proud. Cara could indeed lie when it

was necessary. And it was necessary now. Her friend's life depended on it.

She paused, her eyes shining with righteous indignation. "Because if we don't change the present, Charlie will die tomorrow."

FORTY-TWO

"We don't have a choice," Maude reminded the men surrounding her in the covert transit complex. She wasn't shouting. She was quiet, firm, and in their faces, her index finger poking at Dak's massive chest.

Falah's calming presence was welcome. Tempers were edged with urgency, but the sleeping child in his mother's arms moderated the heated discussion between the remaining conspirators. Their numbers were sadly depleted by the loss of Rick and Gil. And, to Maude's dismay, the remaining men were circling her like avenging knights, her safety their sole focus. And, quarantine seemed their only suggestion.

"We don't have time for a protracted debate," Maude continued. "Quarantine is out. I'm still a Rogue. Gil needs rescuing. And I'm going. Make a hole, Bob, and drop me into it."

The demand startled the Transitor. "The w-w-window w-will collapse," he protested.

"Hold it open, Bob. Find a way. I know you can. You need mass, right? Think, Bob, think."

"This is suicide," Dak snarled. Ever since receiving Hickham's message, he'd been enraged. Dak hadn't shared the contents but his fuming reaction, like a cornered pit viper, was characteristic of bad news. Maude guessed Hick's message was another warning from Chay about future events—likely now about Gil. And if Gil was in danger, she was going to rescue him, and quick. With or without Dak's permission.

"*I've got to try, Dak.* Gil's in this mess because of me. I'll collect Gil, wherever he is, and cart him out on my back if necessary. But we need to launch now. One wrong move and he could trigger a migration, or worse, he could lose his life."

"Drutz. So could you," Dak growled. "Let Rogue Central handle retrieval. Rick set things in motion there. I don't want to lose you this way, Kincaid, and I refuse to permit it."

Falah laughed softly. Nested in a lounger brought down to the complex for her comfort, she looked regal and wise. The collaborators all turned as one.

"You cannot deny her, my love," she said to her husband. "Maude is your creature. Like you, she is brave. She knows her heart. She must heed it as you once heeded yours—against all challenges. You must help her."

Dak's implacable demeanor, his trademark stubborn scowl and fierce gaze, cracked. Maude wanted to kiss Falah. The small beauty wielded words like a warrior's sword, felling her formidable husband with the power of love.

"I c-can do it!" Bob said suddenly. His eyes were bright, his features twitching into a hopeful grin. Slowly, as he shared his inspiration, confidence displaced nerves.

The Transitor's solution was simple and ingenious: Ice, a block large enough to melt over a twenty-minute period.

Dak was outnumbered, Maude noted with relief. Bob's innovative solution would work, he admitted. He revealed that Hickham's message included the transit coordinates. But Dak imposed a stiff condition before agreeing to let her transit.

Quarantine. Immediate, nonnegotiable stasis the moment she returned. Since they wouldn't have Charlie.

"Agreed." She promised without hesitation. Gil's life was in the balance.

Dak still didn't look pleased, but Maude didn't care. The rescue mission was on.

FORTY-THREE

The smell of coffee roused Gil from his nightmare; Brother Nehemiah brewed it strong enough to wake the dead—like the vagrants who had spent the past dark hours lumped together on the worn linoleum in front of the blaring Philco. But as Gil shook off the dregs of sleep, he quickly realized that the horror was all too real. He was still in Dallas, 1963.

He groaned as he surveyed the Ebenezer Baptist sleepover crowd. Brother Nee's generosity had netted quite a few scrappy souls, and he fit in with the grizzled group. Homeless and rudderless, he wasn't sure where his next meal was going to come from, or whether he was going to survive to see another dawn.

Was he stuck in the past forever? Would Core bail him out?

Also, he wondered if this trip to the Big D had unleashed an A-bomb in Earth's history. The minor time line errors that Rick had mentioned might be major now.

Perhaps his impact on the continuum hardly rated recognition. He hoped so. Rogue Central had clearly concluded the same, because none of the retrieval squads had bothered to hunt him down and haul him back to the future yet. But that just didn't seem right.

Six hours later, Brother Nee proclaimed, "You'd make a good short-order cook."

Gil laughed and flipped the last of the golden griddle-cakes Brother Nee's larder had provided for the multitudes. Expanding on his earlier sermon, the holy man had confided in Gil that he'd seen his share of men just passing through and weathering hard times, and for some of them a dose of salvation and a little pocket change made all the difference.

"The Piccadilly uptown could use someone like you," Nee added as he splashed hot syrup on a short stack for himself.

Gil thanked Nee. He'd put it on his list. Rescue didn't seem imminent. After existing moment to moment for forty-plus hours, a little long-term planning seemed prudent.

A hot shower and full belly had lifted his spirits somewhat. But time to think only magnified his concern about Maude. Another hour in 1963 without any news from the future. He glanced at the cracked red face on the old Coca-Cola wall clock. How many hours did Maude have left? Was she safe? Had she consented to quarantine? It was her only option, because contacting Charlie had been a bust. Hands down.

Gil still didn't get it. Charlie had stiffed them.

Then again, the whole JFK-assassination scenario hadn't fit the profile of the other two. The arena, for one, didn't match. Outside versus inside. The scale of the kill zone, as well. The distance between perpetrators and victims differed drastically. It just didn't make any sense.

The Philco reception went haywire again. Groans from the few vagrants who remained vigilant, transfixed by the perpetual broadcast, spurred Gil over to the set. Grabbing a remnant of tinfoil, he started to adjust the rabbit-ear antenna. The familiar sight of the interior of the Dallas City Jail froze him in his tracks.

Oswald.

It all suddenly made sense, the pieces falling into place like a slot machine jackpot. Gil knew exactly when and where Charlie was going to be in 1963. They hadn't missed him. Charlie hadn't stiffed them. Bob had sent them to the wrong event.

Oswald's assassination fit the pattern: Close confines, a tense situation. Charlie had to be there, if he hadn't gone on to his next event—and Gil seriously doubted that he had. He was sure Charlie would be in the Dallas jail testing his accursed prototype when Ruby fired the fatal bullet.

Yes, Gil *knew.* He knew it as surely as he knew he would love Maude for the rest of his born days, past or future, dead or alive.

Adrenaline gushed through him like he'd just touched a live wire. His flesh prickled. His palms itched. And his heart pounded in his chest like an elephant was giving him CPR.

Did he have time?

He glanced at the clock again. He squeezed his eyes and slapped his forehead. When had Oswald's assassination taken place? The reason for the prisoner's transfer eluded Gil, but the central details about the day Oswald died didn't. Sunday. Jail. Ruby. Fatal bullet.

But when? What time?

An update from the Philco supplied the data. ". . . Oswald's transfer is scheduled for 11:30. . . ."

Bingo. He had less than fifteen minutes to hightail it over to the city jail.

He would make it. He had to.

FORTY-FOUR

For a man in love, she was hard to miss. Despite her cloaked garb, the beautiful, statuesque Maude didn't blend well into a 1963 Texas streetscape. Oddly enough, no one but Gil seemed to notice her. Pedestrians brushed past as she measured his approach on her wrist unit.

He would have crossed the continent just to glimpse her smile. And he would have stomped through fire to kiss those lips.

They didn't speak. They just walked into each other's arms and made the world go away for a heartbeat.

"What are you doing here?" he asked gruffly, at last pulling away from her moist mouth.

"What I do best," she returned. "I'm rescuing you."

It didn't sit well with him. She was risking her life to save his. He gripped her arms and gave her a little shake.

"What about your SE?"

"Ten rotations left," she said brightly.

Ten days. Barely enough time to cure a cold; not

nearly enough to fix a terminal diagnosis. And heaven knew how many days had been chopped off by this transit.

Gil's nerves snarled. He had hoped against hope the moment he caught sight of her. But her SE alert wasn't resolved. Charlie hadn't curtailed his testing and returned with the accursed Superman prototype. Maude was still in danger, and the clock was ticking.

"I've got to get you out of here," he said. Tucking her arm under his, he started trolling the immediate area for a ride. "What if the amount of time you spend here is related to your lost rotations?"

A car with keys in the ignition would be sweet. A hotwire candidate would do too. It might be 1963, but this was his home turf. Locating swift transport to get Maude beyond the no-transit zone for retrieval would be a cinch. Yep. Stealing wheels and hauling ass? He could handle that. And it was more important than anything else.

"Whoa, cowboy. Bob's got our retrieval covered," Maude cried, and tugged at his sleeve for him to stop. "He's holding open the window. We've got twenty minutes till the ice melts. Check your wrist unit. The coordinates should register now that we've made contact."

He stopped so suddenly that she bumped into him. "Twenty minutes?" he repeated dumbly.

"Stop scowling," she whispered against his mouth after a reassuring kiss. "And stop worrying. It's not hopeless. I gave in. Plan A. Quarantine. Bob's bringing us directly into Romeo, and I'll check into Dak's stasis pod."

Gil could see the concession was huge. Her shrug and smile were fakes. Quarantine? He knew about her paralyzing fear, a fear so great that she'd risked death to avoid it.

His own fears for her had his thoughts racing. Heroes created options. He had zilch.

Use your brain, he chided himself. Maybe rapid multiple transits had fried his wiring, but twiddling his thumbs for twenty minutes didn't sound smart. He always defaulted to action.

He glanced up the street. The pending Oswald transfer had attracted a crowd. The city jail was a madhouse.

Retrieval in twenty minutes?

After he had Maude repeat the fact and confirm the window parameters, Gil checked the local time. One glance at the dashboard clock in the dented Belair parked at the curb sealed the deal. They had time.

"Want to take another crack at it?"

He knew she'd be game before he even asked, and Maude's questioning frown cleared as he explained Bob's mix-up regarding the two assassinations.

"It's possible," she conceded. "Maybe he misread Charlie's path. Collective errors can displace readings as well as arrivals. Our transit to the theater was off-target."

"And Rick and I were off, too," Gil said.

"Bob's using untested technology. Practical applications will work out the tolerances, but for now . . . we have to trust *this*." Maude tapped Gil's chest. "You know Charlie is going to be at the jail. You feel it, don't you? It's our last chance to contact him. Let's do it."

Gil was bowled over by her trust. His proposal would take her into a known kill zone, a tight one, within spitting distance of a deadly weapon and a bullet with Oswald's name on it. If anything went wrong . . . He repeated the facts with emphasis.

"Understood," she replied. There wasn't a single reservation detectable in her frame, not a quiver, a blink, or a gulp.

Gil glanced back at the jail. A car snaked through the crowd, driving them back a bit from the lip of the Main Street ramp. Oswald's transfer was imminent. It was now or never.

* * *

Maude was flushed with hope. Rescuing Gil made her feel like a Rogue again rather than a cowering victim. And being teamed with Gil and doing something to save her own life was empowering.

Heady and exuberant, she locked steps with her beloved. Together they could do anything.

They moved steadily along Main Street, adopting a smooth, swift gait that would attract no untoward attention but still would get them to the top of the ramp in short order. Gil's briefing had been precise. Gaining entry to the jail would be tricky. They couldn't blend into the crowd. Too many eyes were trained on the scene for them too pass unnoticed. But newsmen and press support had access, and Gil had a plan.

If the plan didn't work, Maude was ready to run the gauntlet, level her stunner at Charlie, and haul him back to the future via Bob's retrieval coordinates. She was finished with covert contact efforts. Stunning Charlie was a sure thing.

Zat the laser recall message. And *drutz* Core regs. If their penetration into the historic event caused a rift, Rogue Central would just have to fix the mess. She wanted that prototype. She wanted to live.

Two blocks of confusion surrounded their target edifice. Onlookers and uniformed police collected curbside; camera crews ferried equipment to and from their double-parked rigs. The clamorous noise generated by the entire assembly echoed off the tall facades lining the canyonlike streetscape, adding to the tension of the moment.

Gil tightened his grip on Maude's forearm. It felt great. His protective gesture reaffirmed his partnership with her. She'd been solo for most of her Rogue missions. She had preferred it that way, until teaming with Gil. Novice or not, the decisive man would double her effectiveness, backing her up with muscle and brains.

Zat. The cowboy seemed to almost read her mind at times.

"It will work," he said, repeating the plan and reassuring her as they headed toward the media vehicles. "We'll pass ourselves off as camera assistants."

Maude thought he was probably right. Numerous networks laid claim to the patch of sidewalk adjacent to the jail. The jumble of their extra gear provided a distracting maze for the competing broadcasters. Support crews in coveralls shouted into bulky walkie-talkies and shifted equipment with focused concentration.

Yes, Gil's plan would work. They could blend into the industry without rousing alarm.

Maude's blood was pumping. The mission looked good. Felt good. One last check to confirm Charlie's signal, and they would be good to go. She received a positive signal. Charlie's coordinates were on target.

She started to retract her wrist unit display but stopped. A bio alert had popped up on the split screen. The steady red glow was abhorrent. Her brain revolted, and her knees buckled from the sudden disconnect.

Her stumble caught Gil by surprise—surprised both of them, actually. Gil muscled her forward, gripping Maude firmly and keeping her upright as they continued.

"Got him?" he asked between heavy breaths.

"Affirmative," Maude replied, and Gil stopped adjacent to an unmanned media panel truck. "Charlie will arrive in the jail in sixty seconds."

Gil grunted an acknowledgment. As planned, he rifled through the extraneous equipment.

Maude waited. It astonished her that she could speak or think. Leaning back against the vehicle, she closed her eyes for a second and caught her breath. The implications of her data display sank in slowly. It expanded and settled firmly like the smell of death. The bio alert was unmistakable.

She checked her wrist unit again, and then retracted the screen; she didn't need it anymore. Her Scheduled Expiration indicator was at zero.

Zero. And, zero rotations meant only one thing.

I am dying today.

The realization was sudden and profound, pieces of a puzzle snapping together and crystallizing with certainty. She couldn't save herself after all. Her fate was fixed because Charlie's prototype was flawed.

Everything made sense now. All of it.

Charlie had seen her recall signals in Rome and Ford's Theatre, but he had ignored them. This was his invention; only he could fix it. The dedicated inventor ignored the recall because he was committed to his primary objective: racing against the clock to perfect and test his bulletproof shield before it was too late to save her life. And she knew without a doubt that he was resolved to die trying.

She almost laughed at the absurdity of everyone willing to sacrifice themselves for one another. And at Charlie's folly. No one, not even he, could match a resolute Rogue intent on rescue. And she was one of the best.

"Ready?" Gil hissed, tugging on a monstrous camera unit and starting to roll it toward the ramp.

She nodded and added her own strength to the effort. She didn't trust herself to speak. If Gil suspected what she was about to do, he'd stop her or try to take her place. But she wouldn't allow that. She embraced her destiny as surely as she embraced her profound passion for the man beside her. In this moment, they were one and the same, both driven by her unconditional love. Gil had given her the best days of her life, and had shown her how true heroes acted.

She was dying today. And now she knew why—to save Charlie.

FORTY-FIVE

"Stand aside!" Gil bellowed as he marched down the ramp, pushing the bulky TV camera. Maude held fast to the other side. She kept her head bowed, her eyes lowered, and her mouth shut.

"Let me give you a hand," a media technician shouted, edging past the uniformed barricade at the jail's garage entry. "That damn unit is worth more than a year's salary."

The madhouse inside seemed to swallow them whole. Man and machine constricted the fume-soaked garage. A line of lawmen in Stetsons, massive camera dolleys, and sweltering spotlights that seemed to be frying the faces of reporters caught in their glare formed a narrow path between the waiting transport vehicle and the basement entry to the jail. All eyes were riveted on the glass-paned double door. Inching into the space was easier after they ditched the helpful technician and the TV equipment and ducked low.

Gil silently gestured to split up, as his plan dictated.

He blew her a kiss and cut to the right, backing against the brick wall and picking his way toward the jail's door. Maude moved left, her search for Charlie's familiar profile unimpeded as she inched around and over the snarl of cables and light stands.

As soon as she saw the area, the intimate confines of the kill zone, her last hope was dashed. Stunning Charlie wasn't optional. The shoulder-to-shoulder density of humans precluded anything but a shot to his head—not recommended for anyone, and especially not for a superbrain like Charlie.

She'd have to take the bullet for him.

Awareness returned in a flash. None of this had been random. She wasn't a victim of fate after all. Time travel wasn't just what Rogues did; that wasn't her real job. This moment was the difference between knowing and living the oath. Her whole life came down to this moment. This purpose. This choice. Her choice to die.

Yes, this was the level twelve mission she'd trained for. She recognized the progressive elements to prove the prototype, and Charlie had reached its final stage of testing. Now came confirmation, exposure to a single round at point-blank range.

And there he was, on her side of the crowd. Charlie's lopsided grin stretched his features into fond familiarity. Maude pressed forward, slipping around bodies and under obstacles until she could almost touch him.

"Here he comes!" someone shouted as the double doors opened and a short, sweater-clad figure emerged, sandwiched on all four sides by stalwart men with scowling countenances.

That must be Oswald, her brain registered. She glanced to the right. Where was Gil? Where was the assassin?

The crowd convulsed with energy, surging forward and pressing into the path of the handcuffed prisoner and his escorts. Charlie moved too. His long limbs windmilling through the humanity, he fairly swam toward his target.

Color faded into black and white as the brilliant lights from the stand of television cameras concentrated their beams on Oswald.

At ten paces, Gil had said, the assassin would lunge in from her right. Gil's description had been flawless. Her gaze instantly picked Jack Ruby out from the others. His suede hat was pulled low, his puttylike features shadowed by the brim. Ruby's telltale blocky body moved furtively, swelling from the ranks of witnesses, bowling over human obstacles as he pulled out his revolver, extended his arm, and aimed.

Maude's instincts took over. Honed to react with speed and finality, she launched herself at Core's chief asset, this grinning fool with his brainchild prototype. She connected with a thud, slamming Charlie to the floor just as Ruby fired.

A bullet smashed her wrist unit and tore into her gut. It burned tissue with the heat of magma, and severed her alliance with reality. She fell slowly, tumbling like a broken sparrow to the gritty basement floor. She was numb now, feeling nothing but a biting chill as Charlie cradled her body in his arms. His friendly features swam before her eyes. His mouth hung open, a gaping hole of wordless shock.

Pride warmed her from within, and she smiled.

She'd done it. She'd saved Charlie.

And as a delicious darkness descended, she heard one voice above all others cry her name in anguished horror. Claiming one last pleasure from that man and his passion, she echoed Gil in reply.

"Love," she whispered, and tumbled into the sweet abyss of unconsciousness.

FORTY-SIX

Gil's ears roared from the gun's report. The crowd tumbled away from the carnage like dominos, allowing him to see Charlie slap a transit tag on Maude's chest and blip her limp body into oblivion. Then Charlie ran for it.

He caught up with the man at the mouth of the ramp, easily evading the contingent of Dallas lawmen who were disarming Ruby.

"Whoa, Big Brain!" Gil roared as he tripped up Charlie to slow him down.

The chaotic scene within the basement barely registered with Gil. He didn't give a gnat's ass about Oswald's fate, and any impact on world history was beyond his sphere of concern. He only had one thought and one goal: Maude—getting back to her before it was too late. And he needed Charlie to do it.

"You're coming with me. I've got a shortcut to the future, and I need your body mass."

"Gil?" Charlie cried as he scrambled to his knees. "Did you see her? Did you see what she did?"

"Yeah, you imbecile. I was there," Gil growled, and

clamped on to Charlie's arm to pull him to his feet. "Let's go."

Thankfully, Charlie didn't protest, because Gil was prepared to take the hapless inventor along to Bob's hole-punched coordinates alive *or* dead.

"Confirm Bob's transit window," he yelled as they dodged the stew of humanity boiling out onto Main Street.

Charlie complied. "Got it," he said, and took the lead. "The window is collapsing. We've got fifteen seconds."

Gil howled, leaping past a knot of terrified Texans scrambling into their Belair for their own getaway. Two more giant steps, and he was in the transit window and hurtling through time.

She must have passed out, because the atmospherics had cut off. Gone were the sounds of spring and the comforting warmth from the heat lamps. But she wasn't dead yet. The cold comfort of the soot-coated tile floor was her first clue. Maude moved a muscle to be sure.

"*Gigadrutz*," she growled through clenched teeth as another wave of pain spiraled through her. She'd never before endured such agony.

With two hundred missions logged on her identilog and countless brushes with death, her time had run out. She wouldn't survive the hour. She couldn't. She'd lost too much blood. She'd given up trying to staunch the flow pulsing from the wound in her belly, but she hadn't quite given up on rescue. Not entirely.

"Help?" The cavernous dark space swallowed her voice. Then she remembered, the communications relay at the tram station had been fouled with grime and was nonfunctioning. Her cry for help couldn't be received by Core.

What a day, she thought. With her transmitter smashed—the first casualty of the bullet that had also sliced through her flesh—her emergency and impending expiration would be a well-kept secret from Core.

Maude grimaced as another wave of agony buffeted her senses. She fought the urge to give in, and to pass out again. It was a struggle, but by applying her Rogue skills she managed to briefly detach from the pain.

The darkness was deadly quiet and smelled like Hades. The noxious odor of rotten eggs indicated elevated magma activity and threat, a pending pyroclastic surge of heat or burp of poisonous gas, she guessed. From countless evacuation drills, she knew it wouldn't take much to shift this volatile Outskirt region from safe to lethal, and her avenues of escape were diminishing by the second as the threat level increased.

Auto safeguards had already shut down this section of the sub-orbital tram system. A logical assumption—she had been stretched out on the tile for an indeterminate time and a tram hadn't arrived to transport her sorry carcass to safety.

And walking was definitely out.

She rolled her head to one side. Out there in the darkness, beneath the station, was lift storage. If it contained a charged unit, she could still save herself. Her instincts were strong. She wanted to survive. Now more than ever.

Gil's image flared in her brain, and a smile tugged at her mouth. Love mattered. Loving Gil had changed everything for her—her dreams, her loyalties, her commitments, and her sacrifices. She had loved once, and loved well. What she had shared with Gil had been brief but profound, a transforming passion that burned bright and sure.

If only . . . Regret more bitter than the wound in her belly twisted her heart. There were no tomorrows for her. She had made her choice in Dallas and sacrificed her life for Charlie's. After all efforts to the contrary—machinations of muscle, harnessing brainpower to outwit and overpower the fickle forces that prophesied doom—she had freely chosen death.

Life ebbed from her body. And her options to staunch the flow were nil. One, because she was short on inspiration. And two, because even with a grand scheme, there wasn't time for implementation.

The stench of sulfur tickled her nose. The planet was belching death. All the symptoms of an impending surge coalesced in her thoughts, and she suddenly realized: *Chay was wrong.* A chuckle shook her frame. The bullet wasn't going to kill her; before that happened, she was about to be fried stem to stern by a Mother Earth hot flash.

Gil's first coherent thought was recognition of the incongruous pink-fog welcome at Transit Station Romeo.

"Where is she? Is she okay?" Gil shouted as soon as the blast panel lifted. He charged through the dissipating mist and leapt off the transit pad, nearly knocking Dak flat.

"What the *zat* happened?" Dak replied as Gil skidded to a stop before him.

"Maude's at Juliet," Charlie wheezed. He joined them by the transit console. "I used Bob's emergency auto-transit tag. When she got hit, it was the only way I could get her out of there fast."

"She's hit?" Bob cried. The Transitor staggered back. "A b-bullet?"

Gil whirled on Charlie, seething with outrage. "You fucking bastard. She's gut-shot and dying, alone in that godforsaken place."

"I can save her," Charlie countered. "If you can get her here in time, I can save her."

"I'm holding you to that promise," Gil snarled, and he started for the tunnel.

Dak stalled him with a shout. "I'm going with you."

"Negative. I need you here, Dak," Charlie commanded, and continued with more rapid-fire orders. The men all mobilized and cleared the transit area.

"Get the stasis pod ready, Dak." Charlie's tone stalled all challenge. He turned to the grim-faced Bob. "Contact Central; bypass all protocols. I'm going to need supplies and a med-tech team from Reacclimation, fast. Better send for Hickham too."

More details for essential action followed, but Gil didn't hear the rest. After a crash course from Charlie on gut-wound triage, he was on the move. Packing a med kit, he scrambled up the tunnel to the villa and the lift storage above it.

He was also packing guilt—a dump truck full. He'd brought the damned mountain to Mohammed when he'd taken Maude to meet her bullet.

Era essential? Ha. Another mystery solved. The odd measurement on his bio screen, the decreasing percentage, the crimson warning, and the symbol for time had been resolved. Now the statistic was bright green and at 100 percent. Gil had fulfilled his destiny.

Although he'd led his lover to her deadly encounter, he hadn't counted on Maude breaking rank. Bull-headed, sacrificial, harebrained female that she was, oh no, he hadn't guessed that she'd pull the very stunt he'd planned to pull if given the chance. It was a reprehensible act, but a lengthy venting of fury would have to wait. Right now he had another mission. He had claimed the primary task, collecting and delivering Maude. He could—*would*—do it, and fast. He only prayed that he could also deliver her alive.

FORTY-SEVEN

"The surge," Maude cried, and pushed him away from her. "It will kill you. Leave me. Go—you don't have time for this. I'm dead already."

"It's my turn for stupid heroics," Gil snarled. "You can't hog all the glory."

It was easy to quell her protests; she kept fading in and out of consciousness. Not a good sign. She had lost a hell of a lot of blood.

Was it too much? Was he too late? It hadn't taken long to find her, but she didn't look good.

He slipped his arms beneath her and slid her onto the lift.

"How are you doing, love?" he crooned as he rechecked her pulse. It was thready but holding. The med kit's miracle foam had worked; it had covered the wound, staunched the bleeding, and stabilized her for transport. Now, apparently, all he had to do was outrun a lethal surge.

He'd bypassed a safety pod bunker on the way in. He hoped to Hades that he wouldn't have to use it. Any delay, even to escape this surge, would probably be fatal for Maude.

"Gilly," she whispered. "I saved Charlie."

"Rogues. You're all wacko," he growled, and kissed her brow as he quickly finished tethering her to the transport. It was going to be a fast and bumpy ride back to Dak's.

In the few moments since his arrival, the environmental quality had degraded. The fumes here made his eyes tear. His every breath was labored.

"You understand, don't you?" she insisted. "I had to do it." She grabbed his arm and held fast. "I didn't want to die so soon. I wanted a life with you. I *love* you. But, I had to save Charlie." Her feverish eyes bored holes into him. "It was my choice."

Gil cursed. He understood, all right. All too well. The good of the many outweighing the good of the one, wasn't just a throwaway line in a *Star Trek* movie. Sacrifices like Spock's were real and necessary.

But not Maude. And not now.

He was enraged enough to want to shake her senseless. But he wasn't angry with Maude; he was more furious with himself. He should have seen this coming.

"So much for my natural Rogue talent. I should have stopped you," he muttered as he climbed aboard and activated the hoverlift's propulsion unit. He'd known she was a dedicated Rogue, loyal and true, but he'd underestimated her courage. Packaged in lush curves and soft smiles, he'd forgotten she was a beauty who walked . . . well, not softly, but carried a big stick; she was a bundle of dynamite with more balls than a Special Forces detail. If and when he got another chance, he'd never underestimate her again.

"I should have prevented it or taken the bullet myself," he added, gunning the transport's engine.

Maude closed her eyes and laughed as the lift jetted away from the station. "Over my dead body."

She meant it too. If only one of them survived to carry on, Maude was glad it would be Gil. The man beside her mattered.

Gil must live and love again, she decreed with her last conscious thought. He possessed so much potential, including the determination to banish the darkness lurking within a lonely heart. Thus, as a grateful Maude clung to life, she was blessed with the grace and tranquility to accept her fate.

Totally, with every fiber of her being, she glowed with joy. Her life was no longer empty or unfulfilled. Gil's love made it wondrous, promising, and complete.

Sunlight woke her. Maude felt it kiss her flesh, inching higher on her body till it teased her eyelids. She opened one eye a crack. The molten orb was winking at her from the darkened horizon like an exotic dancer stripping off the cloak of night.

The crisp scents of a summer dawn freshly washed with dew stirred her memory. So did the sound of the sea, the frothy rush of the tide scampering up the sandy shore before the ocean called it home again, sucking it back into its briny depths.

Gil. She and Gil had planned this scene together, saved it, but had yet to use it. Her pulse quickened at the thought. Love on a beach at dawn.

She opened her other eye and blinked to focus. The sun was higher now. A fan of golden light skimmed across the surface of the sea and sparkled with each cresting wave. A hot-cold breeze stirred the dune grasses and swirled over her flesh.

This is Gil's beach. A delicious bud of desire unfolded in her core. She felt alive.

Was she?

"Did you save me, Gil?" she whispered. "Or is this heaven?"

A mass of heat next to her body stirred and chuckled. "A little bit of both, my love," a voice said, propping his head up on one elbow and blinding her with his smile.

"Gil!" she cried, and moved to embrace him. A tangle of leads and monitor nodes peppering her flesh prevented all but the smallest of movements.

Gil laughed and kissed her soundly. "Thought you might enjoy an unconventional wake-up from Reacclimation. I've got some pull with the Med-Prep staff."

"How long have I been in here?" she murmured against his neck. His flesh was warm.

"Too long," he countered. "I've been missing you like crazy."

Maude was still fuzzy—fuzzy enough to feel dumbfounded and overwhelmed. "Are you okay? The surge?"

"A-okay. And we outran the surge by the hair of our chinny-chin-chin," he quipped. "Ready to rise and shine and bust outta this joint?"

She glanced around, and quickly oriented her mind to the pod parameters, the recessed monitors, and innumerable med gauges edging the cushy pad. *Reacclimation?* It looked like a treatment pod in the Med-Prep block—one with deluxe accommodations.

"I'm alive," she said, and laughed. "You did it!" She managed an awkward embrace and a delightful, toe-curling kiss with her bunkmate.

"*We* did it," Gil corrected. "Your SE is resolved. We're done with hole-punching missions and the quest for Charlie's bulletproof prototype."

She yawned broadly. "And Charlie and Rick?" she continued. Scattered thoughts sparking at random, were triggering questions. "And Chay?"

Gil interjected some order into her mental chaos. "I'll summarize what's been going on while you've been catching up on your beauty sleep," he said. "All is well with everyone and everything. Pretty good, huh?"

Maude nodded. "Good," she murmured, and relaxed against him. Gil's words slid in and slowly restored peace and equilibrium as her body roused from its long healing slumber.

"The continuum is okay too," he added. "Core averted a time rift in 1963—thanks to Mackenzie. She doggedly tagged the errors as we created them. Rick and I have been helping the Rogues fix them one by one. It's an ongoing labor of love."

"That's nice," she replied automatically.

She didn't force anything. Processing all of the data in her current state was still a challenge. Her trauma had been significant, the pain unbearable. And standard treatments at Med-Prep would have addressed both by suspending and isolating her life and cognitive functions for the duration of repair and restoration—*quarantine*.

She'd endured stasis, and her greatest fear had not been realized. She hadn't outlived humanity. And her Adam was very much alive, too, and he was beside her.

It was heavenly having him wake her, hold her, and return her gently to the demanding world that awaited them both. For now, what mattered most existed within Gil's embrace.

Heaven had some discomfort. Her belly was itchy, inside and out. She had peeked at the wound once and dismissed it. The small oval mesh patch indicated little about the damage she had sustained, but plenty about the skill of the Med-Prep staff to restore her to rights. If she had a scar—and if Charlie had anything to do with her treatment she wouldn't—it would be minimal.

She glanced at Gil. No, sorting out the Rogue cleanup related to her SE wasn't paramount—yet. And neither was the punitive accounting she would eventually face for her illegal activities. For now, she was off duty and no longer racing to save her own life—thank goodness. But, one thing couldn't wait. This man. His future and hers.

Did they have one? Together?

She scrunched up her nose as she thought about it. "You and Rick are fixing the errors?" she asked. "You're going on missions?"

"Nope. I'm more of an available know-it-all on assassination trivia. And helping repair this time line is an opportunity I didn't want to pass up." Gil stopped and winked. "Core extended my guest privileges indefinitely."

Maude gasped. "But you're an EE."

"Resolved too. My era-essential moment for the continuum was in 1963, and I'll tell you all about it later—much later—when I've got you exactly where I want you."

Resolved? Maude blinked. That sounded promising. Could her heart's desire be fulfilled? It was beginning to sound more and more like a guarantee.

"For now, trust me. Core may have technology, but interpreting the data isn't foolproof."

He reached up and adjusted her oxygen flow. "I think you're ready for one hundred percent now."

The boost helped banish the last of her grogginess. "Mm, much better," she said as she stretched. "When do I get out of here? I'm hungry, and not just for food."

Gil's satisfying kiss was cut short when the delightful atmospherics abruptly ceased, replaced by the pale blue backlighting for the pod instrumentation. He pulled away with a growl and nodded at the prominent monitor above their heads. Charlie's scowling countenance glared at Maude from the screen.

"Stop wiggling around, Kincaid," Charlie snapped. "I want an accurate bio read."

Maude's brow furrowed. She felt great, but Charlie's severe expression could only be equated with trouble.

She glanced at Gil. "What's wrong?" she hissed. "Am I damaged?"

"You're fine," Gil replied, and nodded toward the monitor. "But he's not. Charlie is still grumpy about that bullet. You gave him a scare, and he probably aged ten years just trying to save your life."

Oh? Maude leveled her gaze at the scientist and tried not to fidget. She thought she could see a bit of the old Charlie lurking behind the stern mask as he completed the test, but for the moment, worry controlled his features.

"I'm not sorry," she announced to her beloved mentor, and watched him flinch as she added with extra emphasis, "I did my job."

Charlie harrumphed. "I'm not deaf, you *zatting* Rogue."

"He's angry," she cried incredulously, and gasped when she saw that Gil was too.

"We all are," Gil explained. "Face it, Maude. You are stubborn and a lousy team player." He waggled a finger at her.

"I am not," she protested, and waggled one right back.

"Are too," Charlie chimed in, then added yet another remonstration. "Stop wiggling, I said! I need to backwash the supplement from your system. I want to discharge you and climb into my own pod for a fortnight."

She flopped back again, huffed, and stared at the blue ceiling for about a half a second, then tugged at the leads. Impatience was a good sign, and probably meant that she was healing.

"Not much longer," Charlie added. His tone was weary but a bit of the sparkle returned to his kind eyes.

Nerves were frazzled all around, Maude realized. Her own short temper could be a byproduct of Reacclimation. That could explain away some of her irascibility, but not all of it. To be honest, the truth hurt. She *was* stubborn and rash. Especially when it came to rescuing people she loved.

"You weren't a one-woman show in Dallas, you know," Gil continued, in a tone more patient than she deserved. "You were part of a team. And you dropped the ball."

"Huh?" She twisted around to face him. Her ill humor was back and starting to spike. "I dropped what?"

"The prototype works," he said. "Taking the bullet for Charlie wasn't necessary."

"Superman works?" She was stunned and humbled in an instant. "Oh, Charlie," she whispered. "I thought . . ."

"I *know* what you thought," Charlie returned sharply, and shook his head. "Foolish, wasteful, *drutzed* Rogue heroics nearly killed you." He continued to grouse as he concluded his outprocessing tasks. Maude suffered it all in silence, swallowing her pride and pressing her lips tightly together. She felt like a raw recruit again, rightly chastised and upbraided.

"Thank you for saving my life," she managed. She'd been wrong—very nearly *dead* wrong—and Charlie had patched her up.

He snorted. Tweaking a few more dials, he popped their bio leads and flushed the pod with a fresh blast of purified air. "Thanks for trying to save mine," he said, his lips waffling between a smile and a frown. "But you're not going to get a second chance to make that mistake."

"What?" Maude's vitals jumped. She struggled to keep her voice neutral. "What do you mean?"

Gil shook his head and laughed. "Let me translate. "Your solo days are over, Maude Kincaid," he said.

The declaration registered as a full-body shock. But Maude's snarl of rebuttal was cut short.

"If you and I are going to be a team," Gil continued, "I demand equal status. That means equal risk and equal glory. Grandstanding won't be tolerated. And sacrificial flies are out. Do we have a deal?"

Drutz. It was too much for Maude to take in at once. She kicked at the padding and balled her fists. Another wave of anger washed over her, tugging at her tongue and body, tempting her to lash out in defiant protest.

Grandstanding? Sacrificial flies? What the *zat* was Gil talking about?

She started to ask. But when the rest of his statement suddenly fell into place, she gasped.

"A team? Gilly! Do you mean a Rogue team?"

"Affirmative," Charlie supplied from the monitor. Most of his grumpiness had dissipated. The corners of his mouth inched up, a begrudging smile to be sure, but one that heartened Maude all the same. "If he passes on the Scio offer, that is. They tried to recruit him from his Reacclimation pod." Charlie paused and snorted for effect.

"Gil can train to be a Rogue or a Scio if he wants. His Core residency option is no longer blocked. His era-essential status cleared with the Dallas 1963 mission."

"No memory purge?" Maude whispered.

"Nope," Gil assured her, and tapped his forehead. "It's all stored up here, crystal clear. Even the memory of Ruby drilling you with a bullet."

Gil's features shifted. His sudden fierce scowl could compete with Dak's any day. "But I'll consent to a purge and hightail it back to Big D," he said with a growl, "if you and I can't make a deal. What's your answer? Are you my past or my future?"

"Teamwork?" she replied. She chewed her lip for a whisper of a moment. Her smile started deep and spread through her flesh and blood like a firestorm, searing a path of utter gladness that left breathlessness in its wake. She nodded.

"Future."

FORTY-EIGHT

"Glad to be home?" Gil asked as he sealed the portal to her flat and activated the residential console.

Maude couldn't nod. This cold pristine shell offered no welcome for her. She closed her eyes and sniffed the sterile space, feeling like a stranger in her own abode. That bullet had claimed her life after all, she realized.

Her world had shifted. Altered by terror, enriched by the sacrifice of friends, and empowered by love, she had been transformed. This tiny refuge and hiding place had sheltered her innocence, but it couldn't contain the joyous woman she had become. It was too late. She couldn't go back to her old life or her old ways. Detached and independent, self-absorbed and reckless—none of these words described her now. Loving Gil had forever changed her.

She called to him, wondering something, and Gil's heart-stirring grin supplied the answer: Love had changed him too. Their timeless connection had been fostered by passion and tested by fire. She had no doubt. It would endure.

"You have a life in the past," she said quietly.

He chuckled. "Not exactly, love," he replied, then set the stage for romance.

The heat soared and lights dimmed. A chorus of crickets and bullfrogs blended with the whispering breeze. Then the shell of Maude's flat disappeared, replaced by a velvety night sky sprinkled with stars. It was a bayou cabin and a hot Southern night.

When he joined her beneath the heavenly display, Maude slipped into Gil's welcoming embrace. *This is home*, she thought, and sighed with utter peace. This man, this soul.

"I have a job and a family in the past," he said as his lips grazed her brow, her nose, and hovered above her mouth. "But my life is with you—past, present, and future." He whispered it against her lips and kissed her slowly and purposefully, invading her spirit as well as her heart anew.

She moved with him, meshing flesh and bone, thought and deed, until they were one. Her smile mirrored his as the intoxicating bliss lifted her up and away from all worries and cares.

Their previous foray into sensuality had been merely a teasing prologue to what now followed. The quest to save her life had unleashed a powerful passion—a separate and distinct force that could move mountains and stop time. They had both heeded that passion's demands, carved a space within, a safe harbor for love and a fertile field for lasting commitment. And the moment of surrender and utter commitment to the man beside her had arrived.

Wondrous. Maude sighed as love radiated from her every cell, swelling up and out, bursting forth until she fairly glowed like a great molten sun. And her whispered promises sealed her fate to the man she embraced without reservation.

Later, when their passion had crested for the hundredth time beneath that starry, starry night, they both giggled like children, drunk on joy. This was a new beginning. A lifetime awaited them, Maude realized. Each day would be a gift, ever deepening the dance of devotion they both had created from love.

FORTY-NINE

"What are you doing?" Maude cried as Gil disengaged the autopilot and nosed the hoverlift down toward the underground waterfall. "We're going to be late for the review at Central. My career is at stake!"

"There's more at stake than your career," Gil growled, and he docked the transport beside the lush pond and dropped the force field. He wouldn't say more as he snagged her hand and pulled her along in his wake. Racing up the rocky path to the crest of the falls, he ignored her halfhearted cries of protest.

She gasped with delight when they reached the top of the precipice. "How did you find this?"

Luck was with him again. The sparkling spray and fake sunlight had created another breathtaking rainbow, just when he needed it most. He wasn't going to take another chance with this futuristic enchantress; before another rotation passed, before another Rogue mission took precedence, before time and the continuum converged on their lives again, he wanted to hear it from Maude's lips. Promises whispered in the darkness weren't foolproof, and Gil wanted an airtight, sunlight guarantee from his ladylove about their future.

He scrambled up onto the heat-soaked ledge, an overhang with a thrilling prospect of one of Core's natural wonders, and pulled Maude into an embrace before she could catch her breath. "Marry me," he demanded as the misty spray swirled around them like liquid diamonds.

The roaring waterfall limited any plans for sweet-talking her into a lifetime commitment. But that was okay. A simple yes or no was all Gil was looking for. It wasn't exactly a now-or-never ultimatum, and he wasn't opposed to flat-out begging if this first approach didn't work. But he was crossing his fingers and toes that coercion wasn't going to be necessary. He wasn't opposed to blunt-force trauma as a last-ditch tactic.

I'm ready. Without a single doubt. And he hoped to high heaven that Maude was too.

She blinked, looking stunned. Her mouth hung open, a surprised O that could mean either *yes* or *no way, no how.*

"Damn," Gil said when she didn't immediately jump at his offer. Pushing her down on the nearest boulder, he assumed the classic bended-knee position and cleared his throat. "Marry me?" he repeated at full volume. Hell's bells, the thundering falls were problematic, something he hadn't considered when picking the scene proposal site.

Slowly—too slowly to spare Gil a jolt of concern—Maude reacted. Her mist-spattered features wrinkled into a grin of comprehension.

"You are asking me to *marry* you?" she returned, and cocked her head to one side. Her bright blue eyes studied him with a mix of amazement and curiosity.

Gil scowled. It hadn't occurred to him until that moment that perhaps the future society of Core had abandoned ceremonies that formalized loving relationships. If it had, he might be in big trouble. Lassoing the stellar beauty to his sorry-assed hide for fifty or sixty years might be impossible.

Still, even if the two-ships-passing-in-the-night formula worked for Core couples, it didn't work for him. Gil was definitely old school. There it was. His stubborn streak. The all-or-nothing ultimatum came out of nowhere, bowling him over and blasting away any hope of compromise. Marriage, he realized, was nonnegotiable. He wanted—and was darned tootin' gonna get—the "through thick and thin" and "growing old together" variety of commitment with Maude. He couldn't live with her any other way. His whispered promises had been straight from the heart, pillow talk with the power of a blood oath. And he wouldn't hold back from enlightening the object of his affection as to the scope of his intent.

"Yeah. Marriage—that's what we call it." He tapped her finger. "A ring. A ceremony. A honeymoon. You and me together forever, cohabitating, making babies, till death us do part. That's what I'm offering. Take it or leave it."

"Yes," Maude replied with a laugh. "I know."

Gil's brows shot up. He'd been sweating bullets since he'd hit his knees, thinking up persuasive arguments for matrimony. He jumped on her affirmation. "You said yes." He squeezed her hand—expectant, hopeful, and borderline desperate for confirmation. "*Yes?*"

Maude shook her head. "Men," she groaned. "Mackenzie warned me about you bullheaded cowboys."

Gil nearly looked at his wrist unit to check his vitals. He was pretty sure his heart had just stopped.

"Explain," he said.

"Maybe you didn't notice, but I said yes a long time ago," Maude replied and she slipped her arms around his neck. "But get this straight. We call it a 'commitment ceremony,' and for most Core residents it is a covenant for life."

"Commitment ceremony?" Gil repeated. "For life?"

"Yes, for life. I've heard that some people in your time don't take the commitment seriously. But I'm *for life*. Am I scaring you off?" Maude asked against his lips. "I know what I want. And I want you for life. Are you in or out? Yes or no?"

He scowled for a split second. Somehow Maude had turned the tables on him, matching him with a dose of attitude. But he found he was loving every second of it. He wasn't in danger of apoplexy now, unless joy could kill.

Maude's nonstandard response to his proposal of marriage proved yet again that the gal could yo-yo his heart like no other female on the planet, past or present. And, whatever lay ahead for them as a couple, life would never be dull.

"In for a penny," he whispered against her lips. "In for a pound."

"What?" Maude jerked back and stared at him with confusion.

He shook his head. "Women," he groaned. "Rick warned me about trying to tango with an independent female."

Maude raised one brow in a silent question, and Gil had to laugh. He didn't attempt to explain. Who led on the dance floor in this marriage was always going to be up for grabs. Tit for tat. He wouldn't want it any other way.

"It's a deal," he finally said.

They both laughed and sealed the promise with a kiss. Marriage or commitment, they were in delightful accord about the outcome.

Together, forever.

FIFTY

The Inquisition was over, and Maude silently cheered as the collaborators collected in the social hub in Rogue Central. She could finally relax her ramrod-straight spine, unclench her teeth, drop her defenses a smidgen, and eat real food.

Charlie's menu was limited, but no one complained. The burgers and fries were sizzling under heat lamps, and the rank and file of Rogue personnel gathered to celebrate Charlie's return and Maude's deliverance from the dreaded SE were fast exhausting the supply of foodstuffs. It had been an arduous journey for everyone, Raymond and the Rogues included. Mercifully it was at an end.

The official inquiry had been witnessed by all critical service personnel. And the event might have been unnerving for Maude without Gil by her side. She had leaned into his stalwart strength when hers flagged.

The investigation had begun with a summary of all actions executed to resolve the time migration triggered by the bullet event. Maude's heroics hadn't altered the assassination outcome as initially perceived. The lethal slug that had pierced her body cleanly had still found its mark. The subsequent death of Oswald from the fatal round lodged in his gut remained unchanged.

However, the Rogue cleanup—including a purge of eyewitness accounts and imagery documenting time travelers within the event—proved challenging. Although Maude's presence on the killing scene had been documented on film, the light-refracting qualities of her garb had converted her into a blurry spectral figure seemingly passing between Ruby and Oswald for eighteen frames. It had birthed a new conspiracy theory about all things connected to the JFK assassination, this one involving avenging angels and ghosts. But as determined by the Consequence Factor, it had failed to trigger a significant change to the course of human events. Still under way, the project to monitor and restore true events was deemed a high-priority effort for Core.

When the inquiry finally addressed the cause of the time migration, Maude became the focus of all in attendance. Defending her actions was exhausting, but she wasn't alone. Dak, Bob, and Rick shared the spotlight of scrutiny while an august body of Core's decision-makers conferred on their fate and delivered a judgment.

Surprisingly, the censure was limited. Punitive measures were light. As a unit, they were both criticized and commended. Their rebellious reasoning was debated at length, but their innovative solutions—especially Bob's hole-punching transit window—were lauded by the Transit Think Tank and key Scios.

"Adversity births invention," Hickham had offered in their defense. "Core itself was just such a creation," he had reminded everyone. And so were countless other discoveries through time.

Maude had been wide-eyed with wonder at Hick's strident appeal and admission of culpability in her flight. The bastion of science had embraced more risk than she had ever imagined.

Hickham's final statement had been stunning. His Eve One programming, a contributing factor to the crisis—and also its successful resolution—had been similarly scrutinized and absolved. And he had beamed with pride when Cara added her defense to his.

Chay's report had effectively turned the tide of recriminations into newfound respect for the collaborators. The half-human, half-machine prototype encouraged the cautious governors swimming in their sea of legalism to balance their reasoning with decisions of the heart.

"I have seen the future," Cara announced. "I am the future. And my humanity is not in conflict with my programming. Sacrifices that preserve life, even one life, are essential for our society."

When the review committee agreed, Maude had exchanged a nod of gratitude with her old friend. They weren't even. She couldn't begin to repay the debt to Cara, but she hoped one day that she could.

"I owe you," she remarked as they claimed a common slab in Central's social hub.

"Good," Cara replied, and cautiously sampled Charlie's newest replication, a mock Blue Lagoon slushie. "Planning for phase two is under way. It's another LR 50."

"How far into the future this time?" Maude asked, mopping up some juicy crumbs from her second burger.

"Fifty years. It's another Charlie and Hickham collaboration. I'm collecting data on epidemics for a super-antidote."

"That explains *my* next mission," Rick said as he leaned in and stole fries from Maude's pile. "That is, the one after we finish with the Dallas '63 mop-up. Charlie just assigned me to a data collection project that includes the Black Death and the 1918 influenza epidemic."

Gil closed in on the group and hopped up on Maude's corner of the slab. "After what we've just been through, if you think Mackenzie's going to let you transit into a plague zone, you're whacked." He snorted.

"A transit isn't necessary," Rick countered. "It's pure research. Similar to what you and I are doing to reconcile the assassinations. Besides, my transit days are limited until my partner is free to join me. I'm strictly a team-player Rogue."

Maude laughed and leaned against Gil's handy chest. "I am too."

Rick nodded and laughed. "I figured that out the first time you slapped that auto-transit tag on his chest. Well, that you would become one. You two are made for each other."

"I agree," Cara cut in. Her eyes were wide with an abashed awe.

Perhaps there was a new awareness in her friend's human condition, Maude noted. And as Bob 13 joined the group, her suspicions about Cara's emotional prospects were confirmed: Chay's lovely features flushed, she couldn't look Bob in the eye, and her tongue tangled on a question about Maude's plans for a commitment ceremony.

"Gil calls it a wedding," Maude offered. Chay looked relieved, and snapped her mouth shut as Maude continued. "It includes a honeymoon—whatever that is."

"They're great," Rick supplied with a hearty chuckle. "And an essential component of the matrimonial event. I highly recommend a long, leisurely one."

"Someplace sunny, warm, and far away from Core," Dak interjected, claiming a central position among them and settling in.

Maude grinned. The kingpin of the Rogues was back. His transit tethers had been terminated, his punitive sanctions lifted, and his mentoring and advisory status at Central restored—along with his dictatorial charm. Folding his arms, he scowled at her.

"You deserve some time off, Maudie. Clear up your certification with Central, settle this outstanding business with your cowboy, and I'll put you on active duty when you get back."

"Ah." Rick nodded and spoke up. "We're getting to the heart of the matter. What are *your* plans, Gil? Are you staying here or coming home? Mackenzie is getting antsy. She can't hold down both your job and hers much longer."

Maude's smile flagged when Gil didn't respond right away. She could feel his heart thudding against her ear. Did she imagine that it skipped a beat?

She dared a glance in his direction. Gil looked smug and confident, resplendently self-assured and wiser than she felt at that moment. If he had an answer for Rick, she couldn't guess what it was. They were a team, but she didn't have a clue about their future. Beyond the commitment ceremony and her reinstatement as a Rogue, the impact of her new partnership on her day-to-day life was a mystery. If Gil already had it figured out, she sure as zat needed to know what it was.

Charlie's toast of thanks to a wizened and visibly relieved Raymond short-circuited any reply Gil was about to offer. Raised flasks and cheers for the acting director's efforts reverberated throughout the space.

But for Maude, the sounds of joyous celebration flattened into discord as her raw passion for Gil slapped up against cold hard facts. Life had changed forever with her commitment to her hero. Decisions weren't hers alone. She wasn't solo anymore. It wasn't an unpleasant realization. But it was strange.

A brewing excitement percolated within her. It outmatched the thrilling anticipation of a Life-Risk 50 mission. In fact, she happily admitted, commitment to Gil equated to the ultimate life-risk rating: 100 percent. As a thrill junkie, the promised challenge and adventure of the vast unknown that awaited them exhilarated her beyond reason.

The next round of toasts welcomed Dak back to the Rogues. And the next, Maude.

Gil's arm slipped around her waist, and Maude shivered with pleasure from his touch. No, she didn't know Gil's decision about permanent residency in the past or the present, but his unflappable confidence about their union had totally banished her concern. Without a doubt, she knew one thing: sharing eternity with the devilishly defiant and courageous cowboy was going to be the mission of a lifetime.

FIFTY-ONE

"What's wrong?" Maude cried.

The alarm was deafening, and the sudden silence after Raymond stalled the sound was equally terrifying. Technicians and Rogues alike rushed forward and clustered around Maude's body scan unit.

Gil reached her first, stepping forward to demand an answer. But explanations weren't necessary; Raymond's ashen features told the story.

"I flunked another scan," Maude whispered.

She glanced at Gil, her stoic hero and rock of reassurance, and her terror slipped away. Whatever it was, they would face it together.

He squeezed her hand and then confronted Raymond. "Tell me it's a screwup. *Damn* it."

"Nope. Maude flunked it," Charlie confirmed as he strolled over from his console hub and looked over the scanner display. "Thought she might."

"She flunked," Gil repeated in flat tones. He was everything Maude needed in that moment—calm, direct, and fearless.

"Is it another SE?"

"An SE?" Charlie's friendly features were twisted into a curious grin. "No, no, nothing like that," he assured everyone crowding the console.

Maude hissed. Charlie's jovial demeanor wasn't appropriate for the situation. Flunking a body scan wasn't a minor setback; it was a career-busting event. And a major impediment to her life plans too. The commitment ceremony and honeymoon were scheduled to commence in two rotations, as soon as Gil completed his first phase of Rogue training and implants. But losing her Rogue status again and stalling her marriage plans both paled in comparison to another terminal diagnosis.

"Get me out of this contraption," she growled.

Charlie tapped the display and released her from her gel encasement. Gil tossed her a thermal tunic, elbowed the curious away from the console, and studied the data himself.

Maude sat up and slipped the garb over her head, watching Gil closely for a reaction. His brow furrowed for a moment, and Maude held her breath. His frown deepened as his gaze zigzagged across the screen that displayed her scan imagery.

"Does that mean what I think it means?" he asked suddenly.

Instantly, Maude's mouth went dry. Her pulse switched from a skip to a gallop.

Charlie nodded. "Sure does," he replied.

"This changes her Rogue certification, doesn't it? She can't stay active, can she?" Gil asked.

"Affirmative. Not until it is resolved." Charlie winked and slapped Gil on the back.

Resolved? The leads restricted Maude's movements but not her sudden temper. "What the *drutz* is the matter with me now?" she howled.

Gil offered her a devilish smile, one that reassured

her and spiked her curiosity. "Time for another team decision, love."

"What do you mean?" she cried, scanning the faces still clustered around the console.

The males were mush-mouthed with emotion, all of them grinning like they were overstimulated on intoxicants. Including Gil. He crooked one finger in her direction.

"Come see for yourself," he said.

Maude jumped off the slab in a huff. "Men," she growled under her breath, tugging and dragging her leads along as she stumbled over to the display.

Normal. Normal . . . she silently noted as she surveyed her vitals. They were all good. And then she saw it. The supplemental reading. The *second* heartbeat.

She didn't faint. Nonetheless, she was sitting on Gil's lap, sucking on a flask of nutrientlike sludge, and leaking tears by the time she recovered her voice.

"A baby?" she whispered, and swiped at her cheeks.

Raymond offered her a wedge of gauze and a relieved smile. "Congratulations," he said. "To both of you."

"Thanks," Gil returned, and pumped Raymond's hand vigorously.

Maude struggled to respond, and finally nodded her thanks. Absolute joy had robbed her of all speech. And her rapturous smile was no longer her own; she shared it with the tiny miracle within.

A baby. Gil's baby. *Their* baby.

Such simple words weighted with dramatic implications. She didn't need another message from the future to alert her to her altered fate. By opening her heart to love, she had changed her destiny again.

Love had saved her life. And it had blessed her with a family of her own.

EPILOGUE

"No more business," Maude cried as Gil's cell phone beeped with another text message, the third in the last hour. She glowered at Gil. If he didn't turn off that drutzed phone, they might just experience their first marital disagreement—in public.

She didn't budge from her chalky boulder at the Artist's Point vista of the Grand Canyon. Gathering with the other tourists for another paint-box sunset was a sacred ritual that she adored, and she refused to allow a zatting box of beeping buttons to intrude on the mystical setting and disrupt the tranquil moments before darkness shrouded the magnificent abyss.

A week at the south rim of the Grand Canyon had temporarily made her a believer, an antitechnology convert. A vacation without gizmos, as Gil called them, had been freeing. No wrist units, transit tags, identilogs, chronometers, or stunners allowed.

Gil's nightly ritual, however, involved a handy but rather annoying gizmo. Checking for messages via cell phone at one of the few areas in the canyon where he could get service was an intrusion from the outside world that Maude begrudged. She had adopted his "out of sight, out of mind" adage for the duration of their honeymoon. And so had Gil, with this one exception.

"Remind Rick that we're on our honeymoon, and turn off the phone!" she demanded.

Gil laughed and held up the offending object. "This one isn't business, love. It's family. Mine. *Ours*. They all want meet you and officially welcome you into the Gillespe fold. Aunt Willie won't be denied, and is thick into plans for a no-holds barred wedding reception when we get home," Gil added. "A regular Bacchanalian feast with barbeque, bluegrass, and barn-dancing."

Maude's tummy flipped. It wasn't the baby—yet—but her own childish glee at discovering a delightful and unexpected present. Family. Lots and lots of family. It was an overwhelming and intimidating prospect for an orphan from the Cabala to consider.

Her smile wavered a bit when Gil's phone beeped again. His silent apology before he checked the message was a small consolation. Curtailing business was one thing. Family, however, was entirely another.

Gil's explosive cheer spilled into the vastness. "I knew Rick could do it," he said as he sent a text-message reply, turned off the phone, and pocketed it.

Rick? Work again. She fumed for a split second.

The novel experience of all play and no work sans technology had been bliss. She had learned countless ways to love her lover, explored the euphoric union that exists between a husband and wife, and thrilled to the timeless tether of the seed of their love: their child, growing within. But a week after they made their lifetime commitment, Maude realized she was eager to start living it. And, though she hated to admit it, she was itchy for news and eager to face the next challenge with her new teammate. In short, she was ready to get back to work.

She hugged her knees to her chest and pressed her lips tight. But keeping her curiosity in check about Rick's message was grueling.

Sunset was nigh. All across the vividly hued expanse, long fingers of shadow climbed up from the depths. A chill seeped into the warm winds whistling about the scrub and rock vista. The cloudless molten sky promised another night for stargazing lovers. Soon the temperature would plummet and chase away all but the hardiest people from the rim.

"You knew Rick could do what?" she finally asked when Gil settled behind her and slipped his toasty warm arms around her body.

"Hm?" Gil replied, as if he had no idea what she was talking about.

Gil wasn't obtuse. It was deliberate, Maude decided— another indication that Gil was one of those wily men from the West that Mackenzie had warned her about. A male endowed with both the physical and mental prowess to exasperate and exhilarate his ladylove like no other on the planet.

"Rick's *message*," she prompted with a growl.

"It can wait," he returned, and rested his chin on the top of her head. "Beautiful sunset, isn't it?"

"Yes." She gritted her teeth.

It was beautiful. They were all beautiful. From the first one a week ago to this one, their last in the park.

She twisted around to face him, hating that she had to admit it. "But I can't wait. What was Rick's message?"

Gil laughed and kissed her nose. "I knew it. You can take a gal out of the future but not the future out of the gal—not entirely, anyway. It's something to consider before we decide whether we're staying here for your pregnancy or in Core."

Maude smirked. "Cut off from Core and the Rogues for the duration might be difficult. But I'm keen on avoiding Charlie's prenatal sludge. And Mackenzie's offered to mentor me through my maternity mission."

Gil shook his head and laughed. "I've never thought of it in those terms, but I like them. This will be our first official mission together."

Maude had to agree. Teamwork had everything to do with the LR 100 mission developing in her womb.

He thumbed her ring finger. It was still bare, something Gil had been adamant about rectifying with a preacher and another public ceremony upon their return to Dallas.

"Rick found Brother Nee," Gil whispered.

"He's still alive?" Maude replied, fully aware of the significant role the generous pastor had played in Gil's jaunt to 1963.

"He's in his seventies, but he's still in the business of saving souls and marrying folks." He grinned. "Can't think of a better God-fearing fellow to bless our union."

She loved the idea, and squeezed his hand as a delicious shiver cascaded through her body. The night chill was advancing swiftly, but joy warmed her heart.

Beyond the lip of the vista point, the sun—now a richly crimson blister—slipped beneath the ebony horizon. She leaned back against Gil's chest again as a blanket of peace settled over the scene.

"We don't have to decide immediately," she said quietly, astounded anew by the glorious thriving world that existed aboveground. Nothing Core could manufacture or simulate with atmospherics could ever replace the utter magnificence of this moment.

Gil nodded in agreement. "We don't have to decide anything yet."

Maude noted the love in his voice, deep and mellow, and it surrounded her thoughts with a warmth that welcomed her trust and faith. He had been gentle, easing her into his world and his time. Sharing the beauty and the adventure.

She was seriously considering a temporary relocation to the past for the duration of her pregnancy. It was a team decision, and a good decision. Understanding Gil's era of origin was essential to appreciating the cowboy who had forsaken everything to help save her life.

The velvet night settled over the yawning canyon, and the swirling winds slid over her flesh like her lover's sigh. She felt a kinship with this seemingly natural transit vortex. Her pulse raced as adrenaline surged through her body, metering the pace of pumping blood at her temples and wrists till she felt like she was purring.

In spite of the chill from the Arizona night, sweat from her energized body soaked through her clothes. She could feel Gil's grin against her cheek, his seductive chuckle teasing her ear.

As if reading her mind again, he asked her, "Feels like we're about to transit, doesn't it?"

She nodded and took the hand he offered. "What's our destination, Gilly?" she returned.

"Doesn't matter, does it, love?"

No, it didn't, she decided promptly. She smiled as he settled his lips over hers and rocked her with one of his bone-liquefying kisses.

She didn't have to ask if Gil was ready; the cowboy was born ready. She had found her heart's desire, her ideal Rogue.

And, palm to palm, their fingers entwined, they faced the unknown together.

GLOSSARY

Analysis station
Scio treatment pod facilitates scans of Critical Services personnel, records and analyzes data, and reports results.

Auto-syst check
An automatic systems check function. Diagnosis and troubleshooting for implanted technology.

Auto-transits
A default safety protocol for automatic transits to Core.

Auto-transit tags
A button-sized device that initializes auto-transit to Core when activated.

Body scan
Data collection function targeting biological systems and implanted technologies for multiple purposes.

Buffering implants
Safety protocol nodes that limit sensory overload.

Cabala Children's Settlement in Edgeville
Core's orphanage. First home for Maude Kincaid and Cara Chay.

Critical Services Department
Mission statement: "Protect the future—Preserve the past." Primary service units: Rogue Central and Scios.

Diagno-med techs
Rogue Central's primary diagnosis and medical technicians.

Drutz
Expletive.

Dust bots
Aerial models include garment cleaning functions.

Edgeville
Primary on-grid settlement abutting the sparsely populated Shelf Cavern region.

EE or T-code Echo Echo
Era Essential. Transit code classification for residents essential to their era of origin. Time travel restrictions.

Eve One prototype
Cara Chay. One-of-a-kind cyborg. Lone survivor of Lima Transit disaster, salvaged through TTT intellect and Scio wizardry. Mesh of flesh and electronics.

Feeder leads
Reacclimation pod equipment. Tubing apparatus that physically connects patients via mesh circlets and metal tipped nodes to diagnostic and treatment services.

Flash
Supplemental illumination device usually incorporated into wrist-units.

Frontier region
Vast subterranean area loosely defined as unstable and hostile and largely unmapped.

Frontier Zone
Specified training arena within the Frontier region utilized by Rogues and other Critical Services classifications.

Governor of the Western Sectors
A key Core administration position.

Hoverlifts/sleds
Silent propulsion air/ground transportation conveyances. Performance envelope: limited speed, altitude, and range.

LR
Life Risk. Rogue mission rating scale. LR 50 equates to a high risk mission and is dubbed a "lethal ride."

Monitoring marker
Akin to a GPS device attached to "tethered" personnel identification chips to track their locations.

Mop bots
Domed cleaning droids utilized in both residential and com-

mercial settings, programmed to activate on schedule and on need.

Navigational buoys
Flashing proximity devices identifying hoverlift hazards.

No-transit zones
VIPER restricted locations on Earth's time map.

Outskirt
Former settlement region within the Shelf Caverns. Abandoned when Core developed safe time travel and instituted a relocation plan to safely house residents in Earth's past. Serviced by an unmanned sub-orbital tram and archaic communication systems.

Particle beam
Laser application to capture, restrain, or move objects from a distance.

PEC
Personnel egress chute. Cylindrical vacuum conveyance system. Facilitates vertical transport within Core's multi-storied structures.

Procreant
Maude. Prototype for a Central Services program. A genetically engineered human created by Scios from DNA harvested in Earth's past. Successful result of the endeavor testing the viability of non-Core DNA sources, securing alternative measures to perpetuate the species as a function of the Scio mission.

Proximity buffers
Adjustable settings for cleaning droids and bots to expand or limit interaction with environmental elements.

Quarantine
Isolation and Stasis storage for Core's communicable and terminal population.

Reacclimants
Personnel currently processing through post-transit protocols.

Reacclimation

Post-transit personnel protocol. Side effects include heightened sensory acuity for indeterminate duration for processed personnel.

Recovery

Post-reacclimation personnel protocol. Indeterminate duration. Interval between post-transit and before Reassignment and Relocation.

Retrieval squads

General personnel collection service team. Time travel capable.

Returnees

Post-transit general classification applied to Core population arrivals upon completion of a durational residential assignment in Earth's past.

Ring unit

Limited range monitoring device. Application: personal GPS tracking unit. Stone settings (jewels) programmed with an "identifier code."

Rogue Central

Time travel service delivery unit for Core's Critical Services Department. Chief service classifications: Time Rogues and Time Transitors.

S.C.R.U.B.

Sensory Cerebral Restoration and Unification Bot. Microscopic robotic medical treatment device.

S.E. or T-code Serria Echo

Scheduled Expiration. Time code classification. Auto-alert trigger for personnel with thirty rotations or less remaining on their bodyclock. Time travel restricted. Mandatory Quarantine.

Scios

Scientific service delivery unit for Core's Critical Services Department. Core's community of scientists. Expanded mission: identifying, evaluating, and protecting human life, including the collection and safeguard of unique genetic material for preservation of the species.

Shelf-caverns

Habitable region with sparse settlements and off-grid homesteaders. Buffer between Core's heavily colonized sectors and the Frontier region.

Stowage sled

Large extended range hovercraft. Utilized to convey bulky cargo.

Sub-orbital tram system

Unscheduled surface transportation route through the sparsely populated and off-grid sectors within the Shelf Cavern region.

T-code

Time codes. Identifiers for transit status.

Tethers

Personnel and cargo constraints. Variations: safety—for personnel and cargo on hoverlifts and sleds; punitive—blocks or restricts personnel from selected activities including but not limited to transits. Tether implants are programmed to expire.

Time Rogues

Elite time-traveling rescue, recovery, and repair squad. Conduct all public and covert operations essential to maintain or restore the Continuum. Certification levels for experience: scout to mentor, and service: full-time to "on-call."

Time Transitors

Time travel controllers. Initiate and retrieve all transits for Core's time-traveling population. Critical Services personnel. Interdependent partners with Rogues. Commitment to protect the future and preserve the past.

Trams

Personnel and cargo conveyance units utilized in Core's horizontal mass-transportation system for surface and sub-orbital routes.

Transit tether
Time travel transit restriction device. Punitive constraint. Blocks transit capabilities for specified personnel.

Treatment Centrifuge
Charlie's Rogue Central treatment facility. Houses essential staff and equipment to support Rogues.

Triad
Critical skills catalog maintained by the Transit Think Tank.

TTT
Transit Think Tank. Core's intellectual community.

Tunics & Tees
Garments embedded with sensor-feeds. Auto or manual adjustments maintain optimum body temperature.

Tunnel system
Network of natural and manmade tunnels facilitating hover-lift and sled travel between Core sectors.

V.I.P.E.R.
Viability Index for Pollution of Eras and Restrictions. Utilized to calculate, govern, and restrict transit pollution resulting from time travel. Designed by TTT to buffer significant historic factors such as people and events and prevent contamination, as a function of its mission to safeguard the present and protect the past.

Zat
Expletive.

Zed scale
Risk measurement formula applied to transit related activities. Calculates less than zero values and exponentials as they relate to personnel life risks.